The New MONTANA STORY
AN ANTHOLOGY

Compiled and edited by
Rick Newby

*To Montana's storytellers,
past, present, and future*

IN MEMORIAM
James Welch

The New Montana Story: An Anthology

Published by Riverbend Publishing, Helena, Montana.

Copyright 2003 by Riverbend Publishing.
Introduction copyright 2003 by Rick Newby.
Cover painting, *Prairie Storm*, from an original oil by Dale Livezey,
copyright 2001 by Dale Livezey, website www.dalelivezey.com

All rights reserved.

Pages 334-335 constitute a continuation of this copyright page.

ISBN 1-931832-29-3

Cataloging-in-Publication Data on file at the Library of Congress.

Design by DD Dowden, Helena, Montana.

Text set in Sabon.

Manufactured in the United States of America.

10 9 8 7 6 5 4 3 2 1

Riverbend Publishing is pleased to donate a 5 percent royalty from sales of
The New Montana Story *to the Montana Center for the Book,
in support of the annual Montana Festival of the Book.*

RIVERBEND
PUBLISHING

Contents

Rick Newby, What Is This "New" Montana Story?
An Introduction ... 5

Acknowledgments ... 11

Deirdre McNamer, "Virgin Everything" ... 13

Paul S. Piper, "Snow Country" ... 25

Ruth McLaughlin, "Haircut" ... 28

Ralph Beer, "At the Edge of Things"
from "Lady," a novel in progress ... 36

Caroline Patterson, "Fruit in Good Season" ... 42

David Horgan, "A Lot of Living to Do" ... 57

Debra Magpie Earling, from *Perma Red* ... 73

Matt Pavelich, "If It Is So Far"
from "Our Savage," a novel ... 77

Pete Fromm, "Cranes" ... 96

Florence Williams,
"The Difference between East and West" ... 104

Tom Harpole, "My Cat Chuck" ... 113

Melanie Rae Thon, from *Sweet Hearts* ... 122

Elizabeth H. Wood, "A Black Convertible" ... 127

Aaron Parrett, "Side of the Road" ... 130

Maile Meloy, "Four Lean Hounds, ca. 1976" ... 141

DAVID LONG, "The Last Photograph of Lyle Pettibone" ... 151

PHIL CONDON, "Dogs and Dogs" ... 169

KRYS HOLMES, "Warrior" ... 183

NEIL MCMAHON, from "Journeymen,"
a novel in progress ... 197

ALLEN MORRIS JONES,
"A Fine Spring Day, with Regrets" ... 208

FRED HAEFELE, "More than a Hiding Place" ... 222

SANDRA DAL POGGETTO, "Relict" ... 226

NOELLE SULLIVAN, "New Deal" ... 230

ROBERT LEE, "Big Ears" ... 240

RON FISCHER, "Manus Dugan" ... 247

MELISSA KWASNY,
"A Woman among Them, Painting" ... 263

BILL BORNEMAN, from "Bill's Bongo Party,"
an endless loop ... 275

KIM ZUPAN, "Shelterbelt"
from "Why Do the Heathen Rage,"
a novel in progress ... 283

ELLEN MELOY, "A Map for Hummingbirds" ... 300

TOM ELLIOTT, "Journey of Small Deaths" ... 307

LYNDA SEXSON,
"This Is How We Got to Be Three Pods and a Pea" ... 319

About the Contributors ... 329

What Is This "New" Montana Story?
An Introduction

"Make It New!" trumpeted Ezra Pound, that native-born westerner who fled Idaho at age two and never looked back. Pound tells us—in his Canto 53—that Tching Tang, an innovative leader of ancient China, wrote "Make It New!" (a Confucian precept) on his bathtub, where he was sure to see it every day. Morrison's *Chinese Dictionary* defines the phrase Tching inscribed on his tub thusly: "Fresh . . . to restore or increase what is good." In Canto 53, Pound further refines—in the context of his efforts to invigorate the literature of his time—his understanding of the Chinese ideogram:

> Day by day make it new
> cut underbrush
> pile the logs
> keep it growing.

Pound's slogan, drawn from the deep past, became the rallying cry for literary modernism, but often it was interpreted to mean that the past has no value and that only the new—which represents an absolute rupture with earlier artistic styles and notions—can possess life, energy, substance. However, new scholarship indicates, as art historians John E. Bowlt and Olga Matich put it, that the new in twentieth-century art and literature "did not suddenly 'arrive' . . . but [instead it] maintained organic connections with the more remote and recent past and then nourished what came thereafter." Pound, who venerated many traditions, felt similarly; he sought to renovate his own literary tradition by reattaching it to its roots and enriching it with elements from other cultures. He wanted to increase what was good and, above all, to "keep it growing."

In compiling *The New Montana Story,* I have tried to bear in mind this vision of "newness." Some of these stories represent more radical breaks with the immediate past than others, but most of them skillfully extend a tradition that has yet to show signs of flagging—it is, after all, scarcely one hundred years young.

The New Montana Story showcases the works of what I am calling the third wave of modern Montana storytellers. The first wave, of course, included such legendary western writers as Frank Bird Linderman, Mildred Walker, Walter Van Tilburg Clark, Grace Stone Coates, A. B. Guthrie, Jr., and Dorothy Johnson. Through the 1950s, these masters, together with prescient educators and editors like H. G. Merriam, Joseph Kinsey Howard, and Leslie Fiedler, nurtured a small but vibrant literary community and laid the groundwork for the Montana storytelling traditions that flourish today.

With the advent of the 1960s, a new wave of extraordinary Montana writers emerged, some of them native born, others settling under Guthrie's Big Sky in search of quietude, natural beauty, cheap rents, and the comradeship of the ever-growing community of fellow writers. This second wave boasts such talents as the late Norman Maclean, Ivan Doig, William Kittredge, Mary Clearman Blew, James Welch, Annick Smith, James Crumley, Jon Jackson, Thomas McGuane, William Hjortsberg, Richard Ford, and Cyra McFadden. By crafting world-class stories, stories that resonate with readers everywhere, this band of writers set a high standard for all future Montana storytellers.

The third wave of writers—most at mid career, though some are considerably younger—range from such well-known names as Pete Fromm, Melanie Rae Thon, David Long, Deirdre McNamer, and Ralph Beer to writers just emerging like Maile Meloy, Noelle Sullivan, and Aaron Parrett. Some are the students or protégés of the preceding generation, but others come from quite different backgrounds, bringing new strains into Montana literature. Their stories—and here I define "story" as narrative prose, whether fictional or not—include short stories (some very short, indeed), excerpts from novels, memoirs, and personal essays.

My selection process for *The New Montana Story* has been highly personal, colored by my own tastes, this historical moment, and my background as a poet and editor (who happens to relish a good story, wherever it may appear). Another editor might have chosen quite a different group of stories. That said, I have—in making my selections—operated on the principle of inclusiveness, although no anthology, of course, can be truly inclusive. This means that I have tried to assemble a genuinely diverse group of stories, diverse both formally and in terms of subject matter and tone. The one restriction I have allowed is that every story must, in some way, relate to Montana reality—however each author prefers to define that reality. My goal has been to achieve a balance between humor and drama, tight plotting and acute psychological portraiture, fabulist excursions and pure realism. Due to length limitations and financial realities, I have had to exclude scores of fine Montana writers, and to them I offer my heartfelt regrets.

Not only are the writers of the third wave "new" in the sense that many have not been previously anthologized—nor have their works become widely known outside a small circle—but they also craft stories that renovate the rich Montana tradition—*keeping it growing, increasing what is good*. They take on new subjects, for example, keeping us abreast of shifts, both slight and profound, in Montana reality. Some of the stories, like Dee McNamer's "Virgin Everything," take into account—to satirical *and* heartbreaking effect—the displacements and distortions brought on by technology and globalization, Montana's status as a vacation wonderland for the world's elites, and the dire condition of our economy. Others, like Ellen Meloy's "A Map for Hummingbirds," underscore the migratory nature of our 21st century lives, while still others, like Pete Fromm's "Cranes," explore the emotional impact, even in isolated Montana, of AIDS, that postmodern plague.

Another aspect of the new has to do with tone, with a lessening of anxiety and an infusion of humor. Ken Egan, writing about A. B. Guthrie and what he calls the "Siren Song of Apocalypse" in Montana literature, notes, "It's difficult to imagine a less humorous tradition of writing than that practiced in Montana." In "Landscape with Figures: The Georgic in Montana Literature," an essay published in 1996, Maile Meloy notes that Montana's modern writers have been "anxious about language, its excesses, its uncertainties, its playfulness" and prey to an "underlying fear of appearing 'mouthy'." The result, as Bill Bevis argues, in a reassessment of *The Last Best Place: A Montana Anthology*, has not been altogether negative, far from it. It has brought us, in Bevis's words, the "endurance, the realism, the various forms of terse eloquence" that have distinguished Montana writing.

But that tendency, admirable as it has been, appears to be diminishing. Many of the stories here—balanced by a number that are powerfully dark and terse and grave—sport plenty of humor and verbal play. Tom Harpole's rambunctious and affectionate "My Cat Chuck," for example, recalls Montana's hilarious folktale tradition, collected in anthologies like H. G. Merriam's *Way Out West: Reminiscences and Tales* (1969) and *An Ornery Bunch: Tales and Anecdotes Collected by the W.P.A. Montana Writers' Project* (1999). David Horgan's "A Lot of Living to

Do" is a joyous take on questions of aging and memory and the creative spirit. Other stories, like Robert Lee's "Big Ears," use humor to ward off, and cope with, a failure of courage. Lynda Sexson's "This Is How We Got to Be Three Pods and a Pea" is an exercise in sheer play—a magisterial parable as mysterious and dense as anything in Kafka, but infinitely lighter in spirit.

The new Montana story is increasingly told by women. As Melissa Kwasny has pointed out, scarcely fifteen years ago, the Contemporary Fiction section in *The Last Best Place* included only four women out of its twenty-three writers. Since then, Mary Clearman Blew, almost single-handedly, has worked to correct the balance, both by spreading the good word about Montana's women writers in essays and talks like "There Ain't No Such Thing as a Woman in Montana" and "Writing and Fire" and through editing, with Kim Barnes, the anthology, *Circle of Women: An Anthology of Contemporary Western Women Writers* (1994), which included more than a dozen Montanans.

Fourteen of the thirty-one writers in *The New Montana Story*, I'm happy to say, are women, and their perspectives render the new Montana story that much more diverse, adventuresome, and truly open to the farthest reaches of Montana experience. To mention only a few: Caroline Patterson chronicles, in "Fruit in Good Season," the downward spiral of a woman implacably out of step with the constraints of her community. Debra Magpie Earling offers her own haunting brand of magic realism on the Flathead Reservation. With "A Black Convertible," Elizabeth Wood has crafted the pure expression of a yearning for broader horizons, for the open road. Melanie Rae Thon speaks, in astonishing prose, of unbreakable familial ties and tensions. And Noelle Sullivan appropriates the voice of Margaret Bourke-White as she photographed Fort Peck Dam, and the people who built it, for the first issue of *Life Magazine* in 1936.

Rural existence has always provided rich material for Montana stories, and here Ralph Beer, Tom Elliott, and Kim Zupan spin widely divergent tales about life on the ranch. These writers know whereof they speak: Beer and Elliott are long-time ranchers, and Zupan spent a decade as a professional rodeo cowboy. It is a pleasure to re-encounter Beer's muscular prose, studded with particulars and rich with that terse eloquence Bill Bevis has celebrated. Among the first of the third-wave Montana storytellers to reach a national audience (William Kittredge and Steve Krauzer included his story "Riders" in a special "Western Stories" issue of *TriQuarterly* in 1980), Beer tells the story of a Métis ranch hand who honors the bonds of friendship, even unto death. Mortality, in its myriad forms, is the theme of Tom Elliott's "Journey of Small Deaths," as it takes us from the home ranch in central Montana to a Texas café to the realm of dreams.

For me, the fiction of Kim Zupan was among the most bracing of my discoveries as I edited *The New Montana Story*. I'm only sorry that I hadn't discovered his work earlier. His story here, "Shelterbelt," excerpted from the unpublished novel, "Why Do the Heathen Rage," appears at first glance to resemble the Gothic work of southern writers like William Faulkner and Cormac McCarthy—his prose is an overpowering onrush of language, filled with neologisms and archaic phrasings, "writerly" in ways that Montana literature has generally not been—and yet as I entered Zupan's world, I found myself astonished and deeply moved by his evocation of the austere beauty of the Missouri Breaks and of "an old man grieving with such perfection."

Themes of grief and loss shape many of the stories in *The New Montana Story*. In "Four Lean Hounds, ca. 1976," Maile Meloy traces, with great subtlety and emotional insight, the impacts of an accidental death upon those left behind. Paul Piper, in his story, "Snow Country," recounts—within a brief span—the process of a dying that is hauntingly beautiful and full of hope. Aaron Parrett, in unadorned, unrelenting prose, tells of another kind of loss, another kind of hope: the leaving behind of an abusive father. Neil McMahon, in an excerpt from his unpublished novel, "Journeyman," portrays a champion boxer who learns what it is to lose, while in Allen Jones's "A Fine Spring Day, with Regrets," a young fisherman discovers the true meaning of ownership. And in "Dogs and Dogs," the story of a homeless man and his canine companion, Phil Condon explores the redemptive power of letting go.

Non-fictional voices have grown increasingly important in recent Montana literature, and I've included personal essays and memoirs in *The New Montana Story* to represent this vital trend. With considerable humor, Ruth McLaughlin tells of growing up poor and resourceful on the northeastern Montana homestead settled by her Scandinavian grandparents. Native New Yorker Florence Williams discovers her Jewish roots in her adopted home of Helena, and Fred Haefele ruefully examines Montana's often bizarre image in the national media. Painter and bird hunter Sandra Dal Poggetto attempts to reconcile "my attraction to gun powder with my love of powdered pigment."

Montana's past has long served to stimulate the imaginations of Montana's storytellers, and I've included stories that make skillful use of that rich and conflicted history. In "The Last Photograph of Lyle Pettibone," David Long tells the complex story of labor struggles in a northwestern Montana lumbering town early in the twentieth century. In an excerpt from Matt Pavelich's novel-in-progress, "Our Savage," we witness the migration of Serbian immigrants upriver from New Orleans to the mines and brothels of brawling Butte. And in "Manus Dugan," a profile of genuine heroism, Ron Fischer takes us inside the horror and exaltation of the Speculator Mine disaster.

I have included, too, a few stories that stray far afield from the realistic tradition. Maile Meloy traces the origin of this postmodern impulse to William Kittredge's memoir *Hole in the Sky* (1992)—"what Montana literature sounds like when it makes its first attempts at playfulness and self-consciousness." The formal experiments I've chosen—"mouthy" and anti-narrative—include Bill Borneman's infinitely looping and loopy "Bill's Bongo Party," a meditation on rhythm and language and place, and Melissa Kwasny's lyrically fractured "A Woman among Them, Painting," which tells of the love between two women—who meet again and again through history and around the world, in an empty room in a small plague-ridden city, "in a stone village in the most civilized country in Europe," "over a hundred years ago on the plains of Montana." In "Warrior," Krys Holmes reveals how a child's grief and fear of loss can stimulate her imaginative powers, even her sense of play.

Playful and grieving, men and women, open to the new but steeped in tradition, the writers of the third wave of modern Montana storytelling—shaped, challenged, and instructed by the rigor, ambition, and sheer accomplishment of their forbears—have been writing a new Montana story that is richly diverse, often altogether surprising, and as a clear mark of their Montana citizenship, superbly crafted. The new Montana story is, as it always has been, many stories: some rural, others urban, some about deep roots, others about the loss of any sense of home, some boisterously funny, others sad beyond bearing. This is as it should be. With skill and heart and power, Montana's storytellers continue to tell us about individual lives in ways that touch us all, no matter where we live or what our experience. In Norman Maclean's phrase, their stories, perhaps now more than ever, are "true of Montana and of the world beyond."

    Rick Newby
    Helena, Montana
    May 2003

Acknowledgments

COMPILING *THE NEW MONTANA STORY* has been a great challenge and pleasure. The experience has been infinitely enriched by the many individuals and organizations who helped in myriad ways. First, I want to thank Chris Cauble of Riverbend Publishing, who offered unqualified support for the project—and whose initiative in reprinting Montana literary classics, in cooperation with the Montana Historical Society Press, has been an inspiration. I want to thank, too, Megan Hiller, the first editor to believe in *The New Montana Story*. Her insights and support helped push the idea to fruition.

I want to thank Mark Sherouse and Kim Anderson of the Montana Center for the Book (a program of the Montana Committee for the Humanities) for their hard work and vision in putting on the annual Montana Festival of the Book, where many of the writers featured here have the opportunity to present their works to their natural audience. And I'm particularly pleased that Riverbend Publishing will donate 5 percent of the royalties from *The New Montana Story* to support the Montana Festival of the Book. I want to thank, too, the Montana Arts Council's Individual Artist Fellowship program for bringing a number of these talented writers to my attention.

The writers in my own community, especially Melissa Kwasny, Bill Borneman, Sandra Dal Poggetto, and Florence Williams, offered invaluable advice and moral support during the editing process, as did my old friends Paul S. Piper and Matt Pavelich. The writers in the Helena Narrative Strategies Study Group, Krys Holmes, Barb Cosens, and Liz Gans, helped shape my thinking about stories and storytelling. Charlie Atkins suggested writers whose work I was unfamiliar with, as did Neil McMahon and Tom Elliott. And Maile Meloy, Melanie Rae Thon, Pete Fromm, Ellen Meloy, Deirdre McNamer, and Debra Magpie Earling went the extra mile in helping me obtain permissions.

I thank all of the writers included in *The New Montana Story* for their generous willingness to be included, their patience with the inevitable delays, and their powerful voices. I want to acknowledge, too, all the writers in the third wave of modern Montana storytellers whose works I was not able to include. There are more than enough of these—among them such celebrated voices as Judy Blunt, David Quammen, Rick Bass, David James Duncan, Kate Gadbow, and Kevin Canty—to compile a second anthology of equal size and quality. That this is true only underscores the vitality and richness of Montana's storytelling community.

Underpinning Montana's storytelling tradition are the editors, writers, and scholars who have written about, compiled anthologies of, and celebrated (and criticized) Montana's writers. These comprise a long list, but I want to especially honor Joseph Kinsey Howard, H. G. Merriam, Grace Stone Coates, Paul C. Phillips, John W. Hakola, Steven Krauzer, William Kittredge, Annick Smith, Mary Clearman Blew, William Lang, Richard Roeder, James Welch, William Bevis, William Farr, Kim Barnes, Russell Martin, Deborah Clow, Donald Snow, O. Alan Weltzien, Allen Morris Jones, Megan Hiller, Alexandra Swaney, Elaine Peterson, Sue Hart, Ron McFarland, Mark Sherouse, and Ken Egan.

Finally, I thank my wife, Liz Gans, partner in all things, for her encouragement, patience, and love as I compiled *The New Montana Story*.

Virgin Everything

Deirdre McNamer

ELISE LAVENDER'S CLASSIFIED AD began very simply: Buy a Home for Your Best Self. Below that, in a sprightlier typeface, her most attractive recreational properties of the moment were evoked in her own words: mountain vistas, fawns in the dawn, leaping trout, highway access, friendly covenants, the heart of the heart, terms.

Elise sold real estate to people who wanted a foothold in the last best place, as more than a few of them bashfully put it. She dealt in rather substantial footholds, small ranches you could say, most of them within twenty minutes of town and most of them worth at least half a million. Elise steered away from less expensive properties because they seemed to attract buyers who weren't as confident of their bankers' good will as she liked buyers to be. She appreciated the tanned intensity of people who worried about whether a particular purchase would improve an already salutary life, but she didn't want any worries about whether they could actually come up with the money. Selectivity was one thing. Raw hope, crawling out there like a bald baby, was quite another.

During the closing moments of a sale, however, even the most assured buyers could get edgy and start asking questions about snow removal and airline service. That's when Elise started telling stories. She had several, but the one she liked best was a fiction she had concocted around an actual person, her old friend Lily. She found this story consistently effective with buyers on the brink, their faces so hopeful and frightened, so eager for the transforming plunge.

Elise had no small amount of charm. She was a plump, honey-haired woman, fortyish, whose day-to-day Montana look was Santa Fe/Sundance: calfskin boots, broomstick skirt, concha belt, chunks of turquoise, a poet's blouse. Occasionally, she liked to change gears and appear in knockout slit-skirted black. Her Former Life outfit, she called it. She was in Montana by way of Tuscaloosa, Briarcliff, Manhattan, and Santa Barbara, so she had access to a number of different dialects and former lives.

"I want to tell y'all a little story," she'd say, making it a question, as she brought in cappuccino from the New Riders coffee gallery next door. "I have a friend from prehistoric times named Lily. She is beautiful, intelligent, and successful in her field."

Then she would describe a trajectory that had produced an unhappy and frustrated Lily—terminally single, recently mugged, consumed by an editing job that was all scramble and no heart. It was a frazzled Lily, Elise said, who had arrived one day for a Montana visit.

"She looked awful," she said sadly. "I literally poured her into the Cherokee and we drove out to our ranch, and it was the most fabulous day you could imagine with the sun flashing off those big peaks and I believe it was six deer jumping off into the forest, right before our eyes."

That was the overture. Elise then went on to describe a dinner for eight in front of a crackling fire and Lily's instant bond with one of the guests. Sometimes Elise made him a visiting screenwriter who was an expert fly fisherman and looked like David Letterman if David Letterman had spent time in nature. Sometimes she made him a war photographer with an Oxford degree who had returned to his Montana roots to raise buffalo and llamas. In all cases, this man and Lily decided they could not live without each other, so they enlisted Elise to find them a piece of property where they could start their new life.

Which she did. Forty pristine acres, walking distance to a blue-ribbon trout stream, twenty minutes from town.

"And no," Elise always added, "they're not giving up their professional lives. They'll do their work from here. They'll fly where they need to fly. They'll e-mail and voice-mail and fax."

The moral of the story was that Lily's Montana move, her willingness to take, the, plunge—Elise tapped the words out with a rosy fingernail—had saved her from a vacuous, soulless existence. She had discovered her own authenticity, Elise said. She had found real love and a true life.

After this speech, they generally signed. But if they still balked at the idea of a full move, if they felt it impossible to simply pick up and move to Montana year-round, then Elise could tell them about her other business.

Her other business, her sideline, was to prepare Montana homes for the visits of their absent owners. At Christmas, say, when a family wanted to fly in from New York or Arlington or wherever they happened to live most of the time, Elise and her helpers would make sure the family's Montana retreat was warm, that a Christmas tree was up and decorated, that the cupboards and refrigerator were stocked with cheese, wine, special requests, and so on. On the morning of the client's arrival day, a plate of cookies appeared on the coffee table. A fire was built that needed only the touch of a match. Magazines and that day's newspapers were scattered casually about, and a few bottles of wine were opened and recorked. The house now looked invitingly tousled; convincingly lived-in.

Elise's business of relaxing other people's homes, as she called it, had made her more critical of her own—hers and Dave's. Theirs was a handsome Mission filled with bold and inviting decorative touches—all of it working together to create an eclectic, well-traveled look. Elise had tried to make it a home that looked confident and curious, sophisticated and unaffected. Something was missing, though. She would come home from relaxing someone else's house and she'd be chafed by a kind of stiffness she felt in her own; their own.

She hired some very expensive and overbooked carpenters to get rid of the skylight in the living room because it got grimy and seemed so unsparing. That helped. She fanned out magazines on the coffee table and ordered Dave to stop bunching them back into soldierly piles. She created a more amiable seating arrangement around the fireplace and propped a beautiful old hand-tooled saddle across the staircase banister. On a leather footstool, she placed a big dictionary, open, so that it looked as if it had just been consulted by a flock of breathless Scrabble players.

One day, in a small burst of inspiration, she moved the maple rocker over to the picture window and bought a handsome telescope to place next to it. She tossed a Pendleton lap blanket over the back of the rocker and put the Moroccan footstool in front of it, replacing the open dictionary with a first edition of the Lewis and Clark journals. The telescope was brass, on a tall brass stand, and it looked beyond the trivialities of the open field and the rooflines of the neighbor's house, beyond all that to the timeless mountains; the engraved immensity of the Gallatin Range.

The arrangement looked, to her eyes, as if a curious and reflective person sat by the window much of the time; someone who had simply stepped away for a moment. She seemed sometimes to detect the barest of movements in the rocker, to smell the place where his head had rested against the blanket as he walked his eyes along the tops of the mountains; the glittering mountains that she, Elise, had helped him to see, as if for the very first time.

Elise had gone into real estate about the time she and Dave knew they were going to stop trying to have a baby. Thousands upon thousands of dollars and two trips to Seattle for *in vitro,* and they had had enough.

It was ironic, because they had moved to Montana in the first place to start a family—had simply assumed it was on the agenda—and then it hadn't happened. One of Elise's tubes was scarred. Dave's count was slightly low. Nothing that made a baby impossible. But it hadn't happened; it had actively not happened, had resisted them. And they were, when that fact sunk in, as stunned as good children who'd been written out of the will.

Eventually they agreed, tacitly, to a briskness of response; a turning away from their fervent, incantatory privacy to the larger world. Elise hung her own shingle and threw herself into recreational properties. Dave kept his copy-writing job at Big Sky Graphix but announced to Elise that he had signed up for biology and chemistry courses at the university because he was going to follow through on a new dream, to become a big-animal veterinarian.

For a while it worked. They felt the clarity of diminished options, a certain relief from the presence of that shadowy third.

Elise spent twelve hours a day in her office or out with clients. At home, she was on the phone to potential buyers. Dave was either at work or at the university, and in the evenings he studied or drove into town to drink beer with other pre-vets half his age.

Elise was taking care of a buyer's baby. The buyer, a suave woman named Francesca, had put the baby in Elise's arms so she could look through a photo album of properties. Somehow Elise misplaced the baby. It was simply no longer in her arms. She looked around frantically for it and found it very quiet in a corner and—this was the strangely obvious part of the dream—fading before her eyes. Within seconds it had turned into a smudge, a silvery ashen mark on the white wall.

Shaken to the core, she went back to the room where the mother of the smudge was leafing through photos, to explain the situation. To own up. And everything, to her immense relief, was still fine. Francesca didn't seem to mind about the baby and, in fact, urged Elise to discuss real estate with her and not burden herself with babies, smudges, anything else.

Elise was infused then with feelings of conclusion and accord. They stayed with her after she awoke, all through the day. That evening, she poured herself and Dave glasses of a good merlot and told him about the smudge-baby, trying to convey the rightness and peace of the dream.

He said, "Good for you, Elise." He said, "No really, Elise, that's good. That's comforting. That seems like a resolution." His words marched. He drank the wine too fast. The furrow between his eyes didn't disappear when he smiled. It had, she noticed, become permanent. He took the last sip and smiled again, and he toasted her with the glass.

On Halloween, Elise found herself home alone. Dave had gone down the road to see his new friend Link Runyon, a hatmaker who lived on his father's small ranch in his own two-room house. The old man had once raised bucking horses for rodeos; he knew horses. Dave had an idea about buying a few horses to put on their own place.

It began to grow dark. The phone was silent for once. Elise sliced a tube of refrigerator cookies and baked them. It seemed a kindly country thing to do on Halloween—add a warm cookie to the kids' candy—and it would also give Dave a domestic smell to come home to for once.

Just after dusk, four children came up to the door for candy. They didn't run shrieking as Elise seemed to remember herself doing, flapping through the dark, lipsticked and rampant. These children were efficient. They wore glossy store-bought costumes that left no questions of identity. They were Ninjas and Power Rangers. They requested their loot with no delight or threat in their voices, then marched like commuters back to the parent's car that hummed and glowed at the end of the drive. A parent figure waved in the near-dark, but Elise couldn't see who it was and wasn't sure she'd recognize anyone if she did.

For the next hour and a half, no one rang the bell, which surprised her because Meadowbrook Estates was only a quarter mile down the road. The subdivision had gone in two years earlier. Elise thought the houses were gaudy and shoddy, and the extra traffic on the frontage road had made her own trip to town a good ten minutes longer at certain times of the day, so she had a habit of disparaging the place. Tonight, though, she thought of the children she'd seen wheeling their bikes around the raw new houses, and she wished some of them would show up at the door.

As if on cue, two boys on a single bicycle appeared in the glow of the tall yard light. They wobbled up the drive, flashlight bouncing and veering, then dropped the bike and ran toward the house. She went to the door and watched them through the security eye.

One was nearly a teenager and had a sharp-chinned, mottled face. A small child, a brother perhaps, held the taller boy's shirt tail and extended a plastic pail with the other. Neither wore any discernable costume.

"What are *you* supposed to be?" Elise asked as she opened the door. Her voice was playful. She dropped two warm cookies into the pail.

"We're supposed to be kids out on Halloween," the taller boy said in a cracking adolescent voice. He said it flatly, without a flicker of a smile. The smaller boy, still grabbing the shirt tail, thrust his pail out further. Elise reached for the big bowl of candy and offered him a few miniature Baby Ruths.

The taller boy watched her hand, then moved his eyes up to her face.

"What are *you* supposed to be?" he demanded. The small child bent his head and snickered.

Elise felt slapped. A peculiar shame washed through her, then clean fury. At the bloodless boys. At the choppy, lonesome evening. At Dave for not being with her to joke with the kids, or be stern, or do whatever seemed to be called for. She herself had no idea what that might be.

She shut the door in their faces. "I am supposed to be someone who can shut the door on rude, ungrateful, ugly people," she murmured. She watched at the peephole as the boys walked back to the single bicycle and moved it down the driveway and on to the frontage road, turning toward Meadowbrook Estates.

After they'd gone, Elise sat for a few moments in the chair by the telescope, hoping to see a few deer in the moonlight to calm down. But she began to feel like a window display and she had a small vision of the boys circling back, sneaking through the woods, so she lowered the woven shade and made a drink and leafed through her *Bon Appetits*. There was an article about the perfect country Thanksgiving. She studied the menu; imagined the food and how much work it would amount to realistically. You'd have to start a full day ahead, but it looked worth it. She read the entire article, then moved the magazine closer to the lamp and gazed upon the people gathered around the big feast.

Jonathan, the host with the carving knife, was a former stockbroker who now had a small company that restored old farm houses in Virginia. His wife Rose-Ann was his business partner and a genius with simple fresh foods. Jonathan and Rose-Ann's friends included a wine broker and a gallery owner and a tawny-haired couple who raised merino sheep. They all seemed to be about Dave and Elise's ages, maybe a shade younger, and looked incredibly handsome and full of high spirits.

They seemed too intelligent and alert not to have had occasional conflicts, maybe outright misunderstandings and disloyalties, over the years. But for now, at the beautiful table before a crackling fire, they were relaxed. They glowed.

The doorbell rang again. Elise peered through the peephole upon a small pair of ghosts. She opened the door. Their young mother or a babysitter sat smoking in the car and didn't even look Elise's way.

The children were like penitents, pigeon-toed and anonymous, draped in last-minute costumes. Their sheets were belted at the waist. They clutched plastic pumpkins, silent as monks or executioners.

Elise dumped the last of the big bowl of candy into the pumpkins, filling them to the brim. She wished them a brisk good evening and shut the door, turned off the outdoor light and watched them fade, palely, into the dark.

She ate most of the rest of the cookies and made another drink, a short one, and then she called Lily in New York to invite her—for the first time—to Montana.

In 1974, when they all lived in Manhattan, Lily had worked for a magazine called *Caesura* and had dated a sculptor named Damon, accent on the second syllable, who was constructing a series of conical iron mono-somethings on pedestals.

One day, Damon returned from a month at Yaddo to announce that he was moving to a village in upstate New York to live with a fellow colonist who taught dyslexic children at a preschool during the mornings and worked on a biography of Amelia Earhart's navigator in the afternoons. Damon told Lily that he thought she, Lily, was sheer dynamite in every way, and always would be, but that he couldn't ignore what he had with this other woman—a feeling he described by making what Lily called "a gnawing sound."

Lily vowed a year of celibacy and sublimation. She and Elise were roommates then, and Elise had just started up with Dave Lavender, a copywriter at the ad agency where she worked in accounts. For a few months—before Lily began to see another sculptor named Pete—the three of them spent at least an evening a week together at a play, a restaurant, an opening, or just lounging around Elise and Lily's apartment, cooking and drinking wine.

On Halloween of that year, they went to a party disguised as each other. This was Lily's idea. They all wore black jeans, black turtlenecks, loafers, watch caps. Their masks were wonderfully lifelike moldings that incorporated color photos of their faces, a little sideline of the art director at *Caesura*.

Elise and Lily both wanted to wear Dave's face, so they flipped for it and Elise won. Lily went as Elise. Dave went as Lily.

In the cab after the party, Elise and Lily huddled against Dave's impossibly great great-coat, as he called it—he dressed beautifully and extravagantly then—and he imitated, perfectly, the greeting of their host, a man named Edwin Early, who was co-owner of a gallery with the art director at *Caesura*.

They leaned together as the cab took a corner. Elise clutched Dave's knee.

"Could you believe that Marie Antoinette?" Lily cried. "Her? Him? Any guesses?"

"Him," said Elise. "Definitely."

"Her, I think," said Dave. "A big-boned her."

What they were all thinking about was the moment when Marie Antoinette had drawn herself or himself up tall, and extended a white-gloved arm to beckon a thin tuxedoed bat. The bat's mask ended in a point at his top lip. He had faced the imposing and frothy Marie Antoinette—she held a piece of cake in one hand—and he had spread his huge bony wings and wrapped them around her powdered white shoulders. Then they had engaged in a drowning kiss while the person the bat had arrived with, a glossy butler with frozen downcast eyes, held the tails of the bat's topcoat.

They were reluctant to let that scene disappear, so it was still with them when they arrived at the apartment. Wine was uncorked; candles were lit; a slim joint was passed around. Lily rested each hand on the opposite shoulder, making a lovely, self-mocking X across her breasts. "Maybe some olives?" she said in Elise's drawl. And she walked slowly with a beautiful little sway to the refrigerator and brought them back in a blue bowl with a silver rim. She set the bowl before them, and bowed her head ceremoniously. "Hmmm?" she said.

The radiator pinged. Sirens cried in the distance.

The mask of Elise's face hung from Lily's wrist like a handbag.

At the beginning of the evening, they had lined themselves up at the closet mirror. Curvy Elise with Dave's intent, carved-looking face. Tall lean Lily with her pale fingers adjusting Elise's full-mouthed smile. Lily's perfect oval perched atop Dave's rangy body.

They had put the self-timing camera on the dresser and taken half a roll of film, arms around each others' waists—photos that would remain, for all their long lives, the documents of their brief and perfect equipoise.

The jet wavered down through the bright light bringing a fresh cargo of Thanksgiving visitors. It had been a completely hectic day for Elise. She had had to supervise the relaxing of eight homes—give her helpers the keys, get the keys back, get their reports, and so on. As soon as Lily stepped off the plane, Elise was calling it quits for a few days. She would leave the world to her answering machine and enjoy her old friend's company; show her what kind of life she and Dave had managed for themselves.

She felt a small wave of defensiveness already—fear that she and Dave wouldn't seem interesting anymore, though Lily was always saying on that phone that she envied them, and everyone she knew was on Prozac, and the only reason she didn't get out of the city was that she was too tired to make a move, to face a move. For a couple of years, she had described herself as exhausted to the core.

Elise had rushed home an hour and a half before Lily's plane was due; rushed fifteen miles out of town to throw together a beef bourguignon and turn it on low. She wanted that winey, wintry smell to be filling the house when Lily walked in the door. And thank God the day was cooperating too. It was white and sun-blasted, surreal with sun, and the mountains were perfect. You had to be impressed.

Lily stepped off the plane, serene and chic in a long-skirted black riding suit. She looked exactly as she had the last time Elise and Dave saw her, four years earlier, after Santa Barbara and before Montana.

Looking at her now, Elise felt the lumpiness of her own thighs, the jaggedness of the caffeine she'd been fueling herself with all day, the bulk and orangeness of the sheepskin coat that had cost her a mint, the five years' difference in their ages.

She felt betrayal. If Lily was tired, it was about as good-looking as tired got.

"I am so stressed out it's unbelievable," Lily said as she retrieved her first sleek suitcase from the conveyor belt. "The worst. I had to simply sit myself down and say, 'Do it, Lily. Get out of here. Let them scream.'"

She looked past the mounted animal heads, through the tall windows at the searing brightness, the blue and white mountains. "Very nice," she said.

They piled Lily's three suitcases into the back of the Cherokee and talked a little about the Atlanta airport and airline food.

"And Dave?" Lily asked. "What about Dave? I'm dying to see that man because I have a question for him. How can he want to be an animal doctor, when he couldn't even keep a gerbil alive in that dive of an apartment he had back when?"

Elise shrugged cheerfully, trying to remember the gerbil, trying to remember the three of them in Dave's apartment. Trying to picture the occasion.

"Didn't that gerbil died of some mysterious cause and we always thought it was a fatal act of neglect—the wrong kind of little gerbil wheel, or food, or something? Something obvious that we'd just missed?"

Elise shrugged again, uncomprehending. She pulled up behind an unmoving Trooper that had the left-turn light and honked furiously.

"Dave's fine," she said when they were moving again. "I should know. I pass him a couple of times a week in the driveway and we wave hi. I couldn't say with absolute certainty that he is absolutely fine, but he does seem fine from a distance."

Lily looked closer at her. "Really, Miss Elise," she said. "How are you-all?"

What to say? That there was a quality to Dave these days that made Elise furious and broke her heart? No. Maybe, somewhere into Lily's visit, she'd simply offer her this one small story. That she had risen at dawn one day and made a batch of blueberry muffins. That Dave was out in the subzero cold fiddling with the incubator they had bought and which they planned to use for a small chicken operation. That she had put on her big down coat and walked out into the rosy light, the glowing quiet of that first hour when the day is still so unlived.

She thought she would call Dave in to warm up, have a cup of coffee and a warm muffin. Listen to NPR and talk a little and then they would drive off to their busy days, having had that small thing, that small time, between them.

She had come around the corner of the garage, squinting into the sun pouring off the top of the mountain, and she had seen Dave leaning against his pickup, his head in his arm as if he were asleep. He didn't move; just stood there, eyes in the crook of his arm, like a child counting while the rest of them hid.

"Dave," she had called softly and his whole body had jumped. And when he turned to face her, he looked as if he'd just finished a furious argument, and that he had lost.

It was a perfect intimate dinner in front of a crackling fire. Link Runyon was at his most charming, in part because there had just been a big feature in the *New York Times* about his stressed cowboy hats—how meticulous and time-consuming the construction was. He was a real cowboy himself, the article pointed out, and his father before him. He therefore knew what a hat was going to look like over time, and he could create that look, right down to the sweatmarks, before the hat ever left his shop. A hat from Link would never have to look brand-new.

He had just gotten a big order from an upscale outdoor concern in Manhattan. They were flying him out to introduce his hats, in person, because he had the right range-weathered looks.

Everyone was animated. The food was interesting and delicious; the wine inspired. Dave put his arm around Elise and kissed the bridge of her nose. He laughed with her. They'd been telling Manhattan stories and he seemed restored to that earlier version of himself.

Elise knew it was the presence of Lily that called up this earlier Dave, and she now knew that she'd invited Lily to Montana to do precisely that. Calculating the risk, she had taken it.

Lily put her fingertips on Link's forearm and tilted her glossy head toward him. She wore a white cashmere sweater that looked electric. Elise left them before the pretty fire, and took a bundt cake and a carafe of decaf into the living room. She plumped the pillows on the big couches, lit a few candles, raised the woven blind to see snow made bright by a high moon. She heard her husband murmur something she couldn't quite make out, and she heard Lily's silvery laugh. She called them happily away from the table.

As she waited for them, she moved her face close to the window to peer beyond its reflection. What she saw then was a simple picture of a simple moment. It is late-afternoon, winter, and the last sun of the day is flashing off the snow. She is standing at this same window, calling over her shoulder to the man who sits in the rocker by the telescope. She tells him what she sees: A man and a woman and a small child in the far distance, walking through the wild light toward her. They wear anoraks that float around them like sheets. They wave at her. Dave waves. Lily waves. The child waves.

They stop, still small in the distance. The tall ones sink to the height of the child, say something, stand again. The three of them turn slowly. They begin to fade. Hands aloft, they strike off across the impeccable snow of the new century.

Snow Country

Paul S. Piper

THE SNOW IS VERY FAST. Two inches of cold powder on an icy crust. Fifty yards ahead of me I see your red parka disappear into the trees. Then my skis catch the slope and start to float. I take the S-curve through the fir staying in your tracks, the shift of weight as I cut the turns, and I'm in there, on top. Then it opens up and the bottom drops out. I'm in the sky, the closest I've come to flying. Blue air. Above the roar I hear Katrina's voice pound in my head. "Don't fight it. Shake your control. Let it go."

Here in the snow country we watch out for each other.

Carol and Jessie take care of the angora rabbits, the goats, and our malamute Al. Keep a fire going so the plants don't freeze. Steve picks up the mail. Others ask if there is anything they can do. Kirby drives us in his old dodge truck with the radio eternally tuned to C&W. Returning from Spokane, I think of them all and thank them silently. Clouds obliterate the mountains. We pass white fields just coming to light, cut square from dense lodgepole that cover the valley floor. Split rail fences and horses huddled head to rump. The tests were conclusive, the bone marrow transplant failed. This doctor, Erlington, a young guy with a permanent tan, pulled me aside in the hall. Four months at the most. He holds my arm for a moment then walks away. The highway is snowpacked, chitinous in the wavering headlights. Three crows fly low over it looking for carrion. Snowbanks eight feet high. Kirby sucks on an unfiltered camel and squints into the fading night. Tire chains slap the wheelwells. No one talks. Huge flakes begin to fall as we reach the Goat Creek turnoff and the one wiper that works squeaks into action. Almost home. Katrina begins stirring on the bumpy road, her blond hair thrown back, her thin face peaceful. As I watch her she opens her eyes, stretches, and softly begins to sing along with the radio. A nameless country song. Her throat thrust slightly forward trembles, catches the light of the dash. Her voice is so clear it startles me. I look over her head at Kirby who meets my eyes and smiles faintly, sad and sweet. In this way we enter another day.

Here in the near dusk on our down quilt Katrina softly scrapes my chest with her nails and whispers in my ear. She is leaving soon, she says. When, I ask? Soon, she says. Overcome with sorrow I shiver in her arms. We have been over it and over it. To her, it is a matter of will. Be brave, she says, I will visit. In the night coyotes come within a hundred yards of the house, floundering in deep snow. They howl at the sliver of moon that slides in and out of the fast-moving clouds. Al picks up their song.

Although our country is known for snow, this year is an exception. The first flakes fell on August 28th and didn't stop. Twenty-one inches by Thanksgiving. It is now January 8th and almost four feet have fallen. Snow clogs the fir and silences the sky. Closes us down, returns us to intimate spaces lit by candle, kerosene, propane. When I reach for Katrina in the long night, under the heavy covers, an emptiness, a slight depression where she lay, is all I find. Instantly awake, I sit up, see her, unaware, staring out the window into the radiant moon reflected off perfect snow. So thin her clothes seem to hang from her like cloth from a tree. Her body is a hole in the light, a shadow.

I crack ice with an axe, dip the pan, and carry it into the cabin. Icy water from a metal cup reminds me this life stings with clarity. The Swan peaks are immediate, so clear Katrina says, they're right here in the room with us. They move in and out of us like air. Her hand is hot in mine as we stand watching the sun fall behind them. At night when I am inside her I confuse our movement with the soft shushing of skis. I see the tracks shine behind us. The light in the holes the poles leave is blue.

At night the wind howls in the stovepipe and fine snow rakes the windows. Katrina's fever is unremitting now, a new symptom. Smoke rises lazily from a bay leaf candle that flickers on a book she was reading. Unable to sleep, I watch shadows turn to memories on the log wall. Watch them fade into the soft shudder of her breath. Her sudden coughing like someone shaking a gourd. The next morning she is baking blueberry muffins and singing. I am filled with joy to see her like this. I put my arms around her from behind and we stand holding each other. So thin, she is becoming air. Our twelfth winter together.

In dream we ski at dusk. Katrina's tracks are illuminated ahead of me. I watch her powerful thigh and ass muscles compress, spring open in perfect one-two rhythm. She disappears ahead of me over a small rise. I ski faster, desperately trying to catch her but when I top the rise she is gone. Dusk closes in fast with the north wind and I sense fear. I yell her name over and over but it is torn from me by the wind. Then I realize the tracks will always lead me to her. I wake laughing, joyous. The bed is soaked from her sweat. I get up and go outside. Shining a flashlight up into the snow I watch it hurl down like a meteor shower, let it bury me in disorientation. Biting black cold, no wind. I feel Katrina's heat begin to fade. In the Snow Country we come to know death intimately. No different than sleep, its dreams are the same. Its season never changes. It seems the reason for our lives.

Sun after four days of snow. Everything glistens. Bran waffles smothered in maple syrup for breakfast. Norm stops by and has coffee. We listen to some jazz. Talk. It is like always. A flock of chickadees in the alder outside the window scatters. Days go by and Katrina doesn't leave the bed. When my tears fall on her bare back she wakes, asks if it is raining. Is it spring yet, she asks?

In the Snow Country we are like family.
   Bonnie uses the horses and Norm keeps a spotlight on the ski tracks. Ernie, Alec, Ralph Townsend, Carol, and others use skis. The rest wade through waist-deep snow in the wake of the horses. We know what we don't want to know, but also what we must do. With unbelievable strength Katrina has climbed the south face behind the cabin to the ridge, climbed the ridge until trees thin out and the steepness of the slope stops us. An avalanche chute breaks off on the left and plunges five hundred yards to where it cliffs a hundred and seventy feet above the river. There is no way down but death. Sky and stars, dwarf fir buried in snow. Norm turns the spotlight off and we watch her tracks illuminated by moonlight cross the bowl, then veer sharply, dropping straight into the chute's darkness.

Haircut

Ruth McLaughlin

I knew I was lucky to be Georgia's friend. I was her friend because I could make her laugh. Otherwise I had nothing going for me: no money for clothes, no looks. But I could make Georgia laugh. Once in ninth grade, when she looked across the aisle at me, I straightened into the stance of Teddy Roosevelt in our chapter picture as he gesturingly delivered the speech about carrying a big stick. Georgia laughed. Then she wept. She had to get out of her purse a handful of Kleenex, digging around in lipsticks, chapsticks, two pretty combs; paraphernalia I admired. Georgia wasn't pretty, but her sister, a cheerleader, was. That Georgia's sister was a cheerleader, and also that she had the money for nice clothes and hair, canceled out what Georgia really was: a fat girl. I felt lucky to be her friend.

Georgia ignored my cheap clothes. I tried to keep up on hair, though my curls sprung out of their pageboy. Most of the other girls had perms, out of the question for me. But with natural curl I didn't need it. At the end of school each year my mother hacked my hair off Dutch-boy style; by the beginning of school it was long enough to roll under again into a pageboy.

Then in my junior year of high school everything changed. A cheerleader (not Georgia's sister) came to school with hair cut short, layered in soft curls. A razor cut, she called it. Everyone gathered around.

Georgia and her sister got new haircuts and perms right away. I thought Georgia's face looked even rounder with her short hair. She was always jolly, like a mascot to all the boys on sports teams and to the cheerleaders. At basketball games in the overheated armory that was our gym, she milled around the cheerleaders after the game, waiting with them for the players to come up from the basement showers all decked out for their dates. I watched from the stage where the pep band had played, drawing a swab through my clarinet. The boys said things to Georgia that made everyone laugh all around before slipping away in the frosty air with their dates.

All the girls started getting razor cuts. Our high school was small, not even 100 students, so no one was a stranger. Whenever anyone came to school with a new haircut—usually Monday morning—girls who had already cut their hair gave even freshmen knowing smiles.

Once a year my mother got a haircut and perm in town. But it was a necessity: my mother had the straightest, awfullest hair, as she often said. By the time of her April birthday it had grown all the way to her shoulders where it hung stiff as a broom. The lady who cut it liked to say that her hair had the texture of steel wool. As her hair lengthened so did the row of bobby pins my mother used to keep it from her face. On April 29th, her birthday, we were all glad when she came home from her trip to town alone in the car; new short hair in a knotty perm.

But I had curly hair, fine-textured, in a nice shade of brown. From articles in my mother's *Ladies Home Journal*, I identified it as my "best feature." Even when it sprung out of its pageboy into curls, Georgia admired it. When we loitered in the school's basement lavatory after lunch, waiting to rush to class at the insistent buzzer, Georgia liked to run a comb from her purse through my hair.

Georgia no longer dug around in her purse after lunchtime for her rattail comb or the large pocket comb to draw through my hair. She rearranged her new curls at the mirror. I waited beside her for the bell to ring, listening to the sighs of leaking toilets. Georgia finished her hair and smiled at both of us in the mirror.

I didn't even dare to ask for a layered haircut in town. I knew how tight things were. On Saturdays, we sometimes drove the ten miles to town for supplies. I followed behind my mother on her snail's pace through the grocery aisles. It was shopping by rejection: not ketchup but mustard, not real vanilla but the imitation; everything else off-brand.

My only spending money came from occasional babysitting for a neighboring well-to-do rancher. One late night I craved a snack and opened up a cupboard door. The contents of the cupboard seemed strange; the rancher's wife didn't bake. She may have baked. But not biscuits, muffins, cookies, cake, pie, sometimes doughnuts, and all of our bread like my mother. I looked for crackers in the cupboard. At home I was allowed a cookie a day from the cookie jar, and all the saltine and graham crackers that I wanted. I ate saltines and grahams on alternate days; sometimes for a change I put them together in what I called a brown-and-white sandwich.

At the top of the cupboard I spied something we never had at home: hot dog buns. Cozy in their plastic bag shaped just for them. At home we had hot dogs often, minus the bun. And the ketchup. I pulled the bag down from the shelf just to look at it. I saw that two buns were missing. Why not one more? I thought. I worked a bun free; unlike my mother's bread it was feather light in my hand. I decided to sneak a look in the refrigerator for ketchup. It was right in front, tall among milk cartons (the ranchers didn't have to milk a cow). I twisted off the cap and laid a band of ketchup all along the bun. My mouth watered. Suddenly I heard a sound, and turned to look into the wide eyes of a six-year-old: "What are you *doing?*" I crushed the bun and scooted the little girl back to bed.

After the haircuts began there was a change one day at school. We switched seats in typing class; Mr. Grissom couldn't see the faces of some of the shorter kids in the room. I was moved behind Candace, a cheerleader. Not Georgia's sister, but the one who had started razor cuts. We had four cheerleaders, the royalty of our school.

We had lots of down time in typing class. Mr. Grissom explained that we could learn as much about typing reading our manuals. Or studying our keys. He hated racket.

The typing tables were narrow front to back; students sat close. Right away I stared at Candace's hair. I knew she wouldn't turn around and catch me, someone beneath her radar. In the long boring minutes—Mr. Grissom said that he wouldn't start a time test till the hour, and suggested that we practice typing in our minds—I studied Candace's hair.

I broke it down: layering meant that all the hair was the same length. About three inches, I gauged, moving my pencil dangerously close to a blonde curl.

"Begin!" Mr. Grissom shouted. Fumbling my fingers onto the keys, I missed a few precious seconds of the one-minute test. I crashed through the test, making mistakes that I knew would dearly cost me: three words subtracted for each mistake. But I was jubilant. I had got Candace's hair. Then at the end of the test, like frosting on the cake, Candace turned her head to gauge her progress on the wall chart. I had time to memorize the side of her hair down to its jaunty spit curl.

On Sunday afternoon, in front of my mother who was baking, I removed one of my dad's razor blades from the cupboard above the kitchen sink. I went to look for the tape to cover one sharp end. I also found the scissors in their drawer.

The tape, the scissors. Ours was a household of single things. Also "the chapstick," and until this last year when I had used babysitting money to buy my own—"the hairbrush."

In my bedroom I squeezed myself into the space before my mirrored chest of drawers. I pushed back my little figurines—puppies and kittens ranging in play all across the chest of drawers—and removed Goldie, the goldfish, to a safe place on the floor.

I'd already washed my hair in the kitchen sink; I stood ready before the mirror. My dad was outside doing chores; my mother still baking. I picked up a reed from my clarinet. I'd thought the discovery that my reeds were three inches long a good omen.

I stood the clarinet reed on my scalp and drew up a hank of hair—about six inches longer than the reed. I sawed with the razor blade at the reed's height, and the hair fell off. My haircut had begun.

Piece by piece I cut my hair, watching myself in the mirror. I carved off long strands, each releasing a curl that tumbled forward on my scalp; perky and pretty. I wondered if that was how Candace felt every day: perky and pretty.

Hanks of hair drifted onto my crowded cat and dog figurines. Some fell beside Goldie on the floor, who darted around her bowl in the excitement.

I kept waiting for trouble. But in a little over twenty minutes the part of my head in view looked as good, I thought, as Candace's.

Then it was time to move to the back. I parked the clarinet reed on my scalp and looked into the mirror. The reed and the hand that held it had disappeared behind my head.

I gripped the reed that was trying to slide down the slope of my head, and lined up the razor by feel. I sawed, and a hank of hair fell onto the floor. A tingling arose in the tip of one of my fingers.

I set up another strand of hair. The second stroke of the razor sliced across my thumb. I took my thumb down to look at it. The cut was across the joint, which resisted bending. I went out to the cupboard above the kitchen sink to find a Band-Aid, feeling a little rising panic.

The house was quiet. My mother had absented herself outside in chores. She had glanced at me when I took the razor blade, freezing in mid-stroke as she pushed muffin batter into the gaping mouths of little fluted paper cups. I gave her a broad smile; she didn't need more worry.

I wrapped the Band-Aid tightly, numbing my finger, and picked up the razor blade again. I went on. I cut, blind, row after row across my head. I cut my fingers repeatedly. I switched hands, sawing at strands of hair left-handed. I cut myself immediately and switched back.

I cut and cut, settling into the feeling that the blood and pain were normal; the razor's cut a not unpleasant stinging.

At last I was through. All of the hair I could feel was short. The curls in back weren't perky, but matted and sticky with blood.

I doubted that my mother was in the kitchen, but I couldn't take a chance. Kneeling beside the tub in our sinkless bathroom, I rinsed pink water from my hair.

Before it was dry I wrapped bunches of hair around plastic rollers, securing straggly ends with bobby pins. I had no idea what I had done.

From her sentry post on the school's front step Georgia spied me stepping off the bus. Everyone mingled before school began, and Georgia liked the top step to pick out friends to greet. I saw her mouth drop open.

On the bus ride to town I'd tried to get used to my new hair, touching it with my fingers. I couldn't feel it through the bandages and it worried me. What if it was awful? Though I didn't think so. My mother's jaw dropped when she saw what I'd done. As I pulled the rollers out before school she said it looked fine; she tried to look at the hair instead of the bandages. Four of the fingers on my left hand and one on the right wore bandages.

"Kid!" Georgia shouted. "It's cute!" Others turned to stare. Georgia was smiling. I walked closer, waiting for the smile to fade.

Georgia squinted all around my face. Finally she said, "Who cut it?"

I looked at her. It was a normal question; she did not look horrified. I tried to smile. I was waiting for her to make the connection between my Band-Aids and my hair—hacked fingers, hacked hair—but suddenly Georgia disappeared, ducking to view my hair from behind.

In the silence as Georgia stood behind me, I promised God that if I could get away with it just this once, I would never again try to cut my hair.

Finally I heard Georgia say from behind: "Vicki?"

Vicki—the youngest, prettiest hairdresser in town! Not the one my mother went to. I felt Georgia fluff my curls; I smiled as she faced me again.

But she was studying the Band-Aids and at any moment she would guess. I decided to give her a hint; as if I wanted her to know. "My favorite hairdresser," I said. "Very exclusive."

"Shirleyann?" Georgia said. Then the only other hairdresser in town, the one who cut my mother's hair: "Louise?" I shook my head.

Just then the big orange Dane Valley bus rumbled into view. "Oh, honestly," Georgia said. She was smiling at the mystery of my hair or at someone disgorged from the bus. "Oh, never mind."

I watched her drift off. She was my best friend.

Had she guessed, I decided, I would have told her. But I would have spun it into something to make her laugh—as though it were hilarious even to me that I had become my own hairdresser.

That day in typing class Candace turned her head all the way around to look at me. We were between speed tests.

My haircut was so late that she had gotten hers trimmed up once. She stared at me.

She looked at my bandaged fingers. No one had yet remarked on the bandages, looking like a suicide gone berserk. Candace looked all around at the hair on my head, our matching spit curls—then she smiled.

It was the first time she had smiled at me. It was the first time I had looked her in the face. I saw she had tiny freckles across her nose that she probably hated.

I had practiced the smile I would return if a cheerleader ever noticed me. I saw a little light of friendliness in Candace's blue eyes.

We were nearly twins in spit curls and shirtwaist dresses. Candace's dress was blue, highlighting her eyes. Mine was a woven red plaid with brown tones the color of my hair. My secret was that, for a fraction of the cost of Candace's dress, I had sewn my own.

I stared at Candace across a cluttered landscape: of our family's cramped house; my hands rough from outdoor work; my imitation suede leather shoes, balding. Parents without distinction: my father arriving in muddy overshoes at a classroom door to hand me my forgotten clarinet. My mother dulled by two years of crop failure; even her cheerfulness seeming to come out of a misery in which she had parked herself so that there could be no more new surprises.

I did not smile back at Candace.

"Begin!" Mr. Grissom shouted. Candace turned around. I hurled my fingers onto the keys and banged hard. Pain shot up through the bandages. I didn't care. I hit the keys hard enough to murder them, and at the end of the minute I had to count my words twice. With the ringing of the machines still in my ears, I found that I had typed 93 words with only one mistake: a new top score.

As the class watched, Mr. Grissom lengthened my red line on the chart with his colored marker. I had passed Candace, the queen of our typing class.

In the lavatory following lunch Georgia resumed combing my hair. She liked to plump my curls with the handle of her rattail comb, sometimes removing the little mirror from her purse for me to admire it. I tried to keep us talking while she did my hair. I didn't want her to start wondering about my hairdresser. We talked about boys—which ones were cute. Because of her associations I deferred to Georgia's judgments, though neither of us had ever had a date. We talked about what teachers were cute. I cracked her up by trying out her name with Mr. Grissom's—"Georgia Grissom." I said he'd saved himself forty-five years just for her, though he hadn't managed to save much of his hair.

Georgia laughed and laughed.

Each day I kept my secret was a triumph.

Then I broke my promise to never cut my hair again. Christmas, and our holiday concert, loomed. My curls were drooping, dangling. I set aside a Sunday afternoon. I tried something new. I dug two mismatched church gloves from the discard clothes on the floor of my mother's closet. Readying to cut, I studied myself in the mirror. My left-hand glove, holding up my hair, had a tiny row of fake pearl buttons. I looked like someone out of my mother's magazine: ladies who dressed up in gloves even for visits to the hairdresser. But I had to abandon the gloves—one pale pink, one white. My hair slipped in them, making my cuts jagged.

The remaining year-and-a-half of school I cut my own hair. On a Sunday afternoon I arranged my tools on the cleared chest of drawers as if for surgery. I found a better technique. I pre-bandaged my fingers, dulling—but not altogether omitting—the razor's slash. I hated to waste the bandages.

Through the rest of high school Georgia stayed my best friend; waiting for me on the front steps, or just inside the door in frigid weather. She started wearing lipstick, making her look slightly clownish. In the high-walled lavatory she tried it on me: I couldn't smile back at her in the mirror; I thought I resembled my mother.

Georgia never asked who cut my hair. I believed I had fooled her.

Candace never smiled at me again.

At the Edge of Things
from "Lady," a novel in progress

Ralph Beer

He stands in wind and morning light watching claybank tablelands to the north where wheat-farmed dirt rides warming air. He wears work clothes, even on this most festive day, a dun Resistol stained along the band, jeans pale with age, broken West Coast loggers and a denim shirt, the cuffs twice folded, exposing walnut forearms that reach to hands hard-veined and scarred. He leans against the bone-white handles of a walking plow cantilevered toward the county road, transom for a mailbox bearing in faded letters the name Countryman.

At his back a shelterbelt: six horseshoe-shaped rows of stricken spruce and olive that enclose an orchard and the buildings hidden within. Among the trees a pheasant bells. Blackbirds come from cattail sloughs, winging toward the weed-bound farmland he faces, their shadows lancing his like so many missiles. Across the road, a sign nailed to a sawhorse reads:

FARM SALE!
FREE LUNCH

Dust rises above the section road to the west, and beneath it, bunched as if for protection, a ragged column of trucks and pickups, a few pulling fifth-wheel trailers, others trailing phantoms of boom and bust. They come in rattletrap sedans and third-hand flatbeds, vehicles distorted into rubbery motion by corduroyed road and heat as they top the last hill, a column of neighbors and other unfortunates—a parade of the crazed, who can tell?—come all this way to feed at auction.

They slow, downshifting to make the turn, some drivers nodding or giving two-fingered salutes from steering wheels to the man at the plow, who dips his chin in return—bland acknowledgment of one to another, each and all children of this place, their necks cracked like mud flats by the same sun, pale eyes hardened by the same hard miles of loss. No two among them friends.

Stragglers arrive alone or in pairs. A fox crosses, as if directed by a traffic signal. The aluminum lunch wagon passes, high school girls aflame in its windows, yearning for escape. A Dodge diesel turns in, followed by a Blazer with star decals on doors and hood, which stops, backs, and stops again beside the plow with a metallic pong of transmission jammed into PARK. The driver's tinted window comes down an inch, two, then the rest of the way, followed by a cool wash of air from within as the deputy leans out to spit.

The pearled Stetson shades a nose gone to bloodshot mush from youthful violence and latter-day drink. Hard fat over muscle packed into a shirt a size too small. Leopard's eyes. In a voice almost resigned: "Horn, you going to be your natural self and give me some grief here today?"

The man so addressed slides burled hands into hip pockets, leans down. "You'll sure be the first to know, Bob."

The deputy coughs a faint snort far back in the clogged passages of his ruined nose. "Sure," he says with a twist of his head that brings them eye to eye, one tribe of hunter facing another. Then he sighs, taps the steering wheel with his wedding ring, drops the Blazer into gear with a meaty hand, and pulls languidly away as the two men exchange wolfy grins.

Lastly a boy treadles past on a bicycle, sweating, thin legs in jeans tied about at the ankles with twine to keep his cuffs from the chain. It is a girl's Schwinn, balloon tires nearly bald, yet the boy dismounts beyond the mailbox as if from a roping horse sitting back on a calf. A sunny boy from a jelly jar label, scion of the failed come out from town, where he summers with his dead folks' kin. He looks at Horn, almost stops, then continues down the weeded lane toward the amplified shrieks of a PA system gone wrong. Horn knows the boy, was present the day he was named and blessed.

In the dirt yard between house and sheds a rude platform has been cobbled from plywood and two-by-fours atop an iron-wheeled hay wagon. Beyond it, stretching to either side and backed by the westerly run of shelter belt, stands a row of tractors, trucks, and implements, which men climb upon or kick with impunity. Off to one side, an almost new Gleaner combine. And for antiques, a galvanized threshing machine with wooden spouts; a sulky plow and middle buster with fenestrated iron seats; a fanning mill, half-filled by the nightly labors of trade rats with bolts and bones and sticks. Directly beneath the auctioneer's dais, two zinc-covered milkhouse tables, littered with household items, hand tools, a half-dozen rifles, and assorted tack draw those in need of gossip and a chance to bid, if bids stay small.

With bear-like quickness the auctioneer heaves himself onto the platform where a young woman gazes beyond the rows of hats and caps at God knows what as she waits with a grinding of teeth for the sale to begin. The pitchman waves a bullprick cane, holds a microphone to burgundy lips. "Boys," he says, puffing his cheeks and cocking his head as if to listen, "she don't get much better than this. The machinery has all been shedded, the vehicles got one name only on the pink slips. The buildings are sound, and the land speaks for itself. All this place needs is a good woman, some kids, and a little sweat to bring 'er around. Hell, you know that."

He takes off his lid, mops his face with a rag, sets the hat down low over pinpoint eyes. "It's gonna get hot up here," he says with a cheesy grin, "so let's get her sold. Item number one: A 1970 Ford, ton-and-a-half truck with eighteen-foot bed, grain box, and hoist—be just the ticket for a spare during harvest. I need fifteen hundred to get us started. Fifteen, gimme fifteen, five . . . ." The roundness of his voice grows richer, spreading in volume to encompass those listening and those gazing blankly about. A voice full of promise that half there assembled recognize as the self-same venal pronouncement of greed that whispers to them of their most secret lust, which is the need to claim, to grasp, to own.

Yet only two men, neighbors and cousins at that, show interest. They stand shoulder to shoulder, bidding the truck back up from the auctioneer's vexed low to sell at nine hundred dollars.

"Friends," from this hawker in country garb, "let's don't be this way. If we can't sell it here, we can darn sure sell it down the road. What we are not going to do is give it away. Now wake up and come on!" He aims the varnished bull pizzle at an International 2+2 articulated tractor with duals all the way around, three remotes, cab air, AM/FM/

cassette. "Look at those tires. Just been majored, too. There's a hundred and seventy horses ready to go to work, so give me thirty thousand for her and drive 'er home." Again the chanting of amplified numbers spills over the uplifted faces where flies circle and settle at will.

After a while the fat man stops counting backwards and sighs. "Boys . . . " he says, his marbled voice trailing off as a man in a white straw hat and short-sleeved shirt steps onto the rostrum beside him. He takes the auctioneer's paw in his own, swings microphone and hand as one to his mouth, says, "Neighbors, I *know* these folks were well-liked around here. Nobody's forcing them to sell. They just want out. You sure can't help them by treating an honest sale this way, so let's get this over or go home." He releases the auctioneer's hand and takes one step back, clearing the fat man's line of sight, yet keeping his eyes moving from one to another of the men standing below, knowing that among those who recognize him there are some who hold his service in low regard. How many times has he held paper for Dutch there? Or sold ground for guys like Archie? Or helped others like Dale turn a 1031? His eyes stop for a moment on each of them until he comes to a man off by himself, a dark man, one hand tucked to the thumb in his pants above the zipper, the other hanging loose at his side. Some blood there, the broker knows, down from the reservation, looking for work or something to steal.

The auctioneer's voice gains momentum, tongue and jaw ratcheting numbers until someone in the second row waves and the bidding begins. The International sells for nine thousand and change.

Smaller tractors, tumblebug plows, chisel bottoms with rod-weeders; discs, drills, harrows, and the old thresher sell in slow succession, then a Powder River chute with some pipe panels, bundles of fence posts, irrigation pipe, a drill press, welder and torch. No one bids on the combine, though several go after an assortment of bolts and nails in buckets, then two mounds of bent and rust-pitted scrap iron.

Of the items on the milkhouse tables, saddles and harness sell first, the harness still oiled, the saddles ready for use. A .250-3000 Savage goes for a hundred dollars less than pawnshop price. A Model 72 Winchester .22 comes up, and the broker steps forward again, says he'd like to bid on the rifle if nobody minds. "Had one just like it on my daddy's place."

The barker faces around, spreads his left hand as if to sell the broker himself. "Twenty-five bucks," he says. The broker nods, smiling the smile of a deal already done.

"Thirty," from somewhere in the crowd.

The broker shrugs, nods, looks to the auctioneer, who takes a bid of forty, grins with ill-disguised ennui, and twirls his index finger in an upward gyre.

Fifty, sixty, seventy, the price climbs a brief thermal of enthusiasm until the frivolous fold their arms, and those who have shilled the price for fun shake their heads. At a hundred and sixty dollars only the breed stays in, squatting on his boot heels, scratching the dirt with a stick, which he lifts to mark his bid when the auctioneer barks and points his way.

Heads turn back and forth with sly and furtive glances. Elbows find neighbors' ribs. The deputy, corndog in hand, wipes mustard from the corner of his mouth. At two hundred and thirty dollars the auctioneer goes silent, looks at the man beside him, who is no longer having fun. The broker wonders if the buck is drunk, then shakes his head, says, "Nope. Too rich for me."

When nothing remains but dirt, they sell that: four sections of cropland, 320 acres of coulee bottom pasture, and the quarter where the buildings stand. A man wearing baggy shorts buys the whole works. The auctioneer gives half-hearted thanks to those few left and, bending to check the bookkeeper's figures, says, "Aw, shit."

"Well, shit yourself, John," the woman answers, fanning herself with a sale flier with one hand while writing a receipt for a jug-eared farmer with watery eyes who turns away in scarlet confusion.

"I'll be wanting my check," the auctioneer tells the broker.

"Soon as we get ours, you get yours."

Horn yawns, looks from those departing to the orchard and swale of coulee, where he and Mace Countryman shot gophers, spring evenings after school. Mace was about as fair as a kid could get, but they had nonetheless been school bus buddies. Later, friends.

Horn lays cash for the .22 before the auctioneer's assistant, neglects the federal firearms form, and is lifting the rifle from the table when he becomes aware of someone at his shoulder. Horn extracts the tubular magazine, opens the bolt, closes it, tries the safety, which holds. He reopens the action. He remembers the ivory bead on the end of the barrel exactly, and the Redfield peep, too, mounted atop the breech. Where tang met stock, the initials M C lay carved in the oiled wood. He looks at the man in the white straw hat and short-sleeved shirt—held together at the throat with a bolo of turquoise the size of a moose turd—as he slides the empty magazine home.

Horn lifts his eyebrows.

"That popgun mean something special to you, Chief?"

"Yes, sir, it does," Horn says, feeling the muscles at the backs of his arms go goosey, as if straining toward speed. The broker cuts him a look, then waves and calls to someone off to the side.

As Horn walks toward his El Camino he nods to an officer of the law who leans among the tansy against the cold steel of a Butler bin, taking his ease with glugmug in hand, near the end of his shift. Old Bob nods back and winks.

A couple miles down the road Horn catches up with the boy on the bicycle.

"Hey," Horn says, slowing to a stop beside him.

The kid looks at him, doesn't have anything to say.

"This was your daddy's," Horn says, lifting the rifle through the window and holding it, barrel up, by its pistol grip. The boy doesn't move. Wind touches his wheatstraw hair.

"Come on, I'm in a hurry here."

The boy reaches, touches the rifle, takes it awkwardly by the harness leather sling.

"Anybody says anything, you tell them to call Clayton, over on Blanchard Creek. They'll know."

With that Horn pulls the Hurst into low and idles away, listening to the uneven roll of crank and cam as he accelerates over a rise, not daring to look in the mirror until it's too late to see the son of a friend lost at just this time of year, in hills not so very unlike these; a boy standing alone and open faced at the edge of the road in some weeds.

Fruit in Good Season

Caroline Patterson

It's true, all I wanted was to wander the hills around Hope, Montana, but Aunt Dot raised me to tea parties and ladies clubs until a ranch hand showed up on our porch with a handful of phlox and said, "A prayer is a whisper from the heart." He touched my cheek and my blood rose up against years of dim rooms where clocks ticked loudly and my aunt crossed her legs with a wheeze. I threw over those mild men, the clerk and the lawyer, with their shiny suits and dimestore bouquets. "You're trading a good name, Edie," my aunt shook her red face at me, "for a hayseed and a Bible."

Weeks later, we walked down the aisle of a rough wooden church and my aunt cried as the organist made a hash of the recessional, then we stepped out into the world.

But my story really began the night Howie rolled over in bed, pressed his flat body against mine and whispered, "Thou shalt propagate."

"Oh, Howie," I said and pulled my nightgown closer around me for my breasts were sore with nursing and exhaustion flooded me.

"Fruit in good season," he said.

"Daniel didn't sleep," I murmured. "I'm the walking dead."

"The leaf shall not wither," he said. He moved against me, his body still sinewy from the years on the ranch, one long line of tight-bound muscle, except the tiny red teeth marks where the barbed wire raked him.

"Do you know what it's like?" I said, jerking the covers up. "All these hands at you? Grabbing your arms? Your hair? Your breasts?" All the while Howie is pulling my gown up over my head until I'm naked, my breasts lit by a thin June moon and tight with cold. I pulled my hair around me for warmth. "What it's like to walk streets where the neighbors watch me, where phones rattle before I get home, *Howie Deschene's wife, did you see she wore pants on the street?"*

"Rage, rage," he whispered. There was a hoarseness in his voice I'd never heard those long nights he pulled me under the covers and the world bloomed up from our bed.

"Howie," I whispered.

His eyes went flat. He pulled my hair across my face, pressed me into the mattress.

I tightened my legs, pushed against him, and said, "Stop."

He drove against me, reciting Psalms 2, verses 1 through 9. I began to float up from myself. I hovered on the ceiling above us, looking down at my hair sheeting the bed, Howie's spine bobbing over me, white as a ghost's. I thought, *Howie* until the pain between my legs stopped, until each letter rose up before me like the skyline of some nameless city. Pines scratched the windows, and as my limbs turned from wood to ice, I heard the lilting call of a wolf and, from farther away, an answer.

The next morning he turned to me, a cold light stealing around the room, the narrow angles of his face hollowed with hunger and a look that said *help me*. He took my hands. I looked away. He got up and jerked open the window shade, and as it went flapping up, dread rose up in me, then drifted away like smoke.

I got up and started the stove.

In the front room, tight and dark with the curtains shut, I took Daniel to my breast while Howie shoved one book after another in his satchel, the pages opening and shutting like mouths. "Today we cross-pollinate tomatoes," he said, looking away because nursing embarrassed him. He grazed my cheek, closed the door, and frosted air fell to the floor and crept the baseboards.

I opened the curtains, and Daniel and I rocked and looked out at Redbow. Clouds chased down the valley, Mrs. Larsen shook out a mop on her porch, and old Mr. Peterson walked his Scotty dogs down the sun-slicked street. Age had frozen his back straight up and his arms straight out and everyday at 9:00, he took mincing steps down the bumpy road, never looking at his feet.

"Well, Danny boy." I lifted him to my other breast. "There goes Mr. Perpendicular."

Daniel reached up for my mouth and grabbed fistfuls of housecoat instead. A sliver of bologna fluttered to the floor. There was a tingling in my cheek and a stone in my heart, and I could feel myself slipping below the surface of things.

I set Daniel in his crib, and walked to the mirror to repin my hair. There was the doughy face of a peasant and mud-colored eyes, but as I pulled the hairpins, my hair fell heavy across my breasts and shoulders, and I brushed it until my scalp stung, until it haloed my head, and lit the room like slow-burning fire.

I turned to Daniel. "Look."

He lifted his arms to me.

The sun stole over Teacup Mountain and burned the feathery tops of the Ponderosa.

I took scallopeds to Mrs. Larsen that afternoon, but when I handed them to her, she smiled in a way that let me know I was never to come back. A day later, I tried the Merry Mixers. They played canasta, and as they shrieked and howled and plunked down straights and flushes, they looked over at me sorrowfully and said, "You're so *serious,* Edie, don't you ever laugh?" *Watch this.* I curved my lips in a smile and forced a laugh that sliced through me like glass.

Three days later, Mrs. Delano invited me to the Pioneer Women's Philanthropic and Cultural Society. As her Buick prowled the rain-drenched streets, she patted my gloved hand and told me how much I would like the gals. They're a hoot, she said, just the tonic for a gray spring in Redbow, Montana.

We went to the home of Mrs. Whitely, whose husband owned the *Redbow Beacon.* The women my age eyed me suspiciously, while the older ones directed things, pouring coffee, staring the group into their chairs. When everyone was seated, I stood up, brushed the skirt of my princess-style cotton piquet, and stared at the windows until the light hurt my eyes. I said, "I am Edie, wife of the science teacher."

"Science," the ladies said.

"I have a little boy, Daniel," I said and I wanted to add *and a stone in my heart.*

They started discussing a bake sale to raise money for a home for the blind in Billings. A woman across the room was upset because two people had offered to bring yellow cakes, when what was needed was variety. Another woman pulled her skirt over her knees and said quietly that she would bring snickerdoodles, but everyone ignored her. Mrs. Whitely looked at the two women, and said that there was room for two yellow cakes, but she was sure Mrs. Fitzhugh would see it in her heart to make a chocolate instead.

I stared at the rug, at the red birds that flew nowhere and blue flowers that bloomed forever, listening to the chatter, to the tick and clink of cups and saucers. Mrs. Delano whispered, "Aren't they a bunch?"

"Yes," I said. A word or a phrase seemed to burn inside me. I wanted to say *I will make kiss-me-cake.* I wanted to speak their language, to have them turn and smile at me and look at each other approvingly. My aunt raised me to say the words—coffeecake, meat loaf, black jet for evening—but she had never taught me how to speak in the spaces beneath them. How *there always dust* means *lonely,* how *I burnt the chops* is *fury.* My hands and legs seemed to grow larger and larger. My stocking wheezed as I crossed my legs, and when I dropped the cookies, they went wheeling across the floor. The ladies paused, and in that silence, something was decided.

"So nice to have you," Phyllis Whitely said, as we left in a whirl of bobbing hats. She did not say *come back.*

On the way home, Mrs. Delano said, "I'm glad you gave us a try, Edie."

"Thank you for bringing me," I said and watched her pink gloves crank the steering wheel. "Can I ask you something, Mrs. Delano?"

"Call me Carol."

"Carol, do you ever—" I couldn't find the words. *What are the words?* I watched her check the rear view mirror, "Do you ever—take care of diaper rash?"

"Good gracious for a minute there...." she said, her body relaxed into the seat. "Of course. A couple dabs of petroleum jelly and presto!" she snapped her fingers.

The car rolled to a stop at the curb. I put my hand on the door handle, but I didn't move. The blinkers clinked on and off between us. "What do you...."

She unbuttoned her coat, and looked out at the graying street, waiting.

I peeled off my gloves. I twisted my wedding ring around and around.

Suddenly I looked at her and blurted, "What do you do when your husband. . . ?"

"Oh that." Mrs. Delano laughed, but her face looked like I'd caught her naked. "It's his due, honey. We women don't always like it but. . . . " She turned around suddenly and grabbed my arm. "You know what I do?" Her eyes were heated, and the cloth violets pinned to her coat shook. "I just lie there still as a mouse and I think about crazy cakes. I wonder how one would taste with chocolate sprinkles or butter cream. And I wonder why they work. If the vinegar is what makes the cake sweet."

Eight months later, I was sitting in church among the pinched faces of Redbow, hugely pregnant in my red wool coat. The preacher finished his words of hellfire and torment, then stepped from the pulpit to gather the collection plates.

Howie patted my knee, said, "Shall we?" Every Sunday morning of the four years he'd taught Science to loggers' children in Redbow, we went down to the clammy basement of the Faith Missionary Baptist Church where we held plastic cups of watery tea and talked about Armageddon with the townspeople: Gertrude Larsen with her pursed lips, Phyllis Whitely with her sugary put-downs.

This time I didn't move. I'd heard something in the words of the sermon, in *sword of the Lord* and *darkness will come upon the earth* I'd never heard before. Instead of the fire that had stirred my blood, I heard cold, sharp words thrown like a mumbletypeg into the circle between fear and infinity. I sat there until the pew cleared, until even Mr. Schmidt, his radar ears quivering, walked to the back of the church.

Howie turned to me, a question furrowing his face.

"You go ahead. I've can't do it anymore. I'm not going down for my weekly going over by Phyllis Whitely." I buttoned my coat.

He swallowed, touched my hand, and said, "We won't stay."

"No," I said. "You go. They smile at you and talk to you, and then they see big Edie, poor thing, she's just, well, odd."

"Look." He grabbed my arm, his fingers digging into my wrist. "I don't ask much. I ask less and less, a lot less than some, but I'm on the Worship Committee. I have obligations, Edith, and they watch. They keep track."

My face went stiff. I pried his fingers off, one by one, and stood up. He looked straight ahead, erect with God, his face blazing.

"I'll get Daniel." I said. I turned down the aisle where sunlight sent down bolts of color that blurred on the polished floor into the rough shape of a cross, and I walked through it.

Daniel squirmed as I carried him from the nursery out into the street, too startled to cry. I kept on walking past the market, the hardware store, the slant-roofed houses, a chinook at my back as I dragged up Snowshoe Hill. I walked until my breath was ragged, until snow slopped over my galoshes, my feet burned with cold. At the crest of the hill I looked back at Redbow, crisscrossed with rivers and houses and the road that led north to wider valleys, and I began to scream.

At dusk, Howie let me come in, fry his pork chop, nurse Daniel to sleep. Then he picked up a coffeepot and banged it down on the counter.

"Take a good look, Edie," he said, sweeping his hand across him to indicate the sink piled with dishes and the crumb-coated floor. "Look at your life." He looked at me from a great distance.

"Well, you're a fine one, banging coffeepots, and bellowing like a bull," I said. "But I guess it's what you do best."

His face blazed. "You should talk, Miss Runaway," he said. "Where am I going to find you tomorrow? Libby? Think you'll hop a freight to Drummond? Why confine it to the state? Why don't you head off to Tacoma for a few days—just for a break?"

"Who told you I ran away? Miss Phyllis Knows-Everyone's-Business, or Mr. Schmidt Hears-Everyone's-Business? Does anyone in this town have anything better to do than meddle?"

"These people are nice people, Edie. You don't give them a chance. You don't talk to them, get to know them. You just give up. You gave up on this town from the day we came."

"That's not true," I said. "And can I help it if they don't like me? Can I help it if they don't invite me back?"

"Even if they did," Howie said, and he put his hand on his hip and smiled. "You wouldn't go."

He was absolutely right, which infuriated me. I headed for the door. He got there first.

"Kneel down," he said, looking into my eyes. "Kneel down and ask forgiveness."

"I'm not ready for begging. Or forgiveness."

"Get ready," Howie said, for his was not a religion of compromise.

He led me into the bedroom. We knelt on the cold linoleum, and he pressed my hands together, called, "Punish us, Lord, for Satan has entered our hearts!" His voice lashed the dim air, his eyes burned, and I knew, as far as he was concerned, the fight was over.

I vowed the next morning to do better: no running away, no teetering piles of dishes in the sink, no roving dust balls. Moving quickly in spite of my bulk, I tore down curtains and washed them, beat rugs, dusted shelves, scrubbed walls, moving like a dervish through the rooms, while Daniel stared at me through the slats of the crib, squealing and waving his arms when I walked toward him. The first night, when Howie walked in the door, he kissed me, and sent up thanks. But after I painted each room, after four days of moving drop cloths to eat, and sleeping in cold rooms, he got impatient.

"Don't you think you've done enough?" he said. "Can't you stop now?" He leaned over Daniel and wiped his nose with great ceremony. "This is making him sick. We'd better finish now."

But the truth was I couldn't stop, and each time I neared the end of a task, a small panic would grow in me until another arose to take its place. When I thought it would alarm him if I painted again, I got it in my head to build a fruit room.

I pictured looking at my shelves, groaning with huckleberry and raspberry jams, chokecherry syrup, butter beans, dried venison, and the hulking crocks of sauerkraut. Instead of the individual jars, instead of berries we'd picked up Lost Creek or the deer Howie shot in the Cabinets, I thought that the collage of purples and reds and greens would tell me *there is a design*. And if I didn't like the pattern, I could rearrange it.

In the root cellar, I nailed up shelves, hammering one sweet-smelling board after the other, stopping only to touch my stomach and wipe my forehead. Daniel clapped his hands at the ring of metal on metal, reached toward spiders crawling up lacy webs, toward mice scurrying off to dark corners.

A day later, Howie came flying home with a hardware-store bill in his hand. "Edie, you've spent fifty-four dollars on supplies. Fifty-four dollars! Do you know how much money that is? That's half my wages. We'll barely make the house payment!"

"Let me use up what I have," I said quickly, figuring I had enough to finish the shelves.

"No," he said. "Stop." He looked up at me sideways. "Promise me?"

I looked at him across the room, and said in a small voice, "Okay,"

"Put it here." Howie held out his Bible.

I placed my hand on its grainy cover and said, "I promise," and hoped that I meant it.

The night he came home from Prayer Circle, I was lining up cans of tomatoes and green beans next to my preserves, on shelves that smelled sharp and clean as sawdust. I lined them up neatly in rows, the green beans after the peas, the Spam next to the sardines, and in the silvered moonlight, the cans glowed like bullets. The room was thick with the smells of dirt and tin, and I held my belly, singing, "Jimmy crack corn, and I don't care." I kept singing until I could feel him behind me, until I could smell the tang of his soap and feel his breath warm my neck.

He whirled me around and said, "You have broken your promise."

I looked at him, and I knelt down on the cold dirt floor, knowing it would never help. He looked back at me and touched my cheek. "Edie," he said, his eyes shining, "what is inside you?"

Something was coming over me, a kind of heaviness in my bones. It's the housecleaning, I told myself, it's the baby dropping down, pinning you close to the earth so you won't go off. I took to my rocker and asked myself questions about Howie.

I wondered about his religion. I used to believe in its torments for the ungodly, its gifts and trials—it drove Howie's backbone straight up in those early years. There was something bracing about it, something definite. Black and white. No milky forgive and forget, like my aunt's faith. Now all I heard behind the words was rattling.

I remembered those early mornings in Bozeman, when Howie'd go to school, and I'd watch him lope the street in his red plaid jacket, a farm boy taking the world straight on. I watched him till he disappeared, then I slipped our wedding 45s out of their dust jackets, lifted the arm of the record player and set them in place. I closed the curtains and fixed myself a foamy bath, and as I floated, I listened to the scratchy recording over and over again. As Pastor Salmonsen rumbled, . . . *this mystical union,* I slipped underwater. My cheeks filled with breath, my hair swirled around breasts Howie touched, and I came up gasping when he said, *covenant.*

I went over everything: Howie's first job in Malta teaching rancher's children, then Redbow. The day he'd gotten the job, he came home holding the letter over his head and said, "The Lord has spoken." "What did he say?" I said. "Redbow, Edie. He's calling us back to the mountains," he said, for the prairie made him nervous with its openness and constant wind.

Truth was, the longer I tried to think of what was wrong between Howie and me, the mushier my mind became. Too much meanness, I'd think, then answer, *the day he climbed Teacup Mountain to pick a handful of black-eyed susans.* Too much silence, then *camping in the Swans where we talked by a moon, Howie stroking my hair, saying, dream, dream.* Neglect, I'd say, but I had answers for that too.

But when I thought of him coming home, coming home in two years, ten years, his flattop graying, his back slightly bent, his face setting, growing stern, and this new child, another child to dress and feed and love and betray, a leaden feeling coursed down my legs and I thought I would die.

I packed Daniel and the belongings I could carry, and I walked up over Snowshoe Mountain. I picked my way slowly, past wet bushes and larches looming dark and shadowless, to the Oxtail River where the deer were fawning and chickadees were nesting. In a large meadow, I staked the tent, built a fire. The spring sky was pale and cool but cloudless, and I nursed Daniel and put him to sleep.

For three days, I stayed there, watching a shy sun whisk across the grasses, the moon still owned the sky. *Darkness will come upon the earth.* I listened to the river murmur *go back, go back,* and once I got as far as packing up again, when I thought of Howie's hands. Big, rough, patient hands unlocking the door, cutting his meat, pouring the water for tomatoes, pressing together in prayer, folding back the covers on the bed. How in spite of his religion and its fiery visions, the hands took each thing and weighed it and measured it to some exact dimension that was Howie's own.

Red-tailed hawks wound the sky. The deer floated down to the river at dusk.

He walked up through the wide-spaced larch, and I watched his face change, as relief replaced worry and anger replaced relief. He peered in the tent where Daniel held his toes, gurgling. He walked toward me, the weeds rattling. I was perched on a stump, at the edge of the river. He stood over me, and said, his voice tight and low, "What are you doing?"

I didn't say anything. I couldn't tell him about his hands, or about the visions I'd had of watching Mr. Perpendicular walk his dogs to his death, of rocking into an old woman in that front room in Redbow, graying into stone. I said, "I had to."

"You *had* to?" he said. "You take my son and run off in the hills and get half the town worked up and make me sick with worry and all you can say is you *had* to?"

"Yes," I said.

He slapped me.

I pushed myself up. I was so big now it was difficult to move, and I went to stand in an apron of tree shade.

He came toward me.

"Get away from me," I spit. "Don't come near me."

"I'm sorry," he said. He started to cry. "I'm sorry."

"Ssssss," I hissed.

"What have I done, Edie? I work all day and I come home tired and find the front door wide open, and you're gone."

I just stared at him.

"Please, Edie," he said coming closer. "I forgive you. God forgives you."

"No."

"We'll work it out. We'll get a different house. Go to a different town. How about that, Edie? We'll go someplace you like better. Someplace where people are nicer. Where the country is open like you like it. And we'll have a new baby, Edie. Think of it. A new little baby to love and hold and take care of."

I began to cry. "But—"

"Don't you love me, Edie?" he said, fixing me with his eyes. "Well? Don't you?"

I couldn't say it. I couldn't say anything. My hands fingered the wide-plated bark, and I wondered if it ever dropped off in a fierce cold.

"Well, then, what is it?"

"Everything's got tramped down, Howie," I whispered. Suddenly I felt limp, as if his words had pierced something and vital fluid leaked out.

"Let's go home now, Edie," Howie said gently. "Take my hand. That's a girl."

His hand was inches from me now, palm up, and his long, rough fingers were curved and trembling.

I gulped, hung my head, and took it.

Aunt Dot brushed my hair as I sat in bed. Howie had called her when I'd run away, and she'd come to stay until the baby was born.

"You have beautiful hair," she said, smoothing it down my back. "The color of chestnuts."

"I want to leave him," I said. "I didn't know that before, Dot, but I know it now."

"Hush, hush," she said, pulling the brush through great fans of hair that crackled and fell back down my back. "It's just baby-jitters, Edie. You had them last time."

"No, Dot," I said. "This is different. It's Howie."

"Shh!" Dot said. "Your beautiful baby will hear."

"No, Dot," I said. "I want a divorce."

"That's enough." She threw the brush on the bed and wheeled around to look into my face. "Do you know what it's like to raise a child alone? Someday I'll tell you all about it. I tried to talk to you about Howie before you got married, but you'd have none of it. 'I know what I'm doing,' you said. 'I know perfectly well.' You chose your bed, dear, and now you've got to make the best of it."

"I'll do it alone."

"And how, I'd like to know? With a high school degree? You don't even have beauty college, Edie. How do you plan to raise and feed two children and pay the rent? Tell me that? I had Daddy's money. You don't have anything."

"I'll waitress."

"Don't be a fool. What would you do with your children? Sit them in a booth in the corner to draw? Howie's put a good roof over your head, Edie, he's a good father. Maybe he's not what you bargained for, you're no great shakes either, kid, not speaking to the neighbors, running off all over the country."

"Do you know how to get a divorce?"

"I brook no more of this, Edie Deschene. Get off the bed, wipe your son's nose and make Howie supper, and don't say anything again."

"Please, Dot?"

"I said *no more.*" She drew her fingers across my mouth like a zipper. "Keep it here," she said, tapping my heart. "This is your own."

The days stretched on between us. Rising each morning, Dot fixed the breakfast, I fed Daniel, Howie sighed and left out the front door and came back each evening to a dinner served up with Dot's chatter. I spent my days in the rocker, watching the sunlight move down and up the mountain, whispering to Daniel, "We are going somewhere green. Warm. Somewhere there's big, white horses."

Howie grew quiet. His face became flushed and tight as if he were always keeping something back, and some nights after dinner, he'd walk down the basement, where he'd sit next to my rows of preserves and read his Bible. Other nights, he went to the church, to prayer circles and foundation boards, coming home long after I'd gone to bed to kneel on the cracked linoleum of the bedroom and whisper his angry prayers.

"Enough!" I shouted one night, and threw the milk across the kitchen and watched it shatter across the floor. "I can't stand this."

Daniel began to cry.

Howie looked up at me, sprung. "What is it?" he said.

"This infernal silence," I said. "Say something."

"Please clean up the milk," he said.

I knelt on the floor and mopped up the milk. Dot picked up Daniel and rocked him, saying something about Mrs. Hansen across the street, about what a lovely woman she was despite her rude children.

I sat down and put my hands on the table and stared at him. "Tell me. Tell me what you hate in me."

"The things we hate are often the things we love the most," he said and cut the meat from the bone of his pork chop.

"Don't be so Goddamn wise," I said. "You hate something. I can feel it."

Dot excused herself, saying something about how the green beans needed watering. Howie watched her walk from the kitchen and out the back door. Then he whipped his head around. His face was bright red.

"Have you had enough? Are you trying to get me to give you the punishment you have coming from other quarters?" He calmly rose up from the table and looked down at me. "This is in your hands, Edie. I can punish you but you know it's up to you."

"What's in my hands?" I shrieked. "What?"

"You know," he said. He went slowly around the kitchen, shutting the windows. He raised his hand. "You know."

Dot brought me dinner in bed and brushed my hair out and told me I looked like a princess and he came early to bed that night. I stared out at the moonlit garden, barren except for the bean stalks dried around their stakes, and knew I'd pack the suitcase and leave when the house was asleep. I knew I'd steal across the back lots and up Teacup Mountain and walk west. I'd keep walking until I reached some farmhouse where a kind, wide-faced woman in a red apron would open her door, and take me in. She would take me to a back room with high, sloped ceilings and she would let me sleep there, sleep for ages, with only the sounds of the wind in the larch and the far away laughter of birds. I would find this place. I knew it. I touched Howie's back and he turned to me in sleep, and I cradled his head against my stomach, stroked the long line of his jaw till he turned.

My water broke long before the sun rose, and the contractions came fast and hard. Howie packed me off to the two-room hospital, where he sat outside my room, reading his Bible, moving his lips as if he were dreaming.

I was groaning. I didn't let them give me ether, and the nurse thought I was odd, but I believed this baptism of pain would bind my baby and me. That was before things came unhinged. Before the doctor leaned in close and pain cornered and played with me like a cat.

To keep things in focus, I looked at the picture across the room. It was of a young girl opening French windows to cherubs gathered outside. In the wash of gray, she reached out to fat, curly-headed babies as if they would take her away. I watched that picture for hours as the doctor swung in and out of my room, the nurse mopped my forehead, murmured *push, push*. Pain blanketed me. The lower half of my body looked like some distant mountain.

"Let us help the pain," the nurse kept saying, her round freckled hands fluttering around me like birds.

The girl in the picture said no.

The doctor came in, checked my pulse, said, "Time to knock you out."

I kept saying no. He didn't seem to hear me.

The girl in the picture said something. Tears trickled down her cheek. I tried to get up to hear her, when the nurse pressed a button and people rushed in to hold me down, and the nurse said, "Slug it out, Mrs. Deschene."

The girl was moving her lips, but I couldn't hear her above the clanking noise swelling up around me. I shouted, "Quiet." The girl cried harder, and I heard the cherubs singing something so sad and beautiful it made my skin crawl, and when the clanking stopped, the thin, sweet voices, delicate as lace, sang *Heigh Ho, Nobody's Home.*

Something sharp stung my arm, and the room went black.

The nurse came in after I woke, a big smile on her face. "Look what I have, Mrs. Deschene," she said, slinging a tight-bound bundle under my chin. "A beautiful baby girl."

I looked into the screwed-up, purple face, the blue eyes that didn't yet focus and I put the covers over my head.

"Mrs. Deschene," the nurse said and her voice turned cold, "Sit up and take your baby girl."

"Take her and leave," I said.

"Yes, Mrs. Deschene," she answered, and I knew it would be all over town.

I lay panting in bed until she closed the door. I took a deep breath, rang the aide, and sent her for scissors. I struggled out of bed, my groin was numb and huge, hanging like an udder.

I waddled to the mirror. My face was gray as putty, but as I undid the clasp, my hair rumpled down, caught the light from the window, and shone copper down my back. As Miss Cindy chattered about babies, their tiny toes, and how even their poop smells sweet, I cut my off my beautiful hair, hunks at a time, until it tufted my head like straw. Then I laid back in bed and called the nurse.

She walked in and gasped.

"Now," I said. "Give me my baby."

She returned, holding my little girl as if she already hated her, and right behind her came Howie, his eyes widening.

"Howie," I told him. "We'll call the baby Grace."

I steal out of the house to speak my story to the dirt. Thick with thistles and crabgrass, it is warm in my hands. I yank weeds till the bed is clean, till my hands bleed, but the noise inside of me continues. I plant daffodils, tulips, snowdrops, and crocus and think of their small uplifted heads, their slender voiceless throats. How after five years, they will go blind and stop sending up blossoms. I slice an earthworm, and the two halves wriggle away, two round tubes of flesh, each with six hearts move off to start separate lives, and a voice sings, *Our daily bread.*

A Lot of Living to Do

David Horgan

It's the usual poignant scene today at Creekside Manor, Missoula's Premiere Assisted-Living Facility. Nutbags and skeletons everywhere you look. Nutbags being the ones like my grandmother Sylvia—geezers and geezerettes who get around just fine, spry as horses, but can't keep anything straight, such as who they are or who you are. Who persist in thinking, for instance, that you are the long-lost brother murdered by Stalin in the 1930s instead of the grunge-rocker grandson born in 1975. The skeletons are just that—sacks of bones shoveled into wheelchairs, rickety stick figures bent double over aluminum walkers, toothless Halloween creatures shuffling up and down the halls with pee-stained bathrobes, wild cobwebs of hair, protruding eyeballs.

Now don't get me wrong. Don't go assuming that I'm insensitive to the plight of the aged and infirm. Lose that thought. But I dare you—I dare anybody—to walk into this place every Sunday morning week-in and week-out without psyching up in some kind of way.

The people who work here are the true saints, in the words of Dorothy—my mother, Sylvia's daughter—and she ought to know. She comes to visit Sylvia more often than I do, pretty much every day, although unlike me she understands how to keep it short. She's way better at hopping off the conversational merry-go-round. "When you've had enough, just get up and go," she's always telling me. "Just stand up, say goodbye, and leave." Right.

So here I am, yet another Sunday morning, eleven a.m. on the dot, bee-lining my way through the pastel-green cinderblock hallways, inhaling that familiar aroma: Lysol, bedpans, ammonia. I zip past the front station and flick a wave at the two desk nurses. They all know me. If there's any problem with Sylvia, if for some reason she isn't receiving today, I can count on somebody to flag me down. They beam their standard-issue beatific smiles and wave me on down the hall. They're always glad to see visitors, no matter how slovenly and unkempt. There are inmates here who probably never see anybody, not even a slouch-ass grandson reeking of cigarettes and more. I didn't even have time to stop at home this morning, after waking up on a basement couch following an after-hours jam session out in Clinton that's still going on for all I know. The theory is that I'm doing Sylvia some good by showing up every Sunday, tanked up on double-shot espresso, bearing a sad little bouquet of tulips from Albertson's, smiling my phony smile. I wonder sometimes.

I've been doing this for six months now, ever since I came home to, quote, get my act together, unquote. I was gone for nearly two years, first touring with a mediocre rock band, then just hitching around, checking out various places, Seattle, L.A., Austin, New Orleans, exotic names on the map, renowned hotbeds of culture—all overrated if you ask me. The finale was a two-month stay with my old man and his latest girlfriend in their condo down in Reno, watching them watch TV, making regular forays to one mall or another, following him around on his lawyer rounds (he's a personal injury specialist, defending the big hotels from people who slip in the bathrooms and choke on prime rib specials), tagging along to politely cheer him on while he sat in on clarinet at amateur Sunday Dixieland sessions, my least favorite music in the whole world, wondering how to get him to look up and notice that I exist, finding out all over again *that* wasn't how. Not much changed on the Montana home front while I was gone, other than Sylvia getting stashed in this place. Dorothy still works for the title company (I still don't have any idea what that is), is still married to George, the clueless well-meaning silver-haired realtor stepfather, still has possession of our former family home, our all-American aluminum-sided tract house in the South Hills. I shouldn't knock it, since she's letting me store a lot of my stuff in the garage. She moved Sylvia out of her dinky apartment in a building downtown that George owns and stashed her in here when it became "patently obvious" (Dorothy's phrase) that the move was necessary. At first I figured it was because the rest of Sylvia's building had started to fill up with "unsavory characters" (Dorothy's subtle wording once again, by which she usually means Native Americans or Latinos). I thought, How can you do that to someone, how can you just put a human being in cold storage? But it didn't take very long for me to come around. Patently obvious is patently obvious. Besides, it's all covered by Medicaid or whatever. You can't beat that. And the timing wasn't so bad for me, either: her apartment became available. I can have it as long as I keep my nose clean—her euphemism for holding down a day job and not getting arrested.

I'm moving fast down the hallway, keeping my head down, slaloming around nutbags and skeletons, nurses and aides, plus the occasional grim civilian like myself. Sylvia lives in the North wing, which all things considered is the best place to be. It's where they park the ones who can be trusted not to hurt themselves or run away. She has a window with a view out the back side of the building of a little bit of lawn sloping down to the Clark Fork River and a couple of nice willow trees. Her door, third from the end on the right, is wide open, as most of them are this time of the day. I poke my head in quietly, as usual, to scope things out.

There she sits on the edge of her bed in her regular outfit, the blue nightie and pink chenille bathrobe, her slippered feet tracing slow circles in the air. This is OK, this is just fine. She's up, she's alert. Sometimes I catch her still in bed, and then we might not have much of a visit. She'll lie there staring into space, not making a sound or moving a muscle, and you could put on a three-ring circus right in front of her and not get a response.

She has her hands resting in her lap, palms up, and she's studying them closely, her head twitching back and forth as she looks from one to the other. It's much like the posture of a person reading a book, only there's no book. Even from the doorway I can see she's got her teeth in today. Another good sign. Wheels are turning, synapses firing. She might be on a new drug. Her pharmaceutical diet varies from week to week— this is one thing we have in common.

I step inside and go over to her, and without saying a word I bend down and kiss her lightly on the top of her head. This is an acceptable form of greeting we have settled on. It startles her less than if I speak up first thing. She raises her head and watches me with what you might call mild curiosity, while I pick up the small blue vase on her bedstand and throw last week's flowers in the waste basket and replace them with the new ones and get some fresh water from the sink. If she sticks to the regular routine, any second now she'll open the proceedings with some goofy non sequitur from out of nowhere.

"These don't look like my hands," she says—right on cue—holding them up for my inspection, sounding more amused than annoyed, as if anyone could seriously expect her to fall for such a stupid trick: replacing her hands with someone else's when she wasn't looking. "My hands are nicer than these."

"Oh," I say, putting the vase of flowers down. "Hmm." I've developed a repertoire of neutral noncommittal responses, upbeat-sounding syllables that show I'm listening even when I haven't got a clue. "So." I put on a big smile. Then I make my first stab at dialogue: "Well. How are you today, Sylvia? It's nice to see you."

I take a step closer, placing myself within striking distance. She eyes me for a second and then lunges, snatching my right hand with lightning speed that would scare the piss out of me if I weren't fully prepared. Inside I tense up but otherwise don't react in any way, except to keep smiling. Her fingers move quickly up my wrist and clamp on tight. The feeling is somewhat reminiscent of being placed in handcuffs, something I don't particularly enjoy being reminded of. She'll do this to anybody who gets within range—grab hold and hang on as if you're the last person on earth. But I'm cool. I can deal with it, for the moment.

She looks up into my eyes. "It's so good of you to come," she says in her sweet Babushka voice, that cute Russian accent the nurses and staff all love so much. Then she yanks me closer and pushes her face up toward mine, slowly licking her lips. She gazes long and hard, trying to make up her mind who I am. She seems to have forgotten about the problem of her hands. Her breath is hot and sour smelling, and there is a little clump of white hairs sprouting from her chin that I don't remember from last week. I'll try to remember to mention to the desk ladies on my way out that she needs a shave.

I pat the bed with my free hand. "Can I sit down beside you, honey?"

She scoots over and makes room without letting go of me. When she wants to, she can move with the agility of a kid. "Sit," she commands.

"Thanks." I sit down and pretend I'm all comfy.

She looks at me expectantly.

"It's Nick," I say, following our usual script. "Your grandson."

Her eyes get narrower, and she leans back a little to take in the whole picture. Her look says it all: *You're not fooling me for a second, buster.*

"This is nonsense," she announces. "You are a grown man."

"That's right!" I say, with idiot enthusiasm. "I'm all grown up now." Look for ways to agree with her, Dorothy says.

She releases one of her claws for a moment, long enough to reach out and push my hair back from my forehead. Her hand is bone dry and cold. Her watery eyes stare me down. A chill trickles from the top of my head to my tailbone. Her palm scrapes down the side of my face, and then she pinches my cheek and starts slowly kneading it hard with her thumb and forefinger—a technique she's been torturing me with all my life. For a split second I think she's actually going to recognize me.

No such luck. "Isaac, my dearest. You are so kind to come. You are the only one who understands."

 I allow myself a small sigh. Here we go. "I'm not Isaac, Sylvia. Isaac died sixty years ago. He was your brother. I'm Nick, your grandson. Nicky. Remember?" I don't say this with any hope of persuading her to change her mind. I say it, every Sunday, over and over again, mainly just to let her hear me say it, to keep my testimony on record so to speak. Did the Isaac of the 1930s look like me? Somehow I doubt it. With my free hand I reach back and finger my ponytail.

She tilts her head and gives me a conspiratorial raise of her eyebrows. "You don't need to pretend," she whispers, leaning in closer, tightening her grip on my arm. "It's safe here."

"Fine," I say. "Sure."

"Isaac, listen to me. What has *she* told you?"

"Who?" As Dorothy says, don't be afraid to play dumb.

"*Who?* That woman, is who. The one who comes here. What has *she* told you?"

"Oh. You mean Dorothy?" I feign the usual innocence and surprise.

Her mouth tightens, and a shadow crosses her face. "She is a sly fox, that one. She tells lies about me."

"Oh, no, I don't think so. She's my mother, after all. And your daughter."

She smiles now, a big grin that fully displays her enormous gleaming dentures. "Isaac, sweetheart, you are so easily misled. My daughter! For God's sake. She is an *old woman.*" The smile vanishes. Her voice becomes icy. "She plots against me. She tells lies to everyone. What did she say about me? Did *she* tell you she was my daughter? Evil woman. She makes a mistake to think we are so foolish, you and I. Such terrible lies."

I look her straight on and give her what is intended to be a sweet and loving gaze. I know better than to get sucked into this argument. Ten more minutes and I can hightail it out of here.

"Darling." Her voice goes soft again. She leans in and rattles off a few phrases in rapid-fire Russian, an intimate communication meant for her long-lost brother's ears alone—a wild and beautiful sound, long strings of convoluted syllables that fill her mouth with saliva. Supposedly when I was little she taught me to speak Russian baby talk, before I went off to kindergarten and promptly forgot it all. *Nyet,* is about what I remember. *Da.*

"You'll have to speak in English, sweetie," I tell her. "I don't understand." As if it matters.

"Oh, don't be silly." She clucks her tongue and shakes her head in mild rebuke. She knows perfectly well that her brother Isaac should be fluent in his mother tongue. "Tell me, darling. How is everything at the bank?"

We've been down this road before, too. I have no idea if the real-life Isaac actually worked in a bank. Dorothy says this is a total fantasy, but I don't think she really knows either. When I was little, whenever she babysat me, Sylvia used to try to make the case that when I grew up I should go to work in a bank. The bank or—not quite as good—the post office. She was attracted to solid, official-looking places that were built to last, preferably constructed out of massive blocks of stone. The bank was best because if you worked there you could wear a nice suit and the floors were carpeted. I'd walk to her place after school, and she would talk up this plan with me over ginger ale and platefuls of her *piroshke*—little hot meat pies. I'd tell her I wanted to be an astronaut or an Olympic skier or a motorcycle cop and she'd make a sour face, as if I'd farted really loud; then she'd resume her earnest advocating for a bank career. She loved the idea of those rows of solemn and neatly groomed people whose sole mission in life was to take care of other people's piles of money. Funny, but there was never any mention of following in Dear Old Dad's lawyer footsteps. After he split from us, anything he did she automatically viewed as evil.

On another given Sunday, I might say exactly what she's hoping to hear. I might go ahead and tell her with a cheerful smile that everything down at the bank is just totally peachy-fucking-keen. I'll lather it on thick, in lurid detail, how every morning I jump up at the crack of dawn and put on my clean suit with matching tie and handkerchief and spend a thrill-packed eight-hour shift polishing coins and stacking crisp green bills down at the old Comfy Cozy National Bank. Other times—today for instance—I'm not in the mood to play along with this bullshit. Sometimes, I don't know what it is, I just feel like laying the truth on her. Not that it makes any difference. I used to think maybe I could shock her, elicit some flicker of recognition by actually pissing her off, but it never works. Still, here I go. Don't ask me why.

"I don't work in a bank, Sylvia. I drive a forklift in a warehouse out on Reserve Street. I get dirty and sweaty and I smell bad. And on weekends I play in a band, you know? Rock and roll. I play guitar, loud. Very loud. Thrash music. You'd hate it. You'd think it sucks, honestly. Every Friday and Saturday at a bar called the Salt Cellar, a place you wouldn't believe in your wildest dreams. But that's the way it is, honey. I like it. It's the only thing I even halfway like to do."

She gazes at me for a minute, an utterly vacant look, a perfectly clean slate. Pretty much what I expected. Then she turns away toward the window. I honestly can't tell if she knows I'm still here. I decide this is as good a time as any to make an exit move. So, I stand up slowly, allowing my hand to tug at hers of its own accord.

"Well, Sylvia," I say. "Gee. Time sure flies, doesn't it?"

She turns back and stares at the level of my belt, where my head was a moment ago. Her grip on my arm has slackened, but she isn't quite ready to let go of me yet.

"I always loved music," she says softly, sort of dreamily. "I loved to go to parties, where there was music and dancing. I would arrive late, deliberately. I would plan my entrance, just so. When the party was underway, then I would go in. A grand entrance. I would run into the party and jump up, onto the piano. Very dramatic. I would stretch myself out, like a cat. And then—I would sing!" Her eyes have become wide and bright. "And I would dance. While everyone drank, I would dance on top of the piano and sing a romantic song. I could do fancy steps, like a showgirl. I understood how to make them all notice me. I was quite good at these things." Her face cracks a little half-smile, a look I haven't seen very much: sly and self-satisfied. She tilts her head up and our eyes meet again. She sees me this time, I'm sure of it—not Isaac, but me.

"Hey, that's great," I say, meaning it. I'm trying to conjure up this version of her, a foxy vamp dancing on a piano. Singing. I want to picture it, but the best I can muster is a distant memory of her chanting a Russian nursery rhyme, leaning against the kitchen counter in her daisy-patterned apron while she rolled out gigantic sheets of cookie dough. This sexy life-of-the-party routine is way beyond me. But hell, it could be true. Why not?

"What songs did you sing, Sylvia?" I'm hooked, I admit it. My interest is piqued, against my supposedly better judgment. The air conditioning has come on, producing a faint breeze that causes her chin hairs to flutter back and forth.

"*Otchey Chorniyeh*," she says, lowering her voice to a husky whisper. "It means 'Dark Eyes'."

"Sing me a little of it. Please."

Her eyelids drop a notch. She's thinking about it, maybe. And then her face goes flat. Somebody else might not see it, but I see it. For a minute there a light was on, but it just went off again.

"I'm hungry," she says now, in her old voice. "Is it lunch time?"

Damn. Now it's me who doesn't want to let go. I squat down in front of her. "Sylvia, honey, listen to me a second. Sing me a little of that song. Can you, please? 'Dark Eyes'—the one you sang at parties. How about it?"

"I want to eat. When is lunch?"

"Very soon. Any minute." This is true. Lunch is imminent. It's the perfect cue for my getaway. I plan it that way, as a backup, in case I get seriously stuck. So why am I stalling? What do I expect to get out of her now? What I know about her you could fit on the head of a pin. She came to the U.S. from the Ukraine by way of China, then Canada, the long way around, a young widow with her infant daughter. It's always been a mystery to me, a total muddle. Crossing the ocean on a freighter, settling in North Dakota, living off the generosity of relatives. Raising Dorothy alone, sending her off to school in Bismarck, eventually following her to Montana when Dorothy married the old man, a misfit farm kid who played the clarinet and wanted to go to law school. That's the sum of what I know, or think I know. One time when I was maybe five years old, a little hellraising punk, I charged into the kitchen and there was Sylvia down on her knees in front of the stove, wringing her hands at the ceiling, her head thrown back, muttering in Russian what might have been a prayer or could just as easily have been a curse. It scared the hell out of me. I practically pissed in my pants. I backed out of the room and then made some noise in the hallway, to give her a chance to compose herself before I went into the kitchen again. I never asked her what was wrong. I didn't want to know.

But now I do. Sure, I want to know that, and more. I want to hear about her days as a foxy chiquita at parties and nightclubs in Moscow or Shanghai or wherever it was, stretched out on top of a piano. Chandeliers, feather boas, smoke, intrigue. It's so corny it just might be true. I want to hear it. I'm forgetting, of course, about Dorothy's cardinal rule: don't make the mistake of thinking you can engage in actual conversation. I sometimes tell myself there's always next week. Maybe we'll pick up where we left off. But we don't ever pick up where we left off. Every day in this goddamn place starts with a blank page. We always go right back to square one.

"Sylvia?" I say. "*Baba?*"

It means "grandma" in Russian. I've tried this before too. It doesn't work.

"I want to eat lunch."

All right then, forget it. I stand up, inhale a deep breath, and retract my hand out of her clutches. Dorothy would be proud of me. I steal a glance at my watch. I've stayed longer than usual.

"They'll ring the bell for you when it's time to eat," I say to her. "They always do." I bend down and kiss her on the cheek. "Bye, honey," I say. "Maybe next time you can sing me that song, OK?"

No reaction. "Well, I've got to go now. I'll be back next Sunday. See you later."

She looks up again, eyeing me suddenly with suspicion. I'm not even Isaac anymore. I'm back to being nobody. Her chin drops, and she's back to contemplating her hands in her lap.

"OK. Just listen for the bell, sweetheart." I'm backpedaling across the room as I'm talking, leaving her perched on the edge of the bed, her feet dangling like a little rag doll, exactly the way I found her. "Well. So long now, Sylvia." A second later I'm out of the room.

I feel like I'm asphyxiating as I accelerate down the hall: I can't wait to get outside. I'm dying for air, wind, traffic, noise, people, life, such as it is: my dead-end weekend gig, my stupid forklift day job. It all looks good right now. By the time I hit the turn at the end of the north wing, I'm practically sprinting for the door.

I come around the front desk, ten feet from the main entrance. I'm not looking out too carefully, no thought in my head but getting clear of this place, when I slip on the linoleum and sideswipe a roly-poly geezerette who's waddling along with the aid of an aluminum cane, and damn near knock us both down. I manage to catch her by the arm as she starts to go over and then help her get centered and balanced again.

"Oh, man, I'm sorry," I say, still thinking only of getting to the door.

She shuffles her feet unsteadily while she catches her breath. "Jesus, Mary, and Joseph," she says finally. Then suddenly she reaches out with her cane and pokes me in the leg, just above the kneecap, not all that hard. "*Oh, man*, yourself. This is a nursing home, young fella, not an athletic club." The voice is low-pitched and vaguely southern.

The woman's upper half is draped in a huge Aloha shirt, bright green with yellow flowers. Below, she has on wide black sweatpants and a spanking-new pair of white hightop sneakers. Her face is jowly and pink, and her steel-gray hair is cut short and parted on the side like a man's. She's not young, but not ancient either, definitely on the younger end of the inmate spectrum—if she is an inmate.

"I'm sorry," I say again and then tack on, as an afterthought, "Ma'am." She frowns and leans closer, examining me. "Sugar, do we know each other?" She grabs my chin and turns my head one way and then the other. "Hmm. A former constituent, I'll wager."

Her eyebrows arch and her forehead rolls up into a compressed wad of deep red wrinkles. "Aha!" she shouts suddenly, finally letting go of my chin. "It's Nicholas! As I live and breathe. Nick, my boy, don't you recognize me?"

Oh my God. This lady knows me. I rewind hastily through my past life: teachers, North Dakota relatives, Dorothy's drinking buddies, Sylvia's drinking buddies, counselors, parole officers. I'm drawing a blank. All I want is to get the hell out of here.

"Nick, you little twerp. It's me, Clara McKay. Mrs. McKay."

Mrs. McKay? My piano teacher? It can't be. Mrs. McKay was a stylish, courtly woman of normal proportions, who wore tailored ladies' suits with padded shoulders. She taught piano in the front room of a little brick farmhouse up the Bitterroot Valley. I took lessons from her for a couple years, fourth or fifth grade, but I hated reading music. I learned one Brahms waltz and played it over and over again for every recital until finally I quit altogether.

"Mrs. McKay," I mumble. Can this really be the same person? She would never have called me a little twerp back then—though that's certainly what I was. She's aged into a mountain of flesh, metamorphosed into a barrel-bellied truck driver.

"What are you doing here, Mrs. McKay? I mean. . . . "

She cuts me off. "I live here. This"—gesturing with a sweep of her arm—"is my home." She gives me a look of fierce triumph, as if daring me to open my mouth again.

I steal a look over my left shoulder toward the front door, with its double pane of sun-brightened wire-meshed glass, thinking maybe I can just excuse myself and continue on out. But then Mrs. McKay has got hold of my arm, and she's saying, "Come on, Nick, I want to show you something, come here with me," and she's yanking me back down the hall.

"Hold it now," I say feebly, "Mrs. McKay, I'm sorry, but. . . . "

"Don't worry," she says, pulling me by the elbow around the corner, her rubber-tipped cane socking the linoleum with every other step. "This won't take a minute."

We make another turn and go clomping through the double doors of the recreation room, where a dozen or so people are seated at the tables and on the couches. Up on the wall, a big-screen TV is blaring away with nobody watching it. I could easily bolt right now, make a clean getaway with no trouble. I don't, though—partly out of politeness, some dumb vestige of respect for my former teacher, and partly out of pure morbid curiosity. If Dorothy could see this, I wonder if she'd be proud of me or totally disgusted.

Mrs. McKay leads me over to the corner, where there's an ugly brown couch and a battered old upright piano. She plants me down on the couch and says, "Just you wait right there." Then she picks up a remote control from a side table and points it toward the TV and starts punching buttons. Up there, on the TV screen, a giant face grins at us, an elderly woman with a feathery white hairdo, smooth-looking pink skin, red lips, perfect teeth, and bright blue eyes. Hardly any wrinkles. A Hollywood-style little old lady, some formerly glamorous babe, a geezerette from central casting. She's chattering, in a sweet and delicate voice, about confidence and security and comfort. At first I think she's selling financial stuff, mutual funds or whatever, but then the image pans back to her pulling a blue box off a grocery shelf and I realize it's a commercial for diapers—diapers for grownups. The camera zooms in close on the TV lady's face. Flashing a huge radiant smile, her voice quivering with enthusiasm, she crows, "Because you've got a *lot* of living to do!"

Oh, please. Give me a break. I gaze around the room to see if anyone else might be appreciating this absurdity, but nobody is paying any attention. Other pursuits are underway: checkers, cards, snoozing, staring out the window. "What's wrong with this idiot thing?" Mrs. McKay says, still thrusting the remote at the screen and jabbing at the buttons.

"Here, let me try." I get up from the couch and take the remote from her, then walk a few steps across the room and click off the TV.

"You just needed to be a little closer," I say, giving her the remote back. Mrs. McKay tosses it onto to the couch. "Hold this," she says, handing me her cane. Then she lowers herself onto the piano bench and pulls up the cover of the keyboard. The piano is an ancient beater, a big upright that takes up half the wall. She looks up and down the keys, keeping her hands in her lap, then turns to me with a frown. Gesturing at the couch, she says, "Sit down." I do what I'm told. What the hell.

"Tell me something, Nick my boy. I seem to remember that you had some musical ability. Lazy, no concentration or discipline, like most kids—but talented all the same. So, I want to know: is music part of your life now?"

A faint buzz has started in the back of my head, a sensation that maybe this isn't really happening. Like maybe I'm dreaming the whole thing up—I could be still asleep on the couch in the basement across town where I was jamming last night, belting out power chords at ungodly volume until whatever time it was—five or six a.m.—when I finally bailed out. "You could say that," I answer, without elaborating.

She smiles. "Ah, that's good. I had my hopes. That's wonderful. Now my friend, listen to this."

She raises her hands and holds them out over the keys, wiggling her fingers in the air, loosening up. Then she begins to play. At first, I figure that her hands have landed in the wrong position on the keyboard or something, that she isn't watching, that she'll make a quick adjustment. But her eyes are wide open, focused right in front of her. She bears down hard with her shoulders and elbows, concentrating fiercely. And here's the thing: it's the strangest piano playing I've ever heard in my life. I once listened to an old piano roll played backwards, which was way cool, and this sounds something like that, but even weirder. I keep thinking I hear bits of recognizable music going by, but in an instant they're washed away by the flow of pure clear craziness. I've heard plenty of outside stuff before, supposedly freeform improvisation that tries hard to be very lunatic and cutting-edge—farting saxophones, synthesized chainsaws, you name it—but nothing compared to this. She sounds so natural and so bizarre all at once. The lady has fantastic chops: hellacious syncopation, jagged melodic lines folding in and out and turning wild corners. Her beat is awesome, pure power, like standing next to a surging waterfall. She builds it up, louder and louder, leaning close over the keyboard with her elbows flaring, sweat coming out on her forehead and her face turning purple.

And then she stops. She just stops, clean, out of the blue, and drops her hands back into her lap. Lifting her head, she sits up, draws in a big breath, and lets out a long slow exhale.

"Huh," she says. "There you have it."

"Wow," I say. "That is really something, Mrs. McKay."

"Oh, boy, is it ever," she says, shaking her head slowly. She looks up at me now. "I thought you might appreciate that, Nick, my friend. When we had our fateful collision, I looked at you and identified a potential constituent." She rubs her hands together. "Most people hear what I just did, they want to reach first thing for the straitjacket. And with good reason, I might add. Because, you know what? That's all I can play anymore. Did you hear me? *I can't play anything else.* I think of a piece I used to know like the back of my hand, something haunting and lovely—the 'Moonlight Sonata,' say—and that's how it comes out. Something bouncy, jazzy—'Maple Leaf Rag,' maybe. Same thing. I sit down with the music right in front of me, same thing—worse, actually. And you know what else?" She points at the window. "It's the same out *there*, too. The real world, I mean. The wheels of commerce, the bump and grind of human activity. It all gets mixed up and twisted every-which-way. So, I stay in here, with the basket cases and birdbrains. You see?" She nods emphatically, as if answering her own question.

I could get up and go right now if I wanted to. Nobody would stop me.

"Play some more," I say.

Her face lights up. "You mean it?"

I nod. "Yeah."

So, she plays some more. And the more I listen, the better it sounds. OK, yes, sure, it's warped, it's insane, whatever. But if she could have taught me to play like that back in the fourth grade, I swear I never would have quit piano lessons.

She stops again. "All right," she says, not exactly talking to me, staring at the keys, catching her breath. She's actually panting. "All right," she says again. The woman is obviously in a major groove.

And then the idea hits me.

"Can you wait right here, Mrs. McKay?" I say to her. "Just wait right here, and I'll be back in a flash."

"Don't go!" she bellows, but now I'm heading out, on the run. Across the rec room and through the double doors and down the hall. Out the front door into the fresh air and naked sunshine, down the sidewalk to the parking lot, along the row to my car, and I pull out my keys and open up the trunk, where I happen to have my acoustic guitar, a cheap clunker which I pack around for spontaneous occasions. This is about as spontaneous as they come.

It's a glorious crisp spring day out here, the first truly beautiful post-winter day of the year. Mount Jumbo looms over this end of town against the stark blue sky, looking a lot like the haunches of some huge sleeping animal. On a day like this people all over are frantically loading up their recreational gear—kayaks, rafts, canoes. I could easily be one of them. Instead, I carry the guitar back into the building. Yes, indeed: entirely of my own volition, without so much as a second thought, I march straight back into the place.

The bell for lunch must have gone off, because the hallways are filling up with inmates in their multitude of shapes and sizes, shuffling, hobbling, wheeling, staggering their way to the dining room. The smell of brown gravy is in the air. Lunch is a major attraction, the main event of the day, second only to dinner. The dining room is directly across the hall from the rec room.

Mrs. McKay is waiting at the piano where I left her. She doesn't look like she's moved a muscle. I head over to the couch, throw down my guitar and haul it out of the case, and grab one of the red plastic chairs and pull it over beside the piano.

"OK, here I am, Mrs. McKay," I say. "Do it again. I'll play along with you. We'll jam. Come on."

She looks at the guitar, then back up at me. "Well, I'll be," she says.

And so we jam. We get it on. Mrs. McKay dives right back in, wilder than ever. First I listen for a minute. This is ferocious stuff, demented, totally bonkers. I close my eyes and let it hit me, and then—I take the plunge. We rock out. We bang heads big time. She isn't playing in any actual key that I can determine, so I just go at it where it feels comfortable on the neck of the guitar. I have to play very loud to keep up, as loud as I can, slugging away with my heaviest pick, strumming like a maniac. Mrs. McKay hunkers down, her face beading up with sweat and glowing bright red. We are grooving, we are making a righteous racket. And along the way I have another wild thought: if the old man could only hear this. How would Mrs. McKay and I stack up against those toe-tappin' Dixieland jazz Sunday brunches down in Reno? Would he love it? Would he think it was interesting and innovative and daring and cool? Somehow I doubt it. He'd be scared shitless. He'd run from the room screaming.

I look up and see that we are not alone any longer. Behind us has gathered an assortment of pajamas and robes, several rows of craggy faces. We have attracted an audience. We have drawn the curious. So much the better. In the double doorway to the hall more heads poke through, necks crane to see and hear, eyes wide, mouths agape. A couple of orderlies, short chunky Latino dudes in blue coveralls, elbow their way into the room, shoving aside a couple of wheelchaired inmates. Faces grim, their duty clear, no doubt they are charged with the task of shutting off this racket. I stand up and put my foot on the chair with my knee up to support the guitar, so I can give it more elbow grease. It takes everything I've got to keep up with Mrs. McKay's firepower.

The orderlies are upon us. But now they hesitate. Maybe the sight of me: I could be trouble, this could become an incident. *Guitar-Wielding Intruder Incites Nursing Home Mayhem.* All around the room I can see we've got genuine fans—nutbags are digging it, skeletons are moving to the groove. One old gummer, flashing a toothless shit-eating grin, dances on one leg in the middle of the room, fingers clamped to the top of his bald head. Just then I catch sight of a small figure powering through the doorway, cutting between the robes and pajamas like a scrawny miniature running back: Sylvia. All right, this is getting good. My own diminutive grandmother, fighting her way through in her blue nightie and pink robe and fuzzy slippers, face fiery and mouth grimacing with crazy joy or animal fury, I don't know which. For a split second I catch her eye, and she catches mine: *Yes!*

Mrs. McKay and I crank it up another notch. Faster. Louder. Sylvia comes diving forward, arms outstretched, picking up speed through the crowd. When she passes the orderlies, one of them reaches out to stop her, puts out a hairy arm, and snags her under the chin. At the same time Mrs. McKay hits a huge two-fisted chord over and over, like big iron bells, and without a moment's hesitation I do what I have to do: turn the guitar around fast and with a high backswing bring it down square onto the head of the dude who has hold of Sylvia. The noise is nothing, a crackle of wood, a small whimper from him, the rattle of loose guitar strings, absorbed by the clangor of the piano as he releases her and goes down. Mrs. McKay—bless her heart—doesn't miss a beat.

I stand back now, my job finished, clearing the way for Sylvia. She doesn't see me anymore. I don't matter. Breaking loose, seizing her opportunity, a perfect match for Mrs. McKay's beautiful musical wrath, she darts by me like a feral animal tasting freedom. She takes flight, untouchable, headed right for the piano.

from
PERMA RED

Debra Magpie Earling

THE BIRDS STAYED AWAY FROM THE WEEDS where she and Baptiste hid from Charlie Kicking Woman. They sat up on the hill in a thatch of rustling grass where they could watch Highway 200 and the Flathead River. To the east, Louise could see the Mission Mountains, the distant threads of snow that marked them. She could see the corner of her grandmother's house. Baptiste spotted Charlie first. Charlie's first stop was her home. She strained to hear the voice of her grandmother, the knock of the closing door, but she heard nothing. He soon appeared again, walking the fields to the root cellar. In the red dusk light of fall she could see the shine of his blue-black hair.

"Didn't take him long to sniff your trail," Baptiste said. "He wants you." Baptiste tapped her knee. She felt annoyed by him. She could see Charlie, how he circled the fields. They watched him for a long time and Louise yawned. She didn't believe he was going to be close to them before darkness closed the valley, if he found their trail at all. She watched Charlie Kicking Woman stop. He stood still for a long time and then he was walking back toward her grandmother's house.

"Cold," Louise said. "You're getting colder."

Louise lay back in the grass. "If he's looking for me," she told Baptiste, "I don't think he has a clue." She was exhausted from running, tired of it all. The wind had picked up and the tall, sleepy grass swept over her. The powdered moon was almost invisible. She began wishing that Charlie Kicking Woman would just go away and not only because she didn't want to be caught. She didn't want to make a fool out of Charlie again. She had seen Charlie drinking coffee in the Perma store. He was sitting with a group of suyapis, all of them in their uniforms. State police officers and Charlie the Indian by himself. Louise had stopped just outside the screen door to listen to them. The white men were talking about Indians as if Charlie wasn't an Indian, or maybe Charlie wasn't a cop, or, worse yet, as if Charlie wasn't even there. Louise had snuck up to the window to watch Charlie. Their conversation was loud. It wasn't long before one of the white men stood up and put his hands on his hips. Charlie stood up then and put his hands on his hips too. He was nodding and laughing with those men like he had been places he'd never been. Charlie Kicking Woman began making fun of Indians himself when he looked up to see Louise. He had stopped talking then. He had taken off his hat and fumbled with some change in his pocket. He had shamed himself. Louise knew his shame. She had tried to pass herself off as white too many times so that she could spare herself ridicule and discomfort. She had denied her family and herself so she could have a drink with a white man. She didn't know what would happen if Charlie did find them. Baptiste always seemed to get the better of Charlie. She didn't want to be witness to Charlie's red-faced fumbling again. It would be better for all of them if he didn't find her.

Baptiste was still keeping watch, rigid and vigilant. She began to feel grateful to Baptiste, but when he tapped her leg again there was a rise in his voice that told her he was in this for himself. Baptiste liked to trick others. She looked up to see Baptiste rocking. He rubbed the top of his head. She could hear the whistle of his breath and when she sat up, Baptiste sidled up behind her and wrapped his arms and legs around her. Charlie had suddenly changed direction. He was moving up the hill quickly, with purpose. When he kept coming in their direction, she bucked up against Baptiste's arms, ready to run, but Baptiste had captured her tight. "Easy," he said to her, and she felt like he was talking to Champagne. She couldn't stop her heart from racing. She could feel Baptiste's voice at the nape of her neck and she strained to hear what he was saying but he was not talking to her then.

Louise watched Officer Kicking Woman as he walked a straight-line path to where they sat hidden in the weeds. He knows where we are, Louise thought and pressed the palms of her hands flat to the ground, ready to run again. Baptiste leaned his chest into her back, and snipped off a milkweed stem, split it open to white foam with his broad thumbnail. He took the watery milk and rubbed it on his hand. Charlie walked a distance away from them and then stopped. A web of grasshoppers shot up behind him. Charlie's shoulders pulled up tight to his ears. He glanced backward for a moment so short he must have felt the muscles stretch behind his eyes.

Charlie was close. She hid her face. She did not want to see him. She could hear a crease of wind slow. Baptiste turned to her. "He cannot see you, Louise," he said. "He is blind to us here." Louise did not believe Baptiste. She pressed her fingers to his lips to quiet him but he kept talking. She put her hands over her head and scrunched herself down into the weeds.

Baptiste's voice was heavy in her ears. Charlie would hear Baptiste and take her back to Thompson Falls. Weakness pressed deep into her chest. Her hands were trembling like the honeyed saplings at the thick base of the hill. Charlie had stopping walking. He rested his hand on his holster. And still Baptiste kept talking. Charlie was close enough to hear Baptiste, to see them in the weeds. But Charlie only tilted his head up as if he were hearing something far away. Louise looked down at Charlie standing in the open field. The sudden wind had brought back the heat of summer. Clear heat shuddered the long September grass, a heat that looked wet in the distance, a wavering, filmy heat that seemed to wash over him. Louise wrapped her arms around her knees and watched Charlie. Charlie began walking toward them again. She breathed through her mouth. "He can't even hear us," Baptiste told her, but Charlie kept walking steadily toward them.

She believed Charlie was playing a trick on them. He was letting them hide like children, letting them play their game, but as Charlie got closer she could see his face and she knew. His eyes watered with the hard setting sun. Baptiste tapped Louise's hand. "We are hidden," he said. He pointed toward the stiff juniper that lined the river. She looked carefully.

"See that," Baptiste said. "See."

She saw the large herd of deer as if she were imagining it. First a twitch. Then a rolling haze. A great shuddering movement like wind on grass.

She could see the gray highway, the stuttering light on the river. She could see light cradled in sweet grass. She could not remember seeing light as if it were more than just light. Silver light channeled down the rock face of Revais Hill. Light glanced off Charlie's smooth face. Louise wondered if the sun itself shed its skin to hide all the animals. "That's right," Baptiste said, and she wondered if he was answering her.

In this field, these hills, the sun ached over red leaves, hid bear and deer. In the Flathead River, trout slept in the hazy shadow of early evening, safe. She wanted to believe she was safe too, that there was a place for her to hide from all of them, from Baptiste, Yellow Knife, from Mr. Bradlock, from Charlie Kicking Woman's chase.

Charlie's shadow darkened the spot where Louise sat with Baptiste. Louise was close enough to Charlie to touch his gun. She felt like a snake coiled and ready to strike. She could feel the heat of his leg, smell the singed heat of his wool slacks. She looked up, saw the wind stiffen the hair up from Charlie's forehead. Baptiste looked up too. Charlie was so close Louise could hear the tight squeak of his leather holster. She drew her knees tighter to her chest and heard the blood beating in her throat. Charlie shook his head and kicked at a rock beside her, his boot skimming her thigh. She felt laughter curdle her stomach. The idea that Charlie could not see them in the cover of the weeds began to fill Louise.

Charlie scanned the base of White Lodge Hill. When he left, he walked carefully, turning back to gaze in their direction with eyes steady and unseeing. She thought Charlie held only the vision of certain trees, a few rock swells he could not distinguish from dirt, everything blending to nothing. Maybe Charlie saw the curve of her hip as only another slope of land, her fingers stark as the weeds that surrounded her. Maybe Charlie could not see the meadowlark in the pine branches, the distant white heat lifting, the separate river rocks, the sleek dark shale that rose from the hill. Louise could feel a low shifting breeze. Charlie turned his broad back to them. Baptiste held her safe. He was talking to her, telling her a story. She wanted to lay back in the prickle of weeds beside him and listen to his dry voice. She could still see Charlie but then he began running, running as if from a cold place where the only name spoken was his own.

The sun had moved behind them, a yielding light now that carried a tint of coolness. She began to believe she was there by herself. Alone, listening to her heart, the sound of far water.

IF IT IS SO FAR
from "Our Savage," a novel

Matt Pavelich

SHE FOUND NOTHING TO LIKE in New Orleans. Stoja followed the hajduk off La Tintina Nova's brow and through a file of black stevedores ferrying hawser line on their backs and singing, some of them, as if their own and all the world's troubles were only a mistake. Their singing caused her to quiver. "The ground here quakes," she observed. "Where have you landed us? Is this Butte, Montana?" The hajduk told her that there were fluids still coursing through her inner ears and that it was muscle memory that caused her feet to clutch at solid ground. It was, he said, a rare sensation, and she should enjoy it. Butte, he said, lay far inland and to the north. Because she had not seen him acquire this information, she doubted it. "I'm not mistaken," she said. "I am sick at my stomach."

Her husband conferred with official looking men in a tremendous room where the machinery for lathing ships' masts was still in place. They were made to dump their tote sacks, her trousseau, into red bins that their few possessions did not begin to fill. "We have nothing to declare," the hajduk told her. Whatever this meant, it was mixed news. A little fellow in a well-made uniform smiled at them as they restored their goods to their luggage. They passed on to another room where a number of papers were pressed on the hajduk for his signature. Savage read aloud from them in such a way that the customs agents laughed with him. He translated a single passage to his wife: "Do you intend to overthrow the government of the United States of America?" When Stoja gasped at this, the customs agents permitted themselves a little more friendly laughter and handed them the documents that made them the country's guests. Now she was deeply suspicious, a very small sea change for Stoja.

While she had been sick at sea, God had taken advantage of her special attentiveness to tell her that He had stoked her fierce, that she was a thorn of His perfect rose bed, and that she must always be angry. He told her that He would forgive her almost anything so long as she was never angry with Him. There was license in this arrangement, but she hated it. What was His forgiveness to her when she herself lacked the capacity to forgive? She was unable to overlook anything in anyone, including the smallest of her own multitude of faults. For her prayers and penances she had been granted a life as a dark disturbance. She too had bargained for a departure, which she had received, and for a fresh start, which she had not. Her anger, it seemed, traveled well and would find its fuel in any company.

To be helpless in the hands of the hajduk—only he could read the road signs, and only he could offer her any direction through the thronging, sweltering streets. In the first mile of their overland passage he stopped three times to eat, once at a saloon to buy two small glasses of an amber liquor that appeared expensive to her. The man would empty their pockets. Already she had told him that they could afford to travel only by foot. At nightfall, filled with crab meat, shrimp, and bread, he set out on a pike road at a constant five miles an hour over the long alluvial flat of Louisiana. Stoja ran along behind, shifting the burden of her tote sack so often on her shoulders that she raised welts on each of them. He mounted a levee that ran through a marsh. They went on. A glutinous membrane formed in her throat and pulsed with her every breath. She recalled the distances that Vuk Hajduk was said to have covered as pursued and pursuer; perhaps he meant to run her to death. In the heart of the night the hajduk pulled up suddenly in front of her. Stoja drew abreast of him and also stopped short at seeing a creature athwart the levee. "Now dragons," she said. "You have taken me where the night air never cools and there are dragons."

"It is an alligator. The tail, I understand, is edible."

Stoja found a knobbed stick and ran with it at the animal. It pivoted away from her on its blunt little legs then stopped to make sure of her sincerity. Stoja had not slowed, she had commenced swinging. The alligator slid down the levee wall and into the marsh. Stoja let the thrill of this engagement carry her an hour or two. They passed through a cypress grove, its roots and mosses agrope in the moonlight, then descended again to the pike road where, despite the hour, a fabulous traffic was abroad. In this nation, she saw, movement was the fetish, even the ragged rode by well mounted. A light and some attendant noise labored toward them, a carriage like those she had seen in Genoa and Marseilles, drawn along by nothing but its own racket. The driver, for all his piddling progress, hunched over the wheel of the machine as if to urge it forward, and smiled optimistically beneath the great, silly sweep of his moustache. Stoja ran on, past trusting even her own senses. Lights of no detectable origin appeared before her. Eventually the night produced a final specter—morning, a morning sun that was cruel from its first appearance in the east.

From a roadside shanty, from its sagging porch, a fat man spoke musically. His chin had become enfolded in flesh so he defined the lower edge of his face with a strip of beard. Stoja assumed he must be ill, dripping as he was. At the edge of the porch was built a system of andirons, a cauldron hung from its apex. The fat man stirred at the cauldron with a long spoon. It looked to be silage, but its vapors were stronger. "He wants to feed us," said the hajduk. Stoja heard children singing inside, saw them gathered at a window, skittish. The sick man called inside and a ragged girl with skin and hair of the same beige coloring ran out into the yard. She shooed hens off the crates where they were roosting in the yard and returned to the porch with a handful of brown eggs. She sweetly intoned a few words to the fat man. The fat man spoke in his own honeyed way, to the girl, then to Stoja. "Spring water, ma'am." He nodded toward a pipe standing in his yard and discharging clear water into a brackish ditch. "That's pure spring water."

Stoja understood it as invitation and knelt to the pipe to let it spill into her hands. She drank and the water was very cold, it savored of the bright beard of algae depending from the pipe's lip. She sat crosslegged on the ground and drank until the weight of the water in her stomach hurt her. She wanted nothing else.

The hajduk let the fat man fry him two of the eggs and serve them to him floating on the green sauce from the cauldron. Her husband winced at the first bite, but went on happily, whistling inward to cool his lips. The fat man was seized with laughter. They hadn't yet made a human contact in this oven of a country that did not result in laughter. Stoja had come with her husband into the land of the Lotus Eaters, a place for which he was well suited.

When the hajduk finished his breakfast, the fat man gave him a gazette to read. Her husband sat near her on the ground and remarked, all morning it seemed, on its contents. "Several different models of internal combustion engine are offered for sale here. Here, you see, engines compete for supremacy. That is all to the good."

Trailed by the household's children, they set out north again. The children's games were also song, song apparently all they had. The hajduk joined their singing, seemed to know or divine their melodies. They came to a stretch of road paved in crushed shells and the children turned back. The shells were too sharp even for their tough little feet. The hajduk went on, whistling. At last he let her catch him, and he asked "Bruckner? Do you like Bruckner? Dvôrak?"

"If you must squeal," she said, "squeal. Just don't ask my permission to do it."

The hajduk slowed after that so that she might walk beside him. But they had nothing to say to each other. She let herself fall behind. Her husband forgot her and strode out again. Stoja jogged along briskly and at this pace could not smell herself so much. The front of her dress was white with her body's many salts. She understood herself to be a creature approximately in God's image, secreting foulness. At shorter and shorter intervals new roads met the road they traveled. As pedestrians they were forced to the shoulder by a thickening stream of traffic. Not all the sun and the noise and confusion, not even the pitying regard of mere teamsters, not all of it together was as hard for Stoja as this running in soft dirt. She called to the hajduk's back, "Don't think I don't know that we're lost. We would surely have been there by now if you hadn't lost us."

At last they came to a small rise. They topped it and the hajduk brought her attention to a horizon where the red brick of several prominent buildings was just beginning to emerge. "Baton Rouge," he said.

"Speak to me in our language."

As they neared the city, the pike road began to run parallel with and generally in sight of a wide river, a river she would have called a sea except that she could see it flowing. The hajduk turned down to a boat landing where a scow was onloading cattle. He talked with a herdsman on the dock, and they were permitted to board the thing. They went forward to the bow and a deck somewhat elevated above the one where the cattle were penned. The cattle bawled, gulls dipped at the water, the scow swung out to make its slow passage into the current. Stoja lay down and dreamed of things familiar and things faint and far away until the engine she had slept over shut down and the hajduk was at her again. Again he was saying, "Baton Rouge." They had come to another waterfront. When she stood, when she weighted her right foot, she understood at once that she had somehow broken it during the course of their walk. It had swollen inside her shoe and she found that she could not prevent herself from limping. But she wouldn't allow the hajduk to carry her or to hire them some conveyance. Let no one deprive her of her pain as that was all, it seemed, that she could expect to have for her own.

The hajduk led her to a train depot, a busy little building of naked brick. She lay down on one of the long benches inside, squarely in a draft from an open door. Again she slept. She walked Ilmograd's few little avenues, saw again the walls of her village, the long, soft slopes in them at their foundations, where they met the earth. And she was gentle too in this dream. Gentle and fortunate. She discovered a Roman coin, had it between her teeth and was just about to test its quality when she next woke. For a moment she could not quit her curiosity regarding the coin, but then she was completely among the wakeful. The bench had hurt her. The hajduk was across from her, eating crumbs from a crumpled paper. It was night and their fellow travelers, reduced in number, were draped all around the depot in abject ways. Merciless night, with gaslights and electric lamps. From time to time a man in a blue fez mounted a platform and called like a muezzin through a long cone, at which the depot would stir, and some left and some arrived.

Stoja was not happy, but the effort of moving anywhere else, she knew, would make her less so. "Where are we?"

The hajduk stood with such emphasis that she thought at first he meant to leave her there. But he did not leave. He lifted her foot from the bench and showed her how it had ripened—how useless and vulnerable she had made herself. She felt herself drawn a little closer to her man. She saw it in him. No matter who Danilo Lazich thought he was, or what he thought he might make of himself, he was Prećani Srbi, her countryman, and there was that hatred in him like burning dirt. At least they would always understand each other perfectly. She let him slip his arms under hers, allowed him to lead, then carry her to the far end of the depot. He placed her on the floor there, just before a wall on which was painted a vast tan map with hatched lines, blue and red and black. There was a good deal of infidel lettering. "The routes of the Southern Pacific Railroad," he said. At the bottom of the map, near the floor, a frayed peninsula spilled out into a field of blue, the Bay of Mexico. He pointed to a dot there. "New Orleans, where we made landfall." His finger slid up a bit to a second dot. "Baton Rouge. We are here, just here, having walked much of two days and a full night." He drew himself up to his full height and placed the flat of his hand well up on the wall, as high as he could reach, on a cold gray expanse into which no line or color of the map had ventured. "Butte would lie here. Or perhaps even farther north. And we would be forever getting there, walking."

"If it is so far for you," she said, "then we will ride."

'You've crippled yourself," he said.

"I can make my way. Always."

"And where is your way? Have you the slightest idea?"

"The worst that can happen to me," she said, "has already happened."

He addressed her where she lay on the floor, "I do not admire the uses of cruelty, but with you, woman, to do a kind thing is almost impossible. You said 'walk', and we have walked, so now you see that your ignorance must not be our guiding principle. Never presume to tell me where I am going, or why, or by what means. Avoid that, and we may stay on friendly terms."

"Buy the tickets," she said.

Stoja expected to find countrymen. Many of the ambitious Lićani of her generation had sent money home from Butte, Montana. They sent descriptions of their progress and invitations to those they'd left behind. No such invitation had, of course, been offered her, not that she'd wanted one. She was going anyway. For a woman with a piledriver for a husband, the mines seemed a sensible destination. She settled her swollen foot on the seat across from hers and held both seats for her own against all comers, including the hajduk, whose comings and goings were her most constant irritation. But even Stoja could be lulled by a long train ride.

Savage's mission to the city was more ornate. Gold, silver, copper, and zinc. An immensity of copper in Butte to tax his mind, marketed to a world intent on wrapping itself in copper wire and propelling itself with copper windings. That year the United States of America and all her territories and holdings had produced seven hundred and fifty million dollars worth of ores, and a full tenth of that had come from the richest hill on earth. Butte sat up in a remote country Savage had craved since he had encountered it in Professor Ornbaun's thirty volume treatise on the Americas.

The Silver Bow, Ornbaun had written, *is the uppermost and easternmost of all those drainages that feed the Clark's Fork and Columbia rivers, and ultimately, the waters of the Pacific. By virtue of its altitude, its stony soils, and the terrible toils and contamination man has brought to it, the city of Butte is a blasted setting quite in contrast to the lush upland valleys that surround it for hundreds of miles in all directions, and here wilderness presses close upon an already fabled destination where even the patterns of corruption remain youthful and vital. Wilderness or city, the Montana highlands may yet yield to the stout hearted a fortune* non pariel, *and will surely continue to crush the faint and the merely desperate arrivals to its precincts.*

There are in Butte, to be certain, cultural elements as glorious as anything known to her older sister cities of the West. The ballet that is danced in San Francisco makes its way soon thereafter to Butte. Denver proudly boasts of playing host to three vaudeville circuits, Butte entertains four. The city is the greatest concentration of sporting events on earth, the earth's latest excrescence of new wealth, and always in such circumstances and to such places is a certain breed attracted. It is a place of industry; it is a place of meritless gain. Granite and brick, also abundant near about, are the basis of all its civic architecture. If the city is new, it is not insubstantial. Butte's social structure is one of egalitarian brutality. The have-nots of many lands have assembled here and come into their own. Outcasts gravitate. Ulstermen play fantan with Chinese, Finns enjoy the services of Hasidic tailors.

Winters in the region are typically difficult. However, one descends from any snowbound pass leading into Butte to find a mile-high plain and a hillside ablaze with light that is profuse, profligate, and in no mean heedful of the trackless reaches of darkness in which it rests. Narrowly cosmopolitan, Butte offers every pleasure and every privation yet devised by man. The industry that creates so much possibility here also casts over its environs a pall through which the sun only rarely penetrates. It is a dangerous child of a city, destined to perish of its own exuberance or to some day rule the earth. Neither outcome would be, perhaps, entirely regrettable.

Savage had seen in Ornbaun's passage the face of the twentieth century and wished to see it again, close to hand.

But it was difficult to wait for it, hard to stay on the train. From Fort Worth, he sat behind Mr. Harriman's paired locomotives, and minutes and degrees of latitude fell behind, and marshlands and woodlands and farmlands and prairie fell behind them, and the boundaries of the various states were of absolutely no consequence. Forty miles on this train every hour; never an hour passed when he did not see from his window, or from the top of the mail car, curiosities he should have stopped to examine. Texas, New Mexico. His fellow voyagers, fellow Americans, sought him in the club cars, some with promotions in mind, productions to turn a buck.

"You could wrestle rubes at the carnivals and have a nice living from it." This was McNeil of Iowa's notion. "Or even just by putting yourself on display." Of late, McNeil had been on the road with perfumes, a perilous grift. "'Rub the Gentle Giant for Luck,'" he said. "'Man or Beast? Guess Correctly and Win a Cupie Doll.' Mister, you could be part of many an easy presentation. Remove your shirt," fired by the thought, he made as if to remove his own. ". . . and, there, you'd have done a night's work."

In Colorado, Savage was offered the chance to sell crop and life insurance. Where the mountains rose up, he began to meet men who wanted him to go lumbering with them, partner on a crosscut, blow log jams. Enterprise was all in the nation. America, precious federation. He would be welcome here. He could have gotten off the train at any point and been home, at all points he was tempted. America. Savage was very sorry now to have been given just the one life; he'd never see any creditable part of all that needed seeing.

Skirting the eastern front of the Rockies, the train slowed. From Denver, passengers of their class became part of a mixed freight and were at all hours shunted onto spurs where they waited for their always lengthening train to take on more tonnage. They made connections in Cheyenne with the Western Flyer to wester with efficiency and élan through another several ranks of mountains and on into Pocatello. Then, running brightly behind the engine *Pandora*, they went beside and, sometimes with goatlike patience, upon the mountains' western slopes. Savage was never completely within the train, not during the whole trip through Idaho's fat toe and into the Bitterroots and Montana. He rode on top now, or on the shimmying platforms over the coupling knuckles, and he smoked prodigiously. He thought he was approaching a perfection.

Savage was not an hour in Butte before he learned a useful dread of silicosis. He spent a day down in the mines, hired courtesy of a cousin-in-law, Dragan Prpa, and he spent another at the end of a calcine oven, and that night he hired out at the New Star Saloon to collect a gambling debt. That was the end of Savage in the industrial arm of the labor force. As his first step toward real participation in the fruitful land, he got himself ready cash and its emblements, all the personal finery he could think of. From the haberdashers at Henneseys he ordered a gray homburg, size eight and a half, and a pearled device, a coursing hawk, to pin to its crown. He bought twelve pair of suspenders, as many starched collars and went among the city's debtors, sleek as well as large, and at his first quiet request for it even the most recalcitrant of them assembled some means to pay. Many seemed gratified by the experience, this chance to make good. "Never again," they would tell him. "From now on, I pay as I go, huh?" It was during the first few months of his life as a dun that he began to style himself Danny, a name that particularly struck his ear.

Savage and his wife had settled first in the Cabbage Patch, a neighborhood built on Butte's most weatherbeaten hillside, but when he had the means to do better he rented a suite at the Arlen. Stoja would not accompany him uptown. He lived there without her interference, lived at the charming velocity of easy affluence. And he prospered. Out on the town, bets were made as to the volume of food he might consume at a meal. In Butte, a man's hunger was respected; the ravenous were celebrated. Considered a jack of all the violent trades, he was finally fully fed, and everything was expected of him. He was asked if he would like to conduct bear-baitings, dog fights. His opinions were sought and attended to. In all his haunts women of varying age and persuasion found ways to pass slowly and closely by him. Curious, prettily scented, close. Such a shame, the hours wasted in sleep and waking with just two hands.

To supplement himself, Savage took thugs into his employ. First, despite the rumors, he hired Karl Ullmer. Ullmer effortlessly implied the Teutonic doggedness and did exactly as he was told. Savage took on a man whose *nom de guerre* was at that time Zed Strizich, and who looked the thug but did not sound it. Strizich was garrulous and enjoyed very much the confusion he caused with his Etonian drawl. A remittance man with a tiny Devonshire estate of his own, he owed much of his character to formative years at St. Bosco's, a school whose pedagogical premise was that no well-born boy is ineducable or incorrigible. St. Bosco's approaches to Strizich had fouled completely when it was found that Jeremy—he'd been Jeremy then—rather coveted the good caning to be had for bad behavior.

Savage, his thick-browed staff assembled and loyal, had become a small but persuasive agency. In the twenty square blocks where his group held sway, the deadbeat, that usually ineradicable weed, was all but extinct. Savage and company expanded their range of services, proved themselves indispensable to the resolution of any truly intractable negotiation; they became officers of a court that, while not official, had its jurisdiction wherever he and his cohorts happened to be. His circles of acquaintance arced higher and higher through the several arteries of the city's population; in each of them, as always, as apparently inevitable, he was thought an oddment. But in Butte, in those places where its capital accumulated, most men thought themselves unique. Savage was very little alienated among them, more like them than not. He was, most importantly, a fellow who got the right result, and made a fine associate on the sticky fringes of any business. So Butte curried his favor, and he was content with her, though she was ugly. Danny Savage. Domestically, he was less successful here.

On the feast day of St. Cyril, he rode the trolley in brisk weather over Park Street. The morning cloud cover was unimaginably high, torn to wraiths by winds aloft. "I will meet any man," he heard a child whisper to a pal smeared with axle grease and plum jelly, "on any terms." The boast had been in town several weeks now, wrongly attributed to Savage. He was often misquoted. These boys, he thought, were hoping he would kill one of them and thinking it would be delicious if he did. He was the source of a thousand specious thrills. Infamous to all but the city's law, it was for Savage oysters on the half shell, and champagne and soda crackers and whatever else he might like, and the only blot on it was his continuing entanglement with his wife. She had sent word that he must squander an otherwise promising afternoon.

For the benefit of his admirers, he made a handsome, sweeping dismount of the trolley at the corner of Idaho and Gold. He stopped to assess the progress made by the Orthodox in mending the onion dome above their church. Their first and irretrievable mistake had been to build it of plaster and lath. He went deeper into the Cabbage Patch, toward the place they had once called theirs, though he was paying for it and now only she lived there. Of late, he had been an infrequent guest. Ohio Street, not a daub of paint in sight, and all along it lay the shadow of what by now should be his long-forgotten home. Savage smelled Lika here, heard it, heard what had been the litany of his nursery, the only story Marko Lazich ever told him.

The Srb rides out, century after century from the black forests, never more than a clan at a time, always undermanned, always insufficiently armed. He rides out, wild-eyed and happy to present his bull neck to the Pasha's Guard, the Janissaries. It was the Srb who dulled the Ottoman scimitar so that Northern Europe might have her Reformation, her Renaissance, her Industrial Revolution, while in the Balkans a better people advanced not at all. Where is our reward? Ask yourself, Danilo.

Savage stood on a roadbed frozen hard as macadam. Of course they would live here, find this contemptible place to squat and nurse their grievances. *So for the Srb, Danilo, it comes to this: like Our Cherished Savior you will instruct the world by your suffering; if you are Srb, you are, like Our Christ, available for the killing but very hard to kill.*

Savage had married one of his own kind, of the kind he would not be, and he was determined that his further difficulties should not include anything so complex and wearing as this marriage. All along Ohio Street, dirt the brightest thing in sight. Not for the Srb any investment in temporal grace, and not for his neighbor. The Srb would live just here, oppressed by someone. And his Stoja would live here.

She had bought two new washing machines, there were now seven treadle-drive Sturgis and Philpot agitators fitted into the room. She sat among them in a red mackinaw and a pair of brogans, got, no doubt, through close trading; waiting for him in shoes that may or may not fit her. Each week Stoja built a thirty-quart cake of lye soap in this room and shaved it into flakes. She sank tons of blackened denim, bachelor's clothes, in scalding water and her acidic soap. She had made the room antiseptic. Wringers stood in a row, awaiting her labor. She was an industry, his wife, successfully in competition with the local Chinese. Potent, incurious, awful. The awful woman, his. "My bed," Savage said. "My lamp and stool. My periodicals, my anaesthetic. What have you done with them, Stoja?"

"That corner is not for your use anymore."

"I would tell you to go to hell, but that would be an improvement over what you've done here. You will go after my things and return them to the place and condition in which I left them."

"Why? Why would I do that?"

"What sort of party is it that you'd go to, dressed as you are? What sort of celebration? We must stop somewhere along the way now, somewhere downtown, and equip you like a woman. You've given me little enough to work with."

"I am wearing a four-dollar dress, hajduk. More than good enough to be seen with you. Save your money for the harlots."

"The bed. My bed, I'll have it back, or one of these moonlit nights you will find me in yours. Your little bed, the two of us. What would come of that? Show me another washerwoman who has kippered herring as often as she likes. These biscuits you like so well, these tinned goods, they come from me. I'll have something for them, won't I? In exchange for the small luxuries. Bring my bed back. I am paying for a residence and I will have a residence, whether I choose to live in it or not."

"The man begrudges his wife her little scraps of fish? The idler. What a wonder you are."

"Wonder of wonders," said Savage, "to be sure. Yours is the quotidian, I am not charged with that."

"To speak so on a holy day."

Savage drew two crumpled bills from his trouser pocket. "Again I tell you, come out of this. Move down the hill with me, Stoja, nearer the conveniences. Why do you work like an animal when I can provide for your comfort?"

"I choose to live among my people, where the old ways are understood. So should you. But you are ashamed of who you are."

"The old ways? I see. Then, by all means let's find a cave where we can crouch among the dogs and piss on our feet. The old ways. Come out of this, Stoja. It unsettles me. Come up to the Arlen and have room service, why don't you?"

"I will outlive you. What is mine is mine. I make an honest business. No one will shoot me for what I do. But you . . . when you are gone, then what becomes of me? I will see to my own needs, in my own way, among my own people. You don't have a thing to say about it."

When she wished to reach him, just three occasions in the two years they'd lived apart, she caused one of her customers to call the switchboard at his hotel. Each of the messages had arrived fantastic. *Wife says bring five big buckets and goose today.* And, *Wife says boobonik flag in Butte. Wife says stay away.* The latest: *Wife says St. Cereal day Saturday. Pick her up at ten.* Which meant, he knew, that Stoja wanted him for her seemly escort at the holy feast of St. Cyril. In truth, even his wife's interest in the mysteries and observances of the Faith had grown wispy here. It was for the sake of form, for business, that they should attend the feast as man and wife. To Savage's thinking, not reason enough to mingle with kith and kin. Yet here he was. "Well," he said, "come."

She would not ride the trolley because she believed it brought her near contagions. At the edge of town she prevented Savage from renting them English ponies to ride out on. Horses were afraid of her and behaved badly when she was near. They walked two miles before Savage tired of it and hailed a buckboard. "Climb on," he told her. Then again, adamant, "Climb on." The old sorrel at the head of the rig turned skittish, just as she'd warned he would, when Stoja pulled herself up onto the wagon bed. They went on to Columbia Gardens, the animal straining constantly to see the new thing behind it. An abrasive wind pushed them across the flat and toward the pleasure grounds. They rounded a thumb of the gulch that sheltered the pavilion and the winter remnants of gardens limned in gray and white. There were hothouses here where international banks of flowers were in bloom even now. At the lane's turning a field of playground equipment danced empty in the weather.

Most of Butte's several hundred Srbs had come, and they stood in their clusters on the pavilion's long veranda. Savage and his wife were driven up to, then beyond the crowd, their driver cursing, reining back with little effect. He began to shout at them, "Get off. Get off." They alit at a stiff run, slowed, and turned to walk back to the party on the veranda. As they gained the summit of its sweeping central stair, Stoja identified for him the various factions where they stood. At the end of history every Srb would have his own flag and be patron saint of his own orthodoxy; until that final, perfect fracturing, they were settled into their fraternities. "Those wearing the wide, red and white ribbons," Stoja said. "All from Beograd, all no good. And the ones in the soldiers' jackets call themselves the 10th Srbian Fusiliers. They play like children at soldiers, but I wash for them, wash those uniforms after every wearing. It is necessary. They let Bosnians join them, Muslims. Filthy." Stoja and her husband belonged, in his case by default, to the Precani Srbi. Their little group did nothing to distinguish itself except to stand apart from the others.

Srbs across the river, Danilo. Precani Srbi. The good families massed in 1804, the best families rode into Beograd and made it their own, as it had been anyway. At their head, the noble Karadjorj, the pig-broker risen through the ranks despite his belief that he was too angry a man even for military purposes. But he led us into Beograd and into a golden era of eight years' duration. Then, by a treaty to which Srbia was not signatory, she was ceded back to the Turk. The Ottomans returned to Beograd with their gifted executioners. They impaled us on their stakes, Danilo. Along every street patriots stood impaled, stakes driven rectum to clavicle, but ingeniously so that the lungs and hearts were spared and each death was a long, instructive drama.

So we wait. But for what? Serbia? We'd be strangers there, just as we're strangers here. We wait, but we wait for nothing we could name or put our crooked fingers to. Precani Srbi. What shit.

Dragan Prpa came to them and gave them papers to pin to themselves, St. Cyril's stark, cruciate crest. The cousin had established himself liaison between the Prećani and the other groups at the party. Shamefaced, he reported that no one had a key to get inside. No one was completely sure who should have the key. Of all the food and drink that had been ordered, only the milk had been delivered. Savage saw himself in a window and was pleased at how obviously he did not belong to the assembly—but their language was the language he understood most perfectly, the first he'd learned, and they talked of how hard they worked, as if more explanation was necessary than the sight of their best jackets hanging from their muscled backs. Muscled backs and hollow chests, and no tailor would ever make a suit to hang handsomely on a miner's body. Srbs. In their leisure they talked of the atrocities committed by Hrvati who lived, in many cases, just across the street from them. The old hatreds, they had found, were true and necessary, and old enemies had relocated each other here, become neighbors to make a distillate of the Balkan idiocy; their talk was very familiar to him.

Stoja stood near the veranda's railing as if she were in a sentry box, staring off at the upsweep of the continental divide or, probably, nothing. Savage shuddered. There were times when she appeared wistful, fragile as a hatchling chick. Complaint was general around him, tending now toward menace. Standing out in this wind it was impossible even to roll a proper cigarette, and where was Obilovich? Hadn't Obilovich rented the hall? What of the box lunches, the beer? What had become of the orchestra? They had been wanting a fine day of eating and drinking above ground but were instead huddled in the blistering wind.

Having guessed he might become captive to just such muddling, Savage had bought an *Evening News* upon departing his downtown rooms that morning. He retired to an isolated section of the veranda, pulled the *News* from his belt, and refolded it into a quarter sheet to make it rigid against the wind. He put his back to the wall and slid to the floor. The lead story had to do with the *News*'s discovery of what it was calling the bohunk problem. *There are 3,000 bohunk miners in Butte today, of these 2,175 are working and the balance are being supported by their brothers and are ready to slip into every job where a white man is laid off.* Whole areas of the city were infested by *these black men from across the water* and yet the *News* seemed to feel it should be specially commended for having located them and for having the courage to beard the disaster they represented. The paper's house artist had illustrated in pen and ink the interior of a shanty occupied by crop-headed, hollow-cheeked Africans in long underwear, but the story was more accurate in many particulars. Savage had come with a sorry lot to Butte. Many recent arrivals were living eight to a cabin, sleeping in shifts on their cots or on dirt floors, and paying, each of them, full rental as if they had the place to themselves. There was a class of landlord, men who were also mine foremen and who, in exchange for the larcenous rentals they charged, would guarantee each of his tenants a job. *The bohunk miner,* the *News* reported, *never adapts himself to the American way of life any more than does a Chinaman. Gambling, white slavery, prizefighting, licensed prostitution, horse racing, and every ill, alleged or otherwise, that one can conjure up, palls into insignificance before this black peril which has Butte by the throat and is dragging it down to the level of a grading camp.* An accompanying editorial said that even a city as gregarious as Butte must have some standards, that it was time for decent men to rise up and speak, to encourage these dark people to move on and look for a place more amenable to their brutish ways.

"Alone again. Off laughing again." Stoja stood above him. "You sit on the floor like a poorly behaved child? How am I to hold my head up when you behave as you do?"

"Let's be off now."

"We have only just got here."

"See how unhappy they are? What do you suppose they will be like in an hour when they are still waiting to be let in, still hungry? No one will come to let them in. No one will bring food, and there will be no orchestra."

"Stand up," she said. "When things aren't as you want them, you cannot wait. No, but always, let's be off. As if all things must be arranged for your convenience. You brought me to this, you must stay."

He joined her to stand again among the Prećani Srbi. Nearest them was a group he had seen before, a little cell of Bolsheviks that had been standing just outside the door of a church and cursing as loudly as they could, and smoking, while inside, also loudly, a priest read a sermon over one of their order who had died. Today, it seemed, some doctrinal problem had arisen among them, and they were about to splinter at least in half. Division and division and division, the endless, sexless genesis of political man. Savage was moved to analysis. "Srbs across the river," he told his group. No flattery was in his tone, but they listened because this was, at least, more interesting than the other had been, the waiting. "Did anyone bring a gusla? Isn't it time for sad songs? Isn't it time for *Ladé Capitané*? Sing, why don't you, but never anything to cause dancing, no, keep to your gray little airs, and sing them, and bicker with a neighbor who resembles you, and that is what you'll have in this country, the same you had in the country you left, because that is who you are. While you have been at each other's throats, the world has come to despise you collectively, you and the Hrvat, and even Czechs and Magyars—bohunks here, all of you. A united slavdom at last, united in condemnation. Now you may sing the old dirges because, once again, no other music is coming. Why should the good music of the world be wasted on your ears?"

The Bolsheviks murmured at this.

"How little you know," said his wife. "No music for us? No food? Well, who is that coming now, coming fast because they have made us wait?"

Three open automobiles approached down the lane toward the pavilion. Two of them bore the markings of the Silver Bow County Sheriff.

"Stop that, hajduk. Laugh and laugh when there is nothing to laugh at? Stop it. Do you laugh at me, you mud? You have a sickness."

"Watch now," he told his wife. "We'll have a comedy so broad that even you will be entertained." He raised his voice again, this time so as to be heard by all on the veranda. "Is there even one here who is descended from those heroes who died at Kosovo Polje? Is there one such among this crowd?"

Up came the chin of every man and the several women and children in attendance.

"Then you are Srbs? You did not look like Srbs to me. On St. Cyril's day, Srbs—men—know how to celebrate." Savage leaned out from the veranda and discharged his pistol three times into the endless sky. Similarly armed celebrants, their majority, also fired, dutifully, three times apiece, affirming the trinity. Damage was done to the veranda's roof. The oncoming cars accelerated. The third and most powerful of these wore no official markings, lacked even a license plate, and it was full of riflemen in mufti. The cars came to within fifty yards of the porch and were drawn up in a sort of barricade; the passengers discharged and hid behind them. With his countrymen momentarily fallen silent, Savage could hear the newcomers just distinctly enough to know that they too had taken up some disagreement among themselves. Their shouting reached a crescendo, stopped, and a moment later a single, unarmed man walked out from the rampart of automobiles. The Sheriff

He came to the foot of the grand stair and looked up mournfully. "My name is John D. Boyle, and I am the law. I mean to collect every shiv and sap and pistol and knuckle duster on that porch. If you people think you can go around heeled like an American, then you are wrong. . . . Oh, hell, is there anybody up there speaks a white man's lingo. Yeah, you, Savage, you tell them what I'm saying."

"This is an Irishman," Savage explained. "Who says he wants every weapon in your possession. As soon as he has them, you can well expect to be tithing to his pope. He has come to interfere with your celebration and your manhood."

"Keep it simple," said the sheriff. "I didn't have that much to say."

A captain of the fusiliers stepped to Savage's side. "No. No," he told the sheriff, the only words he had that might convey his desire for peace. To Savage he said, in their common tongue, "Tell him we want no trouble. We'll do anything he likes."

"He says," Savage told the sheriff, "that they have nothing they wish to give you."

The sheriff came up the stairs and walked directly to Savage, rattling as if poorly assembled of the wrong parts. Tired and vicious, he walked like a lawman. Stoja pulled at the tail of her husband's jacket. "I can see what you are doing. You are making a fight. Just for your fun, a fight. I will not mend you if you are beaten, I will not mourn if you are killed."

The sheriff was before them, his badge a tiny nickel star. He decided to take up with Stoja now. "Ma'am, I'll start with you. You can give me that baby pig sticker."

She had made herself a heavy necklace and hung from it a small sheath knife and a small, unreliable compass. These things belonged together.

"He wants your knife, little wife. Says you are to give him your knife."

"Quit laughing, hajduk." She fingered her necklace, the sum of her vanity.

"In just about three seconds," said John D. Boyle, "I am going to disarm one of these others and pistol whip you, Savage. You can't behave any better than this, I will just have to lay you out."

Stoja touched the knife's handle, she slipped it just half out of its sheath. Then, slowly, she exposed for the sheriff her black smile.

"What you want," Savage told Boyle, "you will have to take. And isn't that always the way, Sheriff? Nothing given?"

"I know the nature of your business, Savage. I know who you know. You've gone ahead and made me mad, so who you know doesn't mean a thing anymore. Not to me. But I am everyone's sweetheart, and I don't care to see innocent blood shed. Not in Silver Bow County. This bunch down here, they think this is a shooting party. Wouldn't take much confusion before that's what we'd have. Gunfire, probably a lot of it. Not one of these men with me is interested in the formalities, Savage. So I will have to wait on you. Otherwise, I'd haul you back to town right now, down to the basement of the courthouse. You can shriek down there like you was Nellie Melba, not a peep of it reaches the street. The next time me or any one of my deputies see you—or her—we'll have a warrant in hand. We'd see you the next time you set foot in town. Now, if you are truly curious, big man, about how tough you are, you just let that happen. Let me find you."

CRANES

Pete Fromm

THE CRANES CAME IN, bottom-heavy, wings high, fluttering and tottering on their stilt legs, looking for all the world like barely controlled marionettes. Behind them, the mountains, what little of them was visible, looked heavy and wet, the clear-cuts stark with rotting spring snow, closer than possible in the binoculars.

Hidden beneath the stubble-crusted netting of the blind, Arleen and I watched in silence, having done all of this too long with Simon to need words now by ourselves. But my bones ached in the cold wet, and I guessed that later I'd have to loosen Arleen's knobbled fingers from around the black weight of her binoculars.

The cranes—sandhills, Simon had taught us, feathered the same smudged brown-gray as the sky—rustled their wings, settling in, taking a first few tentative pokes into the mud with their hard bills. With the low clouds, one step short of fog, there wasn't even the chance of a glint off our binoculars giving us away.

So, when the guns' roar split the field, launching the cranes back into the sky, filling the air with their prehistoric hooting, Arleen and I simply froze, as if somehow we were the target. The cranes lumbered up, their great wings taking forever to unfold into steady beats. As they struggled, the guns boomed again and again.

The first crane we saw fall flipped onto its back, one wing still cupping air, the other suddenly unable to hold anything. Crashing the few yards back to earth, its head popped back up, straight and tall atop the slender neck. Another crane followed it down almost immediately, its neck dropping, the body following in a sloppy summersault. Magnified through the binoculars, it seemed I could almost feel the thwump of that big body slapping back-first into the muddy field.

A third slipped sideways and set its wings, only coming undone at the very end, barreling breast first into the mud just when it appeared it might land safely. A fourth and fifth followed them down, shots hammering the sky.

Then the guns fell silent. I watched the surviving birds circle upward, hoping for some thermal to carry them away, up into the rain. One trailed a dangling leg below its body as they vanished into the clouds. I pictured the slim stalk of femur, the fracture of a single searing BB, and wondered how that crane would ever make that bouncing, marionette-like landing, how it would ever return to earth.

In the silence following the shaking blasts of the shotguns, Arleen's cry of, "George?" startled me as badly as the first shot had.

I wrapped my arm around her, hauling her close as she struggled to escape the blind. "Keep down," I said.

"It's spring!" she insisted. "There's no hunting season!"

Then the men rose up out of the earth and Arleen fell silent. They ran in crouches, their guns jutting forward from the dark, slicing lines of their legs and arms. Camouflaged and caked with the field's mud, they looked like something out of Bosnia. Chechnya. One, smaller than the other two, stretched ahead of his partners.

The crane he charged, the one with its head still held high, cowered at his approach, lowering its neck down flat, as if it had a turtle's hard shell to escape within. Hardly breaking stride, the small man grabbed the neck and swung the crane up. Even as he began to twirl the crane on the end of its own neck, the crane's good wing stretched wide, striking at the man's head, his neck, his shoulders.

In the flurry it was impossible to see exactly which flailing blow connected with the little man's head. After he'd already dropped it, as the crane again settled its good wing along its back, began stalking away, (why hadn't it run before?) we heard the childish swearing drift across the mud to us, then, a moment after, the laughing of the other men.

"He's only a boy," Arleen whispered.

I nodded, wanting to turn away.

The boy, close enough to touch in the tight field of the binoculars, rubbed a moment more at the ear the crane had struck. Then, so suddenly I nearly missed it, he whipped up his gun, his little body jerking back as he fired. The crane's wing flipped over its back and it toppled sideways into the mud. Then the sound of the gunshot reached us. The crane did not move again.

The other men, each already dragging a pair of cranes by the necks, the bodies dragging through the cold, soggy mud, waited for the boy. All we heard after the swearing and the laughing was one, "Hurry up!" Then the two men and the boy slipped across the field, disappearing in a fold of land invisible to us even with our binoculars. Swallowed up by the ground.

Arleen wriggled out from under my arm. "George!" she said, so furious it was almost a roar.

I looked at the mud we perched in, my mouth filling with the bitter, metallic bite of anger and fear. "Let's not get ourselves shot, Arleen," I said, reaching again for her.

"We can't do nothing!" Arleen said, slipping away, out from under the netting.

Just following her out made me breathe hard. "Look at this," I said, waving at the bare mud, the stripe of ankle-high stubble we'd hidden in. My joints throbbed. "They'll see us."

"We won't just sit and watch!" She glared at me. "Simon loved those birds."

I looked at the netting, the stubble we'd woven through it last night in our garage, the two of us working so quietly side by side.

Arleen stared at me, her face watery and gray in what light seeped through the drizzle. "Well?"

"Simon loved everything," I whispered.

"Not those men," she spat.

"No," I answered. "Not *those* men."

Arleen reared back as if I'd slapped, and I tried not to think of the man Simon had loved. He'd left the day Simon passed, though we'd told him, if he wanted to stay, it would be all right.

Arleen kept staring at me, as if I wasn't the same old face she'd watched for fifty years.

"Let's wait," I whispered. "Till we know they're gone. Then we'll call a warden."

"And what? Say, 'It was two men and a boy'? What are they going to do with that?"

"You want them to catch us out here? You want them to know we saw them?"

"They're poachers, George. Not murderers."

"So far," I said.

Arleen gave me a look. "I'm going," she said. "I'm going to get a license number."

"I think we should get back in the blind. What if they come out of that draw? Can see us again?"

But Arleen was already off and I had to start after her, my knees shaky, my boots heavy, growing cakes of the sticky mud. "Arleen!"

She waited for me, but no more.

I kept my mouth shut, trudging beside her. The way they were moving, the men would be a long way ahead of us. Arleen and I couldn't move quickly anymore, even on dry ground.

When we both stopped to breathe, I said, "Arleen, I just don't want to be the evidence."

She whirled at me, glared long enough I could see her face was trembling, her eyes watery with held back tears. "We can't just pretend this didn't happen!"

"Okay, Arleen," I said, reaching to touch her, but she jerked away.

I started after her again. "Maybe they need them," I said. "Maybe it's all they can get to eat."

Without turning around, or even slowing, Arleen said, "A second ago they were murderers."

"Either way," I said. "I don't think we need to get in the middle of this."

Arleen skidded to a halt and turned on me, shouting, "Like Simon all over again?"

I stepped back.

But she was off, clearing the last rise of ground before the car. I saw her hesitate there, then start quickly down the hill. She was out of sight in the second it took me to follow, but I heard her yelling, "We saw you! We saw what you did!"

I followed as fast as I could, the mud like leg irons.

When I crested the hill, Arleen was huffing down the other side, still yelling, shouting, "You won't get away with it!"

A battered, dark pick-up ambled along the dirt road past our car, getting farther away, not slowing down. They wouldn't have the windows down in this weather, they wouldn't hear a thing. Seeing our car must have given them a jolt, though. Must have made them think. Made them peer out their steamy windows.

Slipping down the hill my weight gave me an advantage, and I caught Arleen in only a few seconds. I meant to grab her, to shush her, but in the mud and the rain we collided and went down hard together, sliding along on our backs. Before I could sit up, see if I could, Arleen was pounding on me, yelling, "Let me go! Let go!"

But I held on, and just before slumping against my still strong arms, she screamed, "You are such a coward!" and she began to sob.

I held her, patting her back. The rain was too light to pock the mud, just glistened off of it, shining and slippery.

I turned my head, looking around, everything I could see the same as since I was born. Spending your whole life here, the same place your parents spent theirs, and their parents theirs, you start to think of it as someplace safe, someplace yours, as if any threat as alien as AIDS would flare out in a crackling blue flash at the edge of the ranch. You don't lie in bed at night afraid your son, the best thing that ever happened in your life, is going to like boys, not girls, and that someday that will kill him so slowly.

"Cranes," Arleen murmured at last. "What could be more harmless?"

"There was nothing we could do for Simon," I whispered.

Arleen shook her head. "Cranes," she said once more and then nothing. Just lay there against me in the mud and the drizzle, our car only a few hundred yards down the hill before us.

I told her I was sorry, just sorry in general, nothing specific. Through everything, I'd never before thought of myself as a coward.

We were quiet a little while, then Arleen sat up, her hands too filthy to wipe her face. She started down to the car without me.

Watching her slip away, I pushed myself slowly up from the mud, never having felt quite so old in my life. I shuffled to the rear bumper, scraping as much of the fields from my boots as I could before getting in the car. The windows were already fogging over, and it wasn't until I opened the door that I saw Arleen in my place behind the wheel. She stared straight ahead until I closed the door and walked around.

As soon as I worked my way into the seat, Arleen turned the key. I reached over, switching on the heat, the fan to high. I left mud on the knobs.

"Those men," Arleen said, slapping at the shift lever.

I stopped her hand. The car idled smoothly beneath us, and I held Arleen's hand under mine. "Arleen," I said.

"How he would have hated them!" Arleen hissed. Her breath came in gasps, billows of it in the cold, wet air.

I nodded.

"We didn't do one thing for him!" she cried.

"What could we have done?" I said, rubbing my forehead despite the mud.

"We should have done something! Anything! Anything but nothing. He was all we ever had."

I thought of our whole lives together, and I wanted to say, "That's not true," but instead I kept to what I always said, "Arleen, we're going to be all right," the words even emptier in the cold, steamy inside of the car.

"They're innocent living creatures!" Arleen said suddenly.

"Simon?"

Her eyes narrowed. "The cranes. I want those men punished."

I let go of her hand and she started slithering down the road in the tracks of the big truck.

"The boy, too?" I whispered. "You want that boy punished too?"

Arleen's mouth worked, but no sound escaped, and I knew that watching that boy run, outstripping the grown men in his wild excitement, Arleen had relived her own tiny slice of Simon's childhood.

"He's just as guilty," she said.

Arleen slid to a stop at the section road's first T. I could see her straining forward, searching for tire tracks. But the road was a mess, tracks indistinguishable.

"Even if we could find them," I asked, "what then?"

I glanced at Arleen, saw her watery blue eyes squinted to slits, her chin trembling in anger and frustration.

"We're not hunters," I whispered. "We're bird watchers, Arleen. Harmless Audubon types." It was something we'd picked up for Simon, near the end. After a lifetime here, he made us see what had been around us all along, taught us the names of the birds, showed us what they did to survive. How he learned all that when he was so far away I have no idea. Maybe he'd learned it as a boy, when, it turned out, we knew so little about him.

At the very end I carried him to the blinds, though it was nearly impossible not to show how hard it was on me. Once he was gone it hadn't seemed right to stop.

Arleen kept scanning the road. She chose the right-hand fork, toward the Millers, then the Winningtons.

She went right the next time too, and the choice after that. I wondered if we'd circle out here forever, the heater sweating the drizzle off our clothes and onto the windows. Arleen had finger stripes of mud across her cheek, like a child's war paint.

I looked down at my lap, seeing those cranes losing the sky, one after the other, wondering if Simon's long dying had trapped Arleen and me into this kind of thing for whatever was left of our own lives.

I was still looking down, still seeing the falling cranes, when my window rolled down, Arleen's hand on the control.

I shrunk from the cold blast flooding the hot, wet car, but when Arleen asked, "Look familiar?" I followed her glance before I had a chance to think. Beyond the stark, dead cottonwoods of the ancient windbreak, the dark, mud-crusted pickup sat parked alongside the tired, paintless Tillman place, vacant for decades. With Simon home, we'd grown so into ourselves I hadn't even known someone had moved in. I wondered if they were squatters. I slipped down in my seat. "Arleen," I said.

Then, before I could say anything else, before Arleen could tell me what she wanted here, the boy ran out from behind the dead cottonwoods. He still wore his camouflage clothes, still covered in mud. Only now he ran holding a huge, dismembered crane wing in each hand, flapping them as he ran. He shouted as he flew; the strange, karoooo-a-roo of a sandhill, the best imitation I had ever heard. He was playing crane, I realized, no longer shooting and strangling the odd, beautiful birds, but trying to become one. To fly. And instead of remembering the falling cranes, I thought of Simon's short, difficult life, and wondered where in the world this little boy could possibly land.

Hoping I'd blocked her view, I gave a shiver and fumbled for the window button, raising the foggy glass between us and the boy.

"I don't think that's the same truck," I whispered.

Arleen only stared. First at the truck, then, more slowly, at me.

"It's got nothing to do with cowardice," I whispered.

She said, "What?" so distant I didn't know if she'd ever make it back, and I knew she'd seen the boy.

Together, through the fog of the glass, we watched the blur of him climb the rotting stone fence, then run down its broken, ankle-turning length, gaining speed. At the end, he threw himself off, hooting like a true crane, wings flapping furiously at the heavy, damp air, praying for flight.

The Difference between East and West

Florence Williams

THE RURAL WEST IS LITTERED with dead dogs. It is, perhaps, one of the surest distinctions between East and West. I knew I had landed somewhere foreign when I sat across the table from a rancher at the annual dinner of the Routt County Cattlewomen's Association in Colorado. She couldn't have been nicer. She was trying to impress upon me and my conservationist husband her commitment to wildlife. She told us about how one day she caught her two dogs chasing a deer. "I tied those dogs to a tree and shot them," she said.

A Montana rancher I know ran over three of his dogs, one at a time and all accidentally, driving his truck up and down his driveway. These were herding dogs, hence their unlucky propensity to get under the tires. Still, you'd think the guy would have regularly checked his rearview mirror after, say, the second doggie crunch. I don't have dogs and I'm not particularly sentimental about them. But there's nothing like death, even dog death, to make you see where you've come from and where you've gone, and just how far you are from home.

As far as I can figure, this is how it works: In the West, people kill their own dogs. In the East, someone does it for them. When I was growing up in New York, we had a dog named Albert, after my uncle. It was a Lhasa Apso. You won't find many of these dogs in Montana. They look like a miniature yeti. If Cousin Itt of the Addams Family were a dog, this is what he'd be, and he'd be much too embarrassed to show his face in front of the manlier, mangier dogs of the West. Albert was very New York, to the point of being almost androgynous. He went to the hairdresser more often than my mother did, to a place called Groomingdale's before the department store sued for copyright infringement, again in typical East Coast fashion. He wore bows in his neatly combed floor-length hair. One day while I was in high school, my mother was walking him in our neighborhood, on upper Broadway, when she heard a crack. She turned around and Albert was splayed at the end of the leash, his skull smashed in. A man with a stick was fleeing down the street. He was a famous Upper West Side street psychotic, the subject of numerous *New York Times* articles about the Failure of the System. The guy kept getting out of rehabs and detention centers, only to terrorize more small dogs and children. He once pushed a schoolgirl in front of a bus.

That is the New York method of dog-killing.

Years later, in Montana, there appeared a strange convergence of East and West, or so it seemed. I was on assignment writing about the Great Plains. I was south of Malta, home of a 6,040-pound hamburger memorialized on a local billboard. I was visiting a ranch couple at their doublewide miles from anywhere. I was trying to be liked. I brought them a melon, the freshest thing I could find. I wanted to hear their stories of blizzards experienced from sheep wagons, dry water holes, and lovingly restored barns. The couple was still driving back from town, so I took notes while their partner, an old herder from Spain, poured us copious amounts of rosado from a gallon jug and told me about how Butch Cassidy hid out in the nearby hills. The ranch couple came back, and we continued our interviews. Everything was going well.

Then the magazine's photographer screeched down the drive in a brand-new rental jeep. A New Yorker's New Yorker, she was dressed in a black T-shirt and black jeans, had hair that required regular maintenance, and talked as fast as she drove. "Yeah, hi," she said to the Basque by way of introduction. "Is this the brightest light you've got?" Then, not waiting for an answer, "Where's your outlet?" The fact that I was embarrassed meant I had come a long way. I'd been in the West for twelve years, but never felt less like a New Yorker than when I was actually with one. That voice! Those shoes!

The photographer left to return at better light, and the rest of us had just gone outside to tour the barn when we noticed a dead dog by the side of the drive. It was the ranch couple's dog, and its fate was obvious. The couple, childless and in their late middle years, was terribly upset.

It was such a western style dog-kill, but a New Yorker did it, and my photographer at that. I apologized profusely and of course said we'd pay to replace the dog, which was an expensive breed. We mourned the dog. We ended the interview.

I had to call the photographer and break the news and only hope that she would be sympathetic. I had all sorts of diplomatic ponderables. Who would pay? Would she? If not, would the magazine? Would I?

"That is so funny," she said when I called her cell. "I noticed that queer dead dog when I first drove in."

So, once again, the ranchers had run over their own dog. Only they thought the New Yorker had done it, and so had I, and they already hated us and so now what? We went ahead and paid for the dog.

The thing is, New Yorkers and ranchers are not really that different. They're both tough and curmudgeonly. They tell it straight and work incredibly hard. They're both mortgaged to the hilt. Ranchers probably use cell phones even more than New Yorkers do. They both tend to sleep in surprisingly shabby small spaces and spend most of their time elsewhere.

When I said my childhood dog was named after my uncle Albert, that wasn't the whole truth. Uncle Albert (who never fully appreciated the Lhasa tribute) was himself named after my grandmother's stepfather, Albert Loeb. My grandmother's real father died around the turn of the century of something like influenza or tuberculosis when she was only three. Her mother, Aurene, met Albert a few years later at the World's Fair in San Francisco. She had a booth selling lace she imported from Europe.

I knew Albert was originally from Helena, Montana, and family lore had it that he practiced law for a time there with Gary Cooper's father (this turned out not to be true). I'd seen decaying photos of him wearing shiny boots and sitting at a roll-top desk, and of him riding a horse, and later, a Model T. It was exotic and amusing for my mother's family, unreconstructed urban Jews, to contemplate ancestors with roots in the Wild West. When I moved to Helena in the late 1990s, my uncles chuckled about how I was going back to some sort of family fold, only no one knew much about it. If I, who had always felt somewhat out of place out West, had pioneer family connections here, I was determined to find out what they were.

I'm not sure why our family history wasn't talked about more, but it probably had to do with some willful erasure. My mother's family was about as assimilated as they come. Family members are named things like Tertius and Jefferson. We celebrate Christmas and almost all of us married non-Jews, including my mother. When I told my cousin, who grew up a Unitarian, that I was looking into Albert's past in Helena, I was surprised that she asked me, "Was he Jewish?"

Well. Indeed he was.

After the failed European revolutions of 1848, many Jews, along with other central Europeans fleeing aristocratic rule, headed for North America. For Jews especially, who at times were prohibited from certain professions and schools in Europe, the allure of a more democratic society abroad was irresistible. In late 1848, Bernhard Loeb, who had reputedly disavowed his allegiance to the Duke of Saxony, sailed from Mannheim, Germany, to New Orleans. Like many immigrants, the 48ers risked everything to come: bad sea voyages and cholera outbreaks, thievery, wilderness, and poverty. After several years in Louisiana, Bernhard followed the gold seekers and joined his younger brother in Sacramento, probably by sailing to the Isthmus of Panama, trudging overland through the jungle to the Pacific, and catching a boat up the coast from there. The details are sketchy, but the facts outline a life that was typically American, marked by a pattern of failure, perseverance, and gradual, if underwhelming success. The brothers ran a store, it burned down, and they lost almost everything. They moved on to Portland, Oregon, where they ran another store, and it burned down (fires in central business districts were common). Following the miners again, they moved on to Boise, where they ran a store for a while, before arriving in Helena in 1866 after gold was discovered in Last Chance Gulch. The vein was rich, and this time they stayed. Their Main Street store, Loeb & Brother, advertised in the city directory "clothing etc., boots, shoes, trunks & valises, having no rent or clerk hire to pay, we give the benefit to our customers."

The store did well enough that, by 1868, Bernhard went back to the old country to find himself a wife. In Baden, he found Jeannette Kander, who was twenty years younger and game for Montana. I'd love to know how he brought her here, but I imagine the two of them steaming up the Missouri and bumping over stagecoach ruts, stopping in on other Germans settlers along the route and sharing bottles of

Gewurtztraminer brought back in the trousseau. By this time there were some 21,000 Jews in the eleven western states and territories, 16,000 of whom lived in San Francisco. Helena had thirty-four Jewish clothing and dry goods merchants, six clerks, one bookkeeper, four tailors, four bankers, three bakers, two saloon keepers, and two fur-and-hide freighters. Jeannette was recorded in an 1884 history of the state as having been one of the first Jewish women in town. Her first son Albert, born in 1872, was one of the first Jewish babies. By 1878 there were 112 Jews in Helena, and by 1891, when they built a reform synagogue topped by onion minarets, they numbered around 300.

My route out West was a lot less circuitous. Like many recent arrivals, the appeal was initially based wholly on leisure pursuits (if only Jeannette had been so lucky) and only later on trade. Almost every summer while I was growing up, my father loaded me into a boxy Dodge van with two canoes on it and we drove out West. My parents were divorced, and summers were my time with him. Often good friends or one of his girlfriends or wives would join us (Dad is what social behaviorists call a serial monogamist). We'd canoe a different river every day, sometimes spending a week on a long wilderness river like the Green or Yampa. For me it was the perfect antidote to adolescence in New York. By winter I was a stressed-out, be-skirted private-school girl and by summer I was a Grape Nuts and tank-top devotee. I perceived the West with a mixture of awe and disdain. The scenery was unbelievable, but the teenagers in the supermarket clearly had no sense of fashion. And what did they *do* on weekends? In New York, I went to boutiques and clubs and took trendy drugs and listened to bands like the Dead Kennedys. Still, something in the landscape got under my skin, and I could never wait to come back and smell the sage and feel the rivers gurgling under my boat.

Every summer during college I came out West, following river-guide boyfriends and jobs in a kayak distributorship. After college, I got offered a decent job working for a newspaper in a small town. I thought it would be exotic and temporary, like a year in the Peace Corps. Living among the natives, I expected a lonely stint. I brought a crate of books, unfinished knitting projects, my skis. Back then, I thought you had to be either be Eastern or Western, and when I was in one place, I could forget about the other. I would live like the high-altitude hippies and learn how to cook lentils. When it was over, I'd go back to New York and wearing beautiful shoes.

The knitting needles didn't get much use, but the skis did. I sat on my porch most evenings and watched the sunlight change on the mountains. I was fit, happy and I liked my job. When I got offered a promotion, I decided to stick around and one year turned into another.

I'd been living in Colorado for about six years when my half-sister Violet came to visit. She was sixteen and lived with her mother in Los Angeles. I'd only met her a few times because our father had left her mother for a new, younger wife and he didn't have visitation rights. But he thought no child should grow up without some canoeing experience under her belt, and he talked her mother into sending her out. With the narcissism of all older siblings, I was hoping Violet would be like me, and take to the river. But it was too late for her: Santa Monica was not to be overwritten. She showed up for a week of camping with an impressive collection of high-platform shoes. Even her sneakers were high-heeled. She was wonderfully game and cheery, but she fretted over blisters and shrieked at the bugs. On the river, she could barely lift a paddle.

I tried to show some solidarity by letting her paint my toenails electric blue, like hers. "Oh, soooo pretty!" she cooed. But by the third day on the river, she zipped herself into the tent and refused to come out.

It is true that most people are either urban or not. I was entering a new gray zone, not totally comfortable in either place. But it was a discomfort that would come to define me. Albert Loeb made the opposite migration, from Helena to San Francisco. I wonder if this is how it had been for him.

Born less than a decade after the lode was discovered, Albert grew up with Helena. First the miners used rough placer-panning techniques, but deep ore was discovered that required increasingly complex hard-rock machinery and corporate organization. By the 1890s, the city was a center of financial and commercial capital, largely thanks to the Jewish families who ran the banks and stores that supplied the whole territory. Ironically, Helena was far more sophisticated then than it is now. It was known to have more millionaires per capita than any other city. It had regular train service, good schools, an opera house, a dancing academy, a natatorium, and a progressive point of view, according to the memoirs of Belle Fligelman Winestine. She grew up here and campaigned with Jeannette Rankin for the suffragette cause in 1914 and then worked for Rankin in the U.S. Congress. During her childhood, she wrote, Jews were plentiful, prominent, and well organized. Albert, for his part, was the picture of assimilated small-city success. His list of fraternal connections makes him sound like an extra in the Tolkien trilogy: he was a Mason and a member of the Benevolent Protective Order of Elks, of the Woodmen of the World, and of the Knights of Pythias. He was the first president of the Society of Sons and Daughters of Montana Pioneers and was a founding officer of the Olympic Athletic Association ("prizefighting is under ban" read a newspaper account of the club, which furnished a handball court, a set of flying rings, four pairs of chest weights, a rowing machine, an elastic punching bag, a "neck developer," and Indian clubs, among other apparatus).

In 1894, two years out of law school in Ann Arbor, Albert campaigned for Butte copper magnate William Clark, who was battling his political and industrial rival Marcus Daly over the location of the new state's capitol building. Clark wanted it in Helena, Daly in Anaconda. Each side reportedly spent a million Victorian dollars buying votes and influence. In a box my cousin sent me are cracking, yellowed fliers advertising rallies in which Albert is billed as a "stirring" speaker. He rode the state on horseback to make Helena's case. An early advocate of women's rights, he invited women to the rallies some twenty years before they'd get the right to vote. Clark and Helena won. I imagine Clark paid Albert handsomely for his services, and that he helped get Loeb elected to the state legislature in 1897, and then appointed to a post as assistant attorney general, since most state offices were controlled by one man or the other during the long-running Copper King feuds. With the political idealism of his father's generation, he believed in, and fought for, universal suffrage, Native American rights, and low taxation.

So if Albert had it made, why did he leave? As for many second-generation immigrants, his parents' aspirations would only take him so far. Albert wanted more of the American dream: California. Gradually, Helena was becoming less like a big city all the time. By 1893 the silver market had busted. The younger Jews, many by this time well educated, started leaving for bigger cities and better jobs.

Thirty years later, there was barely a trace of them, or of the blacks or Chinese or dozens of other ethnicities who once lived here. By 1920, the synagogue was sold to the state, and later, de-onionized, it became the Catholic Church archives, which it remains today. The Jewish boom in Helena, like all Western booms, was short-lived.

If Albert ended up chasing urbanization, my migration was the reverse. Every five years or so, I seem to move to a town with worse restaurants than the last. In Helena, the big manly dogs bark too much and the only trains are for freight. The opera house is long gone. In some ways, I wish the young Alberts had stayed and left behind better educational and cultural institutions. These are holes I didn't notice so much at first. My relationship with the West is like a marriage. Initially, I was all play and hormones. Now my love for it has mellowed, and occasionally it—the land, the people, the politics—drives me crazy. Sometimes I think I have to leave. This isn't my West, these struggles with cattle and ore prices aren't my struggles, or at least I'm sometimes made to feel like they are not. Most people here don't vote the way I do, they don't eat the way I do, and they don't jaywalk the way I do. Thank God they don't drive the way I do. Until very recently I did not even know the difference between a rifle and a shotgun. I visit the streets of Manhattan, and I'm shocked by how many people look like me. I stare at young women who could be my sisters, and I feel a yearning. But then I remember that I do have a sister, and she hates camping. We're very little alike. She's going to be a nattily dressed Los Angeles lawyer like Ally McBeal.

Violet and I have learned to save our reunions for air-conditioned places in New York and L.A. She is the best excuse I have for going to those cities now. We run around and make up for lost time, both in relation to each other and in my long absence from the city. Mostly we go out to restaurants we can't afford and gossip about our father, who recently announced his fourth engagement. By the end of a week, I begin to miss Montana.

Albert Loeb became an attorney and lobbyist for the budding California hotels industry. He and his family lived in a suite at the Fairmont in San Francisco. My grandmother, a left-coast Eloise, got to ride up and down the elevators of the grand building and make faces at the bellhops. He inspired my grandmother to go to Stanford and become a lawyer, and for awhile they practiced law together. He helped pay for my mother's and uncles' ivy educations, which in turn led to my own. If Albert hadn't left Helena, it's unlikely I'd have moved here. I wouldn't have met my husband, and he'd be out here saving grizzlies by himself.

We live on the edge of the mansion district, where all those 1890 millionaires built their homes just before the Silver Crash. Helena never did recover. Albert's father died in 1901 and the shop closed. Bernhard's brother, Jacob, ended up a bartender. Albert was lucky to get out, to meet my great-grandmother and to drive his shiny model-T along the coast of paradise. But I'm here now, daily lumbering up the slopes of the mountain that rises behind my house. The West's mountains and rivers will always be part of the complicated map of home in my head. I no longer think I have to decide between East and West. Maybe the distance between them has gotten smaller for me. We have a son, which makes me, like Bernhard, related to a native Montanan. The other day I was walking in my neighborhood, ironically called the Upper West Side. And here, in the low winter shadows of the street, I saw a middle-aged blonde woman walking her dogs. They didn't have bows in their hair, but their coats were long and neat.

They were unmistakably Llasa Apsos.

One looked remarkably, achingly, like my old pet Albert. Here were fellow expats trying to maintain some self-dignity under the gloom of Mount Helena. On the one hand, they looked laughably inept for the task; on the other hand, they weren't concerned a bit.

The woman and I chatted, and I told her I don't see many Llasas around here. "No," she agreed, "you don't. But they're from Tibet, aren't they? They're perfect for this climate."

I'm skeptical about how well they'll do in deep slush, but at least they're not trying to herd any cars. Maybe they'll live a good, long life.

My Cat Chuck

Tom Harpole

It's two-hundred paces from our house to our greenhouse, up a gently sloping lane under a canopy of interlaced cottonwoods and bull pines. On the edge of the greenhouse lawn resides a carved redwood grave marker with a gothic peak. The wood memorial leans a bit backward, gravity has pulled it slightly downhill, and it acquires a grizzled beard by summer's end from birds that alight and then void their bowels as they take off downslope. As winter progresses the salt and pepper beard that has formed on Frank's headstone disperses with the cycles of snow and thaw. When the migratory birds return the beard grows again. When I think coarsely about the bird turd beard on Frank's tombstone I want to be reincarnated as a pigeon in Washington, D.C. But, of course, if I were a bird I would no more care about politicians, or the monuments and memorials we erect to them, than Montana songbirds regard their excretions as statements.

The grave marker reads:

Frank
1973–1980
Mordere Equus Caput Demittere

Feigning sophistication for people who remark on Frank's resting place, I explain that the Latin inscription is in the ablative absolute case and reads: "To Bite Horse Is to Lose Head." I think I'm right about that. There are dozens of creatures interred in unmarked graves in the greenhouse lawn. Most of them died when the weather was unremittingly cold and that greenhouse lawn always freezes last and thaws first, so it's the place to bury our winterkilled animals. Over twenty-five years here I have lost track of the number of times that I've arranged cats, dogs, foals, birds, and gerbils in the fetal position at the bottom of a hole in the rock and clay earth and shed a few tears at memories of what all we'd been to each other. Every pet is a broken heart until you end up with the ones that will outlive you. There comes a point where I must tamp the backfill and I always do it barefoot.

My cat Chuck is buried out there alongside Frank, who was responsible for Chuck entering my life in a sort of perverse deal between a veterinarian and I.

Frank was an Australian Shepherd/Blue Heeler cross. He was athletic and compulsive and needed to be worked. I got him from my pal, Kim, a toothless forty-year-old gay sheepherder turned nurse's aide who worked adroitly with Frank's mom and dad, Leonardo and Mona. Frank's parents worked at the Philomath rest home heedfully and insistently minding the Alzheimer's patients. Sheep dogs are born to herd and are crazy to do so. Most breeds, true to their manipulated genes, want only to do their thing, so to speak. Greyhounds; bird dogs; terriers: think of it. Frank's ancestors were herders and heelers and Frank was predisposed, it turns out fatally, as his epitaph records, to nip at heels and to make other animals act against their will.

While I was away in the woods every day, according to Maya, my indignant new-age housekeeper, Frank herded goats away from sheep and then mixed them up and started over again. He'd herd the chickens according to color, then regroup them and sort them by size. He didn't chase cats; he tried to herd them. He was a black and tan wee whirlwind with a heart-shaped blaze on his chest and a yellowish eye and a Caribbean blue eye that enjoyed a life of its own. He was canny and tireless, and Maya was exasperated. I knew he was wearing everybody out all day when I came home to paltry pickings in the poultry house and weary nannies with swollen udders up on my woodshed roof giving Frank the greasy eyeball and bleating goat curses.

I was horse logging, and of course the horses laid their ears back and kept him in their sights whenever he approached. But I started taking him to work with me on days that I wasn't skidding logs with the team. He loved riding in my 1947 International two-ton, for its missing windshield. On fair days he'd position himself on the hood.

The rust and dirt gave him purchase, and I cruised at speeds that let his nose have its way as we tooled up logging roads that I had built.

On those days that I worked falling timber Frank started heeling the toppling trees, biting off flakes of bark as they fell. I was thinning a thick stand of second growth saw logs, and those creekside firs and hillside pines fell slowly as they worked their way down through the neighboring trees in a crescendo of popping limbs and wind. Frank seemed to be aware of the increasing speed as the trees fell, and I wasn't worried about him. Hubris, sure, but I also kind of empathized with him. Some mornings, just to get the adrenaline going, I'd get a tree tipping, my chainsaw spitting chips from its bole, and as it began its ineluctable descent, I'd leave my saw idling in the back cut and jump in front of it with my hands chest high and a shoulder pressed into the abrasive bark, as though I was trying to arrest its fall. Then I'd jump aside and back pedal as the tree slammed to the ground and I'd feel the will to do this deal: kill trees and drag them down mountainsides with indentured horses.

Most loggers are addicted to their own adrenaline. Watching Frank harrying falling trees was like bonus adrenaline for me.

But Frank began to get more aggressive, taking that last-second escape farther than I ever did. Sometimes he'd jump on a tree as it was still twisting and descending through the limbs of the trees along its hammer stroke. As sunlight flooded through the lengthening rent in the canopy Frank would scramble onto the falling tree, barking at it beneath his feet. This timber was averaging two-foot-diameter butts, and Frank, all claws and flexible canniness, rode their big wooden sine waves as the trunks bounced and sometimes launched him unpredictably. One afternoon, after a steadily intensifying day of herding trees Frank stood directly under a big pine, yapping up at it and tearing out chips of scaly bark. A ton of tree trunk was going to crush him in a split second, but the little stud held his ground. It went too far. I kicked him out from under the bull pine just as it began pressing him down.

I caught him with my steel-toed boot towards the top of his left foreleg and we both heard his humerus crack just before the thud of the pine butt. He let out a surprised howl, an acknowledgement of phenomenal pain, and he went down limp. I didn't have to palpate the fracture. It swelled like a new joint below his shoulder. Frank licked his foreleg tentatively and yipped.

I carried him to the truck, oafishly over roots and slash. I couldn't take my eyes off the swelling that grew with every step. He snarled disgustedly at my clumsiest stumbles. I cradled his head in my lap as I drove the hour down into Deer Lodge and the vet's office.

Doc Clancy was a self-indulgent old Irishman who preferred working on livestock, conveying condescendingly, around dog and cat people, that leaning towards the large animal practice was more manly. He looked at Frank's leg, said it was an unusual break, and asked how it happened.

"Kicked," I coughed.

"Huh?" he said, looking up at me.

"I kicked him," I said.

His oily straw cowboy hat raised up like a stretching armadillo as he appraised me. He left the operating room. I thought: "a lecture?... the cops?... the animal authorities?"

I ruffled Frank's ears and picked sticky bark chips out of the short silkies under his chin, and Clancy walked back in through the swinging door with a writhing grain sack that he held well away from his body. "You want a cat?" he asked.

"I'm a vegetarian," I lied, as I will when taken aback.

Clancy slumped a bit and then reflexively held the sack farther away from his pear-shaped torso that strained at the mother-of-plastic snaps on his cowboy shirt. He eyed me with ingenuous desperation.

"Well, sure, doc," I stammered. Recovering a bit, I added, "Mice. You know."

While he set Frank's leg in a cast that we hoped would prove tongue-and tooth-proof I held the grain sack at arm's length. It was lighter than a handful of beans and emitted tiny yowls, but the creature working to break out of the bag felt like it was kicking field goals in there. I straight-armed the sack out to the truck, wishing I had some twine to tie it shut. I folded it over on itself and stuffed the fold into the joint of the seat.

"Safe home," Clancy said, apologetically. He laid Frank out next to me rather abruptly from the passenger-side running board and added, "Keep the sack."

Before I even got out on the road that kitten, a bobtailed Manx, maybe ten weeks old, with ungainly, long back legs and vivid tiger striping in black and white, blew up out of that sack, jumped up on the dashboard, and could have kept running through the missing windshield and right out onto the hood, but he spied Frank. He thickened his silhouette, arched his back, and bouffanted his short hair. He spat towards me, like a head fake, and leaped onto Frank's muzzle. Thankfully, Frank was still sedated. The kitten got ahold of Frank by the ears with his fore feet and milk teeth and he raked his nose a few times with his angular back legs. I grabbed a few fingers full of the loose skin on his back and swung him onto the seat back behind me where he prowled back and forth huffing grouchy murmurs down at the welts of blood on Frank's muzzle.

Every cat I'd ever been around was a self-absorbed nonentity, easily dismissed, but this one had my attention. He ended up standing in my lap with his forefeet on the side window frame watching for anything that moved. Sheep, cows, horses, it didn't matter, he was as absorbed as any predator.

Back home I carried my flaccid dog into the house, sorrowfully inspecting his traumatized face. He flopped his head drunkenly, as though to lick his broken leg, wiping hideous smears of fresh muzzle gore across the white cast. By the time I came back for the cat he was murderously eyeing the chickens from the hood of my truck. I, too, looked at those chickens as nothing more than food and felt an odd kinship with this kitten and carried him into my house.

There was a pane broken out of the living room window that seemed to let out as many flies as it let in, that I hadn't bothered to re-glaze, and I defenestrated him that evening when he peed on the mud-hued rug in the parlor. Seconds later he scratched his way up the cedar siding, popped back through the sharp-edged fracture in the window glass, walked up to my feet, and sprung into my lap. He went from purring to slobbering as I petted him absently. I was reading Kesey's *Sometimes a Great Notion*. "Stamper" came to mind, and so he was named.

The next day, when I got home from work, I changed his name to Chuck, like the cheap steak. I had unloaded the team, slid their salty oxblood harnesses off their slick flanks, and curried the sweat off them and grained them. I was looking forward to frying a chuck steak that I'd left to thaw on the kitchen counter. When I walked into the kitchen the misnomered kitten was sprawled on the drainboard too swelled up in the belly to jump down. He'd spent the day eating my chuck steak, ten ounces of which were clearly visible in his distended gut. I reached for him and he growled protectively over the remaining scrap. Gingerly, I plucked him by the scruff and in three strides had him out across the porch and down two steps, where Frank crouched avidly at my feet, perhaps realizing that this was his chance to maul the little reprobate.

I cast about to rid myself of the eponymous Chuck. In my angst and immediate need to teach him a lesson, I tossed him up at the telephone line in a reaction that surprised me except that I didn't want to just to feed the little slob to Frank. Chuck spied the black and silver wires as he ascended alongside them and when he came back down he snagged the phone line with both fore claws and hung there, ten feet off the ground, bawling at his fate. His softball-sized gut bobbed grotesquely as the wire bounced. His tiger striping blurred as he kicked, trying to swing his hind claws past his bloated belly and into something. I ran back into the kitchen, grabbed a chair, and hustled back out and set the chair in the thatched grass under him. I stood uncertainly on it and tried to pull him down off the wire which, now, he didn't want to release. Then, with the alacrity of a drowning cat, he twisted down and sunk his claws and teeth into my forearm as the chair toppled. Aversion training, I thought, as the sod rushed up at us, can hardly be carried too far with this cat. But I took the fall on my back.

Every time I caught him on the kitchen counters I'd pursue him relentlessly, grab him, whisk him out the door, and toss him up toward the telephone line which, like a port in a storm, he'd reach for desperately and then ruefully realize that he wasn't much better off. I'd scoot inside, grab a kitchen chair to stand on, and retrieve him. I got better at the chair part, and Chuck got better at sinking tooth and claw into my arm. Throughout my seventeen years with Chuck he continuously disfigured me, inflicting festering scratches and bite marks on my hands, arms, chest, shoulders, neck, and lap.

After just a couple of weeks of the high-wire aversion therapy, however, he quit pillaging my kitchen counters and began augmenting his dry food diet with increasingly successful hunting forays in the grass and weeds around the house and barnyard.

One morning I walked into the barn to grain the horses and harness them prior to loading them in the truck for the hour ride to the logging job. I grabbed the rope handle on the grain bin, lifted the lid, and fished for the coffee can I used to measure out grain portions. My hand bumped something that didn't belong in there. Before I could look or react I felt a powerful pressure and sharp pain. I pulled away from the source of the pain. As my hand emerged from the bin, the pain became lively. To this day, I admire the jaw pressure that rats can exert. This rat was shaking my middle finger, undulating his whole body as he attempted tear off an edible-sized portion. His pink tail lashed my bare forearm and wrapped around it, and then he got all his claws buried in my skin. Utterly revulsed, I plunged my arm and the rat back in the grain bin and whipped it like I had immersed it in acid. I lowered the lid. He let go with his cold tail and claws but still held with his incisors. I pulled my arm purposefully out of the bin, through the dark gap under the lid. The rat let go when he figured out that my next move would be to squash his head. He'd chewed right through to the pulp under my fingernail, I noticed, as the random curses I'd been shrieking settled into self-pitying invective.

Regardless of the horses, I entertained thoughts of getting my twelve gauge and just blowing the shit out of the grain bin. Then little Chuck strutted into the barn. Most cats would flee such ructions, but not Chuck; he always wondered what might be in it for him when some sort of trauma was occurring. He was about three months old, a bit bigger than the rat. I baited him up to me with my bloody finger, and sensibly, I reasoned, I lifted the grain bin lid a hand span and tossed him in.

Chuck's hissing and spitting muted as I dropped the lid, then I heard a muffled growl in there, then the scuffle in the shifting oats got louder, bodies thumped against the plywood walls. I harbored unworthy misgivings about Chuck's valor. Then I became increasingly compelled with the variety of squeals and screams a rat in a wooden box issues over the course of a minute or so as it is fighting, losing a fight, and dying. When I lifted the lid Chuck was straddling the limp rat. He looked quickly up at me and growled and went back to making a bloody mess on the rolled oats.

After winning the great coming-of-age-grain-bin fight, Chuck would take on anything anytime anywhere. He went after fleeing rabbits, with his long back legs pushing him as hard and fast as the rabbit. He'd either drag them down with a forepaw or tackle them by the neck, digging in with tooth and claw like one of those educational channel lions. I'd see Chuck and a rabbit bounce up out of the bunch grass out in the pasture, joined in a flailing furball, and they'd skid to a stop together in a compact cloud of dust. Almost daily he'd strut into the barnyard, head and stubby tail high, carrying a rabbit carcass big enough that its feet drug in the manure. He'd lay around feeding on its hindquarters and eyeballing the numbskull dog, who sidled closer, absorbed by the waft of fresh meat. But Frank was never stupid enough to try to do any rabbit grabbing, even as the old killer slept with his prey.

Chuck became such an unrepentant hardass with dogs that I began to think Clancy gave me that cat to insure his own job security.

I had a large porch overlooking the county road, where I often entertained pals from the logging and ranching communities. Someone had added some old school bus seats to my couch and overstuffed chair out there, and my porch was a gathering place for an eclectic group of workers in the extractive industries who convened for card games, conviviality, cold beers from the aluminum cooler, and quiet talk. My guests often had dogs with them. Any dog with the temerity to strut on our porch or make some sort of nuisance of himself while Chuck lounged on the rail, ended up at Clancy's animal hospital for stitches.

Using the move he'd put on Frank on his ride home from the vet's, he'd leap directly at the dog's head, the dog would duck reflexively, whereupon Chuck would dig his teeth and front claws into the dog's head, neck, and ears while the claws at the ends of his long back legs slashed repeatedly into nasal passages that burst into gore and improbable canine screams.

Chuck became adept at riding howling dogheads around the porch. Although he never got as good as, say, a professional bullrider, and stayed on for an honest eight seconds, he began going longer and longer, sometimes pausing in the muzzle shredding to regain his balance, and then raking vigorously again with both hind legs. I believe he began experimenting with driving and steering the dogs. The whole deal would last a few seconds, then Chuck would bound across the dog's back and settle back onto the porch rail to regard what he had wrought: a stunned dog owner cradling a bloodied muzzle in his lap, and the beer-swilling jades who'd seen all this before, who tacitly admired Chuck's swift and sure enforcement of porch decorum.

At the risk of reverse anthropomorphization, I feel that Chuck had intuited a sense of propriety from the lads and me. Loggers seek low-toned small talk after a week of moving huge weights around with a modicum of control. Those of us who had survived that business for a few years regarded longevity as a matter of pure chance. We didn't stretch our luck getting wound up and acting loud and bulletproof during our leisure time. At least the crowd that passed the jug on my porch didn't. Somnolent dogs raising their noses into breezes never provoked Chuck. It was those feckless dipshits who disturbed the serenity of the porch that got the nose job.

I kept a few of Clancy's business cards handy and gave the victims' owners directions to the clinic. I always offered to pay for the doctoring if it ever happened again. No dog ever stepped on the porch unbidden after encountering Chuck. After a few years of the same friends and their dogs coming over, there would always be a dolorous pack of cow dogs and curs watching Chuck from the yard. They looked related, with their matching, livid scars running down their muzzles, like a pack of mutant baboons. To his credit, Chuck allowed the deferential hounds under the porch roof. They had to keep their tails down and appear to placate him.

Chuck, in his dotage, slowed down and got skinny. Hunting, I presumed, became less rewarding as the risks increased. But he'd still disappear for days. I don't remember the last time I saw him alive in the spring of 1990. The daughter of one of my old cronies found him submerged in our creek in what became a poignant vignette at one of our Mothers' Day Maypole parties when three wee wide-eyed kids alerted me to Chuck's demise in Warm Springs Creek. They watched me kneel and stroke Chuck's body under six inches of water. More kids showed up, murmuring to one another. I don't know why, maybe because a bunch of kids were watching, wondering if they should be horrified, but I unbuttoned my shirt and lifted Chuck's dripping cadaver out of the water and tucked him next to my skin. I walked up to the greenhouse lawn with him in my shirt and dug his little grave with a coterie of solemn kids watching and told them a story about Chuck and the grain-bin rat. Then I barefooted the backfill.

There are so many critters buried under the greenhouse lawn that I hesitate to dig there anymore for fear of exhuming a skeleton. But I know exactly where Chuck is buried, next to Frank, near that gothic marker with the Latin inscription in the ablative absolute case.

from
SWEET HEARTS

Melanie Rae Thon

IN UNCERTAIN LIGHT

Let us say it is a late afternoon in October. Five months ago, or five years—what is time to a girl who has lived always in one place, on a lake wide as a sea, in a white house with a green roof, in a room down the hall from her father?

Imagine a golden light slanting through dark pine and yellow tamarack. The father emerges from the woods wearing a red flannel shirt and carrying a hatchet. His blue shadow falls behind him.

Another day: this time it's deep winter. An old man slips on a patch of ice and flails like a clown, struggling to regain his balance. He hunches against wind-driven snow. Would he be ashamed or angry if he glanced toward the house and saw his daughter watching?

This is my father: short white hair, stubble of white beard morning and evening. He stays smooth only a few hours. He rubs his hand over his face. All these years, the same, but the sudden growth still bewilders him. He says, *I don't know why I bother.*

My father. Thin legs, chapped hands. He keeps a dozen pairs of gloves in a drawer in the hallway, scratchy wool or supple deerskin, lined with silk or fur or cotton. He has no preference. Though his skin cracks, he forgets to wear them. The black leather ones lined with the fur of a white rabbit lie wrapped in a silk scarf, both saved for some special occasion. Perhaps he imagines his deaf daughter married at last. Perhaps he hopes to give her away some chill afternoon in January or November. With gloved hands, he will guide her.

Father. He looks like a tall man in the distance. Strong, sturdy. For example: when I am in the kitchen of the house and he stands high on a ladder propped against the motel, repairing the gutter. He can repair anything—the dock, the boat, the roof, the plumbing. He can replace a broken window, cracked tiles, blistered linoleum.

He can pull a double-sized mattress out the narrow door and up the muddy hill, then heave it into the back of the El Camino. Once he carried his limp daughter out of the woods. If he found me that way again, I do not doubt he would still attempt to lift me.

He'll let me help him unload the new mattress. But I have to ask. I have to guess what he has in mind, or I have to catch him.

Hours later, when we stand in the same small space, he seems shrunken. Maybe he is washing his hands at the kitchen sink and I am putting plates and glasses into the cupboard, maybe I am close enough to measure, to see that the daughter he once carried is now half an inch taller than he is, that his faded flannel shirt hangs loose across the chest and shoulders, that his belt is cinched a notch tighter than it was when I looked the last time.

And when was that? A month, a year? Is this shrinking slow or sudden? Does he know? Is he sad or grateful? Often I have thought he would be glad to leave me, his small crime, his silent burden.

If my mother had awakened my father, if one of them had called good Doctor Dees in time, paramedics might have rushed me to the hospital in Kalispell, sent me speeding down this dangerous road in an ambulance; they might have sensed how serious the fever was and called for a helicopter to take me all the way to Missoula. Some thought-troubled doctor making night rounds might have envisioned the mysterious way each infection leaves a child vulnerable to another: encephalitis, pneumonia, meningitis. No drug or human hand could have spared me from the first, but murmuring nurses quiet as nuns might have pumped my veins full of antibiotics, swaddled me in white sheets, and stopped the second disease before it moved through blood from lungs to spinal fluid.

Then my family would have a different story, and I would be able to hear it. Imagine.

My father and I live like ones long married. Ones who have learned not to touch, no matter how closely their bodies pass as she makes the tea and he stirs the oatmeal. Ones who know what the other wants—salt, butter, wrench, mallet—without asking. Ones who read lips and hands and eyebrows. Ones whose tenderness is a ghost between them.

When I think of his touch, when I dream it, it is the rough hand cupping my face that I most wish to feel. His eyes are not closed. He is not afraid of me.

Daddy.

Now he is here. The air in the house shifts, a faint, cold wind traveling from the living room to the kitchen where I stand chopping onions and celery. He leans in the doorway watching my back, my long dark hair in one braid dangling, my large hand on the knife chopping. I am a tall woman, thin and bony. Wide in the hips and at the shoulders. Not delicate like my blond sister Frances. Not supple like my smooth mother Rina. Not lovely, this daughter who hacks vegetables so swiftly.

The father pretends the deaf girl is oblivious, though they both know if he raised one hand or made one word, she would somehow feel it. But what word would it be? This is an ordinary day. Let us say June, or March, or September. A day like today, a day like any other. There is nothing to swear or confess, nothing to forgive because all is forgotten. There is no reason to be particularly kind, no reason now or ever to be cruel.

The good daughter, the false wife, slices carrots and shreds chicken, then scoops them into the pot of bubbling broth with the celery and onions. She will not turn until she feels space open behind her, until she is certain the doorway is empty.

When I imagine my father making the sign for love, he paces the beach, shaping the word *penance*.

ON DROWNING

My mother swims and drowns and swims and drowns. I do nothing to stop her. These things happen forever. Blistering sun, green waves—she's not tired. She strokes toward the island of Wild Horses, as if the horses call her. Rina. My sister and I gather wishing stones, smooth as eggs, dinosaur birds. Careless girls, we forget to watch. Mother. So we'll never know where or when we lose her. Each stone has a band of white, a seam of quartz, but not a place you can break open.

These are my hands, the lines on my palms. The black-haired woman in the carnival tent says broken lines mean bad luck. As if I need her to tell me. She leans close; she speaks slowly. The nuns say Mother is an angel. I dream of her, fins instead of wings: this mother grabs my ankles; this angel drags me to the bottom of the lake, where the temperature is always thirty-four degrees, summer and winter. Her long hair tangles around my throat. She kisses my eyelids. Nobody will find us.

Searchlights swing at dusk. Fools. Our mother who sinks in heaven laughs with her mouth full. Light does not permeate water. Don't they know this? One by one the men return. But not our father.

The moon reflects: its silvery image shimmers and stretches. This long, bright path could bring my father back to shore where I stand waiting. I cannot call. He cannot see me. He rocks in his wooden boat, still believing Rina might rise up and want him.

FIRST WINTER

It is easy to judge a life if you don't have to live it. Easy to think that the father makes the deaf child come and lie down beside him. That he clings to her in his grief, half forgetting. She is not his wife and not a woman but she is his and he is hers, and nobody sees how they live here. They are alone, the first winter. The nuns have sent the deaf girl home because her fits scare them. Benevolent women, they will keep the younger child in their care, will hold her distant and dear until the day Sister Beatrice catches little Frances stuffing her mouth with holy wafers.

The father does not come to his daughter's room. She believes she senses the rhythm of her name in the dark, but he does not call—even if he did, she would not hear him. She chooses. She is the one who floats down the hall in her white nightgown. Who comes to him.

With deliberate intention. She glides like a sleepwalker. Brings him water and flushes his pills and unloads his gun and hides it in the closet. She could sit on the edge of the bed. Like a good girl. She could wash his hot face and hot feet. Yes, he sweats. He tosses. And yes, she does sit; she does wash. But this is not enough for her.

Every language depends on the one who uses it. The word for *love* can be full of scorn or full of sorrow. You make the sign with an open palm or a closed fist, close to your heart or close to your head, soft and sweet, or hard and fast. Now, when I make the sign for my father's love, I strike my own chest.

Did he touch my hair?

Did he kiss my face?

Did he weep?

Did he whisper, *Darling*?

Did I feel his breath close to my ear and understand the sacred word his lips were shaping?

Yes, yes, yes, all this I am not confessing.

He was the one who stopped. Who locked the door. Who stood with his gun behind it. Who said to the deaf girl who could not hear him, *Go now, please; I'm tired.*

You think I am lying.

You think I want to protect him.

No, I want to go back there.

I felt his footsteps as he paced, so close, so separate, the locked door between us. I felt his hands against the wood. I said, *Daddy*. I said, *Please, let me*. Yes, I mean this. Out loud. I said. I said. I said. So he could hear me. Idiot girl, I raved. I didn't care that my voice was shrill and foolish. I felt his forehead against the door. He stood there, gasping. And the word in his brain was *no*, and the word stayed *no* forever.

I knew it was my mother's fault. She spit black water into his mouth. She said, *I'll drown you*. The dead are selfish. Don't tell me Mother is an angel. I know her. Her thick tail breaks the waves as she swims away from us.

A Black Convertible

Elizabeth H. Wood

Okay, so what I want isn't appropriate for my age. But when is it? When you're young, you're supposed to go to school and then get a job. I almost did that. But really, a woman was expected to have a family, too, and since I didn't have a good job, I let the easy thing happen and found myself married with a bunch of kids. 'Course, when you have kids, you learn not to want anything too much. I mean, just 'cause you're beat and want a good night's sleep it doesn't matter, not if your youngest is up heaving her guts out in the toilet. And so what if you're tired of cooking? Or want a night out? Try to fit that into ball practice and Scouts and swimming lessons. So, it gets beat into you, year by year, 'til finally you get it. There aren't any choices left. Just the work, and that's usually for somebody else. I guess that's why the idea of the car caught my fancy.

It looked so pretty parked there on the corner of the lot, a hand-painted "For Sale" sign propped in the wide front window. Lovely long and black; a shiny 1960s Buick convertible. And I wanted it. Now, I know you're not supposed to do that if you're a fine responsible adult, and what you really need is a station wagon that gets thirty miles to the gallon. But "thirty miles to the gallon" didn't move me the way that black convertible did. To wind a scarf around my head, slide on a pair of dark sunglasses, and drive, top down out across the long prairie—that's what I wanted. Stormy cumulus clouds and blue sky, and drive straight under a double rainbow and away. Anywhere away.

But instead I drove right by the car and on to the grocery store. The ache in my gut receded, some. It was recognizable now, I had a place for it, with lots of other things.

"Mommy!" her cry, a screech of fear, interrupted me.

"Sadie has a bird! Mommy!" I run outside. The sunlight startles me, confusion of flower colors.

"Mommy!" She's over by the garage. The cat crouched at her feet, growling, something in the cat's mouth. I walk softly, long quick steps, and snatch the cat, forcing her to drop the bird. Flutter of yellow feathers. I throw the cat into the garage, latching the door.

"Now wait, Lindy, let's see if she can fly." More flutter of feathers into the tall catnip. A large dark eye watching me as I come close. I scoop up the yellow bird, holding her in my two hands, shielding her eyes. The tree house is where we put them, to give them a chance to recuperate, while Sadie stays locked up.

Using my elbows, I climb up the ladder and on the wide floor of the tree house I release the tiny bird, quickly ducking down, and hoping she won't flutter away and off the far edge. Down the ladder and looking up, I wait, with Lindy. No yellow bird comes tumbling through the branches.

"Come on, honey, let's take Sadie inside for awhile."

In we go, some milk for Sadie. "She's just doing what's natural for her. She's a hunter, Lindy. She kills things." Some milk and cookies for Lindy. And for me? I go back to the porch window, stand in the sunlight, hoping all is well out there in my summer garden. Afternoon storm clouds are pushing in, low from the west. Maybe later the rain will come. But for now, it's all flowers and bees. And birds. I should probably start the barbecue early tonight.

I don't know which kid let Sadie out of the house, but later I find a scattering of yellow feathers in the catnip by the garage. Only the head with a dark eye is left. It doesn't seem to make much difference any more. I just go through the motions, trying to save small things from hurt. Sometimes it works.

Hot dogs and corn on the cob outside in the backyard. The rain never did come. And all through dinner, Lindy looking up, searching for the yellow bird. Afterwards, they want to play in the tree house; Lindy climbs up there with the big kids. I clear the table and turn to check her. Lindy looks down at me. She smiles, real big. I smile back at her, before going inside.

The next day is Sunday, and when I drive into town, I look for the black convertible parked in the gas station lot. But it's gone. Maybe the owner took it home for Sunday. Or maybe somebody else has seen it, and they want it just as much as me. And maybe they're out there, right now, driving long, summer light under blue sky cumulus clouds.

Side of the Road

Aaron Parrett

My father had trouble keeping jobs when I was a kid. It wasn't so much the drinking as that he simply had trouble staying interested in anything that involved the same tasks day in and day out. He worked for a carpenter until he found that the construction company used the same set of blueprints for practically every house. The same held true for jobs like plumbing and wiring—he quit when he realized that the only challenge consisted in working around someone else's errors. He needed work where the scenery changed, where the prospect of the unexpected could keep him from walking off the job to look for the nearest bar.

I was probably twelve years old when he found something he could stick with for more than a few months. It didn't pay a lot, and the title was hardly flattering—"Highway Maintenance Detail"—but it seemed to keep his interest. He still drank, to be sure, but he knew enough to pace himself on weekdays. Most importantly, the job kept him outside, where he could watch the clouds collect over the mountains. We lived in a dry climate, and he was always worried about the snow-pack melting too rapidly. He had a weird reverence for weather. Walking along the road in the early morning collecting trash alongside the highways gave him a chance to keep an eye on the world.

He had lucked into steady employment late one evening in early winter. The three of us—my mother and he and I—were playing cribbage around the wood stove in the kitchen when the telephone rang. I'm sure my father would have let it ring had it not been for the look of concern that clouded my mother's brow. She had a brother who was always in trouble with the law, and a call at that hour usually meant a trip to the county courthouse.

It turned out the call was from a friend of my father's, a fellow named Jim who worked for the Department of Fish and Game. A moose had been hit by a car a few miles out of town on Highway 12. Jim knew that the old man was often out of work, and he thought we might appreciate the meat. So Dad threw a butcher's saw and some knives in our old truck and I rode with him out to meet Jim and a couple of road workers at the kill.

The blood was frosting over on the highway when we got there, but it was still sticky enough to coat my boots like paint. I left red prints, one foot in front of the other, on top of the white shoulder stripe as the two of them gutted the carcass. The moose had been a big cow, and I wondered whether she had had a calf that might be lurking in the woods somewhere, watching us. Jim helped peel the hide back so Dad could saw through the ribcage. A few cars slowed as they passed, their headlights eerily illuminating my father and Jim hunched over with knives in their fists. They talked while they worked.

"You know, Roy, I put you in for a good state job that's coming open here next month. When Johannsen retires, they'll be looking for a road comber."

"Why the hell did you do that?"

"Come on, Roy. A man's got to work."

"I'm young. I have my health. What would I want to work for?"

Jim shook his head. The old man grinned. I knew he would be glad to get the job, but he would be damned before he let anyone know it. His pride worked in mysterious ways. Like a lot of men who had grown up during the lean years of the Depression, he had seen both his parents worn down and defeated, and any suggestion of good fortune made him suspicious. I always got the sense that he felt cheated by fate, because he often spoke of how much better things must have been a hundred years ago. His nostalgia for a remote past he never actually experienced was just one more indication of his loss of equilibrium when it came to living through the present.

On the way home he stopped at a liquor store and bought a bottle of Kessler Bourbon. Back at home, he made me play piano while he sang the chorus to "Bye Bye, Blackbird" and "Little Brown Jug" over and over. I didn't mind, as both he and my mother seemed in good spirits about the way things were looking up. My father had hung three quarters of a moose in the garage and had a line on a pretty good job. They sipped whiskey until they glowed, and sang together while I fumbled at the keyboard. For some reason, everything seemed to come out in waltz time, in spite of the old man poking my shoulder with the bottle and grinning.

"Foxtrot, goddamn it. Play it like a foxtrot!"

Eventually he grew bored of the few songs I could play and he and my mother got out the cribbage board. I wandered off to bed, shutting my bedroom door to stifle the wretched glee of the Mitch Miller and the Gang records my father had stacked on the turntable.

I was awakened a few hours later by the sound of glass breaking and my mother's screams. When I ran into the kitchen, the old man was straddling her chest and cuffing her head with his open palms. He looked up at me when I yelled at him, his eyes soaked red, the lids heavy and slow. I'm not sure he even recognized me. He watched me warily as I circled him. He was too slow to turn, and when I got behind him, I dragged him off my mother by his hair. He made an uncoordinated effort to fight back, but I curled my arm underneath his jaw and squeezed with rage. My mother had eased herself upright, and through her tears begged me to let him go. I backed him over to the couch and dropped him. Adrenaline had charged my valiance, but suddenly I was scared that anger might sober him up enough to whale the hell out of me, and I jumped back. He collapsed on the couch, eyes out of focus, mumbling curses.

"You dirty bastard. You dirty bastard."

I asked my mother if she was all right. She nodded, crying. I stood there in my underwear and looked around. The room was a mess.

The window above the sink in the kitchen was broken out and I could see my breath as I stood there panting. I looked around, surprised that I had slept through most of the fight. They had often yelled and screamed at one another, but this was the first time I had seen things go this far. The table had been overturned and broken dishes were scattered on the floor and the countertop.

"I'm sorry." My mother sobbed. "You have to see this. I'm so. Sorry."

I just looked at her, unsure what to say.

The old man had passed out on the couch, drifting from mumbled curses into deep rattling breaths.

I picked up the empty bottle and looked at the label, orange and black as Halloween. The portrait of Mr. Kessler peered back at me with the stern and searching stare of a cardsharp.

I threw the bottle through the broken window out into the snow.

I often rode beside the old man in the cab of the truck the state provided him to make the rounds. It was a three-quarter ton Chevy truck of dubious vintage (though the manual in the glove box said 1953). It was painted a warm orange color, with "Highway Maintenance" stenciled in black on the doors in a gentle arch above what was left of the state seal. Years of weather had left only the painted outline of a circle and the barely legible motto *"Oro y Plata."* My father seemed to think that the state had given him the truck when he took the job. He drove it around on the weekends, and left it parked out in front of the house rather than at the lot behind the County Physical Plant.

The dashboard of that truck was a display case for the odd trinkets and gewgaws we culled from the borrow pits and gutters along the highway. It was surprising how often we would come across objects among the garbage that were still useful. Tools, for instance. He had a theory that on your average Friday, thirsty workmen paid little attention to putting their things away, and wrenches and hammers left idly on tailgates or running boards would fly off into the ditches as the trucks took the curves carelessly.

The other useless trash we threw in the back of the truck and eventually shoveled out at the county dump. They had a lost-and-found shed next to the scales where we occasionally stored things that we thought someone might come around looking for, though I never heard of anyone actually bothering to track down a missing spare tire or lost umbrella.

I watched from the tailgate as my father reached down into the weeds and lifted out a sun-faded shoe attached to what looked like a folded golf club. Around us the wheat fields whispered above the drone of crickets.

"Look at that. Now how in the hell does a person lose a thing like that?"

The shoe was connected to a narrow leg of black pipe, hinged where the knee went, and ending in a cushioned pad with buckles and straps. My father turned the object over in his hands like a sculptor holding an uncarved billet of marble. He was eternally fascinated with the things that people let slip away from them along the highway.

"Maybe he was dangling his leg out the window and a car or something knocked it off," I suggested.

"Well. A thing like this, you'd think he'd come back and look for it. I mean, Christ. It seems like you'd miss your goddamn leg pretty fast. And why the hell would you put your leg out the window in the first place?"

"I don't know. You know how Mom does sometimes. To cool off, I guess."

"Use your head. A fake leg don't need cooling off."

He continued to shake his head as he turned the device over in his hands. Eventually he shrugged and tossed it into the back of the truck with everything else we had collected that day—a few old tires, a stump of firewood, a length of log chain, and the usual quota of bottles and cans. Afterwards, he invariably pulled into a bar to drink boilermakers and swap lies with the afternoon crowd before heading home.

I learned to live with the contradiction of mixed impulses. Around the house, instinct usually told me it was best to stay well out of his way, but I liked to walk with him along the highway, finding things in the weeds. As often as he gave me the chance, I took it. My bedroom became a museum of my salvaging. Sometimes my pockets jingled with coins I found along the shoulder. Once I even found a pretty good camera. It was slightly banged up, but it worked and took good pictures. How someone could lose a camera while driving mystified me.

"They left it on the dashboard like anything else," my father explained. "Centrifugal force flings it out the window. Simple physics."

My father demonstrated with a paint can half filled with rainwater. He looked absurd, standing alongside the highway, whirling the bucket over his head. I was grateful the traffic was sparse.

"See? The water doesn't fall out because centrifugal force is throwing it against the bottom of the can."

I understood the principle, but it didn't seem to apply here on the long straight stretches of road we policed with our burlap trash sacks. For that matter, how did any of this stuff end up here? Did people actually throw chairs and pie plates out of moving cars? Eight-track tapes? Loose change? The trash—the cans and bottles and candy wrappers—could be explained away, but so much of it made no sense.

Maybe the driver even watched something blow out of the back of the truck and cursed it in the rear view mirror, but was in too much a hurry to stop and circle back. People's lives were eluding them, their histories unraveling behind them in the record of trash they let escape onto the side of the road. Their cast-off furniture and knick-knacks would have collected in the borrow pits in piles as forlorn as leaves frosting over in a winter gutter, except that we were there to sweep up after them.

As his affliction progressed, my father became on occasion a brutal man. He said things to those who loved him that no apology would have assuaged, but more often than not, he offered no apology. He had always been gruff and liable to make cutting remarks. But he had begun to hone the working edges of what he said, and whatever shred of ambivalence his words might have formerly had to soften them were now straightforwardly cruel. Perhaps it was only that I had started to lose the ingenuous faith we tend to have in our parents.

I was old enough to be injured by things he said, and young enough to still believe that he was unable to stop himself. I wanted to help hide him behind the excuse of whatever clinical term existed for his condition, though "alcoholic" failed to capture its essence. Drink was as likely to soften him as it was to fuel his cruelty. The doctors simply told us he had "a nervous condition," and declined to elaborate. But the medications they prescribed my father he either forgot or refused to take, saying that they only made him sleep late. Nothing soured his mood like waking up after first light when he preferred to be out prowling along the road by dawn.

My mother suffered him along with everything else. She took his abuse with the unconscious magnanimity of a child. If she cried, she cried alone, and I seldom heard her. She never complained of his behavior in my presence, though on more than one occasion, dinner was salted with tears. And she had long ago learned not to meet his pointed attacks head on.

"Mary, this goddamned hash isn't fit for a hog. Jesus Christ. I guess anything you don't knock over or spill on the floor, you just piss in."

She offered no rejoinder but the occasional weary sigh, aware that no words were the right words. Sometimes she would flash me a pained smile, and in an unspoken conspiracy of hurt feelings, we would agree to ignore him together. When he saw that he couldn't antagonize us enough to precipitate a fight, he would either storm out of the house to look for a bar, or wander out to the garage where he kept a bottle under the workbench. Either way he tended to mutter curses at the table while my mother cleaned the dishes.

As I grew a little older, I wondered about their courting days. Had there ever been a time when the old man's insults had been buffered by irresistible charm? Perhaps he had even been kind then. As for my mother—it was natural for me to want to imagine a time when she was younger, when her face was not clouded with lines from worry, when her eyes had been bright and certain. I imagined her at my age, when girls wore saddle shoes and wool skirts, laughing at a drugstore counter with her friends, sipping ice cream sodas.

It is impossible for a child to divine his parents' motives for choosing each other. It is even more unlikely that he can ever understand the desperate attraction that holds them together, however warily, like lonely planets in one another's orbit. Of course, all other complications being equal, I understood that my arrival in their world had changed things. I grew up believing that my presence in their lives was an index of limited options—as much a point of tension as a product of ancient attraction. Life is merely a series of other people's compromises, which we are expected to endure; some of us because of some limitless capacity for forgiveness, others by way of a nearly divine power to forget. For others of us, the trick is simply akin to how the fox caught in the woodsman's trap will gnaw off his foreleg to get away.

I left home when I turned sixteen and could legally drop out of school and join the Marines. I was a shy kid with bad acne in whose future the guidance counselors seemed manifestly disinterested. I wasn't a delinquent, but I wasn't college material, either. The few friends I had would inevitably end up working their family businesses, but I knew my only hope was to leave town. I was sent to Parris Island for boot camp, but I wasn't particularly worried about Vietnam. Most of the soldiers still there were on their way home. By 1975, the war had all but petered out, and volunteers like me were offered tours of duty in Japan or Korea. Eventually I was stationed in California.

I came home whenever I earned a furlough, not because I missed the place, but because I really had nowhere else to go, and I felt like I needed to check in on my mother. The old man had been hitting the bottle more steadily since I had left the house, and my mother had lost interest in keeping up with him. It seemed like whenever I called, she was in the middle of sweeping up a broken vase or some other mess he had made, and he was usually too hungover to talk on the telephone. The two of them seemed chronically tired and unable to shake the habit of their lives.

I saw them for the last time one year at Christmas. It had been two years since I had spent the holidays with them, and my mother had called me at the barracks over Thanksgiving to let me know that they were looking forward to having me home. The season didn't mean much to me, but I could hear the pleading in her voice from fifteen hundred miles away, and I worried that I might be the only happiness in her life. It caused me a certain amount of guilt to think that she was proud of me, though I was a high school dropout looking at a drab career in the service. And so I threw my duffel in the back of a '64 Comet with a peeling paint job—a car I'd acquired with my first paycheck as a private first class—and I drove home.

The house still smelled slightly of old newspapers and woodsmoke in an oddly comforting way. Each piece of furniture remained rooted in the same spot it had occupied when I was a kid, though I could see where my mother had crocheted slipcovers for the cushions and had draped antimacassars over what were certainly the otherwise threadbare arms of the couch and my father's chair. The place always looked worn, but clean.

I got up early with the old man and accompanied him on his highway run, something it seemed I hadn't done since I was a kid. I had forgotten how much I had liked walking along the road in the pinkish light of sunrise. The brisk air was invigorating, though my father seemed to move more slowly than I remembered. His breathing was labored, and it bothered me that he openly sipped from a flask of whiskey nearly every time he got in or out of the truck.

"Don't you ever worry about driving drunk?" I asked him.

"I'm not drunk," he said, a little defensive at my bringing it up. "I'm drinking a little, sure. That's all right. You'll know when I'm drunk."

He drove his rounds carefully and shoveled the truck out at the dump every day before noon. We stopped at Eddie's Club to have lunch.

He ordered a tall beer with a couple of eggs broken into it and a BLT. It was a routine I recognized, though it didn't feel particularly comforting to observe. All his gestures seemed rehearsed, but unfocused.

"The army treating you okay?"

"The Marine Corps. Yeah. They treat me fine."

"Well. That's good."

After we ate, we sat at the table. The old man drank several boilermakers while I sipped a coke that was slightly flat. He did his best to keep my interest in the stories he was telling that were the same stories I seemed to hear every time we were together. I supposed the bartender and the fellows at the bar were sick of hearing them. It was his way of avoiding conversation, I figured. I was content to let him ramble on. By the time I pulled the old orange truck into the driveway back at the house, he was pretty well lit.

My mother had the house all decked out with pine boughs and tinsel. I didn't remember such festive decorations being a part of Christmas when I was a kid. Some years I don't think we even had a tree. I now sensed apology in all my parents' gestures—as if they were trying to make up for time lost. Whatever fragile peace they had arranged when I was a kid had been defeated by my leaving, and the holidays were now just exercises in futile nostalgia. I felt sad for them, but I did my best to appear appreciative.

Not that the holiday stopped my father from immediately pouring himself a drink and flopping down in the recliner the moment we entered the house. My mother turned the television on for him and pulled me into the kitchen.

"He's drunk again, isn't he."

"You seem surprised."

"You'd think he would slow down for Christmas. I even made us a nice dinner."

I saw the tears welling in her eyes, and I hugged her. It occurred to me that the only reason she had put up with him over the years was out of consideration for me.

"Jesus Christ, Ma. It's not like I'm a little kid any longer. You don't have to stay with him, why do you do it?"

I was chilled by the answer she gave me as she wiped the tears from her face with the back of her hand.

"Because he needs me," she said softly.

At nineteen, her words gave me an intimation of what happens when love, for better or worse, outlasts romance and age itself turns us fragile as onionskin. I may never again stand so clearly in the presence of beatitude, but at that moment I understood our need to invent Heaven. Since that moment, I have had to live in the faith that somewhere a world exists that is equal to my mother's grace.

A few days later it came time for me to leave, and I waited around for the old man to come home from work so I could say goodbye. My mother and I waited in the living room, watching the sun sink behind the treetops, sipping lemon tea, wondering why it was almost January and there was so little snow. We didn't say much to one another, but that was okay. I felt the relief of already having reached an understanding with her. She seemed content to simply sit quietly and I no longer felt the need to make her see reason.

When we saw the old orange truck sidling slowly down the street, my mother stood up and hugged me. I sensed that she was about to cry.

"You take care of yourself," she said.

"You take care of yourself, Ma."

She slipped into the house as the old man climbed wearily down out of the truck.

I walked down to the driveway and put my duffel in the backseat of my car. I walked around and met my father leaning on the hood of his truck.

"I guess you got to ship out, eh?"

"I guess I do, Dad."

"Well." He coughed. "I got you a little something for the road."

He reached back into the cab and brought out a bottle in a brown paper sack.

"Have one with your old man before you leave." The seal was already cracked on what I could see was a cheap bottle of whiskey.

"Sure, Dad."

As he hoisted the bottle and threw back his head in one smooth, practiced motion, he struck me as one of the old cartoon boozehounds. All he lacked was the battered hat and the bubbles drawn in around his head. Still, I raised the bottle to my lips and took the first and last drink I would ever share with my father.

We stood in the chilly air for a few moments looking at each other. Then I climbed into my car. I tucked the bottle into the glove box of my car.

My father gave me a weak salute. "Watch out for all the maniacs on the road," he said as I pulled out of the driveway and onto the street.

I left town on Highway 12, headed west. At the outskirts of town I recognized old buildings I had explored while my father collected trash along the road. I remembered walking with him in the soft light of early morning and seeing his breath lingering briefly over his head each time he bent down to pick something up. I remembered all the odd things I had found myself, walking behind him, poking in the weeds at the side of the road.

A few miles out of town, I pulled over on the shoulder and just sat in the car with the hazards on, remembering. I reached over and retrieved the bottle from the glove box and held it in my hand for a long time without opening it, though I took it out of the paper sack.

Eventually, I leaned over and rolled down the window. Gently, so that it wouldn't break, I tossed the bottle out into the weeds, and then I drove on.

Four Lean Hounds, ca. 1976

Maile Meloy

THE FIRST TIME HANK SLEPT WITH KAY—the only time—was the night her husband drowned. Her husband was his best friend, had been for years. Duncan was a great diver, a crack shot, a good storyteller. He seemed to like being in the world more than most people did. He'd married Kay on the grassy bank of a lake up in the Swan River Valley, and everyone danced barefoot and camped out for the weekend. The way Kay looked at Duncan, it was like he was the whole world. Everyone who saw them knew that.

Hank and Duncan had started an underwater-welding business together, and they worked freelance on hydroelectric dams. In the last week of July, they went down to look for earthquake damage on the Hansen Dam, but it seemed fine. They kept looking, eighty feet down where it was so cold Hank's bones ached, and found nothing. Duncan waved him back to the surface, and Hank peeled off his wet suit on the gravel bank, getting the sun on his goose-bumped skin. He stashed all his gear in the VW bus and started making notes for the report, but Duncan didn't come up after him. Finally Hank tugged the cold wet suit on and went back down. He found Duncan at the bottom, weighted down by his belt, staring empty-eyed inside his mask. Hank shouted at him, stupidly, bubbles escaping around his regulator and clouding everything, and he looped an arm around Duncan's chest to drag him to the surface. On the bank he pumped his friend's sternum so hard he felt a rib crack, and forced his own air into the sodden lungs. He kept trying long after he knew Duncan was dead.

They were miles from any town, and Hank didn't know what to do. It was too late for an ambulance. He didn't know if you were supposed to move a body, or where he would take it. He finally left Duncan there, and called the cops from a bait-and-beer store on the highway.

His hands were shaking and blue, and the woman at the counter eyed him. He didn't know what to say to his wife, and he couldn't call Kay. The woman at the counter kept watching him, so he left, driving north to Duncan and Kay's cabin as the idea that Duncan was dead sunk in. He was dead and Hank had left him alone on the lakeshore, after leaving him alone down below, but now getting to Kay seemed as important as getting back to Duncan.

He found her alone at the cabin, hanging laundry on the line. Their four-year-old, Annie, wasn't there, and Hank was glad. Watching Kay hang the clothes, with the blue mountains in the distance, he felt weirdly calm, as if everything had settled down into a space Duncan didn't occupy anymore, a space that would never be any different than it was now.

Kay didn't cry right away; he had never seen her cry. Duncan used to say Kay's father was the strongest small man he'd ever known, and had never said more than eight words together. Kay was her father's daughter: she hung the last pair of Duncan's jeans, then went inside to call her brother, to ask him to keep Annie for the night.

They drove in silence back to the reservoir, and as they approached they could see Duncan's body next to a police cruiser. One officer snapped pictures while the other sat sideways in the open car door, talking on the radio. Hank wished he had waited to call them, so Kay could have been with Duncan alone. She knelt by the body and pushed her husband's hair from his forehead. Hank answered the cops' questions, feeling awkward and angry. Yes, he had surfaced first, alone. When he found Duncan there had been no pulse, and CPR had failed. He felt the cops' contempt for him, for letting his partner die. Finally they took Duncan away.

The sun was down when they got back to Kay's empty cabin. Hank laid his coat on the table Duncan had made from a cable spool turned on its side, and she pulled the string that turned on the light. Kay was pale and dark-haired, with a thin face and strong hands like a man's. Her eyes were red-rimmed, though she still hadn't cried. Hank had never heard the cabin so quiet. The threading hole in the middle of the table was filled with Annie's stuffed animals and toys. Hank stood there looking at the toys, and Kay stood looking at him, and then he comforted her in the only way that made sense at the time. She put her arms around his neck, and he lifted her to the tall pine log-frame bed Duncan had built, and he undressed her and held her, still feeling the calm in Duncan's absence that seemed to ring in his ears, until she cried out and clung to him, her body wrapped around his own, and then she began to cry for real. It wasn't the thing he would have chosen to happen, but he felt strangely relieved. They'd broken the dead space Duncan had left behind and it seemed that now things would start changing.

The funeral was in a cemetery so forgotten that it was just a field, grown over with sweetgrass and bitterroot. They'd fought the mortuary to be allowed to take Duncan there themselves, in a pine box loaded in his own pickup truck. Hank helped dig the grave, and the sky threatened rain. His wife, Demeter, was stoned. She was at her worst when she was stoned, and she'd been at her worst a lot in the days since Duncan had died.

After they got the hole dug, Hank opened the door of the VW bus and looked in at Demeter, who'd been crying. "Put your shoes on," he said.

"I can't." Her hiking boots were on the floor, her socked feet tucked up on the seat. She had a hole in the toe of one gray sock.

Hank shut the door and left her there. She'd been singing to herself on the drive up, a song that started "All in green went my love riding." Demeter had a voice on her, but this wasn't one of her songs. Her songs were Texas trail songs, Lone Star laments. The drive to the cemetery had taken a good forty-five minutes, and the whole way she sang, "Four lean hounds crouched low and smiling, the merry deer ran before." She was singing in her low voice; Demeter's low voice meant trouble when she talked, and Hank didn't like hearing her sing in it. But there was no telling Demeter to stop. The song went on and on, and when she seemed to finish she would start over, as if it were all one long song.

Hank thought if Demeter could get her head on straight, she'd be all anyone could want. Long ashy hair, freckled shoulders, Texas in her voice. Her rancher father had named her for the harvest goddess, and stressed the first syllable, like Demerol. She was the first girl who kept Hank's mind from wandering, so he'd tried to keep hers from wandering, too. But lately Demeter had a look in her eye like he'd failed.

Hank opened the tailgate of the pickup, and Duncan's yellow dog Blue jumped in, circled around next to the long pine box and whined a little. More people had arrived from town, and Kay's two brothers helped Hank pull the box off the truck and carry it to the hole in the field, near a low iron fence with grass fields beyond. The box rocked with their different gaits. Kay trailed behind, in jeans and a red rain poncho, with dark-headed Annie in tow.

The coroner had said Duncan's heart had stopped, and he had drowned as a result. He said Hank wasn't to blame, but Hank blamed himself. Kay had always wanted Duncan to stop diving and do something else: take a state job, run for office, raise sheep in their pasture. Sometimes she'd been teasing but mostly she hadn't. The night they saw Duncan dead, she told Hank she couldn't believe it had happened, because she'd worried about it so much; you worried so a thing wouldn't happen, and then it did.

Demeter managed to get her shoes on, and made her way across the cemetery. Her cotton dress was slipping off her shoulders, and she wore no jacket in the wind. She picked up Annie at the edge of the grave, hugged her to her hip and pushed the girl's hair from her eyes. "You look like your daddy," she said.

"Jesus, don't say that," Hank said.

Demeter gave him a slow, sideways, don't-fuck-with-me look. She turned back to Duncan's daughter. "Your daddy will always be inside you," she told her. "You're a little piece of him." She brought the girl's pale cheek to her lips. With her hair loose in the wind, she looked like a painting: Madonna with another woman's child, in a white peasant dress and hiking boots, the fields behind her clean yellow waves. She carried Annie to the other side of the gaping hole.

Kay watched them go. "Annie doesn't understand all this," she said. "Maybe Demeter can explain it better than I can."

"I don't think Demeter understands," Hank said. "I think she's on another planet."

"She understands," Kay said. She shoved her hands in her jeans pockets under the poncho. "At least as much as we do."

Trying to understand had made Hank miserable and afraid. They'd hired a lawyer to investigate the accident, but there was no one to sue except Hank. There wasn't any insurance because they could never afford it; Duncan had always said his luck was insurance enough. Kay was left with nothing, and she was holding up better than he was.

More cars and trucks arrived, dusty from the drive up from town, and people—thirty or forty now—gathered in the field. There was no minister, so everyone looked to Kay to start. She stood near the head of the grave.

"Listen, I know you all loved him," she began. She wrapped her arms around her poncho to hold it down in the wind. "He'd be real glad you all came out." Her face started to screw up and she wiped her hand across her nose. "I don't really know what to say," she said. "So—Annie made a tape yesterday. It's her talking to her dad." She pushed a button on a cassette player, and Annie's four-year-old voice carried over the grave, sounding like she was stuck in a box, but loud enough and clear enough.

"Daddy, we love you," the voice said.

Released by Demeter, Annie dodged through legs to get to Kay, and pressed her face into her mother's thighs. On the tape, you could hear Kay saying something muffled in the background.

"I have my fish, but they're not swimming," the taped Annie said.

"Duncan got her these little plastic fish," Kay explained, stroking her daughter's hair. "Do you hear your voice, sweetie?"

The men moved in to help pick up the pine box, and Hank braced himself to lower it down. It bumped against the edges and he felt concerned for Duncan, then incredulous that Duncan could be inside. On the tape, Annie kept talking about fish. The box touched the bottom and they all looked at it in the hole.

"Oh, God," Kay said.

"I'm going to be a good girl, Daddy," Annie said on the tape.

Kay had a shovel, and she dropped the first dirt on the lid of the coffin. It didn't thud as Hank expected it to; it was dry and loose and fell evenly, like sand. Digging it out was no preparation for hearing it go back in. All the green of spring, the living grass, had been dried out by a month of high-desert sun and wind. Even the summer thunderstorms were gone too quick to bring the green back, or the wetness to the soil.

Kay gave the shovel to Hank and he dropped his portion of dirt on the box. He looked around the crowd, not knowing who should go next.

"I'm going to sing Daddy a song," Annie's taped voice said. She started to sing in her little-girl voice, "All in green went my love riding, on a great horse of gold into the silver dawn."

"I think Duncan must have sung it to her," Kay said. "I think it's a poem."

"Four lean hounds crouched low and smiling, the merry deer ran before," Annie sang on the tape.

Hank still held the shovel in his hand, and Demeter took it from him. She was coming down off her high, he could see, and she was purposeful in taking the shovel, and in dropping the earth into the grave. Hank stepped back from the hole, feeling he might fall in.

Annie, on the tape, sang, "Four red robots at a white water."

Four red roebuck, he corrected her in his mind. He'd thought of hunting season when Demeter sang that line in the car, the season that would be coming soon, and all the past seasons with Duncan. The shorter days, the gloves pulled off to fire a rifle in the wind, the look of a buck as it stared you down, unafraid, then crumpled and fell. The rush of a shot fired well, and the sad feeling of the heavy body that had to be dragged bleeding back to the truck. Now he thought about how you can not know the songs a man sings when he's alone with his little girl, or with your girl.

"Softer be they than slipper-sleep," Annie's voice sang, "the lee lie deer."

Lean lithe deer, Hank thought. He looked around at Duncan's friends, and wondered what they knew.

Kay knelt next to Annie, who held a fistful of dirt and didn't want to let it go. "It's for Daddy," Kay told her. "It's to help Daddy make the flowers grow."

Annie opened her fist and let the dirt spill down the rough wall of the grave. The boxed-up voice stopped, and there was a fuzzy silence. Demeter had sat down on the ground, away from the hole, cross-legged with her elbows on her thighs.

"Maybe you should say something," Kay said to Hank.

She looked at him, waiting. He tried to think what he would have said before. How Duncan was impatient and saw through people and how he was lucky and felt it. How you trusted him because he saw through everyone's bullshit, so well you couldn't believe he had bullshit of his own. But if Hank said any of that now, he was a fool.

"He was my best friend," he started. He looked at Demeter. She didn't look stoned at all anymore, just sad. "He was my best friend, and he was a good man." It sounded sentimental and stupid to him, but he went on.

"He left behind this family," he said, "and I love them and wish he hadn't died." He kept talking even though his head felt like it was somewhere else, maybe on Demeter's planet. "I feel responsible, you know. I guess you all know I was there when he—when it happened. I didn't make him come back up with me, and I didn't wait for him. I was so close, and I didn't know."

Annie's voice came faintly from the tape, singing another song, one Hank didn't know, though he guessed Demeter did. He couldn't say anything more.

Kay stopped the tape player and put a hand on his arm. "Let's all sing something," she said. "Demeter'll start."

The cemetery was quiet except for the wind in the grass, and Demeter stood up where she was, apart from the grave, and started to sing "Home on the Range." It sounded crazy at first, but something in her voice made it sound just right for a funeral. It wasn't the low, ominous voice from the car, but it was clear and slow, and other people joined in. Demeter closed her eyes and sang in that voice that was bigger than she was, and Hank could hear Kay beside him singing, "Where the deer and the antelope play." Even Annie sang, and it seemed good to have a song Annie could sing. Hank didn't feel close to Demeter, exactly—he hadn't felt that in a long time—but he felt something else he hadn't felt in a long time: that Demeter was doing exactly the right thing. A hawk flew overhead, watching them, and all the voices came together, all the people in jeans and boots and windbreakers and dresses, people who loved Duncan and didn't want him in the ground. There was a secretary who always called Duncan "honey," an old uncle and the uncle's daughter, and an ex-girlfriend who looked embarrassed and sad. They were singing, all together, "And the skies are not cloudy all day."

When the song was over there was a silence and everyone looked at one another, then moved toward their cars and trucks, like they knew there wasn't anything more to say.

Hank helped fill in the grave, and thought about Duncan's body in the sun-bleached wet suit on the bank. His arms ached from shoveling, then stopped aching, and when the grave was filled, there were blisters starting on his hands.

Demeter was waiting in the gravel parking lot. He wasn't sure what he was going to say to her. "Duncan," he finally said.

"He's gone now," Demeter said.

It seemed important to know how long it had been, but it also seemed important not to hear the number of weeks or months or years, not always to have that number in his head. He cleared his throat, but said nothing.

"I just want to get stoned," Demeter said.

"That's my girl," he said, then wished he hadn't. Talking with Demeter had been hard for a while, and now it was going to be harder. Whatever he had felt toward her during the singing was gone.

"I want to get stoned and I want to go home and then I don't know what I want," she said. "I want to go back to Texas."

"There's nothing for you in Texas," he said, but he wasn't sure if that was true. He looked up at the sky, all the rain clouds blown out of it. The hawk was gone.

He said, "He was my best friend," and he didn't know what he was talking about, Duncan's sleeping with his wife or his sleeping with Duncan's, or Duncan's drowning on his watch. He thought again of Duncan's pale face, the sickening feeling of his friend's cold, still mouth under his.

"That didn't make him yours," she said.

Hank shook his head. "Oh, Demeter," he said.

The road wound down into the valley, and there was a thunderstorm coming from the east that might not make it to town: it might hit the mountains and move on, with the wind blowing like it was.

People were going to Kay's cabin, but Hank couldn't stand to sit around that cable-spool table where the four of them had sat so many nights, eating food they'd shot or caught, smoking the communal stash and singing Texas songs to Demeter's guitar. He used to go outside with Demeter after those nights, and if it was winter she'd be wrapped in a shearling jacket with the collar up so her hair bunched out of it like cornsilk. He'd have kissed Kay good night, on her smooth bony cheek, and Demeter would have kissed Duncan—years of that—and the sky would be so bright with stars, out where there weren't any lights at all, that it made him dizzy with the bigness of it. Demeter's breath would hang cloudy in the air, and she'd hug her guitar case and laugh, and Hank had felt so lucky on those nights, especially early on—he didn't think any man had ever felt luckier. Duncan said he was born lucky, but Hank had come into luck.

Demeter leaned her head against her window and her eyes flickered at the fence posts and telephone poles going by. There was a load of firewood stacked up on a tarp in the back. It had seemed like a good thing to bring to Kay, and splitting it had taken his mind off the accident. He could forget the lawyers and funeral arrangements and think of the next swing of the ax. The wood was hard and dry and split cleanly; he only had to pry a few logs apart with the blade. If they didn't go to Kay's, he was stuck with the wood. If he went alone, later, nothing would happen between them. He was only a friend to Kay, and their sad awkwardness in the cabin would prove it.

"Let's take her the wood and unload it," Demeter said suddenly, as if she knew what he was thinking. "Then we'll have been there. We don't have to go in the house."

Sometimes the Texas came out in Demeter, not the singing Texas, but the Texas that got things done. At the cabin, three cars were parked in the dirt driveway, and Kay's old aunt carried a covered dish into the house. Hank backed up to the woodpile under the eaves, and Kay came out, drying her hands on a kitchen towel.

"I didn't think you two were coming," she said.

"We brought you some firewood."

"Oh, that's too much," she said. Hank could see her realizing that Duncan wouldn't be around to cut the wood anymore, and he opened the tailgate so he wouldn't have to see that fact take hold on her face.

When he turned back to give Demeter his work gloves, the two women were in each other's arms, holding on tight and dry-eyed, each looking fiercely over the other's shoulder. Hank felt like he shouldn't be there, like he wasn't there: they had no awareness of him. He dropped the gloves, loaded up his arms with wood and tried not to look at the women. Duncan had wronged him, but all he could hate his friend for was that Duncan had been loved. He was on his third armload when they finally let go.

"What would I do without you both?" Kay asked.

Hank thought it might have been better if they'd never met. He said so after Kay went in the house. Demeter looked at him, fine hair down around her shoulders, jacket sleeves hanging loose, hiking boots sticking out below her dress.

"Duncan still would have dived alone," she said. Her nose had started to run, and she held her wrist against it. "Some other woman would've turned his head, and his heart would have done what it did." She shook her head. "Duncan just ran out of luck," she said. "He would have done it with or without us."

Then she turned from him, picked up the work gloves and put them on. They unloaded the wood slowly, like they were underwater, in silence except for the sharp drop of split logs. As they stacked the pile higher, he could hear Demeter's low voice singing in his head: *four lean hounds crouched low and smiling, my heart fell dead before.*

The Last Photograph of Lyle Pettibone

David Long

I took this early on a Sunday morning, the 26th of August, that blistering summer of 1917. I was using a Brownie Autographic, bought for eighteen dollars at the Stillwater Mercantile—you can see where I scratched the date and hour along the bottom of the negative. The people who'd been up all night were gone. Others would soon be rising and dressing for church; stories would crackle through the streets. But I was alone then, or nearly so, crouched on the rails at the west edge of Stillwater, shivering. I could smell the fire on my clothes, and the first light, when it finally arrived, came thickened with smoke. I made the picture, folded in the bellows of the camera, and walked back along the tracks toward home. You asked me how I got started . . . it was then.

I was twenty-one that summer, caught between working as my father's factotum at the Dupree Hotel and being conscripted for the war. Boys I knew had already left their jobs and shipped out; others had fashioned hasty marriages—I'd see them walking through Depot Park with their pregnant wives, heads bent to the grass. I wasn't so gung-ho on the war myself. When the *Clarion* ran the first cull of Sperry County names, three hundred to the man, I was mortally relieved to skim to the end of it without seeing mine. But the relief wore thin before long. Flanders was falling, Russia was going to hell, American recruits were funneling into Pershing's army by the thousands. As for matrimony, the only girl in Stillwater I'd cared for had gone East that May to study piano in earnest. Her name was Marcelle, and she wore a French braid that hung down her back like a bullwhip. Mornings, her picture shone at me from the bevel of my shaving mirror. In her last letter, she told of hearing Irma Kincaid play Chopin at the Opera House in Chicago. *I know you'll think I'm just being dramatic, Willy, but Irma Kincaid has changed my life.*

I spent my free time staring at the town through the Brownie's viewfinder, developing what I saw in a room off the cold storage under the Dupree. I had a picture of the mayor with his foot planted ceremoniously on the running board of his new Saxon roadster, school children poling their raft down McCafferty's Slough, drifters sleeping under a wagon behind the Pastime. "What do you want pictures of old bums for?" my sister Ellen scolded me mildly. "There's enough unpleasantness in life without going out and scrounging for it." I told her I was just keeping my eyes open.

One afternoon I sweet-talked Ellen into sitting for me with her clothes off. We went up to an empty room on the top floor and I made dozens of pictures of her lolling on her quilt pretending she was one of the women on Calhoun Street. She was never a beauty, but her skin was white as bar soap, freckled pleasantly across the bosom, and she was capable of a wicked droopy-eyed smile. "How's this, Willy?" she'd ask, draping herself in a new travesty of wantonness. "You're one to reckon with, all right," I said, and we had a high time, the two of us, there under our father's roof. But when I mentioned the developing and printing, Ellen suddenly glazed with worry and told me she wouldn't allow it. "Promise me you won't print them," she said.

"You look awfully good," I told her. "Trust me."

She said, "I'll trust you to never ever print those pictures," and threw her robe around herself. "I'm not fooling."

And so I left her glaring out over the roofs of Stillwater, on the edge of tears. Later, I made the negatives and looked at them by myself against the light bulb, then put them away in a drawer and never did print them up, more's the pity.

Of course, I took my father as well: a florid, girth-heavy widower of Scotch-French-Canadian stock, a man burdened by an ungenerous nature and nagging social aspirations, and burdened, too, by a daughter who drank and a son he called a runt and a dreamer.

But here's the first picture of Lyle Pettibone. He's down in front of the Montana Cafe, around the corner from where the IWW headquarters had been till that June, when the troopers came one night and shut it down. He's just endured another set-to with Wilbur Embree, who was on the town council, and E. C. Doyle, the banker, part of that high-minded crew that came to the hotel at noon every day to pack away one of Ellen's heavy lunches and smoke Cuban cigars with my father. By the time I got across the street, the shoving was done and Pettibone's copies of *Solidarity* were strewn down the boardwalk. Winded, hat aslant, he collected the papers in silence, waiting for the other men to get on with their rightful business. Men like Doyle and Embree thought harassment of unionists *was* their rightful business.

Pettibone was a tall man for those days, sober-looking as the Lutheran pastor, but it wasn't God on Pettibone's mind that summer. You can see his sawtooth of a nose, those chiseled-out cheeks; his voice was the same, sharp as a sickle, rife with a union spiel that either sickened and terrified you or sliced through all the built-up, half-dead parts of you to a place that was still tender and ripe for such radical encouragement— depending, of course, on how you fell in the scheme of things. I'd heard that Helena had whistled through an ordinance to ban Wobbly organizers from public declamation, but Pettibone had spoken on our streets for weeks, and up in Depot Park as well. I'd watched him with his long arms thrown open to the sky, and I'd watched the people watching him, people of all kinds, in all kinds of costume, but mostly men I didn't recognize, shading their eyes, listening hard, and a few at the back I did know, taking notes.

They blamed the fire on him. Of course they did.

They'd been expecting something like it and then it happened and there was no question who was behind it and what it meant. All summer the *Clarion* had wailed and prophesied against the Wobbly Menace. Back in July, when trouble broke out in Arizona, when they loaded Wobbly miners onto cattle cars and rode them out to the Mexican border and dumped them without so much as a tin cup full of water, Will McKinnon wrote that it wouldn't surprise him if citizens all through the West declared an open season on IWWs. He predicted a reign of terror. He wasn't in a position to advocate such a perversion of justice himself, but the deaf could've heard him pardon it. He worked that vein so hard, none of the *Clarion*'s right-thinking readers could've harbored any doubt that IWWs were enemies of the flag, a plague on the country's war effort worse than slackers or pacifists or the few outright cowards dodging conscription. Of course, the Anaconda Company owned McKinnon, owned him outright, as they did damn near every other editor in the state of Montana, then and for a long time after, but such a distinction was lost on me at twenty-one. The town was afraid, you could feel that for certain. Myself, I was restless, and some afraid, too—though not of Pettibone or what he said, not yet.

Well, I made that picture of Pettibone on the boardwalk and it wasn't until I started to thank him that he came to his senses and glowered at me.

"What're you doing?" he wanted to know.

It was so obvious I didn't know what to say. Nobody'd ever cared one way or the other if I took their picture—except that time with Ellen.

"Who's this for?" he asked.

"It's not for anyone," I said. "I mean, it's for me."

He gave the street a sidelong check, but commerce had resumed around us.

"I liked hearing you talk the other day," I added suddenly, unaware until right then that I'd even listened. An illicit pleasure came crushing over me, so palpable Pettibone couldn't fail to witness it. He laid a hand on my shoulder and bent to squint me in the eye.

"You did," he said, solemn and testing, both. "What did you like about it?"

"I don't know," I said. "Sounded fair, what you were saying."

"We should live so long, you and I," Pettibone said.

Then he asked who I was.

I told him, leaving my father and his well-regarded name out of it.

"Willy the photographer," Pettibone said. "You know there's going to be a strike, at the mill, here in Stillwater."

All I'd heard so far was the wary grumbling talk of the lunch crowd at the hotel, and McKinnon's.

"I want you to come out to the mill and take some pictures," he said. "I think it would be very good if you would help us this way. You think you're up to that?"

I told him I was.

I told him he could count on me.

But a week later, when the strike came, I was at the hotel re-shaking the back roof with my father. He could've paid to have it done—there were plenty who wanted a day or two's wage, but he was deviled to do for himself. He hauled his prosperity up the ladder, puffing and swearing at me. You'd think these might've been prime days for an innkeeper, Stillwater swelled out with newcomers as it was. A generation earlier there was woods here. People still called it Stumptown sometimes, but no one worried anymore that Stillwater would prove another flash in the pan. Even so, these were not peaceable days for my father. Too many of the passers-through couldn't afford the Dupree. Some were family men who'd lost homesteads east of the mountains—honyockers they were called, immigrants lured West by the Great Northern to farm 320-acre parcels of dust. Many were single, though, with no change of clothes and, to my father's mind, unhealthy ambitions, or no ambitions at all. Anyone with a whisper of an accent, or a complexion darker than his own, he suspected of being an agitator. He rented rooms to strangers who could pay, but kept his eye on them, using spies like my sister and the hired girls who served them dinner. What he did with such intelligence as he came by, I didn't know.

We worked side by side on the roof all morning, and I itched to be out at the mill where I didn't belong, but I kept my tongue. I watched the traffic on Main and around the corner on First Street, and it passed for an ordinary day of high summer, though it was hard to pin down what was ordinary anymore. Just before lunch, my father pounded his thumb and cursed the Lord and flung the hammer across the alley, end over end, shattering a back window of the Mercantile. He stood on the ladder glaring down into the jagged hole, slackjawed, as if now he'd surprised even himself.

We'd had strikes before, but nothing since 1909, and the tension was sharper now. What Pettibone was talking about was a general strike Big Bill Haywood and the Wobbly brass had called for the whole Northwest: pickers and harvest hands, miners, mill workers, and bindle stiffs who worked out of logging camps. They wanted five dollars for an eight-hour day and respectable living conditions in the camps. They wanted to run their union without being harassed and shot at and picked up for every kind of petty charge from vagrancy to suspicion of sedition. And they wanted the ones already in jail let go.

They were perfect fodder for the Wobblies. Nobody else was going to stand up for them, that was for damn sure. *Timber beasts,* people around here called them. *Illiterate footloose rabble*. The mills and camps went through men like cans of beans. The Wobbly talk about One Big Union struck home. *An injury to one is an injury to all*, Pettibone and men like Pettibone said. *Live to be an old man or woman and hear the whistle blow for the bosses to go to work*. It sounded glorious, this talk, but the rest of it, the politics, the trashing of capitalism itself, that was only a far-fetched dream. They'd slept forty or fifty or sixty to a bunkhouse, doubled-up on straw-covered slabs, their clothes still rank and wet in the mornings, no match for the ferocious cold. To a man they'd had lice and dysentery, and plenty had bronchitis they couldn't shake even when the summers finally came. And there weren't any over thirty with two hands full of fingers.

The Wobblies said you can forget about the sweet by-and-by, strike now, and they did.

For a few days, the *Clarion* ignored the strike, except for McKinnon's mighty editorializing, his call for federal troops. Then on the 20th of August he announced that the strike had proved a grand failure. It hadn't, though—or hadn't yet. For a time, it tied up three-quarters of the mills in the Northwest. But the strikers were isolated; nobody but the Lumbermen's Association and men like McKinnon knew the facts, how far it had gotten.

Now something let loose in McKinnon, and when it let loose in him it let loose all over the county. Other IWWs before Pettibone had stood up and said this wasn't their war, but this was Pettibone's favorite string to harp on. "Stay home," he preached to his people. "Fight your real enemy, fight the bosses." It was too much for McKinnon. *My friends*, he wrote, *treason is treason*. Nothing short of rounding up every last one of them would do, but authority was dragging its heels.

It was a dry summer, as I said. The streams ran low and the sloughs caked over and the grain heads shriveled before harvest. East of the mountains it was worse, because the land was infinitely drier to begin with, but even here in the valley the long afternoons of sun and the promise of a poor crop added to the strain. Early in August, a timber fire started in Idaho, near the Canadian line, and burned eastward for eight days. It was far away, yet you smelled it every morning and saw the haze backed up against the mountains. Someone called it sabotage;

a few probably believed it, though surely lightning had touched it off. The forest there was government-owned, and the Wobs had no kick against that.

Anyway, sabotage was on people's minds. I never heard Pettibone favor it—his thoughts were on the strike by then, that and the problem of keeping Wobblies from being conscripted. But others had. They called it *soldiering on the job*. Grain sacks would come unsewn. Shovel handles would break as soon as they were passed around. Spikes would appear in logs bound for the headsaw. Whole shipments of cut timber would turn up four inches short. And nobody to blame. Hit the boss in the pocketbook and play dumb, that was the idea. But by August, sabotage had come to explain anything going haywire, from polluted wells to derailings of Great Northern. There were some who swore the drought itself was a Wobbly trick.

That Saturday, a week into the strike, the town was stuffed with people. Common sense said it was too hot to sit in the movie house, but people were braving it to watch Myrtle Stedman in a five-reeler called *Prison Without Walls*. There was a benefit for the Red Cross out at the Pavillion. At the hotel, we had a wedding party in progress—the Upshaws, important friends of my father, had married their oldest girl to a fellow from Spokane. The groom's mother was a disciple of Temperance, so the cut glass bowls on the buffet held a strawberry punch, but the men excused themselves now and again to work on flasks or bottles of ale my father had stowed in crushed ice under a tarp on the back porch landing. Earlier he'd called for pictures, and I'd lined the celebrants up and frozen them for posterity. But now it was stifling inside. Even the cut flowers drooped on their stems. The dining room was cleared of tables; Mort Pickerell's string band played and the guests danced. My sister Ellen looped freely about the room in the grasp of the groom's brother, her shoes off and her eyes half-shut. My father and Matthew Upshaw and the groom's father presided over it all, smiling heavily and dabbing at their foreheads with handkerchiefs.

I'd had enough of noise and pleasantry, and I thought I'd expire without some air. I headed toward the kitchen and slipped up the back hall to my quarters on the third floor where I could sit in the window with my feet on the peak of the porch roof. It was nine-thirty by my watch, just growing dark. The sky west of town was still aglow and overhead was a smear of deepening blues. Some of the mill workers had taken their last roll of wages over to Calhoun Street, I imagined, but most were down below, drinking. Men spilled out the doorways of the Pastime, the Grandee, the Silver Dollar; already there was yelling.

From up here, the town didn't look like so much, a few streets of commerce, a grid of frame houses stretching north to the Great Northern yard, south to the elevators, a little cluster of lights on the valley floor you could imagine snuffed out by the Lord's little finger. In a while, the evening wind came across the roofs. I stretched and breathed it in, expecting the smell of hay, not creosote and burning pitch. I jerked my head up and caught sight of the train yard. All up one siding, box cars and flatbeds loaded with lumber were shooting out flames, full blown at the western end, just getting going down by the station. For an instant, it seemed I was the only witness, then a few figures broke into running, the headlamps of a few cars veered into Depot Square, then, all at once, the people on Main Street began to know.

I hustled back inside, into the hallway and down through the back wing, but a door opened in front of me and a man backed out, latching the door gingerly, as if he'd left someone sleeping. He straightened and saw me and stopped short.

It was Pettibone. What was he doing here? My God!

"William," he said. He looked enormously tired. His shoulders sagged, his hands hung from his sleeves like skinned rabbits.

"The train's on fire," I said.

The words didn't reach him at first.

"The train," I said. "The whole . . . all the lumber's burning."

There's no picture of Pettibone in the hallway, gazing down at me in bewilderment, except as I've called it to mind many times. They say action was Pettibone's long suit, action and oratory. Still, with such a picture in hand, you'd see how the real man was given more to brooding and intellection. You'd see incomprehension letting down into understanding and disappointment and weariness.

Then, standing opposite, we heard the fire bell. Pettibone returned a wayward suspender to his shoulder and peered over me at the empty hallway.

"I thought we were going to have pictures of the strike," he said.

"Well, I didn't make it," I started in, but Pettibone wouldn't have any use for cowardice, so I shut up. *I'll make it up to you*, I was thinking. Pettibone shook his head. He turned and went back into the room and threw the bolt.

By the time I got to the fire, things were already out of hand. Not only were the cars burning, but a storage shed had caught, and flames had leapt from there to a snarl of weeds and torn across them like a dam burst to a garage on Railroad Street. From the platform I heard the popping glass, the whoosh of air, and from all sides commands and argument flaring and jumping from man to man. They'd managed to unhitch some of the cars, but by the time they could get an engine jockeyed to the right track it was pointless to try and pull them all apart.

Some councilmen had arrived, and volunteer firemen, and men who worked the yard for the Great Northern, but for all this authority, nobody was in charge. A couple of hundred others pressed around, many come straight from the dance, the women in summer linen with flowers or hair ribbons worked loose, the men holding jackets and staring. Through this crowd soon pushed stalwarts of the Lumbermen's Association, including two of the mill owners, brothers named Kavanaugh, who'd made it in from a lodge on the lake with remarkable haste.

One boxcar was wheat, and two flatbeds were ties soaked in tar and creosote, but the other twenty-four were stacked full of contract lumber. The two Kavanaughs halted on the platform, observably angrier and more stupefied than the rest of us. They searched the line of fires, then turned and searched the line of flickering faces. In a moment they set off down the spur for a closer inspection, but the heat and downswooping coils of black smoke stopped them short, and they stood silhouetted in the cinders finally, gawking with the rest of us.

The firemen had now turned to that tongue of blaze threatening Railroad Street. The pumper and the chemical truck were pulled up at the edge of the heat. The south wall of Kramer's car barn was eaten away and smoke came chuffing through the roof shakes. If the firemen knew that railroad bums sometimes slept off bad weather or liquor in Kramer's loft, it didn't figure in their attentions. They sprayed down the sides of the next building up the way, some of the water turning instantly to steam. For a handful of minutes, the rest of that scraggly block—and who could tell what else—hung on the whim of the wind.

Then the crowd's first amazement burned off. The men in front got tired of standing around—helplessness offended them. Shoving broke out by the depot doors. By the time I'd wormed myself near, one man had been wrestled to the pavement and held down with a knee to his neck, like a calf for branding, while his friend was restrained by a beefy Sperry County deputy. Their pockets were gone through, their red cards found and held up for all to see.

"No law against being in the union," the friend said, but he was a small man and surrounded.

"Don't give me law," the deputy said.

Someone reached in and kicked at the down man's ribs, and the struggling started up again. A third man, who'd been standing by, was shoved forward.

"Here's another one," somebody yelled.

The depot door opened and the county sheriff stood illuminated by the fire, a man tall as Pettibone but solid as a steer. He eyed the box cars, then popped open his watch and had a look at that, closed it with a patient click, then came striding down through the people to where the trouble was, one hand on his holster. Out the door behind him came two preened heads, the Kavanaugh brothers, but they slipped away into the commotion, and that was the last I saw of them that night.

Maybe it was the sheriff who said it, or maybe the word was spat from some other mouth, but I heard it well enough.

Pettibone.

I won't say I fit this all together at the time, for I was a slow blossomer in most things, matters of deceit included. But I worked my way out from the people and the rising clamor at the station and headed via the alleys toward the Dupree.

I ran up through the shadows onto the back porch and my boot sent an empty bottle ringing across the landing, but no one was left to hear. The party had gone astray. Some guests had dashed off to the station, not being able to stand not going any longer, and some had already returned and were loitering in the big room wondering what kind of mood to take up now. The bride and groom had departed. There was no sign of my father. Even the band had left their instruments on top of the piano and were nowhere to be seen.

I ran up the two flights of back stairs and down to the door where I'd had my sudden audience with Pettibone. No one answered my knock. I put my ear to the door, but was breathing too hard to hear. Next thing, without a thought, I had my third-floor key out.

The curtains flapped into the room indifferently, those strips of cheap poplin my father assigned to his dollar-fifty rooms. The bed was stirred up, cigarettes were snuffed out in a water glass on the window sill, that was it. I tried to fix Pettibone there in the room, that dark lankiness and agitation. And who it was with him—what would possess him to trespass under my father's roof, so near the authorized gaiety downstairs? It occurred to me with a cold rush that I didn't know the first blessed thing about men like Pettibone, where they'd find respite in a town like ours, where they could turn when they had to.

When you thought of Stillwater, you thought of the railroad. You saw the depot in your mind's eye, looming at the end of Main, huge, white-painted, monument to the wheeling and dealing that secured us the GN's northern route, when everyone had expected it to dip south to Sperry. My duty, since the age of fourteen, had been to loiter there, outside on a baggage cart by summer, inside on the curved walnut benches by winter, waiting for the train to disgorge guests for the Dupree.

But tonight, by the time I'd returned, the depot was ringed by men with guns.

Some were police and some were National Guard and some were just men from town. They'd started rounding up Wobblies. The jail was too puny for such a job, so they were herded into the depot's generous waiting room. I climbed onto the back railing and stole a look through the stationmaster's window. Fifty or more were in there, packed together under the lights. They looked as if they were waiting for a train, but where they were going they didn't need bags.

I tried to wiggle the window up enough to stick the Brownie through, but someone suckered me behind the knees and I fell from the railing and my head careened against the concrete. The noise and the lights went dead for a moment, then came pounding back with the bang of my heart. I got up on all fours, but crumpled again with an awful pain and dizziness, and was a moment later hauled up by my shirt and marched around into the light on spidery legs, then searched. The man was in uniform, no one I knew or who knew me. He stood me against the depot wall while he composed himself. I could feel the fires on my face. Burning like that, it seemed like they could burn forever. Nothing in focus, I strayed a few feet toward the tracks, but he had me again and prodded me past the windows and thrust me in.

The smoke was worse inside, trapped under shafts of heavy electric light. One guardsman had the door and one stood in each corner and one more perched in the ticket window with a shotgun cocked over his forearm, five in all, against a roomful of herded-up men.

"What you waiting for, bohunk?" the one at the door said.

I stumbled out into the middle of the room. The nearest men looked me up and down and saw they didn't know me and turned back to themselves. I found space and collapsed to the bench and held my head. Slowly, the pounding lightened and my thoughts began to clear. I looked at the faces around me, and finally remembered the camera, felt it dropping from my hand earlier and falling into the trampled shadows.

After a while, the door snapped open and another man was driven inside. A languid wave rolled through the hanging smoke and broke against the far wall, then the air settled again. He was middle-aged, this one, with a dazed, swollen face and the tails of his shirt blood-soaked. He was as lost in here as I was, and I realized then I knew him, or recognized him, from the photo I'd taken behind the Pastime, when he was sleeping under Von Ebersole's wagon. He was no Wobbly, this one.

For a time it was quiet. The heat grew and pressed in on us and the room took on a mean smell. Some of the men wouldn't sit down anymore.

"You," one was saying, staring the nearest guardsman in the face. "How old you supposed to be?"

The guardsman was hardly older than me, a moon-faced boy in a clean uniform that didn't fit. He jockeyed the gun around in his arms and squinted off above our heads at the other guards, but the haze isolated him.

"Look at what they get to point guns at good union men," the man said, louder, narrowing in on the boy and his gun. Another two steps and he could wrap his hand around the muzzle. I couldn't tell how people would act anymore, what they'd give the most weight to at any particular moment. I could see how the first shot might be touched off in panic and self-regard maybe, or would just expel itself like matter in a boil; then the others would have their reason, they'd lace us in a crossfire, and we'd be in no shape to say boo about it afterwards, though the guards would say plenty enough and McKinnon would write it up in a high style and people would believe it gladly and completely.

"Sit down, Blue," someone called out.

This Blue rocked back on his heels and turned to us. He was drunk, or he'd been started in that direction when they'd caught up with him. His mouth was chapped with tobacco, his eyes were flat and watery as he tried to light on the one who'd yelled at him.

"Shut him the hell up," someone farther back shouted. Blue shook his head, stranded between us and the guard. "You pukes," he said. "You ain't worth boot grease."

There was nothing of Pettibone in him, nothing of entitlement or pride, I understood then, and got a sick feeling for us all.

Pettibone could've told us what they were doing: penning us up until morning when they could march us out in the daylight past the stench and ruin of the lumber train and load us onto cattle cars just readied for this purpose, the idea not even fresh, having been stolen from earlier strife at the copper mines in Bisbee, Arizona, then they'd haul us out of the valley and the county and the state under suspicion of sabotage.

Pettibone could've stood up and told them—*us*—it wasn't his fire, and engendered a silence around him, in which every one of us at the station, Wobbly or no, would get clear-headed and remember that we weren't individually or in concert stupid enough to bolt up this line of train cars with gallon bottles of kerosene and punks, with the sun barely down and the town crawling with people and no realizable good to come from it, only trouble, which had materialized in spades. It's true, Pettibone, by himself, or with the rest of us solidified around him, wouldn't have been able to stop the deportation, any more than he, or any of the others, right up to Big Bill Haywood himself, could stop the War Department from shipping IWWs off to Army camps, but with him there the men could've known the extent of what was going on and kept from going at each other, empty-handed and down in their hearts. But, of course, Pettibone couldn't have risked being there himself.

Now the filigreed hands of the station clock said one-forty. The door to the tracks cracked open once more and the sheriff pushed his way in, a gang of deputies in tow.

The room got quiet again, man by man.

The sheriff looked around for something to stand on, then just raised his voice. "Listen like this mattered," he said. "You're going to line up against that wall for me, that one with the bulletin board on it," he said. "Fast and orderly would be a good way."

After a decent interval, the nearest bunch rose as if their bones hurt and moved grudgingly toward the wall. A few more straggled over and I joined them and then most of the rest came, leaving Blue alone, slouched on the last bench, talked out. The boy guard moved in on him, happily, and pointed the gun at his face.

The sheriff drifted over to the two of them. "Where's Pettibone?" he asked Blue.

Blue didn't say anything. He looked from the sheriff's face to the snout of the gun and down to his shoes.

The sheriff nodded. He picked his watch out again, opened it, and turned to compare it with the clock on the wall.

"All right," he said. He motioned the boy to get Blue up and standing like the rest of us. Blue swung his arm out to bat the gun barrel away from his face, but the boy swiveled the butt around and cracked him in the temple and he went down across the bench and lay there, derelict.

The sheriff walked back over to us. "Where's Pettibone?" he said to the first man.

The man said he didn't know.

The sheriff watched him impassively. "If you knew, you'd tell me, wouldn't you," he said.

The man said nothing.

"I know what kind you are," the sheriff said, still eyeing him. "I know what you'd do."

He moved down the line, one deputy following along with a note pad, taking names. When he got to me he stopped and scowled.

It wasn't Pettibone, I thought, the sheriff hulking over me. *It could not have been Pettibone, even carried out by someone else's hand, could not have been.*

"Well, Mr. Dupree," the sheriff said. "Looks to me like it's time for you to get on home."

And like that, like sleight of hand, or worse, I was outside again, where it was cooler and the air was less concentrated and the crowd had been broken into factions and dispersed. The fires were still going but I didn't want to look at them anymore. I started back to the Dupree, despite myself. Where else was I going to go?

It occurred to me that I might walk up to that third-floor room and find the door open and the bed clean-made, and no vestige of Pettibone except in my imagination. I heard my father's tremulous baritone reiterating in my mind's ear how untrustworthy I was, how weak to give myself over to the made-up instead of the certifiably real and necessary. But, I was thinking, if all that milled lumber was burning and the depot was full of men to be locked inside cattle cars, then anything else could, or could've happened. Salmon could come raining down out of the sky. I was halfway down Dakota Street near the Chinese laundry before I remembered the camera.

I knew I'd find it ruined, the lens shattered and the bellows ripped like a rag, but I had a sudden fierce desire to secure it and carry it home. I snuck back through the elms to the dark side of the depot and pawed through the shadows under the railing, and down in the gap between some packing crates and the wall, then out on the grass, though it couldn't have flown that far. I was kneeling there, stupefied, my hands wet with dew, when a flurry of raised voices from up on the platform drove me back behind the boxes. In a moment, three men came past, one in uniform, the others decently dressed, men I'd seen before but didn't know. They couldn't decide whether to run or walk fast. They crossed to a car waiting along the park and two got in. The other leaned down and kept talking, his free hand like a huge bug against the streetlight.

Finally the headlamps came on and the two men drove off and the third stood looking after them, then did an about-face and peered back at the train yard and up at the putrid orange halo above it. Then he was gone, too. I pulled myself up by the lid of the packing box and it came free in my hands; there, swaddled in shavings, was the Brownie.

Try these other pictures: Pettibone and the woman—for it was now, in my mind, surely a woman, hard-faced comrade and lover under the guise of traveling widow, whose room he had visited in the hotel—hurtling in a car away from Sperry County toward shelter and counsel at the Wobbly cabal in Spokane. Or Pettibone alone—just as likely—striding west on the GN tracks toward the skinny part of Idaho, satchels in either hand swinging like ballast, long legs hitting every second tie in perfect cadence. I could see him halting every little while to listen—for what, for dogs? They didn't have dogs, these officers or citizens who were after him, or have need of them apparently. Pettibone, his head cocked east, just the dimmest smudge of sky-reflected firelight glancing off his face, would hear only the yap of a coyote, most of the timber wolves having retreated to British Columbia by our time, and the clamor of the town not carrying much beyond its boundaries, and the worst of that just spoken between men in voices not meant to carry.

Or picture any of the others I dreamed up, hidden in the lee of the depot, the camera folded against my shirt, not twenty feet from where the sweating-out of Pettibone's whereabouts continued, the sheriff's shadow obliterating each man's night-beaten face in turn. What they'd have in common, these pictures, would be Pettibone in flight, for I couldn't shake the image of him in the upstairs hallway, face abruptly unleavened by the news I'd delivered and all the implication he wrung from it almost instantly. *Battles are won by the remnants of armies*, that was a Pettibone refrain, lifted maybe from an Old Testament litany of suffering and endurance. Outnumber, outsmart, outlast them. I could only imagine him using his head start as a weapon.

And as for the Wobblies inside, it wouldn't matter if they knew or didn't know, if they broke ranks or not—whatever any of them said could be taken as more sabotage, more red-inspired trickery. These thoughts in mind, I tried out a new idea: that I might be forgiven for not telling what I knew, the truth about Pettibone and the fire, that my silence might even be strategic, the better part of valor. All of which was consoling, but missed the point entirely, for I'd managed all night not to ask myself the one question that counted: *If it wasn't Pettibone's fire, whose was it?*

McKinnon was right: it was the end of the Wobblies in Sperry County, beginning of the end even in Butte, union town above all others. "The expected has happened," he wrote in Monday's paper, the rest of the state and the Northwest looking on, meaning not the fire itself, which he decried separately, but the work of the twenty or so free-lance men who located Pettibone and took him into their collective custody, at roughly the same late hour of the night the sheriff finally concluded that not one of those miserable Wobblies in the depot actually knew where he was.

Deportation by boxcar must've been the heart of the plan, as conceived, for the cars were too readily at hand, paid for by the sacrifice of a portion of the lumber train—but not the whole of it, certainly, and not those car barns down Railroad Street, and not the railroad bum charred to futility inside one of them. Nor the combustion of anger—most of all that—in no time surpassing their design. McKinnon played it straight. He passed the buck to Congress for not protecting industry, then turned his vitriol on Pettibone for a final time. "Hysterical," McKinnon said of Lyle Pettibone, "mentally unbalanced, preying on uneducated, unsophisticated laborers—"

I left Stillwater.

The rest I know you're familiar enough with: the staff work I did those years for the *Post-Dispatch*, then my great fortune at meeting Roy Stryker who added me to the group he had at the Farm Security Administration—Dorothea Lange and Russ Lee and Walker Evans and those others making pictures of the croppers blown out of the Dustbowl, and so on, all of it, I can see now, fitting together, aiming me toward that day in 1941, outside General Tire in Akron, when some union men swarmed and beat down a strikebreaker, which was the shot they gave me the Pulitzer for.

It's luck who gets the prize, that's an article of faith. But I took it as an honor, regardless, because even then, forty-four years old, older even than Pettibone had been, I would still sometimes hear my father's grinding deprecations of me and was tempted, despite the evidence, to believe in them. And because luck's not enough to explain what I was doing at General Tire that day, that change of shift. The tire workers, ganging in union regalia, with balled fists and nightsticks, smiles burning into frantic bloom on their faces, and the scabs, this one cut from the pack, bent double under a single thickness of overcoat, nothing showing but a bony hand aimed at the sky like half a prayer. They knew what they were doing, all of them. And I knew my business by then as well, for it's a man's duty to find what he's good for, if he finds nothing else worth the cost of learning it. In all his days, in all his dogged sucking up to men of property and office my father never found this out.

 That Sunday morning in Stillwater, after I'd talked myself home along the tracks, holding the folded Brownie inside my shirt, I slipped down into the cellar of the Dupree where it was cool and no one ever came, except my sister, in search of potatoes for the kitchen, or communion with her private store of red wine hidden among the Ball jars of Sperry County cherries. In a few minutes I had the film stripped, developed, and hanging by a clothespin to dry. I sat in the dark and touched the clotted lump at the back of my head. I heard the morning commencing above me, the wince of guests reaching the bottom tread of the front staircase one after another, pausing on the foyer carpet struck lavender by sunlight spewing through the transom, then crossing the bare floor of the dining room where the tables had been restored. I heard the hired girl's feet clipping back and forth to the kitchen, Ellen's dragging by the stove. I heard waste water coursing down the pipes and in a while I heard the church bells start in. Gradually, the dining room grew quiet. I got up and turned on the light and passed the negative before it. There they all were, the bride and her earnest groom, the mothers, Matthew Upshaw and my father and their friends, everyone shoulder to shoulder, dignified before the camera, and there at the end of the roll, Lyle Pettibone, uninvited, hanging from a trestle just west of town.

Dogs and Dogs

Phil Condon

SHADED GRAY LIGHT ON THE DUSTY CONCRETE UNDERSIDE of the Madison Street bridge. The splash and lap of the river, rushing with spring melt and the tide of night rain. Jen's wet fur, damp and musty-smelling from the early mist. Apple.

Matt cracked his eyes open and squinted beyond Jen at the blossoms on an old half-wild apple tree near the riverbank. On the best mornings, it was like waking up on the first day of a family camping trip, even in the rain. On the worst mornings, it was like waking up on the same camping trip to find your family packed up and gone.

Monday morning traffic rumbled over the bridge. Matt pulled his socks on and knelt while he rolled his faded flannel sleeping bag. He found Jen's torn sack of food and tossed two handfuls on the ground, like a farmer scattering chicken feed. While she ate, licking the dusty ground in the rain shadow of the bridge, Matt squatted by the river and rinsed his face and arms and hands, the water cold everywhere but on the tattoos on his forearms, identical profiles of blue eagles. As he stood up again, he felt the nagging pain in his left leg, familiar as a kid brother.

Across the river he saw a Meadowgold Dairy truck moving slowly along Front Street. Matt had worked at Meadowgold during his week of on-call day labor two weeks back—loading trucks at the meatpackers for two days and then cleaning the parking lot at the milk plant for three more. His leg had bothered him bad toward that Friday, and the dairy dock foreman caught him sitting down with his boot off more than once. He sent him back to the Job Service office. They said they might have ranch work in the Bitterroot Valley soon.

Jen trotted west from the bridge and Matt followed. In the opposite direction on the riverside path, two women in sweatsuits and walkmans ran side-by-side in an easy synchronized rhythm. Matt and Jen roamed from McCormick Park to Jacobs Island every day, bumming along the Clark Fork River, sometimes looping through Missoula's small downtown. On an ordinary day, he bought lightbulb sandwiches and rolling tobacco at Super America on Fourth. On a lucky day, a sixpack of beer, dogfood, and a few Lotto tickets at the Food Farm on Fifth.

Behind the locked-up ice skating shed at the kids' lagoon in McCormick, Jen circled a dumpster and Matt retrieved half a burger from a sack near the top of the trash. A man about Matt's age sauntered across the parking lot. Matt followed the man's gaze upward and saw two ducks, beating through the low gray sky, their wingtips only inches apart.

This guy looked good for a bill or two. His coat was old, but suede. He wore soft leather gloves and low rubber boots that were especially made for walking through water. The ducks disappeared behind a row of tall half-rotten cottonwoods. It looked like it could rain again.

"Say man, how you doing?" Matt shifted his pack and came to a stop with his weight on his good leg.

"Fine enough. It's a beautiful April morning. And yourself?"

"Straight ahead and flat out." Matt set his smile to something near a grimace, an expression he hoped might match his slogan. "Say, man, could I trade you for some change? Jen and me need a meal—post-pronto." He laughed, motioning to the dog, the burger wrapper between her paws like treasure.

The man reached in his pocket and pulled out the first bill he touched in his wallet, a single. He looked at the dog and pulled out a second one. Matt pocketed the money. They shook hands and introduced themselves.

"Roman like the empire?" Matt asked.

"My grandfather's name," Roman said.

"Well, Roman, I've been hanging under the bridge too long," Matt said, as if they had already been in the middle of a conversation before the money changed hands. "I had a day job week before last, but since then, nada. And then my gear gets ripped." Matt sometimes shocked himself when he heard the lies he told people who gave him money. Yet he liked the feeling, too. It wasn't that different from what a painter or songwriter must feel when they made up something brand new. "Lucky I had this old pack stashed. I felt it coming, one of those omen deals. I could trade you a blanket."

"No, no. I have a blanket. I have several blankets. You get yourself something to eat."

"It's a drag being broke, you know? I'm thinking of heading out of this town—this Misery-oula looks pretty boarded-up to me." Matt waited for Roman's smile. "So far I've been in forty states. You ever been to Alaska?"

Roman nodded. Matt turned and gazed off to the north as if he could see that far.

"That's where I'm headed. They still have the room for opportunity up there. Get on the right crew, I hear a man can really sock it away quick. This crap's old." He waved his arm at everything, the concrete, river, sky. Himself.

"The dog travels with you?"

"More than half a year now. Company. People think living on the street's scary or fast, but when you carve it down to the bottom, it's just lonesome. You know?" Matt faked a laugh. He had said more than he meant to.

"Sure, I know."

Matt guessed Roman didn't know. He was just killing time the way people did. Matt liked men well enough but he didn't make friends with them. It took too long. With the right woman, you could get close quick—a kiss or three, a night or two. But men always had to find ways of making sure who was winner and loser first, before there was much room for the friendship. Yet Matt had plenty of time to kill, too. He kept talking.

"Like the other week when I shacked up, see. I met this honey in Super America, renting movies and charging a six-pack on a Friday night, and I think to myself, this one knows the whole book on all-by-yourself. But there was no place for the dog, man. No dogs allowed in her apartment house. A guy down the hall shot her with a pellet gun just for barking. Look."

Matt pointed out the scab on Jen's muzzle. "She's OK, but hell, I don't know whether it's worth getting laid if my dog gets shot."

Roman laughed like it was just a story with a good punchline.

"She's healing," Matt said, "but the dog was shot, see for yourself."

"No, I believe you. I can see it." Roman stooped and patted Jen. He rubbed her neck. "She's a retriever, isn't she? Pure?"

Matt stared at Roman's gloved hands. "I don't know for sure. She's a good dog, though."

"Well, retrievers are good dogs. She'd make an excellent hunter."

"She sniffs the dumpsters like a pro," Matt said. He laughed.

The man stood up, his eyes still on Jen. "That dog deserves better than running alleys and dodging cars," he said. "She may have a bloodline." He drew the word out slowly as if Matt might not understand it. "See how she breathes steady through her nose? That's telltale."

Matt studied Jen. For a second she looked like a stranger's dog. "I don't know about any of that."

"And her eyes are smaller than most," Roman said. "That's another sign. You said you wanted to trade me something. What about her?" He pointed at Jen.

Matt stepped back, and Jen did, too. "For two bucks. Not this year. Do you practice up on that sense of humor, or does it just roll out natural for you?"

Roman made as if to laugh again, but his eyes didn't follow through. "It sounds like I've insulted you," he said. "But I didn't mean for two dollars." He reached for his wallet again and held it in his hand. "I'd give you more."

This time Matt didn't want to look. Wallets and purses—everywhere you looked they were opening and closing like little leather mouths that did the real talking in the world.

"Just because I'm busted don't mean my dog's for sale, pal."

"Fine. I was just offering." Roman turned and waved his arm toward the houses above the park. "But you know, friend, there's dogs and then there's dogs. Missoula's thick with them. The paper has free ones every morning. And the shelter gives them away right and left." He pointed west, downriver, the direction the ducks had flown.

"So how much more are we talking about?"

Roman brushed his gloved fingers around Jen's mouth, exposing her gums from one side to the other. He raised her pads and looked at them. Matt didn't like the way he touched her.

"Twenty dollars more?"

"Forget it. We ain't no walking yard sale here." Matt flashed Roman a hot glinty look and swallowed hard, a metallic, baking-soda taste way back in his throat. He sized Roman up, the placement of his feet, the bend of his knees. He gauged his reach and inched back till he was just beyond it.

Roman kept his eyes on Jen. "Okay." He looked back in his wallet. "I'll give you forty-eight dollars, fifty total, a good deal all around. I could use a retriever come fall. And she'd be a good dog with my daughter."

Matt thought of his day wages—about forty dollars take-home. Fifty meant more than a full eight hours on his feet. He considered palming the money and splitting with Jen. But no, this Roman lived around here. He'd fetch the cops. One thing Matt prided himself on was staying clear of jail. He extended his hand, and Roman shook it again without taking off his glove.

"Thanks for both the Georges," Matt said. "But Jen's not for sale. Retriever or no."

Roman dropped his hand. "I guess there's no helping some people out," he said, stepping away, shaking his head. "Even with the best intentions."

They stood a few feet apart now—outside the circle Matt had imagined—there would be no fight. But Matt didn't want to let him have the last word either.

"Yeah, and there's a golden ladder leads right up out of hell, too," he said. He wasn't sure what it meant, but he had known a bartender in Tulsa who always said it at exactly the right moment. It was the kind of idea that could mean a lot of different things, and people didn't often have a comeback for it.

Roman took another step away. He pointed at the dog, circling Matt's feet. "She's probably past teaching anyway."

Matt matched him with another step back. He tensed his leg to cover his limp. A guy like this you needed to keep up with or he'd find a way to take advantage.

"The best ones are," he said. "That's what you guys never know."

Roman waved his hand as if he could push Matt away from a distance.

"C'mon, Jen," Matt said, turning away, smiling as the dog fell in behind him, feeling as good about the forty-eight bucks he had refused as the two he had pocketed. If you didn't take the little victories to heart, you'd never know a big one when it came your way. He waited. Roman didn't say anything else. One more for good measure. Matt yelled over his shoulder.

"See you at the hunt, man."

By noon the sky cleared and the sun stood straight overhead like a yellow hole at the top of a big blue tent. The day was gathering heat for a run at the afternoon. Coming out of Super America, Matt stopped to charity on a man gassing up a motorhome. A teenage boy watched from the passenger seat. The leather cover on the spare tire read *The Getaway*.

Before Matt even made his pitch though, tires squealed on Fourth Street. Matt looked up just as a blue Tempo knocked Jen to the curb. He dropped his pack by the pumps and ran to her. She lay nestled in next to the curb, breathing heavy like she had run a long way without water. There was no blood, but her eyes flickered from side to side without blinking.

"Easy, baby, easy." Matt lifted her two front legs slowly, one at a time. They didn't feel busted. A woman in fine summery clothes stepped out of the blue car. Matt saw a flash of thigh as quick as a promise, but he didn't enjoy it the way he usually would. She hurried over to them.

"God, I'm so sorry. He ran in front of me. Is he all right?"

"She's a she. I don't know. She don't look good."

The woman reached her hand out. Jen growled.

"Leave her be," said Matt. "We'll be OK. She may need some food though. You wouldn't have an extra few, would you?"

The woman hesitated, shivering in light clothes. "My purse is in the car. Her breathing's irregular. I'm worried about your dog."

"So am I."

The woman went toward her car. Matt listened to the sharp click of her high heels on the pavement. The *Getaway* man came out with Matt's pack at arm's length and set it down. He had a silver credit card between his fingers.

"I'll call the Humane Society. We've got a cell phone in the rig."

"No—don't do that."

"The dog needs help. It took a good shot." The man's trimmed salt-and-pepper hair ran flat and straight, close to his head. Even the creases in his slacks looked first-class. Matt felt messed-up. His life was junk in a world where everything else was combed out smooth.

The trim man went back toward the pumps. Matt didn't say anything else. As he watched the woman click back over with three dollar bills clutched in her hand, he saw Roman standing across the street, staring from the doorway of a used book store.

"I'm short of cash," she said. "Should I call somebody?"

"What?" Matt looked up at the woman. He folded the bills with one hand and put them in his shirt pocket. He kept the other hand steady on Jen, stroking her head. "No need. Thanks."

"Listen, I'm late for an appointment. Should I stop back afterward?"

"We'll be gone by then," Matt said. He looked back across the street, but he didn't see Roman again.

They wouldn't let Matt ride in the Humane Society van—insurance regulations, the driver said. The attendant said the dog would survive—the bumper had just tagged her on the shoulder and shaken her up good. They gave Matt the Animal Shelter phone number and address. It was four miles away. Matt sat on the curb, chewing on a strip of beef jerky he had saved out for Jen.

On the way back down to the river, he stopped at the Job Service, a low brick building in an old residential neighborhood on Third Street. The man at the counter had large sweat circles under the arms of his dress shirt. He told Matt they were still waiting on the call for ranch hands in the valley. The man was in a hurry. He said he had to give a typing test in a few minutes.

After sundown Matt built a small close fire in a low hidden spot among poplar trees and willow brush near the waterline. In the flickering light he stared at the eagles on his arms as if they might take off at any moment and listened to the river rush by like it had a place to go nobody could stop it from getting to. Matt tried not to worry about Jen. Instead he went over the only two other important things he could think of, his plan and his past.

The plan he could put in a single word. Alaska. He had been headed that way for two months, following the spring north and west from a tough, achey winter on a tree-planting crew in Alabama. In a month he would turn forty, and he had made up his mind to be in Alaska on that birthday. It had started out as just a lucky sounding notion, but Matt figured the only real difference between a notion and a plan was in the following through.

As for the past, he was still hoping to get that back. He had lost his first thirty-five years, or all memory of them, which amounted to the same thing as far as Matt could tell. In the spring of '94, he had appeared to himself in a St. Louis hospital mirror, a damaged man with eagle tattoos, a limp in his left leg, and a fresh white bandage wrapped around his head like a turban. He had been found in the I-70 median with nothing but his clothes and one letter in his pocket—a Charlie Brown birthday card that said "Happy 35th to Matt—Love, Jenny." Matt took his name from that card and his birthday from the day they said they found him, May 11.

The police traced his fingerprints, but all anybody could tell him was that he didn't have a police record and he had never been in the Service. Matt had hoped he was a veteran when he saw the tattoos. He thought he might have a pension coming or might be some kind of hero who had lost all his medals.

Jen had stumbled onto him while he slept under a roadside picnic bench outside of Guymon in the Oklahoma panhandle the summer before, and he named her for the mystery woman who gave him a name and an age. There had been enough real women since the birthday card though, starting with Liz Shelden, a barmaid he met the week he was discharged from the hospital. Thirty-five years old, and he couldn't know whether he was a virgin or not, although Liz seemed to think not.

Matt believed his limp brought out the mother in women, and too, they always seemed to want to help him find out about the lost years. The woman he spent the longest time with, JJ Duncan, had promised him it would all come to him one night in her bed, right at the supreme moment of pleasure, she said. He stayed with her for over a year in Trinidad, Colorado, believing she might be right. She waited counters at a truckstop, but she said she had some gypsy in her, and Matt believed her about that, too. She told Matt she saw flashes about his life when they made love—she was sure it was pretty close to the surface. When she got near to her own moment, she would press her palms on either side of Matt's head, as if she could coax all those lost years out into her fingers, like an old-time poultice pulling on a wound.

It turned out when Matt came to know her well enough that she had an awful lot she needed to forget. Her old man had screwed her once every year on her birthday from when she was five until she ran away at fifteen. He told her that if she breathed a word to anyone he would stash her in an orphanage and no one would ever come see her. One night when Matt came in from his job on a sheep ranch outside Trinidad, he found JJ kneeling in a slump over the toilet. Red fingerprints smeared the flush handle, and a bloody wire cheeseknife lay on the tile next to her. When Matt pulled JJ's head up, her face was as white as mashed potatoes and her forearms disappeared into the scarlet water of the toilet bowl. Matt laid her down on the bathroom floor and folded her arms against her chest. He had covered her with two big towels and kissed her cold forehead before he packed and left.

Sometimes Matt thought he was actually the lucky one. A lot of the people he had known in the last five years were spending half their time trying to forget something. And it seemed like it was just as hard for them to forget as it was for Matt to remember.

Matt walked along South Third Street toward the Animal Shelter. For three days straight, he had called from a pay phone to check on Jen, and now he was determined to get her back. They said the dog was all right, but they were concerned she had no record of shots or tags and they wanted to know Matt's address. He told them she'd had her shots in Oklahoma, and he gave them an address from a house near the river on Second Street. The lady on the shelter phone said they would need I.D. or other proof of a local address before they could release Jen.

Two boys on a bike too big for either of them rode toward him on the sidewalk. The larger one pedaled standing up, puffing hard to keep the bike straight, while the smaller one balanced on the handlebars. They looked like brothers, and Matt turned and watched them until they disappeared. The soft-headed feeling children gave him, like the urge he felt to protect Jen, made Matt believe he might have been a father once himself. He had daydreamed about coming across kids of his own by accident someday. He liked to imagine that he would know their names without asking, and that the names would trigger an avalanche of memory inside him, his past falling into place for him all at once, like boulders settling in a creekbed.

As the houses thinned out and the yards grew bigger along River Road, Matt came up with a plan for getting Jen back. He would say the starter in his car had checked out and he had left his wallet in the glove box. No one would press it all that hard over a dog. The wheeler-dealer Roman had said the place damn near gave them away. Matt just needed to show up in person and make his claim.

He had missed Jen bad that morning when he woke up without her under the bridge, and what had awakened him hadn't made it any better. It was a dream about the time in Denver when Jen had been lost for almost a week, the week the smog had been so bad Matt thought maybe the world was ending, the kind of dark, fearsome weather they talked about somewhere in the Bible. In the dream he didn't find her again, though. Instead he met JJ, wandering the streets, looking for him. Her face and lips glowed pale white. She ran to Matt when she saw him and said she'd remembered his past, that she had it all in her head as real as any movie. Her hands stretched out to him like she was trying to clap. She had Matt's eagle tattoos on the inside of both her wrists.

He heard barking before he even started up the long gravel drive that led to the Animal Shelter. An acre of lawn stretched beneath Chinese elm trees in front of the building. Matt nodded and smiled at a woman in white slacks walking a miniature collie.

Inside the office, it was too hot, and the woman at the counter wouldn't budge on the proof of address. Plus she acted put out because he hadn't come sooner. She told him they had already put the red dog—she wouldn't call her Jen—up for adoption.

"That was a retriever, I believe?"

"One hundred per cent," Matt said. The top button of the woman's blouse was undone. Matt checked her out when she bent over to look up the file.

"In fact," she said, straightening up and looking at him with an index card in her hand. Her fingers drifted to her open button. "In fact," she repeated, "you're too late. A family took her this morning. I just came on shift at noon." Matt had looked away, but now he stared at the card in her hand. "They paid for her shots and license. A man with his daughter. A very nice home."

"Nice or no, that's pretty quick, isn't it? Four days?"

"Quicker than usual, perhaps. But the dog had no license or records." She looked at the card again. "Apparently this was someone who had seen her brought in."

"Seen her? Who would that be?"

"We're not allowed to give out any names." She tapped the card against her fingernail. "I'm sorry."

"That's cool," he said. "That's fine. I was just surprised anybody but me knew she was here." He hesitated for a moment. "You ever had a dog of your own, Miss?"

"Mrs." she said. "Why?"

"I just wondered. Working around so many dogs. You must really love them."

"Yes, I do. I'm more of a cat person though. We have two at home."

"Two keep each other company."

"That's true." She smiled for the first time. Matt watched her slip the card back into the file. The corner edge stuck up just enough to see.

"Well, thanks anyway, I guess. If she's out to a good home like you said, maybe it's that much better." He started for the door and then turned back. "Oh yeah, did you all keep my collar she was wearing?"

"She didn't have any tags," the woman said. "What collar?"

"It was braided leather. Just a plain braided collar, black and dark brown. But it was almost new. I'd like to have it back if it's still around here."

"I don't know," she said. "I'll check."

She opened a door and disappeared down a long aisle between cages. Before she shut the door, the animal smells wafted into the office as thick as if they'd been bottled. Matt leaned over the counter and pulled out the index card on Jen. He read the name and address on the card: Roman Cleed, 223 Rollins. He shook his head as he slid the card back into the filebox.

"Sneaky son of a bastard," he said under his breath. He moved away from the counter, but the woman still didn't return. Matt paced the length of the room, looking at pictures of pets on the wall, perfect Springer Spaniels on point and petite Siamese cats with mysterious eyes. A large glass donation jar with a slot cut in the lid stood on the counter, and Matt unscrewed the lid and counted eight ones. He thought of all the animals behind the door. Fifty-fifty felt fair. He pocketed four of the bills and replaced the lid. He stepped away again just as the woman came out from the back rooms.

"No one remembers seeing any kind of collar with the red dog," she said.

"No big deal," Matt said. "Thanks anyway." He walked to the door quickly.

"I don't think there was any collar," the woman said to Matt's back.

"Mr. Bloodline probably stole that, too," he said as he shut the door.

By the time Matt found the house on Rollins, he was short of breath and dragging his leg worse than usual. He limped up three steps and knocked loudly on the door and then pressed the bell twice. When Roman answered, Matt spoke first.

"I'm here for my dog."

"She's not your dog anymore," Roman said. He stepped out on the porch. "You nearly got her killed anyway. It was just a matter of time. And how did you get my address?"

"There's a way to every will, buddy. I don't want any trouble. Just give me back my dog and I'm gone." He pointed into the house.

"First, I'm calling the Humane Society," Roman said. "They need to hear about this. And then if you don't get off my porch right now, I'll call the police, too."

Matt swallowed hard and stared straight in Roman's eyes. "Lots of things can happen between the calling and the coming," he said.

Roman's face went rigid. He looked Matt over as if to see if he might have a knife or a gun. Matt wanted to play it right on the edge, just enough fear to get the dog and go but not enough to get the guy really worked up. He backed up and started whistling for Jen.

As Roman turned to latch the storm door, Jen pushed through it and ran out of the house. She barked twice and threaded between Roman's legs and leapt up on Matt. He grabbed her behind the neck and rubbed her roughly, smiling.

"Hey, Jen, yeah, it's me," he said, "it's me." The door opened again and a little girl stepped onto the porch. She wore a cone-shaped, foil-covered party hat with a thin elastic strap pulled around her chin.

"Who's this, Dad? Is he a friend of Goldie?"

Roman put his hands on his daughter's shoulders and held her. Matt said "Down," in a deep voice, and Jen sat at his side. The four of them looked at each other. The girl's grin looked to Matt as if he had rung her doorbell right between the presents and the candles. He felt the hint of a memory, not a real picture of a birthday party, yet something close, like a twinge and a taste mixed together.

"I'm a good friend," Matt said. "I've been taking care of her."

"This is my girl, Beth," Roman said. "You caught us at a bad time. We're having a little party. It's her half-birthday this Friday."

Beth laughed. "It's not a bad time," she said. "It's a good time. I have a dog. A dog of my own." She grabbed Jen by the neck and put her arms around her. Matt stepped back to the edge of the steps and watched her.

"Happy birthday," Matt said. "How old and a half are you?"

"Ten," Beth said. She looked up at Matt. "Do you know how old Goldie is? My dad says two."

"That sounds about right," Matt said. "You call her Goldie?"

"I named her," Beth said. She looked at Jen and then back up to Matt. "Did she have another name?"

"Well I called her—" Matt stopped. If he didn't tell them her name, it would be like not really giving her up to them. They'd only get themselves a red dog, a retriever. "I called her all sorts of names."

"C'mon, Bethie, let's go in," Roman said. "You don't have a coat on."

She grabbed Jen by her new collar and pulled. They both moved toward the door and then inside. Matt and Roman stood motionless, both looking at the dog until she disappeared into the house. Beth turned around at the door.

"Do you want a piece of my half-birthday cake?" she asked.

"No, I'm going," Matt said, "I'm gonna be going. I'm on my way to Alaska. I just stopped over to meet you and see how she's doing." He pointed in the house after Jen and smiled at Beth. He started down the steps, his pack on one shoulder.

"Bye," Beth yelled. She went into the house, and Roman closed the door behind her. Matt heard Jen bark again.

"Thanks," Roman said. "That was decent of you."

Matt looked up from the bottom step.

"There's people and there's people," he said. He turned away.

Roman shouted a question after him. "You leaving town right now?"

Matt waved his hand over his shoulder without stopping, but then turned around when he reached the front sidewalk.

"You see Alaska anywhere close around here?"

"I could give you a lift to the Interstate," Roman said, pointing at his van. Matt looked at the van, then back at the house. "I'll walk."

"Wait," Roman said. "Hold on just a minute now." He turned and went in the house. Jen came to the storm door and stared out.

Matt could see a little way into the house behind Jen. He couldn't shake the excited look on the girl's face, that birthday look. It almost felt like he remembered someone giving him a dog when he was a kid, but he couldn't tell if it was from a dream or maybe just a TV show he had seen and forgotten.

Roman came back. This time he stepped carefully through the door so Jen wouldn't get out. He was carrying a piece of chocolate cake on a paper plate.

"She really wants you to have a piece of cake," he said, holding it toward Matt. Roman handed him a napkin, too, and Matt saw a flash of green folded in it. With one hand he thumbed the bills, five tens. As he did, Roman walked quickly back up on the porch and stood beside the door. Beth and Jen were at the storm door again, too.

Matt watched the three of them watch him, all facing the same direction, the way a family would. Beth waved through the glass. Matt held up the plate with the cake and nodded toward her. He slipped the bills in his pocket and ate the cake in three big bites and wiped his mouth with the napkin. Roman had gone inside now, but the girl and the dog stayed at the door, still watching Matt, so he waved again, exaggerating, swinging the plate back and forth at the end of his arm as if he was directing traffic or signaling someone far off. He saw Beth laughing although he couldn't hear her. The plate slipped out of his hand, and he bent to pick it up. When he looked again, they were gone and the inside door was closed.

There was no one in sight up and down the block. Matt folded the paper plate up small and stuffed it in his jacket pocket. He didn't look back again until he had turned the corner behind a long row of thick lilac bushes in heavy bloom, and then when he did, he couldn't see the house any more. The bushes next to him smelled sweet, and as Matt walked away, he imagined he could hear the girl's laughter, drifting on the breeze.

Warrior

Krys Holmes

I RECEIVED MY FIRST SPIDER BITE and had just finished choking on an apricot pit on the day that Chinggiz Khan rode into the Elkhorn Mountains. The spider bite formed a welt on my back, soon rubbed raw by the elastic waistband on my pants. We were staying at a cabin on Crystal Creek, a place to park the kids while my father visited my mother in the hospital at Helena, where she might die.

From the porch of the painted log cabin you could almost throw a stone all the way into the creek, where we got water. In those days we'd never heard of giardia. We drank from every stream. The stand of pines around the cabin opened up into a broad field where sunshine poured out of the sky and baked the dry grass and where everything smelled like cattle and light.

It was across this field that Chinggiz Khan came riding up on the most muscular little horse you ever saw, his scarlet robe billowing in the wind. He wore heavy black pantaloons and felt boots that turned up at the toes just like old cowboy boots do. Over his shoulders flew a thick cape gathered across the front of his chest by fasteners that clinked and jangled. He dismounted and strode over to me. He carried a long staff that reached up toward the sky and from it dangled a hoop with nine ermine tails. The silver helmet on his head, decorated with cascades of fur, made him look taller than any other man but his eyes were about level with mine.

I was still thinking about the apricot pit. To me apricot pits looked just like almonds so I thought they were the same thing, but when I bit into the pit the bitterness that came out made me gasp, and I sucked the pit into my throat and had spent the last few moments hacking it back out again. It was a moment you hoped nobody else saw.

He grunted a little. Then the silence stood up between us like a third person. His eyes looked folded over, like sea shells filled with black liquid. His face was huge and round with high cheekbones and a big, fierce jaw, but a little fringe of crazy bangs poking out from his helmet kept me from being terrified of him. I had been taught it was impolite to point or to ask someone who they were, even on the telephone, and since that was the only question I could think of, I remained silent.

He turned to his horse, untied a leather bag from its harness, held the bag up in front of the horse, and squirted some thick milk into the horse's open mouth.

What's that, I asked.

Kumiss, he grunted. His voice was deep as a bear's growl.

How'd you get him to do that? I asked, wrinkling my nose at the horse, who stood with its mouth open to catch the fountain of curd.

Thirsty, he said.

I was blessed with the kind of childhood that contained few memorable moments, such was its consistent happiness. As a result I remember almost nothing of the past and choose, instead, to fill my head with terrors of the future. Otherwise I am sure I would go mad with nostalgia.

As a result, most of what I am telling you is false. The characters are real, but the details have been changed to protect myself. Except this: The afternoon my father called me inside from my play in the back yard of our eastern Montana house and, standing me between his knees, said, Your mother's been in an accident. Over in Helena. He looked deep into the backs of my eyes. But everything's going to be all right. Broadside collision, broken back, internal injuries. Everything's going to be all right.

How old are you, he asked

Eleven, I said. How old are you?

Seven hundred and sixty-three, he announced, as though that number put every other fact in the world to shame.

What are you doing here? I asked him.

He planted the butt of his staff in the soft ground, right next to a lupine, which shivered. He said, Due to circumstances beyond my control (he cleared his throat) I have just learned of this new land, a world beyond the edge of the world. I have come to conquer it.

Hm, I said. I was thinking of my father. He was practically the only person in Montana who publicly protested the Vietnam War. He marched on Washington. He even marched on the Billings courthouse lawn, when only two or three other people showed up. He was not going to like this.

My father was at the hospital for the day. Mother was not doing well. In those days they wouldn't admit children into the intensive care ward because children were a nuisance, and had runny noses. I had not seen her for a month.

You and what army? I said, looking at the cows in the field and the wooded hills beyond his ermine-lined shoulder.

He thrust his shoulders back and, speaking with a great voice directed over my head, said, In the Year of the Blue Fox, the shaman Kukch͟, announced to the world that the Everlasting Blue Sky, Möngke Kökö Tengri, had with his own hand raised up the noble Timujin, orphaned and deserted at birth, to the highest position among humans. On that day the Everlasting Blue Sky, Möngke Kökö Tengri, proclaimed the humble Temujin to be his representative on earth, Chinggiz Khan, universal ruler of the *Yeke Mongol ulus*.

Where are your Yeke Mongol ulus? I asked politely.

He looked at the ground. Over the years they have scattered, he said. I must call them together in a great *kuriltai*. A general assembly of chieftains, he added for my benefit.

Do you think they live near here? I asked doubtfully.

I understand this is a land of great warriors, he said, sweeping his arm across the silent landscape full of cows and chokecherries and a few old logging roads.

I think all our soldiers are already at war, I told him quietly.

Where? he demanded. I shall join them. I will bring down into their presence the golden might of the great arm of the Ruler of the Universe.

I thought the news that we were dropping bombs on Southeast Asia might offend the great Khan, who was Asian, so I simply said, Boot camp, somewhere.

Soldiers, he spat. Are not true warriors. I seek the other. Warriors of old who once ruled in splendor over the vast steppes of the Rocky Mountains.

Like the Blackfeet? I squinted up at him.

Blackfeet, he pronounced. His mouth moved over the name like a hungry man chewing on a little snack that wasn't going to be filling, but better than nothing.

Piegan, I said.

Ah, *Piegan*, he said, with more relish.

I learned about the Blackfeet and all of Montana's other Indians in school. Fifty miles off the Crow reservation, all I knew of Indians I learned in books. Once in fourth grade my teacher had told the class that if it wasn't for smallpox in the army blankets the military had sent upriver to the Indian camps, about half of us in the class would have been probably Blackfeet or Crow, and everyone groaned and said, Ick. She also told us the real name for the Crow people was *Apsa'alooka*, which meant Children of the Large-Beaked Bird. It probably meant raven, she said, but calling them crow people made them seem less fearsome.

Maybe you're looking for the *Apsa'alooka*, I said to Chinggiz Khan, trying to make the word sound fierce.

Apsa'alooka, he shouted toward the broad chest of Casey Peak with his powerful jaws thrust wide open.

The day of the accident I was sent to my friend Robin's house to stay for a few days so Dad could drive the 250 miles to mother's hospital room, where she was about to have emergency surgery. I don't remember where my brothers, both older, were farmed out to. Robin's father was a minister, like mine. When I walked into their living room and told Robin's father, Jack, that my mother had been in a car wreck in Helena and was about to have an operation, he yelled What! and leapt to his feet. Until that moment, I believed my father's calm: everything would be all right. After Jack made several phone calls—car accident, surgery, months in the hospital, nothing to do but pray, food of course, and someone to take care of those kids—it dawned on me that these are the calls preachers make when someone's really in trouble.

Nothing had ever really happened to me before. As I said. I'd broken my wrist in third grade, and we almost lost our dog once, but we found it. My parents were the ones who took care of others, counseled wives who'd been cheated on, took in troubled kids, moved us onto the floor so some itinerant or battered woman or kid applying for conscientious objector status could get a good night's sleep. Things happened to other people, and my brothers and I were not encouraged to ask what they were. Things never happened to us.

I remember once lying on our back lawn looking up at the dim blue eastern Montana sky and its small herd of unremarkable clouds. The grass itched the backs of my legs. I looked straight up at the sky and tried to see everything my eyes could see, clear out to the edge of my peripheral vision, including the little fringe of my bangs and the vague hump of nose you can see in the lower corners if you concentrate. I tried to take it all in at once.

I exist, I thought, for perhaps the first time. *At one time I wasn't, and now I am.* The sheer unlikeliness of being one of those accidents of nature that becomes a human being with thoughts, at this particular place and time, baffled me. I held my hand up and contemplated it against the sky. *My* hand, with me inside it, and yet all that it indicated—the intricacies of bone and nerve and artery, its silent metamorphosis since infancy, this unique and personal grafting of my father and my mother—seemed so far beyond my comprehension that my own hand began to look foreign to me. As though it and the sky and the earth below and the whole undiscovered universe were made of something divine and magical, and I was only peeking at them through wide-open eyes.

What are you going to do? I asked Chinggiz Khan.

I would like a drink of water, he said.

Life at the cabin was simple and hard. We made it hard. We believed in the doctrine my brother Tim had read in *Gospel of the Red Man,* by Ernest Thompson Seton, about the ways of Indians who, because they were persecuted, were practically saints. We had to walk silently through the woods without breaking any twigs or if you stepped on a wildflower you propped it up and apologized so you could be one with all things. There was a little fireplace but we didn't use it, because if you wasted resources just to stay warm, what would make you strong when real hardship came? For the same reason we washed our faces in the creek, rather than heat water with the propane. Once Tim and our oldest brother

Steve went backpacking and at suppertime wrapped their meat in an old leather bootlace they had found, and cooked the little package over the fire. When it was charbroiled they ate it, bootlace and all. They had inner fortitude. I tried, in their presence, not to be too much of a girl.

For that reason I was not about to show anybody my spider bite no matter how much it hurt. Besides, the rising welt was irritated by the elastic of my underwear and to show even a glimpse of white cotton to the boys was too shameful to think of. My father, of course, had other things on his mind.

They had plucked shards of dark green glass out of my mother's forehead with tweezers, after her sunglasses shattered against the car door. Of all her injuries I thought that one the most horrible.

The next time I saw Chinggiz Khan he was out in the middle of the field lying underneath a cow, squirting milk from its teat straight into his mouth. I stood over him until his head emerged from beneath the cow, squinting up at me. He gave a little kick with both legs and leapt straight up onto his feet. He was smiling. His round face looked grandfatherly, not like a Mongol barbarian at all. Little eyebrows danced far above his eyes.

Fat cows, he said. Most awkward I've seen in the history of the world.

Yep, I said.

They look like it hurts them to walk, he said. How do they pull your carts?

They don't pull anything, I said. They just sell them for meat.

Their milk tastes funny, he said as he walked back to his pony. I expect it's the grasses here.

Why do you rattle? I asked him.

He grinned, and parted his cape, which was fastened all across the top of his chest and then hung freely almost to the ground. It was made of thick felt, trimmed with silk and white fur. On a leather belt inside his cape dangled an entire arsenal of wicked looking weapons. He pointed at them one by one.

Shash-par, pyazi, kistin, tabar-zin, , he named off his array of maces and spears. He also carried a sabre, a lance, a quiver with some strange-headed arrows, and a fish hook made of bone. Then he said, Ah, and retrieved from a belt behind his back an enormous battle-axe. *Baltu!* he said reverently.

Could I see? I asked, pointing toward his quiver of arrows. I hoped he would give me one. He selected an arrow, dropped one shoulder out of his cape, shrugged a short bow off that shoulder and into his left hand, and in one gesture swept the arrow back into the bow and let fly. The arrow cut across the sky emitting a terrifying scream. Chinggiz Khan laughed, and pointed at a series of tiny holes carved in the tails of his other arrows.

To panic the enemy, he said. Listen.

He whipped another arrow into the bow and shot it; this one whistled low, like a mourning dove. I looked at the round-cheeked warrior.

This one signals all the other arrows to follow it straight to its target, he said. Then he trotted off across to the far hill to retrieve his arrows. I thought of the little town of Helena nearby, and my mother lying helpless in the hospital.

Are you going to wreck our town? I asked Chinggiz Khan when I caught up to him. Because there's an Air Force base nearby. Immediately his smile disappeared and his eyes went cold. Mongrel pigs, he said. I have seen those cowards fly overhead like shrikes and drop their weapons behind them and fly off again. *Karachu*, he spat. A true warrior, a *baghatur*, looks his enemy in the face. Your modern warriors are not fighting each other. They are trying to destroy the land beneath each other's feet. They only maim each other, but they leave great gaping holes in the land. Do you see these?

He pointed at an enormous six-flanged mace hanging from his belt. *Shash-par*, he said. All my weapons leave a mark only at the point of contact. He closed his cape and turned down the corners of his mouth, exhaling through his nose.

I am a *baghatur*, son of a *baghatur*, champion among civilized men, he said.

What about the catapult, I asked. Didn't the Mongols invent that? That's a long-distance war machine. What about gunpowder?

Given to us by God! he bellowed. If the Mountain of Life from which all Rivers Flow chooses to make us stronger than our enemies, to have dominion over all the world, who are we to argue?

I looked at the ground.

But destroy the fields and farmlands? Burn towns to the ground? he went on. Then he took his own helmet off and looked at the ground, too. These things I have done in my ignorant youth, he confessed with some remorse. But not since the year 1222, when I was taught by my Muslim advisors that it is the farmers and the craftsmen who comprise the lifeblood of a civilization by their diligent toil, have I committed such a barbaric act. For seven hundred and forty-six years I have righted my ways.

That doesn't really count, I said quietly. You're dead. Technically.

Ah, he said, and shoved his tortoise-shell face into my face. You know about death?

I bit both my lips together and watched a carpenter ant scale a long blade of grass until it bent over and dropped the ant on the ground.

What do you know about death? he demanded, planting his standard in the earth like a challenge.

I squinted to keep my eyes from filling up with tears. I know that people are only alive a short time, I said. That before you are born you are not alive, but you are waiting to be alive and hoping that you will get to. And after you die. . . .

After you die, what? he asked me in his growling voice.

But my chin gave way and the tears burst out and I ran. Down the slope, leaping over gopher holes, I ran as fast as a Mongol pony dashing across the steppes. The blurred world jiggled before me. And behind me: horse's hoofbeats, closer and closer. Suddenly his great scarlet sleeve swept around me and he lifted me off the ground and over the flank of his horse and with his harness bells jingling and the wind whistling through my ears and the smell of horse sweat rising up we rode and rode and rode.

What else can you see from where you are? I asked him. Besides the air force dropping bombs on little children, and the forgotten warriors of North America?

Xo, he said—it was a kind of grunting exhalation. The sun started to go down.

Everything I trained my eyes to see in life, I continue to see in death, he said. Strategies of war, patterns of agriculture, loyalty wherever it abides, new ways to increase strength, and the happiness or unhappiness of my people.

Are your people happy? I asked, thinking of *Life Magazine* photos of hundreds of Chinese children in gray pajamas lined up in perfect rows.

My people, he said proudly, will always be happy because they have befriended their own death. Once you have befriended death, nothing can harm you. It is my greatest legacy.

I squinted into the setting sun. Sounds morbid, I said. I think we're supposed to love life.

Chinggiz Khan reached over and tore a button off my shirt. Hey, I said, give that back, it's mine.

No, he said. It's mine now. I am more powerful than you, I have taken it away from you, and it will never again be yours. Even if I give it back to you, you will only be borrowing it from me.

I looked at him like, you're crazy.

A thing is only truly yours if it can never be taken away from you, he said. Every warrior knows this. If you fear death, then whoever threatens to kill you holds your life in his hands. Then you are very vulnerable, and forever you are only borrowing your life from whoever wants to kill you.

Nobody wants to kill me, I said.

Your death is always at hand, he said. You could choke or freeze or eat a bad mushroom, or get hit on the head. Always your death is right behind you, trying to trip you up.

How can you be friends with that? I asked. I thought about my spider bite.

When we are young boys training for battle, we fight against our best friends, Chinggiz Khan said. Everyone knows you see the enemy only through your own weaknesses but through love you see your friend's weakness clearly, and so in battle you take advantage of it. You become his greatest teacher, and he yours.

Chinggiz Khan, who had been lying back with a stalk of timothy grass between his teeth, sat up and looked directly in my eyes. You must face death squarely as though it were your best friend, he said. You must give your whole life to your death.

We're supposed to give our life to God, I said.

Same thing! he said. If God is life, then God is death also. See? Nothing to be afraid of. Slap it on the back. Give it a wink! Once you make friends with death your life will be your own, and no one can ever take anything away from you. Hee hee! he rolled onto his back and kicked his feet in the air. And it scares the hell out of your enemies, he said.

After a moment he rolled up onto one elbow and said, That is the reason my people are happy. That and, of course, we always taxed the wealthy according to their wealth, so as not to overburden the merchants and craftsmen, who are the lifeblood of any economy.

Of course I had to walk home. It was a long way.

Your shoe's untied, Steve said as I came up the path to the cabin. He let the screen door slap shut behind him, and sat on the step. Dad's here.

Inside, my father was stacking up firewood by the hearth for the next guests to use. Tim was stirring some glop over propane. Nice of you to stop by, Kry-ystal, Dad said. It's not my name, but his name for me. I heard the jokey part at the beginning. It was many years before I would hear that, when he gave the 'y' a two-syllable sound, it meant he was upset and trying not to sound like he was.

He said that the following day we would get to go visit our mother. No, she wasn't much better. He looked at each one of us in turn. It might be your last chance for a while, he said. His voice was soft and strong. His own mother had died when he was ten—was taken to the hospital and died there and buried, and he never saw her again. My father will be saying goodbye to her forever.

But it won't be easy on you, he said. She's very sick.

Needles. Pumps. Loud machines. Tubes down her throat, so she can't talk. Scars and bruises everywhere, so we can't hug her or squeeze too hard. Very fragile, even after a month. But, thank goodness, not on the stomach pump any more.

The cabin took on a solemn air, as though we were facing a grave danger or about to receive a great award. There was no kidding around. Over dinner we said positive things, trying to make each other feel better—mostly trying to make Dad feel better because the better he felt the more faith we had in what might happen. We told him about adventures we'd had at the cabin in those few days, clever things we'd done to outwit squirrels or sabotage the entropy that plagues an unused place out in the living landscape. When the talk ground down he'd say, What else? and we'd start up again.

That night in my bunk I thought about a sky full of Chinggiz Khan, and if he felt small coming back to earth again. I thought maybe I could show my bug bite to my mother, and even if she couldn't talk, maybe she could write me a note to tell me what to do for it.

There are things mothers do everywhere. Many they do with the backs of their hands—sweep hair out of their faces, push on the water faucet, open the refrigerator door—because so often their hands are full or wet or sticky. I practiced using the backs of my hands for things. I learned how to tuck the phone to my ear by crooking my shoulder. I even said "We'll see," though without authority. In that time I practiced these things.

In the morning I woke up feeling important and older than I was. We got in the car silently, and drove in silence to the hospital. When we did speak, we spoke quietly, as though we were in church. We tried to make our footfalls silent on the long wooden floors of the hospital hallway. Our father led us gently. He tried to act like he was not in a hurry to get there.

He stopped us outside a closed door. Are you ready? he asked us. We all nodded, silently. He pushed the door open and we stepped in.

First, a smell of camphor and alcohol, of body odor and blood. Tubes running into and out of the bed gurgled and spat, their machines whirring and choking and pumping rhythmically. Tiny wisps of hair splattered against a pillow. And beneath it all, a small spiderlike body that perhaps belonged to my mother. Tubes ran into her nose. Her mouth gaped open in an expression that looked like an old woman, near death. We all stood back from the bed.

I've brought the children, my father said to her, caressing her white and tiny forehead. She strained to open her eyes, strained to shift her focus to the side to see us. She grunted.

Stand over there where she can see you, he told us. My brothers and I shifted positions in tiny unison steps. Her hand lay on the bed.

My mother's hand lay on the bed. An IV tube was bandaged to it, but it was my mother's hand. I reached for it and put it against my face. My mother's hand smelled funny, but it felt the same as always.

Her face looked gray and bandaged and awful. But her hand was the same. I bent my face down into the cup of her hand, and I whispered into her palm, Mommy, I have a spider bite that hurts and itches at the same time. I want you to come home.

Suddenly the machine that clicked and whirred beside her bed began to gallop. It galloped like the steed of Chinggiz Khan as he raced across the pasture. I heard that galloping and I looked up at the machine. I think I saw in that moment that my mother was a warrior, too, racing across some pasture of her own. I began to see that only a small part of my mother remained there, in the bed, and that some bigger part of her was engaged in a battle we could not see, and was galloping and galloping. The machines stared blankly down at her from her bedside. She also did not blink. She is not dying, I thought. She is looking death in the eye. And after that she will come home.

Why so silent? asked Chinggiz Khan that afternoon. We were sitting by the creek, and Chinggiz Khan was dipping his enormous round toes into the cool water, over and over.

Thinking about my mom, I said. I threw a grass blade into the wind and it blew right back and stuck in my hair. I squinted up at Chinggiz Khan from where I lay. His round warrior's face looked soft and sad.

Are you going to cry? I asked him.

Yes, said Chinggiz Khan. I am going to cry out in a voice the seven heavens can hear. I am going to cry for my people and for all warrior people, because there are no more warriors alive on the earth. Everyone of merit has been killed off, vanquished, or destroyed.

What are you talking about? I asked him.

I have been to the land of the warrior people, said Chinggiz Khan. The *Apsa'alooka*, whom you call the Crow. I went there with honor, I gave them audience with dignity. I proffered myself as their advocate, their great father, and, of course, their conqueror. For what greater honor could I bestow on a noble warrior people but to be conquered by someone as great as me?

Chinggiz Khan's head fell against his chest and waggled back and forth.

But there are no more warrior people, he said. Even the mighty *Apsa'alooka*. They have been conquered by something so foreign to themselves they had no hope of fighting it. It has torn them from their own heritage.

Chinggiz Khan's head fell to his chest. No one cares about warriors any more, he said. I may as well go home.

Don't worry, I told him. Maybe their time hasn't come yet. One day they will be strong enough to fight you, and then you can be happy again.

I looked deeply into the backs of his eyes. Everything will be all right, I told him.

Chinggiz Khan looked at me. His eyes were black stones behind buttonholes, gleaming. Children! he spat. The only creatures on earth braver than warriors!

Chinggiz Khan peeled a blade of grass out of my hair. He held it between his thumbs and blew hard, making a wheezing whistle that lofted on the wind. In a moment his meaty little horse cantered up, its war regalia shimmering in the afternoon sun. Chinggiz Khan pulled on his felt boots, leapt astride his horse in a graceful arc, righted himself smoothly, and galloped off across the pasture, bellowing some ancient jibberish.

I watched him almost fly across that hillside, his horse taking barbed-wire fences in long leaps, scarlet robe billowing behind him, his voice gusting across the spaces in whoops and cries. Soon he was just a dot on the horizon, still galloping.

That night my spider bite began to ache fiercely. Finally fear overcame shame, and I decided to ask one of my brothers to look at it. I chose Tim because, though Steve was older and knew more, Tim spent all his time outdoors and probably had been spider-bit himself. I considered him almost an Indian, he was so knowledgeable about outdoor survival. He might even know an ancient Indian remedy made of charcoal and spit and pine sap, or something. I waited till he was brushing his teeth out on the porch of the cabin, spitting into the weeds like a native. He liked the way the toothpaste glowed a little in the dark after you spit it, but he was careful to pour his swishing-water over it because you should always leave nature the way you found it.

Would you look at something, I asked him timidly.

What, he said. I handed him a small flashlight. Though the cabin had electricity, it was considered sissy not to rough it without. I pulled down the waistband of my pajamas and bent my spine around so we could both look at the funny-shaped welt topped with two bright-red dots.

Spider bite, he said. On your butt. He snickered.

Not on my butt, on my back! I said. What do I do about it?

He looked at me, considering. It'll probably go away, he said.

But it hurts! and itches at the same time! I whined.

Okay, he said. The thing you do is rub it really really hard. The harder you rub it the faster it will go away.

I thought about this. A remedy that required stoic discipline in the face of pain. It made sense. He handed me the flashlight back and turned to go into the cabin.

You can't die from spider bites, can you? I asked quietly.

Don't be stupid, he said.

It is advice I have tried my best to follow all the years of my life.

from
"JOURNEYMEN"
a novel in progress

Neil McMahon

O N A SATURDAY AFTERNOON in early March, 1962, Dan Allard drove out of Helena, Montana, on his way to the Rocky Boy's Chippewa Cree reservation near the hi-line town of Havre. He was seeded to the finals of the state AAU boxing tournament, where he would fight an Indian named Harold Lives Well Man.

Allard's fiancee was sitting close beside him in his 1958 Ford pickup. Her name was Rae Torgersen. Her father owned the construction company Allard worked for as an apprentice carpenter, a job that provided a living and helped keep him in shape until his career took off.

He had already won the Montana Golden Gloves, held in February. It had been an easy victory; there was no one in the area to compete with him. At six feet, one sixty-four, he was a perfect middleweight. His legs were reliable and his upper body powerful. He was quick, he could take a punch, and he had a knockout right hand. He was favored to win the Golden Glove regionals in Tacoma and go on to the nationals. There had been newspaper articles in his home town of Helena and the larger city of Great Falls, with the sportswriters speculating as to whether he would turn pro immediately or wait for a chance at the '64 Olympics. He was white, in the first big-time sport to be dominated by black men. He had begun to understand the difference between being good and being valuable.

At the edge of town they stopped at Louie's and bought a sixpack of Rainier, victory beer for the return drive. He told Rae jokingly that he was going to bring home an Indian's scalp on his belt. Then they started the four-hour drive to Rocky Boy's, for the last easy fight of the season.

A chinook had sprung up two days before, a freak warm wind that stripped the wheatfields of snow, leaving scars of dark earth through the tired cover of winter. The sky was the color of frost, the horizon impossible to distinguish. In Great Falls they turned north on Highway 87, a narrow raised blacktop road with deep barrow pits and frequent white crosses mounted on stiff wire and thrust into the earth, memorials to those who had died at those places in car wrecks. On Montana highways there were no speed limits, and a sixpack was standard company for any drive longer than a few miles. The crosses tended to come in clusters.

The radio played the Texas swing of Bob Wills, the broken heart of Hank Williams, the music Rae and he danced to when he took her to the Silver Spur on Saturday nights. They passed Fort Benton, lying low in a curve of the Missouri like a scene from a picturebook. The river wound eastward as far as they could see through the bleak empty fields and buttes, its thawing stretches a metallic gray-brown in the flat afternoon light. There was little traffic, an occasional rancher in a pickup or carload of Indians headed for the bars in Great Falls. Miles passed when they would see no sign of human habitation but a tin-roofed shed or a grain elevator. Ahead of them somewhere a cavavan of vehicles carried the rest of the Helena Boxing Club, but even in those days he had yielded to the need for apartness without fully understanding what it was: knowing only that it had to do with the emptiness of that land, especially in winter.

They passed a small ranch, a cluster of neat log buildings with smoke rising from the main house chimney and the windows glowing in the deepening evening. "Let's come back and buy that place when I hang up the gloves," he said, glancing at her. "Be just right for you to keep your horses."

She gazed down at the ranch, studying it as if he were not just teasing. When she turned back, she said, "That seems like a long time off," and Allard heard in her words what he had increasingly been sensing: that she looked at his boxing as she would another woman.

They had not set a date.

She was small, with ginger hair and a Nordic face that was pretty but could look harsh. She wore tight jeans and buff-colored elkskin boots her father got hand-made out of skins he brought back from hunting. At twenty, she was three years younger than he; like him, she worked for her father, a part-time secretary in the company office, but everybody knew she was waiting to get married. She was quiet, often serious, easy to be with, and exciting during their secret sex. He assumed that what he felt for her was love.

He had rationales for waiting, the important events to come: the regionals, the nationals, the Olympics or a professional debut. But underlying all that was the unease she could create in him by disappearing inside herself to a place he could not follow. It was not a simple matter of distance, but of complete departure. It would leave him helpless and alone, but more, it was as if there were something taking place in that other realm that could affect him but he could not touch in return or even glimpse. He had little fear of men, but she awakened in him the warrior's dread of losing his power to that mystery. He saw that she was leaving now, and the half-teasing words of reassurance that had formed in his mind—*I been meaning to ask when you want to get hitched*—remained unspoken. The silence lasted the rest of the drive. He seemed to feel a coolness on his skin.

At the town of Box Elder, not much more than a crossroads, they turned off the highway and drove the three miles to the reservation agency. It consisted of a modern glass and concrete school and several old frame buildings that looked like they belonged on a military base. Pickup trucks and station wagons were scattered all around, more than he had expected, their license plates bearing the numbers of different Montana counties and at least one from Canada.

Night had come. For a moment they sat, watching the shapes moving behind the lit windows of the school gymnasium, and Allard felt the first tingle of what was to come: an emotion that had begun as fear but over the years of fighting had changed to a kind of power more intense than anything he had known, even the anticipation when he and Rae were on their way to a forbidden evening at her parents' cabin. He opened the pickup's door, a swirl of wet warm breeze slipping across his face and high into his nostrils, and then her hand was on his arm, holding him back.

"Let's not go in yet," she said. "Let's drive around some."

"I've got to go check in," he said.

"I don't want to go in there." She spoke with a firmness that approached pouting, a tone she rarely used. "All those little kids beating each other up and their mothers watching like it was something neat. I'd rather stay in the truck."

Allard looked at his watch. It was only six. He would not be fighting for hours.

"Where do you want to go?" he said. They were perhaps fifty miles south of the Canadian border. Havre, the nearest town big enough to have a gas station, lay just halfway between them and Saskatchewan. There was little else for a hundred miles in any direction except half-frozen prairie.

"We could drive up to Baldy Butte. Daddy took us skiing there once when I was little. I want to see if it looks the same." Her eyes were bright in the dim glow of the cab's lamp and her hand stayed on his arm, warm through his shirt, thawing the coolness. He understood that this was a chance to make up his uncertainty. He closed the door and started the ignition. As they pulled out, she took a can of beer from the sack and opened it with the church key he kept in the glove compartment. He was surprised but said nothing. The little ski hill was another seven miles. She leaned against the far door, knees drawn up, sipping from the beer and watching him over its top.

The parking lot was deserted, the lift sheds and little concession building unlit, the hill's snow streaked with earth like the surrounding fields. He cut the lights and engine and said, "You want to get out?" She shook her head, still staring at him; then, as if to underline it, pulled her boots off and tucked her feet beneath his thigh. Uneasy, with the feeling that he had taken a wrong turn on a mountain trail and was about to find himself in unpassable terrain, he said, "Well then, I guess I've seen enough," and reached for the keys. But she was moving too, setting the beer on the floor and quickly, fluidly, draping herself around him.

Startled, he half embraced her and half tried to hold still her squirming body, while her tongue flicked into his ear, moved hot across his cheek, forced open his lips. "Baby," he tried to say, "Rae, we can't, not now," but her fingers were at his belt, in his jeans, and he inhaled sharply, turning helpless as her face fell away and her mouth found his cock.

Then her breath was against his neck again warm and quick, hips wriggling to push down her jeans, his own hands helping roughly, and as she heaved and cawed astride him and he growled in answer, his bootheel slammed the inside panel of the door, leaving dents he would find days later.

―

Inside the door of the school gymnasium a table was set up for selling tickets. The woman sitting at it wore a high school letter jacket with leather sleeves, in the colors of the Havre Blue Ponies. She was blackhaired and darkskinned, heavyset, her eyes bright black. When she grinned a gap showed between her front teeth. "I know you," she said. "I seen your picture in the paper. You go on in."

Rae was still holding his arm tightly, as she had when they walked across the slippery melting ice in the parking lot, and all during their silent drive from Baldy Butte. He spotted his teammates across the gym and started toward them, skirting the ring where a pair of eleven- or twelve-year-old boys flailed at each other with gloves the size of melons strapped to their thin arms. He guessed the crowd at a hundred and fifty, standing or sitting in the bleachers, many wearing bright nylon jackets with the name of a boxing club emblazoned across the back. Young fighters with wrapped hands watched, or warmed up at the gym's edges, shadowboxing or punching at a coach's hands held shoulder height. Some carried trophies, a sign that their ordeal was over.

Mikey Egan, his trainer, glanced up from a conversation with a circle of boys, raised a hand, returned to his talk. A couple of the boys waved shyly at their hero. Allard stopped short of them, feeling his face warm: wondering if it could be seen that he had broken taboo. He sensed Rae watching him and, for the first time since then, met her eyes. They were anxious, but there was something else in them, that had to do with claim. They looked at each other for some time. Then she rose on tiptoe to kiss his cheek. "Luck," she whispered, and climbed the bleachers to join the mothers and girlfriends.

"How you feeling tonight, champ?" Mikey said, clapping him on the shoulder. He was a medium-sized balding man with kind concerned eyes, a schoolteacher, first in a family of Butte Irish miners to get an education beyond grade school. Like Allard, he had grown up street tough and had his first bouts in the service. He made no secret that he saw his primary mission in life as sending his own nine children and as many others as he could along the paths of fairness and honesty. He believed in boxing the way he believed in God, and lying, cheating, and stealing fell into the same category as punching after the bell.

"Probably be a couple more hours before your bout," Mikey said. "Half the kids in the state showed up." His eyes showed his satisfaction. Boys who were boxing were not out drinking beer or stealing hubcaps.

Allard smiled, but his uneasiness remained. "Maybe I'll go take a walk."

"Don't get chilled." Mikey spoke distractedly now, and Allard saw that one of the Helena boys was about to climb into the ring. He looked scared, his gaze searching the crowd confusedly. "I better go," Mikey said.

Allard glanced up into the bleachers. Rae was talking with two other women, young mothers, the three heads bowed together. He wondered what she was telling them. For a moment longer he stood, looking around aimlessly, nodding to a few familiar faces. Then he started for the door.

As he crossed the gym, the edge of his vision caught someone watching him. He swiveled, in time to see the other head turn as swiftly away. It was Harold Lives Well Man, standing with a group of Havre boxers, mostly Indians. He was about Allard's age, taller, his reach longer, but thinner through the chest and shoulders. Allard had watched him lose at the Golden Gloves, coming out at the bell with a violent flurry, but possessing neither stamina nor style. He had already planned the bout: the first minute, waiting for the flurry to subside; the second, tiring him with punches to the arms, shoulders, and body; and every second after that, watching for the slip, the tiny relaxation, that would start Allard moving before his mind was even aware of it, feet shifting, head ducking, driving in to set up that ferocious right that would put Lives Well Man on the mat. He walked on, knowing what he had seen in that instant of quickly twisting heads, gazes that did not quite meet: Lives Well Man was afraid of him. It should have given him another jolt of that power. Instead, he found his shoulders hunching.

The overhead fluorescent lights cast a sheen on the faces and brightly colored jackets that he had seen at other boxing matches and never anywhere else, an enhanced visibility that seemed to magnify features. It was not attractive. The thought came that he could say something to Harold Lives Well Man, perhaps shake his hand. But it would have felt false, with both of them knowing he was going to win. Good fellowship was for afterward. At the door, the gap-toothed woman grinned at him. "You running away?" she said teasingly.

"Yeah," Allard said. "I'm getting out while I can."

She cackled, shaking her head and raising a warning finger. "You better watch out," she said. "Us Indens got tricks white men don't know about." He smiled and walked out into the night.

Except for the warm gusting wind it was quiet, a relief after the yelling and thudding of the gym. The sky was overcast, without moon or stars. The lights of the buildings reflected off the low clouds, creating a sort of luminescent dome. He stopped walking and stood, feeling suddenly disembodied, floating between two worlds.

Mikey had had a number of pro fights before hanging up the gloves. He never said much about it, but his eyes turned cautious when the subject came up. It was different, Allard understood, from the comparatively tame amateur ranks: brutal, frightening, the stakes high beyond his ability to grasp. He had once had a bout refereed by a former champion, an old warhorse with upwards of fifty title fights. Everything about the man was thick: his forehead layered with an inch of callus, his ears and nose like lumpy vegetables, his eyes troubled and distant. In the locker room afterward, Allard had seen him sitting on a bench, staring at a wall, cracking the knuckles of his powerful hands, oblivious to anyone or anything around. But it was the world Allard wanted, whatever the risks. Anything less seemed like a retreat, tasteless and soft as mush.

He put his hands deep into his jacket pockets and started toward the agency headquarters a few hundred yards away. As he got close he heard a sound like tuneless singing. It became clearer, a number of voices chanting in a strange tongue, then abruptly stopped. Three young bucks drinking beer sat on the entrance steps, their hair and eyes dark in the shadows. Allard nodded, but all stared pointedly past him. Two or three times in his life he had gotten a glimpse of the secret world beneath the way Indians ordinarily showed themselves to whites. He had sensed something similar with black men in the service, a way an oppressed people showed their contempt, and it had seemed to him that at least occasionally they managed to have a pretty good time at it. He considered those brief contacts a mark of honor, but clearly this was not going to be one of those nights.

The hall inside was lined with photos and artifacts: fierce, regal chiefs with gorgeous headdresses and metal-studded rifles, glass-encased tomahawks and broken treaties, trophies for baseball and basketball. He passed a concession stand selling beer and snacks, and several more averted stares. The chanting had started again, coming from a room at the end of the hall. He stopped at the doorway.

Perhaps fifteen adult Indians sat crosslegged or knelt on blankets spread on the floor, forming a rough circle, with more standing around the edges watching. As the chanting rose, the players would gather small bundles of sticks in their hands, and at the last shouted syllable, cast them down. A chorus of exclamations, pleasure or disgust, would follow. Allard stood in the doorway like a ghost, noted but not really seen. After several minutes of watching, he had no more idea of what the game's objects or rules or stakes were, or even of who was winning or losing, than when he had arrived. As he turned to go, he caught the first full and direct stare that had been offered him, from an old man with a headband, waist-length gray braid, and a face so sunken and lined it looked mummified.

The eyes were dark and filmy, and he felt them on his back as he walked down the hall.

Not until he was again out in the night, walking toward the gym, did he remember the way the old man's fingers had moved gently over his sticks after he had thrown them down, and realize that the cloudy films over his eyes were cataracts.

At the bell Harold Lives Well Man came out as Allard had expected, swinging with a fury that held desperation. Allard did not try to fight, but circled and dodged, occasionally jabbing, waiting for Lives Well Man's arms to start sagging. As the round passed the halfway point, a part of his mind noted the voice of the crowd, changing from excited shouts to discontent as they realized he was not going to mix it up. In the final half minute, he connected with two hard shots, one to the shoulder that knocked Lives Well Man off balance, and another that smashed his glove back into his face and started a trickle of blood from the corner of his mouth. But the opening did not come.

He remained standing in his corner, a technique intended to demoralize an opponent. Mouthpiece in his glove, he swished water from the squeeze bottle Mikey held. "That a boy," Mikey said quietly. "Easy does it." Allard's stare remained on Lives Well Man, hunched on his stool across the ring. He had three men working his corner, stocky older Indians rubbing his shoulders, dabbing his face with Vaseline, and talking at him excitedly. The stare, too, was intended to demoralize. Lives Well Man did not meet it.

Mikey held out the rinse bucket. "He's dragging that left," he said. Allard nodded and spat out the water. It was bloodless. The ten-second whistle blew. Lives Well Man stood, and the Indians hurriedly pulled the stool out. Allard turned his back, gripping the ropes and bouncing on his toes. When they met in the center, the crowd was shouting again, sensing that this would be the round. Allard circled, easily avoiding the first flurry of punches.

But there came an instant when he felt rather than saw the other man's fear like an invisible knife slashing through him, as if it had turned on him who had engendered it. It stopped his mind and body for just that heartbeat, his gaze went inward, away from the all-important center of the chest, and his own gloves relaxed the fraction of an inch he had been waiting for. He realized the mistake as he made it and was ducking hard and raising his gloves when the punch caught him precisely in the socket of the left eye. It was like a soundless painless explosion inside his head.

In both his own knockouts he had taken the eight-count and gone out to fight again, once three times and once four, before finally going down. But this time, as he lay struggling on the canvas, willing himself to rise, distantly aware of the crowd's violent roar and the referee's shouted counting, the burn of rough canvas against his cheek and the smell of raw wet leather from his own glove beside his face, his body refused. By the next evening he realized it had known something his mind did not.

The next hours and days ran together in his memory, a kaleidoscope of images that still sometimes brought him sweating out of sleep. A particular sound of wood hitting wood on a job, or the tingle of electric current from an improperly wired tool, could have him physically backing away before he realized it. He remembered faces, Mikey's sharp with concern and Rae's near panic; the young boys on the club, shocked and uncomprehending; Indians, yelling and gleeful; and a final glimpse of Harold Lives Well Man, looking, not triumphant, but stunned, as if he had done something wrong. The journey home was endless, slumped against the door of the truck while Rae drove, sipping the victory beer in the futile hope of killing the tearing pain, keeping his jaw clenched against the need to weep. He had assumed it was a bad black eye, a humiliation that would sting but could be overcome.

Late the next afternoon, alone in his small apartment, he had felt something break inside his face. The eye swelled shut so quickly that by the time he got to the bathroom mirror, he had to pry the lids apart. He could not see his left eyeball. It seemed to have disappeared inside his skull. A neighbor took him to St. Peter's Hospital. The doctor X-rayed him, was gone some time, then came back into the emergency room and sat on a table, tapping the sheaf of X-rays against his thigh. Allard got home four days later, with several bones wired together and his eyeball resting on a piece of plastic. The nurses told him that he had come out of the anesthesia hours before he was supposed to and, not yet conscious, sat up ripping the IV needles out of his arm.

His face remained numb for months, the severed nerve tissue growing back at one thousandth of an inch per day. As feeling returned, a new understanding grew with it. He was not exactly a has-been. He was a has-been would-be. He was a carpenter, working for his future father-in-law, and that was what he was going to remain. The thousands of hours alone at night in the old gym, shadowboxing, working out the intricate dance steps of single combat, learning to punch the heavy bag with force and precision and the light one with split-second timing, the endlessly swollen nose and bruised ribs and skinned knuckles—all were as useless and dead as the dreams of cheering crowds and a champion's belt, vanished like scenes from a movie that had once had something to do with him. His former smugness at feeling valuable was like an evil clown that followed him through his days and nights, pointing a finger and leering.

Over the next several months his weight went up to nearly two hundred pounds and his beer consumption toward a case a day. His quarrels with Rae grew frequent. Often he started them, which he had never before done. Inevitably, she offered to return his ring, and although he understood that the gesture was really a plea, he accepted coldly. He began seeing her around town with boyfriends.

One night he punched a man in O'Toole's bar, hospitalizing him. He spent twelve days of a thirty-day sentence in the Lewis and Clark County jail before a judge agreed to let him post bond and jump it. His own money had disappeared in bars, and he had to borrow two hundred dollars.

During the long sober days in jail he came to recognize what had put him there as rage, that the stiff sentence for what at that time and place was a minor offense had come not from the fight itself or even the trouble he had given police in subduing him, but from a look in his eyes. Whether it came from his defeat or he had been born with it and shaped it into the violence of the ring, he did not know. What mattered was that the control he had learned, a dynamic balance of exhausting himself physically during the days by working and mentally at night by drinking, was weakening: that what was left was the memory of that time, a ghost stripped of flesh, that would return more and more over the coming years.

A Fine Spring Day, with Regrets

Allen Morris Jones

HE HAD JUST TURNED SIXTEEN, and was living outside of Great Falls with his mother, who was still a young woman, still someone who liked to watch movies and drink beer and laugh. He'd been growing fast, and carried his new height with the hunched, gangly posture of a water bird: wrists and ankles and an Adam's apple. But underneath this lanky adolescence, this awkwardness, was a hard kernel of observation and judgment-passing that no one, it seemed, had yet discovered he had.

He came in for breakfast to find his mother already standing at the sink, wearing her flannel nightgown and a blue, down hunting jacket over the nightgown. Her boyfriend, Jerry, sat with his long legs stretched out under the kitchen table, drinking beer in bare feet and frayed jeans and a white T-shirt. "Charlie," he said, toasting the boy as he walked in, "welcome to another fine day in America."

Jerry claimed to be part Blackfeet, although Charlie had his doubts. The skin was dark enough, but the mustache suggested Italy. This morning, Jerry's hair still held the lines of last night's comb and he looked tired. His eyes took a few seconds to focus as they settled on the boy.

Charlie went to the cabinet for cereal, then to the fridge for milk, then sat down across from Jerry.

"Jerry here thinks Oly's some kind of breakfast food," Charlie's mother said, hugging her elbows. The room was cold but not uncomfortable.

Jerry put both arms on the table and pushed his eyeglasses up with the back of the hand that held the beer. When he wasn't drinking, Jerry worked as a drywaller, and he always had money to spend. He'd taken to buying Charlie hunting magazines on his way up to the house. His hands and forearms were the thickest Charlie had ever seen: bowling pin slabs of muscle and vein and ligament. And when he turned a beer can in his hands, it was always a delicate motion for such muscles. "Your mother's pissed at me, Charlie," he said. "Know why?"

His mother went to the refrigerator and pulled out a beer for herself, spraying foam across the floor as she cracked it open. "Charlie's smarter than you, Jerry," she said, shaking off the back of her hand. "Don't talk down to him."

"I live like I want to. That's it." Jerry sat back and pulled a small pen knife from his pocket. "Makin' my own life," he said, trimming a fingernail. "Old Indian trick."

"Your uncle Frank called," his mother said. "He wants to go fishing today. Said he found you a new place."

"Your mom's confused, Charlie. She wants red men white."

"I wouldn't mind it if you stayed home today, Charlie," his mother said.

Charlie walked his bowl to the sink. "Did he say what time he'd be here?"

"Nine-thirty."

Jerry stared at his beer, rolling it back and forth in his palms.

Charlie opened the door to his garage, where he kept his fishing gear, but Jerry said his name and he turned back.

"My man," he said. "Catch a big one. It's later than you think."

He sat on the steps of the porch, knees under his arms, the canvas bag with his waders and creel of spoons at his feet, spinning rod over the bag. His uncle's Dodge truck, heavy as a boxcar, worked its way up the graveled drive to their house, switchbacking from empty lot to empty lot, tracing the contours of a subdivision that had never panned out. Frank parked below the steps, engine clattering. Charlie threw his gear into the bed and climbed into the cab, breathing the familiar odors of diesel fuel and cheap cologne and animal hides. "Where we going?"

"I got us a good place." Frank smoothed his mustache and looked toward the house. He was ten years older than Charlie's mother, with hair that was already beginning to gray and a stomach that belled out in loose wads over his belt. Charlie liked to walk by his taxidermy shop after school, to sit on a bench against the wall and sometimes help flesh out the fresh skins. Trophies cycled through the door, cold and stiff, to be disassembled and slowly pieced back together. Glass eyes set into foam, wet skin sewn down from the crest of the neck, faded noses painted black. It had given Frank an early power in Charlie's eyes, this resurrection of animals.

His mother opened the front door and walked down the steps toward them, feet loose in a pair of unlaced Sorels. "Mornin', Frank." She reached up and laid her forearms on the open window, glancing down at the truck's floor, at the dashboard. "Where are you boys going fishing?"

"Got us a good place. You don't know it."

"Where would that be?"

"Up by Pine Butte. Up in there."

"I know about your good places, Frank. Don't get caught."

"Annie." He shook his head.

"I mean it, Frank. Stay out of trouble."

"Oh, sweetheart." He put his hand on her shoulder and leaned close. "You should be working at that yourself."

Frank had a church that he went to in Great Falls, and when he saw the beer cans piled into the back of their little yellow pickup, the broken windows in the garage door, he shook his head. It was probably true that he saw Charlie and his mother as problems to be solved.

She raised a hand as they pulled away. Jerry stood in the doorway behind her, staring at her back.

"This place, Charlie," Frank said, "this place has got rainbows like this." He took his hands off the steering wheel and spread them apart. "And they're trying to spawn right now. They can't, but they try. They're gonna be stacked up against that dam like cordwood."

"That doesn't sound like Pishkun."

"Pishkun." Frank shook his head and took his pack of cigarettes off the dashboard, pulling one out with his lips. "I got us a couple jars of eggs, enough to fill up the freezer with fish. Your mom won't know what hit her." He lit his cigarette from the truck lighter, and reached over to smack the boy's leg a couple of quick times.

His mother had never worried about him much before. Things always happened for the best, was her view, and she'd told him often that luck was on their side.

"How old are you now, Charlie?" Frank slowed and turned north onto the highway, away from Great Falls.

Charlie had turned sixteen three days before, but he didn't want his uncle to feel embarrassed that he had missed his birthday. He liked Frank—he liked fishing and hunting with him—and he didn't want that to change. "Sixteen and a half."

"That's a good age. Maybe the best age."

"How old are you?"

"Too old. It ain't the years, it's the miles. Isn't that what they say?"

"You're not that old," Charlie said.

"You get to a certain age and you think you got no more choices. Probably you don't. But then I look at somebody young like you, Charlie. You got all kinds."

"Like what?"

Frank nodded. "Sometimes you can't see it."

They left the haze of Great Falls behind, finally turning off at Choteau. Ear Mountain rose thirty miles to the west, its bent back hinging the Front, north and south. High sheets of cirrus clouds blew fast toward them over the mountains, curling at their front edges as they hit the plains.

"What do you want to do when you grow up? Maybe that's a place to start."

"A writer."

"Like a newspaper writer?"

"Stories."

Frank drove quietly for a while, biting at his thumbnail. Then he said, "What about a vet? Your dad's a vet."

"Haven't talked to him since he left." Charlie reached up to grab the pack of cigarettes, but when Frank didn't react, he put them back. "Are you going bear hunting this spring?"

"Don't think so."

"Why not?"

"Getting' sick of skinnin' 'em, to be honest."

"They look too much like people. You told me that once before."

"That's just it." He picked his hand up off the steering wheel and flexed his fingers. "They got those paws, you know."

The road turned to gravel west of Choteau, and then to bare dirt, muddy in the swales below the largest drifts. Frank stopped to put the hubs in. They rolled down their windows and rested their arms on the doors. The air was cold, and smelled like new grass.

Frank ground out a half-finished cigarette and lit another, bending down over the steering wheel to look up at the peaks, whistling tunelessly through his teeth. He'd always said that he liked hunting best, but next to hunting he liked fishing, and when he was going fishing the world was a good place for him. The road turned steep, and they shortly turned off it to churn up a bare, untracked hillside. Charlie stepped out to open a gate at the top of the ridge. There was a view of the whole countryside, including the pond where he guessed they would be fishing: a plate of water set flat and blue inside a thousand square miles of rolling dead grass and unwashed boulders and festering patches of snow. Above the lake, the snow gradually increased until, on the highest slopes, the mountain was nothing more than rotting cornices and old avalanches.

They dropped into the ravine below the lake and parked. It was steep country—steep enough for the dam to have become the horizon—and Frank's truck would be hidden from anyone coming onto the pond from above. Frank stepped out, stretched, and walked up to the front bumper to take a leak. Charlie shrugged into his jacket and reached back for his bag.

"You won't need your waders," Frank said, looking at him. "And we'll just be taking my one fly rod."

"Fly rod?"

Frank zipped up and walked back to peer over the side of the truck into the open bag. "You might want that creel, though."

They eased up over the crest of the dam, stretching their necks until they could just see into the water. By the gradual slope of its shores, the lake wasn't naturally deep, but the bottom had been excavated. Piles of gravel and clay lay humped in a ring around the banks like mine tailings. A raft of ice floated in the middle, necklaced by the ripples of rising fish.

"Who owns this ground?" Charlie whispered.

Frank stood beside him breathing hard. "Becker," he said, after a moment. "Something Becker." He stood up straight and put his hands on his belly. "Bill or Bob or Buck or something. Used to be George Rainy had it but he sold out about five years ago for sixty bucks an acre." He shook his head. "Sixty bucks."

They stood above the water, letting their eyes adjust to the glare. Then they began to see the fish: long, dark slivers coasting in pods among the rocks. Even in the lightly broken chop of the breeze, it was possible to see the fins as they cut through the surface, to make out the backs rolling briefly into the air, black as glass, thick as salmon.

Frank grinned. "Do you see 'em?"

Charlie nodded. "Big."

They backed away from the dam and Frank unscrewed the lid from his jar of eggs. "They'll come for miles," he said, winking at Charlie. He pulled the rod from its case and pieced together three antique lengths of bamboo. "Your grandpa left this to me," he said. "Hardly ever fish with it anymore. But on this fine morning. . . . " He filled his chest with air and looked at the sky, the mountains, the water. "It's just what that old doctor ordered. See, you've got to have you a line light enough to float down slow, but it's got to be heavy enough to get out there a ways." He pulled the reel from his vest and screwed it onto the butt of the rod. Age had tarnished the metal into the color of old ice, but it was clean, and the line spooled smoothly when he stripped it through the guides. "Let me test the water," he said, "then I'll pass the rod off to you." He took a step up the dam and then reconsidered, turning back. "You haven't fly-fished before, right?"

Charlie shook his head.

"Okay. That's okay. Now. Watch." Frank crouched on the flat of the dam and reached into the jar of eggs, threading the first one onto the bare hook then flicking the next one out into the pond. It floated undisturbed, bright punctuation in the murky water. He flicked another egg, and then another, until four or five were floating in the water at any one time. Within a few minutes, the eggs seemed to be bouncing as they went to the bottom, jigging to the currents of unseen fish. And then the fish were clearly feeding, some of them striking at the eggs as soon as they hit the water. It was how Charlie imagined tuna to feed in the Pacific: a whirlpool of eyes and tails and white stomachs.

Frank looked back at him, and although Charlie expected him to smile or make some sort of joke, he didn't; he was solemn and wide-eyed and tense. He lifted the rod and made one or two false casts off to the side before sending the line out over the water, laying the egg precisely in the middle of the feeding knot of fish. Charlie breathed, and then breathed again. Frank tensed through his shoulder, lifted his arm. The fragile-looking rod jumped and sawed and bent itself into a horseshoe.

Frank walked down the dam, following the fish. "That's how you do it!" he yelled, his voice booming out over the quiet water.

The fish jumped only once, a loose-boned breaching that smacked against the water like a hand across a cheek. Frank reeled, and let the fish take line, then reeled again, until the fish lay exhausted and rolling on the surface, a few yards from the bank. Frank stepped in after it, even in his jeans, and pivoted from his hips to sling it back onto the bank. It landed with a hollow thump, long as any trout Charlie had ever seen, but chunky, too, like some absurd cross between a snake and a football. How big? Six pounds? Seven? It could have easily gone seven pounds, although memory, like water, distorts. It flopped once, and then again. Frank stepped up and grabbed it behind its gills, his large hands not quite large enough to reach all the way around it. He rapped its head on the rocks. It flopped against him and he rapped it again until it lay still. Frank raised the leader to his mouth and clipped it with his big teeth. "Fish you've caught for yourself taste better," he said, sliding the trout into the back of his vest. The fan of its tail protruded. "Remember that. Now it's your turn." He handed Charlie the rod. "Put on a new hook and give it a try."

A few minutes later, he stood beside his uncle, the length of bamboo trembling in his hands.

"Cast along the dam first," Frank said, "for practice."

They stood parallel to the water, facing the opposite hillside. Charlie noticed for the first time that the dam had tire tracks on it, winding out past the dam and then through the sagebrush flats. "Keep your wrist stiff," Frank said, grabbing his forearm, "and act like you're pounding nails. Pick it up, throw it down. Pick it up, give that line some time to get out behind you, pound it down. But do it pretty hard. And keep your wrist stiff."

The first casts were fine. Charlie kept his arm loose and let Frank show him the motions. But when Frank took his hand away, the next cast draped the line around Charlie's shoulders. And the next cast caught on the grass and accordioned into Charlie's back. "Do it again," he said, giving Frank the rod.

"Watch close, and then we'll get you set up." Frank walked down the dam to undisturbed water, not bothering to hide, not bothering to chum. He cast, and let the egg drift to the bottom, and then he cast again. "See that there? Pounding nails. And watch the line when it goes back."

On the third cast, a fish struck at the egg and Frank's reel was suddenly humming. "There it is," he said, holding his thumb heavy over the line. He glanced up at the sky, at the mountains. "Yessir," he said, "fine, fine day."

This new fish was smaller than the first, and he beached it quickly, hitting it on the rocks and sliding it into his vest. "Your turn again," he said.

Three or four hours passed, and Frank had caught two more fish, each of them over four pounds. But he had stopped fishing to stand behind Charlie while he cast. "Don't worry about watching the line once it's in the water," he said. "They'll take that egg and just suck it on down. It's not like fly-fishing with flies. Just get it out there."

Charlie stepped off to the side to fish over fresh water, casting line in one long, rolling loop. The egg dropped lightly on the surface, laying there for a moment before it began to sink. He gripped the rod handle hard, poised and tense. Everything felt right, but still the egg sank undisturbed. He was lifting his rod for another cast when color bloomed off the bottom. A dull orange roll as brief and sharp as a flashbulb. Then the line's slack was burning through his fist, collapsing his stomach, and drawing the moisture from his mouth. Frank walked up and laid his hand on Charlie's shoulder.

The fish ran fast, parallel to the dam at first but then away from it, deeper, and deeper still. The world had acquired a new center, a pivot around which the lake wobbled like a loose tire. Behind him, the plains began their great surge to the Mississippi. In front of him, the Rockies flared away from the plains in splintered detonations of stone. The fish was the heart of the lake and the lake was the heart of the plain and the plain was the heart of world, outward and outward in spinning revolutions that slung him hard against his own rod. The fish dove deep, and the line hitched as it hit against the bottom. "God a mighty," he said, and grinned back at his uncle.

Frank had taken his hand off Charlie's shoulder and was looking back up the hill. Charlie followed his eyes.

A blue Ford truck stood parked on the rim a quarter mile above them, the afternoon light starring off its windshield, or perhaps a pair of binoculars. As they watched, it began to move down the hill toward them, picking up speed to plow through the first, high drifts of snow. Pastured horses followed behind, head to tail.

"Swing your line over here, Charlie." Frank reached up to the tip of his rod.

"I've about got him," Charlie said, although it wasn't true. He reeled frantically, pulling hard against a fish that was suddenly much heavier. He was already expecting the hook to pull away, already anticipating the sudden, stomach-emptying slack of line.

Frank had a pair of fingernail clippers from his pocket and was reaching for the line. "We got to get going, bud."

"Hold on, I can get it."

"We got to leave, I said."

"Will you hold on?"

There was a moment of pause, a long ten seconds as Frank stepped back. But then he was stepping forward and reaching for the line again, no longer asking. Charlie moved away, keeping the rod tip high, reeling hard, the butt of the rod seated against his stomach. He heard the crunch of Frank's steps behind him, and moved away again. The Ford was closer now, the sound of its motor and the whine of its transmission steadying. They heard the engine shut off, and a car door slam.

Charlie's fish was less than twenty yards away from the bank. He clamped his fingers around the line and raised the rod above his head, backing down the other side of the dam, away from the water, away from Frank. "That's it, then," he heard Frank say. "Are you satisfied, then? Are you happy, then?"

Charlie slipped on the gravel, falling hard on his elbow but keeping the rod high. He slipped again. The fish was still there, still heavy on the line. Charlie slid fifteen or twenty feet in a few long, cascading steps. He was almost at the bottom of the ravine before the smooth texture of the pulling changed into a rough flopping. He dropped the rod and sprinted back up to the water, glancing briefly at the truck at the end of the dam, at the small man in the red woolen jacket walking toward his uncle. Frank stood with his back to Charlie, straight and still, hands in his pockets. The fish lay exhausted on the gravel. Hook-jawed and wide as an open book. A vein out of its skin.

Charlie pried his fingers under the gills, biting at his line even as he was stumbling back over the dam, back toward the truck. The line fell loose, and he ran without impediment, holding the struggling fish at his shoulder, its tail hitting against his thighs and its weight cramping his arm.

He threw the fish on the floorboards and sat over it, breathing hard. He put his head in his hands; he opened the glove compartment. He rolled down the window. Except for the breeze out of the mountains—a breath of wind still somehow fresh and clean—it was quiet. He looked down at the fish between his feet, its sides mottled with the dark, burning colors of an ocean reef. Its head lay on the slope of the gearbox, its tail lay folded against the door panel. He picked at the blades of dead grass stuck to its sides and brushed at the leaves crumpled across one eye. Its gills convulsed and flashed, then lay still. It was so unlike the pale, undergrown trout he had spent the last few years catching around Great Falls and Choteau, those minnows with their oversized eyes and tiny, pinched mouths. This was something he'd never even imagined.

The fish had been lying still for a long time when his uncle finally came back over the dam, vest hanging loose and empty over one shoulder. The man in the woolen jacket walked beside him, and although Frank was much the larger of the two, there was no doubt who was in charge. Charlie stared down at his fish, and then into the hills beyond the lake.

The two men stood talking in low voices at the front bumper of the truck. Frank laid his hand on the hood and listened, nodding and walking a few steps away to light a cigarette and study the mountains. The other man put his hands in his pockets and looked at Frank's tires for a moment, thinking. Then he walked back to Charlie.

"What's your name?" he asked in a Canadian accent. He was a short man, skin-weathered and thin. He wore thick glasses low on a short nose. There was something of the monkey about him. His eyes were gray and cold as cement.

Charlie told him his name, and stuck his hand out through the window.

The man considered it for a moment before deciding to shake it. "Do you know where I got these fish, Charlie?"

"I was wondering."

"British Columbia. Do you know what it takes to bring these fish down from Canada? Did *you* bring these fish down from Canada?"

"I guess I didn't."

"So what did you do to deserve these fish, Charlie?"

"Nothing."

The man put his hand on the truck's rearview mirror and leaned in, his face inches away from Charlie's. "Goddamned right. *Nothing.*"

Charlie stared past him, up to the snow patches and the flat top of the dam. There were still so many fish in that lake.

"Are you going to come back up in here?"

Charlie shook his head.

"Do I have your word? As a man?"

"I guess you do."

"Well, then. That's all right then. Give me that fish and we'll call it good." He opened the truck door.

Charlie lifted his legs, leaving it to the man to reach down for his fish. It slid out onto the ground and the man stepped back, surprised by its size.

"How can anybody own a fish?" Charlie asked suddenly, unaware until then that he was going to say anything at all.

As they pulled away, Charlie reached through his window to adjust the rearview mirror, to watch Becker carry the fish toward the dam. He watched him stop and swing it back and forth to finally toss it, enormous and spinning, into the willows.

Frank drove with both hands tight on the wheel. "You know, seems like buying a bunch of ground like this, buying a bunch of ground and not putting cows on it, letting this pasture go to waste, seems like that's more of a crime than taking a few fish." He reached up and shifted gears. "What'd he want to talk to you about?"

"What?"

Frank breathed heavily through his nostrils.

"He asked me if I thought I owned these fish. He asked me if I thought these fish were mine."

"What'd you say?"

"I said no, sir."

"Was there anything else?"

Charlie thought about it, then shook his head. "No."

"So why'd you run, boy?"

Charlie started to say something about his mother, about staying out of trouble, but Frank shook his head. "Ah, horseshit." His face was flat and hard. "Don't give me that. Don't try to tell me that." He lit a cigarette and shook his head, and that was all.

They didn't talk again that day. Not through Choteau, not around Great Falls, not even when they pulled into his driveway. Frank sat silent while Charlie drew his gear from the bed of the truck, nodding when Charlie lifted his hand. Then he pulled away. And although they went fishing again after that, there was a new absence of trust to everything that they did, or a presence of distrust, and it was never the same.

His mother sat alone at the kitchen table, still in her nightgown and down jacket, smaller than she had been that morning. Her hand lay curled around a half-empty bottle of wine. There was a wine glass on the table filled with cigarette butts. She glanced up when Charlie walked in, then back down.

The right side of her face was a bloom of red, swollen eyebrow to lip. A thin trickle of blood had dried at the corner of her mouth. She had been crying, although she wasn't now. Charlie thought of Jerry's bowling pin arms, and felt sick. He swallowed. His throat worked against nausea, then worked again.

"How was your fishing?" his mother asked.

He sat down next to her, opening his hand on the table.

"I'm okay, Charlie." She tried to smile, but it was all she could do to stretch her lips tight against her teeth, to grimace.

"When did he do this?"

"Damn." She shook her head and took a drink from the bottle. "Goddamnit. I fall in love like foldin' clothes. One man after another. It's no damn good for anybody."

"Where is he?"

"Who knows, who cares." She took another drink, and Charlie knew that her day would end like it had begun, at the kitchen table. "But hey, Charlie. . . ? Promise me you won't fall in love. Hey Charlie?"

He shook his head.

"Promise me." She was very serious now, moving the wine bottle to the side to lean forward.

"All right."

"That's good. That's a good boy. Thank you." She took another drink, and sat the bottle down on the table, hard and off-center. She grabbed at it. "Do you want some wine?" she asked.

He started to stand up, but she reached over and caught him by the arm. She was strong when she wanted to be, and her fingers dug into his skin. "Sit down, Charlie," she said. "Just sit." She let go of his arm and put her head in her hands. "Just sit."

Lately, if his writing has been going well, if he's been looking at the world with the appropriate eyes, he can walk home from his office and see everyone still. The flash of shame that leads—a hammer against his knee—to the faces swinging through and past. Frank as they pulled up to the house: his eyes shadowed, the muscles in his cheeks clenched. His mother crying that night on the front steps. Sometimes, even, he catches a glimpse of himself, the narrow, soft face of a child that has become the unshaven wreck he sees in the mirror now.

At this late age, he finds himself wanting very little. He limps from a car accident three years ago, and his glasses fog even on warm spring days like this one. After the third cigarette, he's breathing hard enough to pause over the idea of his heart, his lungs. The burnt shell of his ribs. Five blocks, and guilt spreads like oil across a pan, leaving nothing but a dull loss; an absence like extracted teeth. It's true for Charlie, as it becomes true for everyone, that he could have done more. That he could have made better choices. But he didn't. And regret floats out of the depths a hundred times a day, and drops again.

His mother died ten years ago, still a young woman as these things go: tired and broke and alone. He had seen her for the last time in a gas station in Missoula, where she'd been working the register. It was snowing outside, and he stood holding his wallet and a Pepsi. He told her that he was taking night classes at the university. She'd gotten another divorce, she said, and was leaving soon for a good secretarial job at the mine in Zortman. He put on his gloves, standing there while she walked around the counter. She hugged him at the waist and stepped back, briefly cupping his cheek in her palm. "Did our luck run out, hey Charlie?" she asked. "I guess our luck might've run out, hey Charlie?"

He thinks about his mother, and Frank, and Jerry. And it occurs to him as an irony that the only advice that has stuck with him, the only wisdom that has come from that day of common wisdom, had come from Bill Becker.

"How can anybody own a fish?" Charlie had said.

Becker had looked at him sharply. But then he had relaxed, smiled, and reached through the window to shake Charlie's hand again. He said that, while it was true that he had bought these fish, paid for and delivered, it was also true that he didn't own them. "But...." he said, enunciating clearly, biting at the words until each syllable stood between them blunt as boards: "But . . . some . . . things . . . own . . . you."

More than a Hiding Place

Fred Haefele

Two weeks ago, my oldest daughter flew into Missoula from D.C. and when I picked her up, I said, Well Kirsten, what would you like to do now that you're here? We could go check out the Kaczynski arraignment in Helena or we could drive over to Jordan and see how the Freemen stand off is going. I mean, it's your vacation and it's up to you. . . .

It was a joke of course, but like many of my friends, at first I took a kind of perverse pride in Montana's unique brand of celebrity. Certainly not because I espouse the causes of Uzi-slinging racists or sociopathic Luddites. But just because, living in a state with barely 800,000 people, how often do you get to hear the CNN anchor say; "Elsewhere in Montana today. . . ?"

So for a while, the gags were coming fast and furious: "Montana—where you're wanted!" or, "Montana: the Last Best Place . . . to Hide!"

Significantly, none of these seem particularly funny now. Things turned sour in a hurry, and helping us toward that end were the hordes of journalists that converged on this state like a hatch of black flies and began immediately to draw a stunningly perspicacious series of conclusions:

—That the natural respect country people have for one another's privacy somehow equates to a kind of complicity. (One columnist from Ohio suggested we didn't watch our neighbors closely enough!)
—That the unrelated incidents at Jordan and Lincoln prove beyond a doubt that Montana is a kind of Destination Resort for every whacko, fliptop, and windchime who ever had an axe to grind.

—That the Jordan stand-off and the Kaczynski arrest are very likely a product of the fact that Montana has no legal speed limit. . . .

A good friend drove past Kaczynski's cabin two weeks ago, when the story was still breaking. He said there was a small army of journalists in the yard, brandishing their boom mikes like medieval halberds, grimly laying siege to the place. Posted at the door was a single FBI agent, who would only let them inside two at a time. There was much jostling for position, and at one point, the journalists were actually trying to out-credential each other in hopes of gaining preference: "Listen, pal," said one. "I should get in next. I've been to Rwanda!"

"Yeah?" said another. "Well, I was in Rwanda and Oklahoma City!"

As if on cue, a rental Taurus suddenly roared into view, bore down on the cabin, hit the brakes hard, and slid to a stop in the gravel. The doors flew open and two journalists bailed out, breathless.

My friend said, "Take it easy, you guys. I mean, you almost hit me."

The driver replied, "Hey. We're on deadline, pal. . . . "

Last weekend, my wife and I loaded our dog and our new baby into the family wagon and drove eighty miles east to have a look at whatever there was left to see in Lincoln.

It's hard to overstate just how small a town it is: situated on the west slope of the Rockies, roughly halfway between Missoula and Great Falls, for years Lincoln's claim to fame was the coldest recorded temperature (minus 75 degrees) in the lower forty-eight. Before the arrival of the High Country Jerky works, the main industries were outfitting and logging. Along those lines, it's worth mentioning that in 1979 I spent my first summer in Montana working in these same woods. It's also worth mentioning that, at that particular time in my life, I was something of a fugitive too. A fugitive from an imploding marriage, from a career gone badly awry. To minimize expenses, my sawing partner and I decided to rough it, and throughout the work week, we lived in a wall tent on site. After a couple days cutting timber we would come into town for a beer, wild haired, covered with dust and pitch. In the end, I suspect, we didn't look all that different from Kaczynksi. Nobody ever bothered us, either. To that small town's credit, nobody even batted an eye.

My wife and I stopped at Lambkin's restaurant in the center of town to get a bite to eat. Aside from some graffiti in the men's room that played off the term "pipe bomb," things looked pretty much the same as they had seventeen years ago. It was peaceful and convivial in Lambkins, and my wife nursed the baby while we ate. I asked the waitress if it was still pretty crazy in town and she nodded emphatically: "Oh yes. We got the boys and girls Class B Basketball tournament going on at the same time."

A heavyset ranch woman in shorts and Reeboks sat across the aisle from us, admired the baby, and we began to talk. The way people do in small towns. At the mention of Kaczynski, she heaved a sigh and scowled. She told us she got so tired of the out-of-towners' disappointment that she didn't know him that she began to tell everyone that she did. "I'd tell them, 'Oh hell yes, I used to shoot pool with Ted all the time.'" She shook her head. "People are so gullible. I mean, I didn't know Ted, but sure, I knew who he was all right. He was just another crazy old guy, riding around on a bike. . . ."

In a box by the register was a stack of freshly minted souvenir T-shirts featuring a tiny silk screen of Kaczynski's cabin with a legend that seemed the soul of discretion:

MOUNTAIN HIDEOUT OF THE SUSPECTED UNABOMBER.

Nobody seemed to be buying them.

By this point, the citizens of Lincoln seem to have had quite enough of the press and Ted Kaczynski. Stemple Peak Road, the site of Ted's cabin, is a right turn at the Conoco station in the center of town. I stopped there for gas, walked in to settle up, and grinned at the woman behind the counter. "So," I said. "Where is it?"

She took my money and, without so much as a glance up, pointed down the road.

In the time-honored tradition of ghouls and rubberneckers the world over, I drove my family three miles down Stemple Peak Road in search of Kaczynski's cabin. It was a brilliant spring afternoon. Ranch families were out burning slash piles and the smoke stung our eyes as we drove along, searching for that now-famous mailbox.

But the mailbox was gone, uprooted for some crime lab. Or to vex the curious, such as ourselves. All there was to see was a Jeep Cherokee parked across the Kaczynski drive. Inside was a bored-looking female agent in a smart flannel shirt and high-top lace up boots that looked to be the J. Peterman Amelia Earhart model. I got out to ask how far up the drive we could go, and she told me we'd already gone that far. I can't say I was terribly disappointed, but I lingered a moment, tried to make small talk. Like you might do with a neighbor. Like we'd just done in the restaurant in Lincoln. But the agent wasn't from Lincoln. Not with boots like that she wasn't. What's more she wasn't interested in the baby or in the fact I'd driven all the way out there with my family. In fact, she gave the impression she'd seen my kind before. She'd seen me through the eyes of CNN, "Twenty-Twenty," "Dateline," and the like. She'd seen that I was another yahoo from the sticks who bore a little closer watching. . . .

Relict

Sandra Dal Poggetto

THE SMELL OF SAGE WAS STRONG as I drew the warm entrails out of the bird and onto the ground. Food for scavengers, I thought.

"To hunt the all-American bird one should have the all-American gun," he said to provoke me as I rose to my feet. I looked with affection at my Spanish side-by-side made by temperamental Basque artisans, and then at the feathery legs of the sage grouse hanging limp from its eviscerated body.

As a painter, I understood the value of having the right tool. Yes, one could hunt pheasant or Hungarian partridge, exotic species that are exquisitely colored, with an import. But the sage grouse calls for something else.

It is a bird plain of feather mirroring its surroundings of bleached umber soil, alkaline whites, and drab sage. Its body swells large at the middle with short neck and tail, like a Greek hydria tipped on its axis. Its sound when flushing is much lower than a pheasant's. Reverberations are hollow and liquid as if the ancient water jar's opening were covered with taut skin, the wing beat drumming and slow to rise.

I had come to love this bird: its plainness, its force, its flavor. It led me into a landscape equally plain, forceful in its empty presence, pungent.

The following winter, at a Helena gunshop, I handled the all-American gun. A Model 12 Winchester pump, made in America like the sage grouse. It possesses a shapely profile, but unlike the Spanish double, is not elegant. It has an economy of form that is pleasing but not ingratiating. And it works well and plainly, leaving the gratifying, if uncouth, metallic sound of the bolt chambering the shell.

My husband's point was not only that the shotgun was homegrown like the bird, but that it held five shells in the magazine rather than the two of the double. Typically, I had learned from experience, one walks miles to locate the grouse, and upon entering the flock the birds flush sporadically. After two shots with possibly one bird taken, they continue to rise. With an empty gun one can only watch as they fly away.

The purpose of a gun with five shells is to bring home the meat. In 1912, Winchester designed and manufactured the firearm for the working man. European gunmakers served the aristocracy and their handmade products were for sport.

While I can appreciate the form of the aristocratic pursuit, the primal joy of bringing home savory and wild meat is what moves me; the primal act of hunting satisfies something ancient in me.

I learn where the animals are, what they eat, and the soils in which their food grows. I learn the shape of their beds and the contours of the land that holds their water. I learn the weather they endure, the predators they suffer. I learn how their bodies are structured by literally taking their bodies apart. In this way, I also learn about myself and participate in what at age five my son called "The Great Charming."

By spring I was standing in the living room of an ex-Marine and veteran of World War II whose Model 12 was for sale. The sixteen gauge felt slim and light in my hands and the focus of the single barrel gave it weight and direction. It was made in 1942 and in excellent condition. It had a cigar-shaped forend, the wood grain was lively, the bore pristine. American guns of this quality were no longer made. There was no question. I wanted it.

He took me into his basement.

The top of his crew cut was as flat and level as the shallow shelves which lined the walls above his work bench. On the shelves were placed useful items, in order. He pulled from a cabinet large sheaves of paper. Each sheaf was riddled with the shot of the sixteen gauge and each looked different and were labeled: twenty-five yards, thirty yards, thirty-five. The shot patterns displayed what he could expect from his shotgun and were evidence that this man was a conscientious hunter.

His voice was soft as he instructed me how to clean the gun. Over the years his care of the firearm was worthy of a Marine and he was trying to insure that I would take the same care.

I watched attentively as he slowly and carefully broke down the gun, so that the barrel was separate and accessible to the cleaning rod. He recommended a certain jig which he attached to the end of the rod and covered with a cloth patch dipped in solvent. He then pushed the rod through the barrel until the bore was absolutely free of residue and the steel shone brightly. I was asked to repeat the procedure. Under his observant eye, I dismantled and reassembled the gun several times: sliding the forend, pushing the pin, turning the barrel until the faint arrows lined up, releasing the barrel from the receiver. The repeated motions became rhythmic and in this way were remembered.

My Montana colleagues tolerate the fact that I hunt and consort with ex-Marines, but the urban artists I know are repelled. They think of my gun as a weapon, my pleasure in eating what I kill as bloodthirsty. They perceive me as a potential redneck and thus question my place among them. An opera connoisseur, European and American bred, summed up the general feeling when he said with disgust, "Why on earth would she want to do that?"

I admit to an unease. I am a woman wielding a gun. Women do not own guns and do not kill beautiful animals. I am a painter who at times finds it difficult to reconcile my attraction to gun powder with my love of powdered pigment. Artists live in lofts, teach at universities; and I do not.

Rather, I move deeper into landscape and the further I go the more distant are my relations with urban artists, the more the gap widens between me and those with an aesthetic eye sharpened by proximity to the great painting collections of the world. This pains me, for it is not only the flesh of the wild grouse that feeds me, but the cultivated mind of the city dweller. To my detractors I am a relict, my atavism proof of their advancement.

There was a time I thought as they, but found I wanted more. More of myself and of my work. This choice they do not and will not understand unless perhaps they *participate.*

I know of one other such person who is taking that step. He is urbane to the bone, but in his marrow he feels the pull of the hunt. An art critic, he wants to touch what lies beneath the great American city.

He sometimes takes to the field with us. When he must cancel, it is with a mixture of regret and relief. Yet he senses and honors why I cannot let go of the hunt. He understands that the pulse of the hunt and of the art are one. They both originate in the great charming.

But do I delude myself? How deep beneath the city streets do I really want to go?

I recently learned that a grizzly bear has taken up residence on the ridge above our cabin near Yellowstone Park. Ranchers who for years have summered their cattle in the area are anxious; one has left it to her husband to fix fence and repair broken waterlines.

Grizzlies can be unpredictable. Will I hunt blue grouse on those ridges as I do every fall? Does the primal tension between the hunter and the hunted lose its charm once I am the prey?

Still, I will hunt. I am not a tourist. And the gun is not my camera. It takes me beneath the city's concrete.

Concrete made of rock and lime.
Lime made of bones.
Bones made of marrow.
Marrow making blood.
Earth making pigment.
Pigment made of blackened bone.
Used in testament.

New Deal

Noelle Sullivan

Deb handed my rye and water over the counter with a grin, knowing I wanted human contact more than the ceremony of drinking. Like everyone else in the Bar X, I wanted perspective and shade from the unblinking eye in the sky. If only the baked clay earth would rotate and pull me into its furrows. I craved a warming darkness, and in the bar's shadows I was glad to see her.

The raw-faced men on the slabwood floor also sought connection, of a more personal nature if they could work that angle. They pushed forward when blonde, bony Deb came near. Reaching out with stained hands, they took whatever liquid reassurance she could offer and dropped coins or government scrip in exchange. I had tried to get the scene on film. In all my time at Fort Peck I took maybe one good picture of that bunch and their true craving, though I've attempted dozens since, in other places. Getting the essence of a night bar on paper is a difficult art, since a crowded saloon has its own structure. The air holds density that doesn't show, and some human column always seems to be getting in the way. Of a hundred soul-seeking men inside such a place, any one can become an obstacle.

"There's Sol," Deb noted that night, "back at his post." Sol was Deb's hurdle. The young man threaded his way toward a splintered pine seat near the kerosene heater from which he watched her each night. She traced his movement with eyes behind reedy, weedy hair. A mere blink in his direction would have summoned him over, and that was the last thing she wanted.

"He's alright," I told her. The darkness had begun to sink in; my hands held my mug tighter as I said it. "He'll leave you alone tonight."

"I wish he wouldn't," she said. It wasn't as it sounded. What she meant to say was she wished he wouldn't hang around there, waiting for her as if she weren't a married woman with a toddler and a public life. As if she had a soft heart that would have allowed her to love a man such as that, anyway. His dark, close-set eyes turned inward to a different god. His stooped shoulders and refracted kindness didn't appeal to her.

"I wish he'd forget about me," she said. There was a wistfulness about the way she wished it, as if she had wanted so many other things that weren't possible.

"I'll talk to him if I get a chance," I said. Deb moved down the bar to fill orders and I finished my rye, opening my notebook to get started. My camera sat waiting, my own ubiquitous eye on the world.

Most of the scabby men and footsore women in the Bar X had come to the Missouri River from the ranch towns of Glasgow or Glendive to line up in work crews at the new dam site. Some of them found barracks in the makeshift boomtown of New Deal rather than in the federal camp a mile upstream. I tried to stay out of their sphere even as I stopped its rotation in my negatives. I wanted to be able to view things clearly, without the haze of involvement. I wasn't yet thirty then. I wasn't a barmaid or a prostitute or someone's wife. I was unfettered. I thought, naively, that I could stay invisible. I carried my huge box camera and tripod like a wooden skeleton in front of me. I crouched behind its all-seeing head.

I had come as far as anyone to reach the dam site and the boomtowns in this Montana river's scraggly cottonwood bottoms. The Bar X sat in an outpost at the end of an unnumbered oil road, a place that few who weren't workers here tried to find. I had stumbled into it for the same reason that all its patrons had: we were in New Deal for the jobs or, more properly, for the money they brought us. My contracted task was to capture images of human engineering as it stopped the flow of the mighty Missouri. I was to send inspiring pictures to my editors back East.

The dam was said to be a necessity. Downstream, in the last flood season, barges had flipped in the river's swollen flows. Then, when the water level at last dropped, boats grounded themselves on churned-up sandbars. The Corps of Engineers came up with the idea of holding water in storage upriver, filling a reservoir in wet years and letting it drain in dry ones. This idea for keeping St. Louis afloat might not have come to anything if the sheepherders of the national stock exchange hadn't sent their herds running downhill. In desperate, depressed hours the President came into his powers. Like a pharaoh, he built pyramids. The dam, held together by earthen fill and federal funding, would elevate him to the gods.

I had been sent west from a glass building in Manhattan to document the President's grandest project to date. My editors chose me to be present at the birthing because my reputation turned on worshipful photos of newborn industrial beauty. Though I had shot pictures of construction sites worldwide, this one was so much grander than any before it. The President had gathered enough men to alter a geography—ten thousand workers paid at government scale, numbered yet numberless like bees.

Buildings and machines aren't complicated in terms of light. They've got solid surfaces and square corners, and with the right shadows it's easy to capture a concrete hardness, a metallic glaze. The dam work, progressing, was harder to fit in frames. At the worksite, the river valley stretched four miles between its sprawling bluffs. From the air, the thin packed-earth barrier the engineers had envisioned bulked like a single hair against the earth's huge face. Shaped like a railroad grade, the embankment held no promising curve. Instead it lay straight, growing with each hour's slurry. Four giant tunnels bored into slate at one side to let the river flow through it when it needed to. Three miles away, a cement spillway slanted down a mile-long grade. A giant's slide, it was too immense to fit into a picture.

So I focused on the workers. I tried to catch men as they moved beside the never-resting dredges and gravel trains. As dawn and dusk brought longer shadows, I aimed to capture men's scratchings at the few outcroppings of steel and dirt. I spotlit welders in the spokes of a steel liner for one of the giant diversion tunnels. Hanging there, they were circus performers on monkey bars. "Hey, Maggie, will my mother be able to see my face?" one of them called out.

Those men were glad to be caught in the act, to have their presence recorded for some future accounting. It was the mindless anonymity of ordinary days that made them flat-faced and rough. That invisibility drove them to places like the Bar X, where there was a ceiling overhead and all men seemed large and human rather than antlike. Inside, away from the radiating sky, we felt less lost. We gathered in the Bar X because it offered us sanctuary, like a tent that could shade our frazzled souls.

Deb had poured drinks behind the bar for five months when I arrived. Her husband, Tommy Maclane, supervised a crew in the gravel yards seventy miles away. She'd seen him last in August, two months gone by. Deb's brother owned the bar but left the running of it to her. She had a fry cook and general hand to help out—mostly he washed the Ball jars that served as mugs, and smoked Deb's hard-earned cigarettes—but she didn't have family with her except her daughter Mamie, who was four.

Mamie was the bar's mascot, though she wasn't usually allowed inside. She stayed in the mudroom off the kitchen until Deb went on break because there wasn't anywhere else to put her. Few knew she was there at all hours. I went to find her sometimes when the smoke or noise got to me and I wanted a child's perspective. Blonde like her mother, she was the happiest one in the place.

Sol knew about Mamie, and about Tommy, but that didn't seem to matter. At first sight he had latched onto Deb's image as if it were a map of where he wanted to go. I don't know what makes a man choose one woman over another, but I suppose it's the same physical requirements and chemical processes that make one picture leap off a page and another sit dull as newsprint. Sol must have thought Deb glittered with an inner light. If the other men reached toward her for the libations she offered, Sol sat back and watched what she was. It unnerved her; it ripped her mask away.

The air inside the bar cloyed once the dayshift arrived. Men smoked and the girls on the floor wore oily scents. Deb left to put Mamie down, and in her absence Sol came over and offered me a smoke. His wrists were thin, his fingers still bent from the day's pounding. I took the butt he held and we talked as we always did, about back home and the Hudson's green corridor in comparison to this dry sink, or about our immigrant relatives, about getting west. We talked around the margins. We didn't discuss the present. Though Deb thought otherwise, I never warned Sol off her and wouldn't have, even if I thought it would do any good. In return, he never asked me why I tried so hard to get pictures of the dime-a-dance women or the prostitutes' lined faces. If the bar was a cloak, our conversations were its lining. We dared not bring some things to light.

Each night a few newcomers would try to figure out what exactly had brought me there. Some tried to use me, coveting pictures they could send back home. Others warned me not to use recognizable profiles. Those men came from churchgoing families who wouldn't have approved of their post-shift activities, especially if they appeared in the pages of *Life*.

The few women in the place, getting what they could from the laborers on the floor and in the bar's back rooms, said absolutely no photos, as a rule. They had told families they were working as typists, not whores. My work wasn't as wearying as theirs, though like a dime dance it didn't require a narrative. Photography is documentation. I aimed at what I saw, but I didn't have to tell the full story. I captured one image, then another, and let the photos speak for themselves. I looked at the world in pieces, through a curving shield of glass.

It was easy for my editors to wire that I was being too proletarian by sticking to the workers, too narrow in scope, but what did they know? They weren't in that windblown western world. They didn't see that the splayed, incomprehensible plains defied portrayal, and that the more important flood at that river site was the human one. I couldn't help but turn to people. I was drawn to their comedies, their dramas in the Bar X, again and again.

To get Deb's attention, Sol had tried so many things. At her second break that night, he put his fist on the counter and made me pry open his fingers one by one to see what he had brought her this time. "You think she'll like it?" he asked. On his palm rested a limestone nodule speckled with tiny, hard points. "It's a petrified fig. Some of the youths digging the tunnels found it." Fossils had turned up regularly as they dug the new watercourse. The men pocketed remains of herbivores, fishes, palm leaves, and other flora of an ancient tropic.

"Passion fruit," I said.

"Ah, go on." He spun the treasured object on his finger and hoped that what I said would be true.

The noise around us ebbed and eddied. Ten or eleven men in beige hats, bent at angles, grumbled at the front tables. They weren't on the construction rolls. They were locals who had lost everything by Presidential fiat. Their fathers had homesteaded the Missouri bottoms, three-hundred-sixty acre tracts proved up in batches. Their uncles had dug ditches to bring the river water to hayfields and gardens. And now they had been bought out, if you could call it that, for market value at a time when the market was at its nadir.

Their arguments rose as the river did behind the dam. Deb didn't like the boys swilling down her booze with their troubles, but neither did she want to turn them away. She had known most of them from childhood. They respected her rule, in general, and so did we. Sol most of all: he kept his distance. It was only because Deb had stepped outside that he could feel free to sit next to me, holding his ovoid, ancient fruit so that it was silhouetted by the dim lights above the counter. "Makes you think about everything we're missing," he said. "Everything that's gone."

"Such as?" I prompted.

"Them dinosaurs. Mastodons. That sort."

"What do you think happened to them?"

"Don't know." He tipped his eyes toward the noisy bunch at the front. "Maybe they found a fermented batch of figs and drank themselves into extinction." He added, in a softer voice, "Who knows. Maybe it was their time to go."

When Deb came in through the kitchen, she saw Sol waiting and flashed me a look that said "Get him the hell out of here." Sol saw it, too, and put a goofy, droop-eyed smile on his face as he lifted his offering to show her. He held it high then left it next to my glass where she could find it when she wanted to. His face stiffened again to a pleasant orb as he pushed his way back to the crowd around the heater.

Deb came out after he'd retreated and went up to the line of men wanting her to pour their nightly medication. "Mamie won't sleep," she told me when she reached for a bottle at my end of the bar. "I can't get her to quiet down tonight. That damn Frank Carlisle's whooping it up next door, too, which doesn't help." She brushed a strand of hair from her sweaty forehead often over the next hour, but she never touched Sol's elegant fig, never even looked at it. After a while I put it in my pocket to show Mamie the next time I saw her. I made sure Sol didn't see me take it. I wasn't going to be the one to drown his hopes.

My editors had cabled that the first photos I sent them were vivid, but not exactly what the President had in mind. I also was dissatisfied with what I'd done. I had wanted to spend more time where I could see frontier emotions, not the mere actions of unnamed men dwarfed by the tremendous country. I had wanted to stay in the shanty towns instead of the supervisors' planned community, where only streets papered with advertisements struck me as good examples of our determination to get something from one another.

Try as I might, I couldn't give up the idea of sending back pictures of those hardened women who worked the floor. There were two or three out there at all hours, from a pool of maybe ten or thirteen. Hurdy-gurdy girls, they made it seem as though women had never come out of the past in spite of the West's promises. They didn't like me much, most of them, although one girl didn't mind talking about how she got there as long as I didn't take her picture. It had been her big break away from Dawson County, she said, and she liked hanging a dress on her shoulders every day. She imagined she might have been stuck in some dry gully, or dry marriage, forever, and this was relatively better. I don't know if she did as most of the others and sold more than dances, but men lined up to take their turns. They left sweaty palmprints on those everyday satins.

The taxi dancers didn't interest Sol. I think it was partly because he had fixated on Deb as the only one who might satisfy him. It was also because he was burdened by guilt: he'd already violated the laws of adultery, coveting a neighbor's wife. A good man by all other standards, he wouldn't break the rules if he could help it. More than that, I like to think he looked for the real person, not the gussied-up husk. Unlike him I loved the dancing women as types, even if I didn't like them as people. I thought that they were brave and entrepreneurial and photogenic. He saw that they were desperate.

After Deb returned, I went back to my lenses. My editors wouldn't have approved of the shots I took, of clay-smudged men clutching jars of draft beer like safety ropes. They stood in groups of like ages or leaned against walls singly, where I caught them. A tall Swede danced with the girl from Dawson County. Ignoring what she'd told me, I pressed my thumb to the button that gave the unexposed film light. My flash burst like gunfire in betrayal.

And then came the flare-up. As I watched, a bubble of unhappiness welled up from behind the couple and the man's head tipped backwards towards my frame. I pulled my camera to my chest just before he fell where it had been. "Son of a bitch!" someone shouted as his swelling face crashed down on the base of my tripod. I couldn't hear him groan as he must have when he hit the hard wood, because the floor squealed and scraped with the sudden shift of chairs and stools. The bar began to whirl.

The fistfight sped up and exposed everyone. All hands were on their feet and kicking with them; every hard fist rose as if to strike. I thought maybe I'd taken a picture of the right man with the wrong woman, but my breaking of a promise was not the focus of the brawl. It had begun instead with those grumblers up front. The local boys had monopolized the taxi dancers as a kind of protest, a way of claiming what should rightfully have been theirs. They pushed the imported day crews out of the way, and one of the less-patient dredge drivers had thrown the first punch.

As the place roiled, I made my way toward the wooden bar, hunching over my camera to keep it from getting broken. It was then that I saw Mamie, half-dressed, at the stool near my knees. At almost the same instant Sol saw her and lunged across the room, grabbing the child's sleeve over another man's flailing arm. We three bent to the boards beneath us as the men surged and swore over our heads. Mamie began to cry in our huddle, more startled than anything, and I whispered soothing words as Sol gripped my elbow and pulled us down in the melee.

A glass broke. Mamie howled harder. A dog barked in a frenzy outside. Sol began to laugh at the strange music and I joined him, and we could not stop it. The noise rang in our ears as the room settled and we finally were rescued by a few men just off the night shift who came in through the back entrance. They formed a denim-covered wall around us. They pushed all who were still hurling fists outside, banging the screen door and setting chairs upright amid Deb's loud cries for order and curses at the whole uncouth bunch. The proprietress was still shaking with anger when she saw Mamie and guessed what had nearly happened. Her face went blank as her cloudy fury cleared to fear. "Oh my blessed God," she said.

Before she picked up her sweet, imperiled baby, that hard angular woman broke her own shell in two. It lay in pieces there, one hard white shield and one soft yolk. In the rising dust, Deb kissed thick-necked Sol hard on the lips and I saw that beneath her crazed surface she had a soft spot for him. I'd even call it love.

Photographers sit at the sidelines and observe, distantly. But what happens when, in spite of all our efforts to remain neutral, we're pulled into the fray? Before I left the Bar X for good, I snapped a photo of that little girl sitting on the bar, intending to print one up for Sol as a memento. I knew even as I clicked the shutter that it would never reach him. More properly, that I would never send it. I wanted it for my own souvenir of a story that had no happy end.

I knew at Deb's kiss that there was a gulf of feeling between them, and that it could never be contained. There was no hope for them. In my few years alone I'd learned one simple thing: admitting a crime never makes it legal. Deb froze up almost as quickly as she had thawed once her swell of fright and motherly instinct was back in check. For the rest of the night she kept Sol at his usual distance. She put the girl up between them, sitting her down right on the counter as she wiped the slowing tears from the child's puffy face. She held Mamie up as a visible barrier, proof of the sanctity of motherhood. Then she built an even larger divider. As soon as the bar quieted again, she placed a call to her brother in Glasgow and told him on the party line that she was quitting. She would go find Tommy at his camp in the morning.

Sol walked out into the dark as soon as she spoke those words.

I packed up my cameras and found him down the street at the Buck Horn Club. He wasn't unconscious yet. I let him sit there for an hour, treating his wounds with alcohol, then took the hand that had held a petrified bit of paradise and led its owner outside. We walked into the chilly October night past the still-clicking engine on the car that belonged to Deb's brother. We passed rows of makeshift bunkhouses and canvas tents and at last reached mine. We leaned into each other to absorb the shock of our movement, hearing nothing but the sound of leather boots against the skin of the road. The predawn galaxies shone against the black beyond.

Inside my tent I wrapped Sol in a gray Army blanket, cocoon against the prairie dawn, and laid him on my bunk. Just before daybreak I took off everything I wore and climbed into that thin trough next to him. I pulled him close and he didn't push me away. Sol and I turned against the changing world that morning with our joints and fleshy curves, dimples and bulging veins. We took refuge from loss in each other, as we'd never taken comfort in others before. We burned ourselves up with a blue heat. We became living wood instead of cogs in a machine.

I left Sol asleep in that darker, better world.

After packing my things, I flipped the tent flaps shut and headed west toward the airport at Billings. I had three hundred miles ahead of me. I hadn't told Deb, or anyone, that my editors had pulled me from the site. I was a woman alone again, lost like a forgotten riverbottom.

The bosses had lifted my pass because the man who had made the grand dam possible was coming to see it. The President wanted to show he was still interested in what happened there. He sought good press for his altruism. He was already on his way west when I got the word. They said I couldn't be trusted to follow through with the right sort of publicity. They pulled me, instead, to focus on the country's already completed diversions. They sent me to the Columbia Basin and its tall walls styled with lofty Art Deco headgates and linear steel beams. I'd find only clean images of progress there. They wanted the ends, not the process.

So I was not the one to document the gauntlet of men who met their leader, hats off, believing he was looking out for them. In someone else's images the beloved President would sit glorious in his open car, waving from the plumped back seat. Another lens caught the men on the job as they gave him a gold-topped cane of willow, and he accepting it without fanfare as his due. I would not see Sol's face in the crowd shots. He would not know my desire to preserve our lost humanity. It was my time to go.

Pictures of half-empty bottles, sloe-eyed men, and working mothers are not what anyone wants to buy. In their magazines, people want glossy fantasies and grandiose constructions. Slick images are a way of pretending the world doesn't wound us; they avoid subjects we cannot approach with words. But the truth, whether it's found in a bar or a photograph or a despairing man's arms, never fools you. You carry it with you for the rest of your days, familiar as a coin or round fossil in your pocket. A hard truth is the only real currency we've got.

Big Ears

Robert Lee

THE GUY HAD REALLY BIG EARS. They were the first thing that I noticed about him, after the gun, of course. I noticed that gun the instant he pointed it in my face. The barrel wasn't very long, but it had a big hole at the end. It was a .44 magnum, they told us after they autopsied the collie, but I don't know anything about guns. I just knew this one looked dangerous pointed right at my face like it was. That big black hole was all I could see.

I didn't see the guy at all until Carol said, "Leave us alone, motherfucker," and he pointed the gun at her. Then all I really noticed was his ears. Christ, this guy had big ears.

Carol says that's bullshit. She says the guy's ears weren't that big. It's just that he had short hair. "You've been doing your aging hippie routine for so many years," she said, "you don't even remember what ears look like."

She's wrong. This guy had big ears. But, when the cops asked me if he had a crew cut, what color his hair was, and if he had a beard or not, I told them they better ask Carol. They said they already had asked Carol, and now they wanted my story. I didn't have a story, except for the gun and the beer and the dog and the guy's big ears. I don't notice all those other things.

Carol likes to say that it's exasperating—that I never notice anything, but I say I notice the important things. "Oh yeah?" she says, and then the quizzes start.

"What color's my hair?"

"Brown." I've been getting that right for months now, but then she wants to know: "What art work do I have on my bedroom walls?"

"Christ, Baby. You change it all the time."

"Like hell. I haven't changed it in six months."

"Well . . . hell, Carol, I don't notice the walls when I'm in bed with you."

"Don't give me that crap. You usually fall asleep before I finish my bath."

"Baby, you take long baths . . . okay, okay, so I don't notice everything. I get all the important stuff. I may not notice what you're wearing, but I know what you taste like."

"All right then, Mr. Observant, just exactly what do I taste like?" She's starting to smile now.

So I think for a moment, but not long enough, and then I say: "Soap. You taste like soap."

Well, the woman up and storms out of my apartment. But it's true. She bathes twice a day. If Eve had spent half the time soaking in the river that Carol spends in the bathtub, all the fish would smell like oatmeal soap.

Still, she's right. There are a lot of things I don't notice. I noticed the ears though, right away, as soon as this guy turned and pointed the gun at Carol. I noticed something else too. Carol was going on and on about this guy being a rotten bastard, and a stupid motherfucker (Carol really has a mouth on her sometimes), but when he pointed the .44 in her pretty face, she shut right up. "Damn," I thought, "that really works."

Unbelievable: Here's this guy pointing a gun at my girlfriend's face, and I notice that it shuts her up. I haven't told Carol that.

Big Ears brought me back to reality pretty quickly though—back to the alley, the scene of the crime. He said to Carol, "What did you call me, bitch? I ought to shoot you right in the face."

Right at that moment, I thought he might. I knew I had to do something. "Hey!" I said.

"Hey, what?" The gun was back in my face now; the big black hole was all I could see. I forgot about his big ears. I forgot about Carol.

"Hey, what?" the guy said again.

"Hey . . . man, what do you want with us anyway? We don't need any of this. We just came out to have a couple of beers. We were feeling pretty romantic until you came along with that gun. What the hell do you want us to do—like you?"

I quit then. I was afraid I'd already said too much. Besides, I was out of breath. And that was the first time I noticed old Big Ears having a conversation with somebody who wasn't there, maybe more than one somebody. He moved his mouth a couple of times, waved his arms around and even closed his eyes once and lowered the gun.

Carol says that's when I should have jumped him. "I would have," she said, "if I'd been as close to him as you were."

"Jesus, Carol, can you imagine me attacking somebody?"

There was a long silence then, and she looked at me in a way I didn't like very much, kind of the way she'd look at a package of beef in a grocery store. Carol is a fussy shopper.

"No," she said, "I guess I can't."

"At least," I said, "not a guy with a gun in his hand."

She looked at me again. "Probably not anyone," she said.

I don't know why that made me so mad, but it did.

"Goddamnit, the guy only looked down for a second. I didn't even have time to think of attacking him."

It was true. I'd been too busy wondering who the hell he was talking to, and what they were telling him. It wasn't a long conversation. Pretty soon he looked up at me. He pointed the gun at me again but at my chest now, not my face.

"Yeah," he said. "I want you to like me. There isn't any reason that you can't. I'm a good guy. I'm just broke, that's all."

So it was a robbery. I relaxed a bit then. I've never had much money, so I don't stand to lose much in a robbery. Carol didn't even have her purse with her. Big Ears might kill us, but I didn't figure he wanted to. I was a bit worried about the voices he was hearing though. I should have been worried about the voice we both could hear.

"Broke!" Carol screeched. "You dumb bastard. Why don't you rob a gas station or a liquor store? Why pick on people damn near as poor as you?"

This time, Big Ears pointed the gun back at my face. "You better tell your girlfriend to shut the fuck up," he said.

"Carol."

"What?"

"You better do what the man says."

"Do what?"

"You heard the man."

"He told you to tell me. I want to hear you say it. You haven't got the. . . . "

"Carol, shut the fuck up!"

"You bastard," Carol hissed, but she didn't say anything more.

Big Ears smiled at me then. "Your girlfriend's got a filthy mouth," he said to me as if Carol wasn't there.

Carol swears I nodded then. I really don't know if I did or not. I remember what I thought though. I thought: "clean body, filthy mouth." Jesus, the thought rang so loud in my mind, I was afraid to look at Carol. I probably did nod. Jesus.

"I've only got twenty bucks," I said reaching for my wallet. "Carol's got a point. You probably should have held up a store."

"No!" said Big Ears, and I swear I saw him shudder. "I can't stand crowds. Crowds make me crazy."

I believed him.

"Besides, " he said, taking the bill from my hand, "twenty dollars is a lot when you don't have any."

"Yeah, I guess I'm about to find that out."

And right then, old Big Ears checked out again, had another chat with the gang upstairs. All the time, jaw moving, arms waving, he was staring at me. Finally he said: "Look, I'll show you I'm not a bad guy. I'll buy you both a beer."

Carol said "No" at the same time that I said "Okay."

Big Ears motioned us ahead of him with the gun. As soon as we started walking, Carol whispered, "What the hell is wrong with you, I can't believe this."

"Hell," I said, "we were going out for a beer anyway."

"You're as crazy as he is."

"Carol," said Big Ears, "shut the fuck up." Then he laughed.

There was a dog outside of the small bar, a collie, and when he saw the three of us, he started barking a loud shrill bark. Big Ears pointed the gun at the dog and said, "Shut the fuck up," but this time it didn't work. Big Ears stood staring. The dog kept barking. I was expecting a shot, but finally Big Ears turned away from the dog and put the gun in his coat pocket. "Come on," he said. "Let's go inside."

Carol tried again: "I thought you hated crowds."

"This place won't be crowded. Besides I'm just going to buy you two a beer. Then, I'm leaving."

The place wasn't empty. There were a half dozen people in there drinking. It struck me that crowded is a relative term. The thought made me nervous. The bartender finished waiting on a customer at the other end of the bar, and came toward us.

"What do you want?" Big Ears asked me.

"How about a Beck's dark?"

Big Ears laughed. "Who's robbing whom?" he asked. Then to the bartender: "Two Miller Lites." "You're getting a little fat," he said to me, as the bartender put the beers on the bar.

I relaxed then, but it was too soon.

The door opened and five more people came inside. The small bar was suddenly crowded. The three women and two men were drunk and loud, and they left the door open. The dog outside barked louder than before.

"Jesus Christ," one of the drunks said. "Somebody ought to shoot that fucking dog."

Big Ears was talking to himself again, and he had the gun out in plain sight.

"No!" Carol shouted. "No, you can't shoot that dog."

Big Ears had started toward the door, but now he turned, grabbed Carol by one arm, and holding the gun to her head, pushed her in front of him.

"Hey!" I hollered.

"Stay there," said Big Ears. "And shut up."

It worked.

They were outside. I heard the dog barking. I heard a shot. The dog stopped barking. "You bastard!"

That was Carol's voice. Then another shot. Then nothing.

Even then, I stayed where I was.

The whole thing with the cops took over an hour. It was nearly midnight when Carol and I got back to my apartment. I made coffee, and we sat at the kitchen table and talked for another hour about what had happened.

"I don't believe he shot that poor dog twice," Carol finally said.

"The second shot didn't matter."

"It mattered to me. And you, I don't believe you—drinking both those beers before the cops got there."

"If I hadn't they would have confiscated them."

"Well, they were evidence."

"They were beers, and I paid for them. You didn't want one, so I drank them both."

"The cops were pissed at you."

"It's not the first time."

"I'm pissed at you."

"Yeah."

"I don't believe you let that creep take us to that bar."

"He had a gun. Besides, I don't really think he's a creep."

"Oh yeah, what would you call him?"

"I call him Big Ears."

"Goddamn you. You always think you're so fucking cute. Even when some asshole has a gun to your head, you have to be clever." Carol was standing up now, putting on her coat. "Yes sir, Mr. Big Ears, buy me a beer. How about a Beck's dark? You're right; my girlfriend does have a filthy mouth. Why don't you take her outside and shoot her?"

She slammed out the door.

It's nearly three a.m., and I'm still drinking coffee. It started to rain a few minutes ago. There's hardly any traffic left on the streets. The couple across the hall just came home. They're arguing. Last night, they were making love. It sounds about the same when you can't see what's going on. I know if I go to bed and close my eyes, I'm going to be staring at that gun again—or worse.

Carol is probably in her bubble bath. I could call her. She has a speakerphone in her bathroom. I even know how the call might start. We've been doing this a long time.

"Hello?"

"Come on back. I feel like a robbery victim."

"It's about time you noticed."

I notice more than she thinks. The trouble is I don't know where the conversation goes from there—where we go from here.

When Carol came back into the bar, after the shooting, she looked small and scared. But I didn't go to her. I couldn't. I just turned back to the bar and started drinking those beers.

The cops were pissed at me, but I think drinking the beers was only a small part of why. They made me go out and look at that dog. I'd thought it was a big dog when it stood in front of the bar barking at us, but it sure looked small lying there dead. One shot had blown most of its head away, but that wasn't the bad part. The other shot hit the dog in the stomach, split it wide open, yellow green bile oozing from a raw red wound. It smelled terrible. The younger cop nudged the dog with his toe.

"That could have been your girlfriend," he said, and I looked at him. "That could have been you," he said.

"I wonder whose dog it is," I said.

Carol doesn't want to talk about the dog. When I asked her earlier, if Big Ears shot the dog in the head or in the body first, she said she had no idea. She said she closed her eyes, and didn't open them until she heard Big Ears walking away. She never did look at the dog, just watched Big Ears until he turned the corner. "He never did run," she said.

I think Big Ears knows he can't get away. If I called Carol right now, and started describing what I saw when the cops made me look at that dog, she'd scream at me. Then she'd get out of the tub with a splash and leave the room, or hang up the phone. I've never been good at leaving the scene. And screaming doesn't help. Being clever only helps a little.

Manus Dugan

Ron Fischer

When a sudden gust of hot air blasted him, Manus Dugan sensed that something wrong had happened in the mine. The wet timbers receding into the dark of the crosscut seemed thin and fragile. Old worries tormented him. His child refused to be born. Madge was ten days overdue. Every night, he went to work with regret and now this. Dry air doesn't sweep down a mine stope twenty-six hundred feet underground, particularly from the direction of the elevator shaft. In the dark silence, Manus could hear the mine timbers creak and felt a shrinking in his bones. He left his ore car on the skid rail and walked toward the shaft to find out what it meant.

He pictured Madge at home lying across the bed. He could hear how the bedsprings would strain and see Madge's fist wad the purple blanket lying on their bed, her other hand clutching her swollen belly, her face grimacing because of a cramp. Desperation made him walk faster. Day after day, she was pregnant. It made him helpless. In the mornings, he came and lay beside her, listening to the ore trains rumbling over the sunlit hillsides of Butte, the day bright against the skein of green window shade. Sometimes she cried softly and he held her, feeling awake, feeling her heavy, auburn hair against his face until he drifted into dreams of the mine and its black tunnels.

"Let the other fools blast themselves to bits," she had said loudly when he had asked her to marry him a year and a half ago. Straight time for the Company, that's what she wanted him to work if she was going to get married.

"But there's money in contracting."

"Two hundred dollars is widow's pay when the mine caves. I don't want a man with dirt so deep on him he's got to let it wear off and who'll live past thirty-five only if he's lucky."

What could he say? She had red cheeks on winter days that put you in mind of the petals on a moss rose. Her bright eyes could glance on him and suddenly numb him all over, like having a hammer smack his thumb.

So he gave up mining, went straight time, and took the nipper's job. Maybe he still worked underground carting steel drills and dynamite to the contractors, but he didn't have to stand under loose rock or breathe the gray dust kicked from a miner's buzzie as it hammered hole after hole. After six months of straight time, she married him. It was the closest thing to gold yet.

Manus stopped cold. A black cloud rolled slowly down the crosscut toward him. Smoke hung about two feet off the floor and billowed around him. There was a fire burning somewhere. The shaft? He took a breath. The air tasted bitter as green willows burning and its ash nudged deep into his lungs where it twitched a cord that made him cough and hack. He backed ten feet away.

He could hear the faraway cracks of explosion and the dull thunder of fire. His neck muscles tightened. He looked at the shell of smoke and imagined bright gold flames bursting the dry timbers of the shaft into ribbons of black ash. The whole shaft, a tower of dry beams and planks half a mile long, was exploding into a volcanic hole. He could picture the glowing cinders and dark smoke rippling from the blazes, blood-red fire balls leaping higher and higher, the long well of liquid blackness roaring with its immolation, and the flames finally erupting on the surface into a blazing geyser, torching the headframe and the elevator cages, spraying the mineyard with white-hot embers, spewing a black cloud of soot into the sky.

In the distance, he heard someone inside the fumes wheeze for air and cough. "Faron!" He called the names of the miners he had just left. "Faron! Ansely! Faron!"

Manus sucked in a breath and charged into the curling cloud. When he needed to breathe again, he stooped over and kept his face in that margin of clear air left between the smoke and the ground. When the smoke filled the whole crosscut, he wrapped his arm around his head and breathed through the crook of his denim jacket. His carbide light was so dim it was useless. He smacked into a stull and knocked himself down. His cheek lay against the warm steel of the tram rail. His eye caught the sequin of his carbide flame reflecting off the worn steel. The mine rock looked gray against the feeble glow of carbide. No one coughed anymore. The air was hot as a furnace. Although he took his breath through his sleeve and held it as he crawled, his lungs flared as if scraped by a rasp. It was all he could do to hold a cough back.

He touched the man's shoulder, then grabbed a whole arm and felt the body flop. He felt for the man's nose to see whether he was still breathing. His fingertips touched something sticky and warm, blood. Had the man torn his own throat to get a gulp of good air? Manus bolted for clear air. He tripped over the tram rail, got up, and ran on, feeling dizzy and blind. The few minutes it took to stumble into clear air seemed unending. Had the entire crosscut filled up with smoke? Suddenly his carbide lamp opened like a small hand of light against the rock and receding timbers.

When he stopped and turned to look at the cloud swirling toward him, he felt like he had stood for years on this same spot. Life suddenly seemed to repeat itself. A drop of water fell from the rough ceiling above him and landed on his neck. His fingertips were stained with small rusty spots. Looking at them, he felt the bones of his spine bristle. He coughed and the phlegm in his throat tasted syrupy.

Trapped. There was no way up. Madge and the baby left without him. He had to calm himself. Staying out of the wood gas meant everything now. Somewhere ahead the other miners of the twenty-six hundred were still working. He had to warn them. He began running down the crosscut, his boots thudding against the rail ties, crunching the gravel of the railbed.

He met a crowd of miners who had also felt the rush of hot air and were making for the shaft. Bill Lucas smiled at him. Bill was seventeen, gangly legged and cocky. Bill's eyes darted from Manus to Leonard McClure, the miner who was breaking Bill in. Leonard saw to it that Bill was paying the price: blisters and backache. Manus liked Bill because he didn't peter out. He stuck to his job. Right now he was sorry Bill had.

"The shaft's on fire," Manus said.

Leonard shoved his hat back and rubbed his hairline. With his hat tilted back like a skull cap and with that leather apron over his trousers, Leonard looked like the barrel-chested Jewish butcher who had a shop on Main Street. Whenever he saw Leonard, Manus saw another version of himself, the man Manus was afraid he would become if he hadn't married Madge. Alone and angry, his best feelings blasted and mucked out years ago. The rich veins of compassion traded for whiskey and the empty pockets the girls on Venus Alley leave a man with.

But what did it matter now? As certainly as he knew the smoke was drifting toward them, he knew that he faced the deepest stope he had ever come upon. This would test all the timber and lagging he had inside him. He couldn't panic. He couldn't let the whole mountain of his being collapse. There had to be a way out. "We got to hole up somewhere and keep the smoke from choking us."

"No," Murphy Shea said. Shea was a Wobbly. He shoved between Leonard and Bill. "The manways. We'll climb out of here."

"What the hell?" Leonard shouted. "We can't climb a half mile out of here." Bill Lucas didn't smile anymore. Spiro Bezersich, Al Cobb, Gozdenica, and the others stared at him.

"We can try," Manus said, knowing the Speculator Mine had a tunnel into the Rainbow Mine on the twenty-two hundred level. "The twenty-two. Just far as the twenty-two. We can walk into the Rainbow and ride the cage up from there."

"Twenty-two," Gozdenica said, "we make." Gozdenica started shoving through the miners, taking the lead toward the raise that had ladders coming down from the twenty-four hundred. As they walked, Manus made out the smudged faces of John McGarry, Spiro Bezersich, Krist Popovich, Joe McAdams, and Al Cobb. Gozdenica, usually smiling-faced, turned to look at them. He seemed expectant and uncertain. The lime dry smell of dynamite lingered near the last drift they passed. Manus' shirt, wet with sweat, clung to him.

Leonard had a way of sprawling his elbows and legs to make himself the biggest man in a room. Bill Lucas butted around Leonard and Manus. Bill had quit school a year ago. Since then, Manus had watched him load ore cars, muck, and even drive mules on the tram. He was a fast learner who worked hard. As Bill walked in front of them, Manus could see Bill had even picked up Leonard's way of walking, high-headed, like he was some kind of wonder man who knew how to break a dollar's more worth of ore than any other miner, how to wash all the dust out of his blood with a couple of beers and hang on a little harder to those ringlet-haired chippies down in Venus Alley. Leonard, who knew stopes where the rock broke easy, bars where the silver dollars squeezed out of your hand like mercury, and girls who slid under you just as easy, was responsible.

In the manway, men bunched up as everyone waited for the fellow ahead of him to climb high enough so the miner's heels wouldn't boot against his head. Manways and stopes, tunnels and shafts, the mine was a honeycomb without honey. At least they weren't on the thirty-two hundred, Manus thought. The manways didn't go that deep. No one there had any chance of getting out. All he had to do now was open his palm and an iron rung suddenly filled it. He was climbing out.

At the twenty-four hundred, Manus followed the miners ahead of him down the crosscut and toward the next manway up. No one spoke. They panted and their clothes rustled, their heels crackled the ground. Manus' carbide and the miners' candles etched the bark-stripped posts into gray bones and fragmented their shadows into dark starlings that flitted and weaved across the rock wall.

Before they reached the manway on the twenty-four hundred, some miners ran into them from behind. Negretto and Worta, Evcovich and Jennis, Jovick, Ned Heston and Godre Galia, and some others—men from the twenty-four hundred. There were many now, maybe twenty or more.

"Gas cut us off," Ned Heston said. His hands looked like fat potatoes.

"How far back?"

"Coming fast."

Herb Carlson behind them stumbled into Manus and apologized. "They're shoving."

"Smoke's coming on 'em," Ned said.

At the manway, Manus heard Leonard shouting, "Keep climbing."

"He won't," Al Cobb said.

"Who's up there?" Leonard demanded.

"Gozdenica."

"That bastard better move his ass!"

Men were strung along the ladder, but no one climbed. "Let them down," Manus said, seeing that the highest men on the ladder were stepping down instead of climbing up. "Give them room."

"Come down," Leonard bellowed. "Get your ass off and let me up."

Steve came into view. "We're cut off. It's all smoke up there."

Manus shined his carbide upward and squinted into the heights. He saw billows of gas. Behind him men in the stope coughed. Leonard shoved to the iron ladder, clutched its rusty railing, and grabbed Popovich's shoulders as if he wanted to fling him against the wall. McAdams, Murphy Shea, and a few others pushed through the crush of men to get beside Leonard and get at the ladder.

"No one goes up," Manus said. The whites of Leonard's eyes bulged and Shea set his jaw firm.

"Stay here and die then," Leonard took the unlit cigar that he chewed on from his mouth and tossed it against the rock wall.

"Stay together." Manus looked at the wild eyes that showed like hens' eggs in his light. "No one can make that climb. Not in gas."

"We go 'til we drop," Leonard said.

"No!" Manus made a fist. "We hole up. All of us, in a blind drift."

"The twenty-four seventeen." Steve waved from the ladder. Cobb and Ned Heston repeated his words and headed out of the manway. Motes of dust rained through the dim light. Everyone else held their ground to see what Leonard did.

"All right, all right." Leonard waved them to follow Cobb and Heston. "The twenty-four seventeen."

Manus believed in his chances of living when he could keep moving. Al Cobb, a short man who wore a woodsman's cap cocked to his right side so that his oversized left ear stuck out like the handle of a coffee cup, led them toward the twenty-four seventeen. When everyone stopped, they were facing forty feet of a dead drift.

"What we do?" Jovick asked.

"For Chrissake. Bulkheads. Two of them. Here and there. Them posts and laggings. Pull that canvas off the vent. Pile up rocks. Dirt. We gotta build us two goddamn walls. One here. One away, about two yards away."

Manus pulled out a pocket knife and cut into the canvas of a vent. "We can use this to line it." La Montague started ripping more of it down. Cobb took a hammer left in the drift and knocked a stull out of a drift set.

They understood. Jovick uncoupled a hydraulic line. "Is there air?" Manus asked.

"Naw, dead."

"Take a couple pieces of pipe."

With the two walls shaping up, Bill Lucas suddenly disappeared down the drift. Manus wondered if he was following Leonard back to the manway. But Leonard was there, shoveling rock and dirt out of the drift and packing it into a mound against the bulkheads. Bill suddenly came back with a small waterkeg left in the crosscut. It was about a quarter full.

"We're gonna need this."

"Get behind the bulkhead."

McAdams and Gozdenica brought boards from the drift set walls. Manus saved a piece of canvas to make a flap for a crawl space between the inner wall and the bulkhead. He had trouble pulling enough saliva together to spit the pasty, sweet dust out of his mouth.

When the walls were finished, he and Cobb waited in the six feet of space between the makeshift bulkheads, plugging holes when they saw wisps of gray smoke seeping through. Where the wall met the ceiling was weakest. One candle burned in the blind drift where the miners sat, backs against the bare rock, and another flickered where Manus and Cobb sat. There were twenty-nine of them. They ripped their shirts, handed up trousers and socks to Cobb and Manus to seal out the smoke.

"That's enough." They settled back, like two rows of bats, their backs against the rock wall. Their naked flesh seemed white as talc in the pale glow of candlelight.

"Take this, for later." Manus gave Cobb a second length of pipe afterward. Cobb cocked his head, his protruding ear a question mark.

"What for?"

"When they come at us." Manus said it dryly. He gripped the pipe, thinking that no matter how hard it would be to swing on a man he had worked with, he'd rather see the miner hurt than dead. "Are you with me? If you can't, I'll understand."

Al hefted the pipe against his palm, then slowly nodded. His calloused palm was black with dirt.

Manus felt the weight of his watch and his nipper's pad touching his chest through his shirt pocket. He wondered whether Madge had had the baby. He took out his watch and checked the time, thirteen minutes after midnight. It would come at a time like this, he thought. They were only into the shift an hour.

It pained every time he took his watch out. Hours became the ballooning of men's shadows on the rock wall, the dank smell of wet earth mingling with burnt wax, the jab of a sharp rock against his back until the nerve twitched, the burning down of a candle until it sputtered and got replaced before dying out, the shuffle of men who took turns at watching the first bulkhead for seepage.

"We hit the motherlode this time," said Leonard.

Manus fingered his nipper's pad where it rested in his shirt pocket and mapped out all the things he wanted to write on it. La Montague reached a cigarette to the short candle flame. His tobacco glowed ember red as he sucked on the scraggly rolled twig, creating the only color in the dullness.

"Put it out," Leonard said, but La Montague inhaled and turned the red glow gold. "You're burning good air." His arm stretched out and he snatched the cigarette from La Montague's face. La Montague cursed at him in French.

"Leonard's right," Manus said. "No one smokes. Give me the rest of it, La Montague. All you pass it up."

He dug a hole away from the wall and buried their tobacco. McGarry mumbled a tune to himself. Henry Fowler had a pack of cards and started a game with Mike Spihr and Atha Stewart. Negretto had his head lowered and mumbled over and over something quiet and Catholic. Murphy Shea leaned back on his elbows and kicked Negretto's feet. "God's a bum bastard." Negretto swallowed and looked away from Shea. Shea grinned, repeated himself, and laughed.

Hours later, Manus took another turn between the bulkheads. The air smelled worse in this small space than in the big chamber. Smoke had seeped through. He couldn't see where, no fumes showed, but the air had fouled. The candle burned dimmer, and his breath came heavy as syrup. He didn't know which to fear more, the gas or the slow poisoning of the big chamber by every man whose breathing stole another fresh gulp of oxygen and who exhaled poison.

Away from the others, Manus took his nipper's pad from his trouser pocket. His partner, Steve Gozdenica, looked at the smudge of white paper Manus held in the dark chamber and looked away as if he didn't want to see it. Manus regretted that Gozdenica saw it. He wanted to write Madge, but he felt that saying anything somehow admitted defeat, betrayed the hope. He didn't write what he wanted to say or what Gozdenica, whose eyes kept shifting away from him, believed he was writing. He wrote just the facts:

> Been here since 12 o'clock Friday
> night. No gas coming through bulkheads.
> Have water. All in good spirits.

He squinted to see the dark pencil marks and held the white paper close to his eyes. He hadn't betrayed their hope.

"What time is it?" Leonard asked Mannus when he crawled back into the blind drift.

"Nine o'clock."

"Morning?"

"Naw, night."

"Saturday?"

"That's right." Twenty-one hours of waiting had passed. Leonard lay on his side without saying anything. Men had shit in the diggings, pissed. Sweat loaded with the sharp adrenaline of their fears had made their bodies smell sour as apple vinegar, and exhaled carbon dioxide soured the chamber even more. They took a turn at the water keg. Leonard passed his up.

The water was warm. Manus dozed for the first time until the rumble of sliding rock shook the blind drift.

"Someone's coming," Bill Lucas said.

Manus felt the ground tremble again, then heard rocks and timbers clunk as they fell against each other.

"It's a cave-in somewhere," Leonard said, "below us. Probably water they've poured on the fire's flooding the thirty-two hundred."

"Won't be long now."

"Won't they be surprised to find us?" Gozdenica said.

"We got to let them know we're here." Nick Jovick began tapping the compressed air line with a rock. Jovick made heavy thuds with a dirge-like slowness. A metallic clang knocked the walls, traveled down the crosscut and, as Jovick and Manus hoped, as far as the shaft, even up the shaft to some listening ear that could pick out his muted throb from all the noise and know it had bubbled up from half-a-mile underground, that someone was still alive and wanting rescue.

Then time became turns at hammering. McAdams took a turn, Ned, even Murphy Shea. Shea's pace settled into the same slow thuds that Jovick had made. Manus could hear the hollow metallic ping travel up the compressed air line. Looking intently serious, Shea hammered with the earnestness of one in true prayer. Maybe that's what all prayer is, Manus thought, the monotonous hammering out of hope.

The pings wore into them. Far off in the mine, rock continued to slide. No one noticed it anymore. Spihr and Fowler no longer shuffled cards but stayed prone, close to the ground to get the good air that had settled there. The candle made only a faint glow now. In his trouser pocket, Manus had just two remaining stubs of the candles he had collected. He decided that when this candle was burned out he would let the darkness settle around them. It would make things worse, but there was no sense burning good air and using up their last hope for light. He wondered whether news of the fire had shocked Madge into giving birth.

"Is anybody gonna spell me?" came Krist Popovich's voice. "I've been at it longest."

Leonard took his place. After a long row of clinks, he hurled the rock against the pipe. It struck a sharp clang and opened every eye.

"It's no use. No one's coming. Not now. Not ever. I say we break the bulkhead and take our chances. The fire's gotta be out. The smoke's cleared enough for us to make a climb. What do you say, Manus?"

"We'll test it. Nobody'll get far in that gas. Me and Cobb'll check it first."

They pulled some canvas from the wall and ceiling. Smoke streamed through the dirt and chinks. Although Al raised a candle, the flow of black smoke wasn't hard to see.

"Close it up." Manus said. "We'll try lower. Maybe it's hanging above the floor." They shoved a pipe beneath the wall. Fumes flowed out of the pipe, even though its end was on the ground. Leonard didn't say anything after Manus told them about the gas.

"Me and you'll timber fifty-feet," Manus said to Bill. The boy had a vacant look on his face ever since Leonard threw the rock down. His open hands lay in his lap, palms up. The white of them showed in the dimness. His face seemed sunk, too hollow for sadness.

"That boy's already learned to tell a ping from a thud. Ain't no loose rock gonna take him out," Krist Popovich threw in.

"He's learned to bar down real good." Manus smiled at him.

"It's dangerous," Bill said.

"She ain't over yet." Manus looked from face to face when he said it.

"I mined. Least I can say I did."

"Damn rights," said Popovich. "We gonna get you home yet so you take the next shift out."

"Ain't no next shift in this mine."

"Be somebody got to put it back together."

Manus closed his eyes. Memory could beat this monotonous waiting, turn the darkness into blue sky with clouds unfurling like sails and driving across the vast open space of a valley—no walls, not even the rank smell of his own breath flowing back to him. After a while, Popovich got the hand-sized rock Leonard had thrown away and began rapping the pipe.

Manus passed the water keg around for everyone to dip a finger in so they could wet their lips. The keg had gone almost dry. After lying in the dirt so long, wheezing for a breath, roasting in the heat of the crosscut, a man became so thirsty his lips stuck together. Manus allowed them just a finger's worth and trusted them with the keg. As the keg passed from man to man, the wooden thumps of hands touching its barrel sounded.

When the keg came back, Manus took out his nipper's pad. He had seen their faces as each man pressed a glistening finger to his lips and he felt a need to explain. They blamed him for being trapped here. He sensed that in the way they looked at him. His pencil whispered across the scratchpad:

> We were caught
> in a trap. Gas
> everywhere. Built bulkheads.
> Could hear rock fall.
> Rapped the pipe continuously
> since 4 o'clock Sunday morning.
> No answer.
> Must be some fire. Hard
> work ahead of the rescuers.
> Have not
> confided my fears to anyone.

The whittle of his pencil sounded on the coarse paper. No one slept, not if he could help it. They would be opening the sky left inside them or just vacant, listening, hearing his pencil whisper its soft words.

"Write my Beth," Murphy Shea said. Everyone had heard him write. "Tell her we did the best we could."

They called out names then. Sarah, Anna, Carolyn, Mary, Rachel. Manus heard only the thin sound of resignation roll through their throats. He thought of stockyard cattle. Leonard stood up. His dark shadow looked like an old grizzly sow's. His leather apron was gone. With his shirt gone, his skin burnished ghostly in the candlelight.

"Goodbyes is it?" He stepped forward as he said it. "I'm not gonna die waitin'."

"Don't make this ugly." Manus rose up and slapped the pipe against his palm, but he understood Leonard. He couldn't blame Leonard for wanting to fight out.

"You'd use a pipe on me, huh? How many are goin' with me? Stand up. Don't let Dugan stop us."

"You're choosin' for all of us if you break that wall, Leonard."

"And just who are you choosin' for?"

"I won't let you do it. It ain't time for that yet." Manus had the pipe poking up in front of him, ready to use it on any man who made for the bulkhead.

"I say it is. Get up." Leonard yanked Yrja Johnson up. James, Shea, Bezersich, and McGarry stood up too. Cobb stood and came beside Manus, flashing his pipe for them to see. Steve Gozdenica made a hard fist and joined Manus. So did Jovick.

"All right, it's us and them," Leonard said. "And the rest of ya? You gonna wait and die in here when the air goes poison?"

Bill Lucas stood up with Leonard this time, getting right beside him. Manus didn't swing on Bill when they charged. He went for Leonard, swung the pipe, and broke Leonard's head open. The big miner fell hard, the side of his face sticky with blood. Manus didn't whack him again but waited to see what Leonard would do next. Cobb shoved Bill to the side and used the pipe across his back. Jovick and Shea pushed and wrestled with the others.

Murphy Shea pulled Leonard away from the bulkhead. The fight was gone out of Leonard.

"I don't want them to hear about it up top," Manus said. "Don't you be saying what happened down here. It don't look good for miners fighting themselves. We got to keep our heads. If we wait things out, they won't have to carry us out of here on slats." He threw the pipe against the bulkhead. It rattled and bounced into the dirt.

Murphy Shea nodded agreement. "Manus is right."

Stretching and flickering to stay alive, the candle flame thinned into a faint wisp. The carbon dioxide from all their breathing had filled the chamber with dead air. The candle sputtered in a last try to draw more oxygen, then went out. The darkness plunged so absolute, Manus felt how near they had come to the abyss. It was like slipping out of his body and pulling the blackness into himself. How can there be anything solid again, he wondered. At first he felt lost. To get his bearing, his ears picked up every saw of breath, even the gurgle of air inside Al Cobb's throat, its gritty rasp against his teeth, tongue, and nostrils.

Without the light, the bulkhead at his back became the only real thing. The darkness settled the weight of inevitability on him. He sensed the others feeling it too. Someone groaned. A hush would pass and then someone else would moan or choke back a cry. Sometimes an outright cry sounded, like a muffled howl that ended in huffs of breath. When men called the names of women, the blurt of their voices stabbed the blackness like sudden lightning. Some prayed out loud and others burst out crying, making no effort to hold it in anymore.

Men pawed the ground to stir oxygen out of the dirt. Manus could hear the scrapes of their clawing. He did it too, scraped a trench to hold his face into, hoping the hollow spot might catch him one gulp of breath to relieve the tightness. It was slow suffocation. But he could breathe easier; scraping freed enough oxygen in the loose dirt to make a difference.

No one rapped the pipe any more or waited between the bulkheads where the gas had grown too strong. They lay weak, almost lifeless, and groaned for air. He didn't want to hear them breathe those last dying gasps. He pictured his own death coming to him as he slumped against the bulkhead—Madge left alone, except for his child. Maybe she had his child by now.

He called Madge's name into the darkness. Then he wrote his last note, using both hands to place each word:

> If death comes it will be by all
> oxygen being used from the air.
> My Darling Madge,
> It hurts my heart
> to be taken from you.
> Think not of me,
> if death comes it will be
> sleep without suffering.
> I ask forgiveness
> for any pain I ever caused you.
> The place is for
> you and the child.

He tucked the note into his trouser pocket. Dying together served no purpose. He didn't want their lives on his hands, not anymore. He didn't want to hold them back. They had waited long enough and now they were waiting for the inevitable.

"Leonard," he said. "Get up. It's time we make a try." Pulling planks away from the interior wall, he made a hole large enough to get easily through. He went to the outer bulkhead. "There's good air in the Rainbow. Head for the twenty-four raise." He forced himself to stand straight. Ned Heston joined him; so did McAdams. Bill Lucas got up but hesitated.

"Go on. Go!" Leonard sunk his head back down on the ground.

"Leonard?" Manus said, "You coming?"

"Go get 'em, Manus. I'll be resting right here, waiting for you to come get me. Tell Katie I want to see her dance naked to the Whiskey Bottle Honkytonk when they bring me up." The others lay prone, passed out, maybe dead or feeling too hopeless to try.

Manus and Ned tore a hole in the bulkhead. Gas swarmed lazily in. They headed down the drift, Manus, Ned, and McAdams with Bill Lucas following.

Manus went to the manway and began climbing the ladder. Only Ned and McAdams were behind him. He could not see Bill Lucas on the ladder. The smoke was pretty thick.

It made me hold my breath to hear that bell. First nine bells rang, then six, then two. The danger signal. Felt like a thunderbolt had cracked heaven open. Nine-six-two, just like that, from out of nowhere. Over and over. Then twenty-four bells. I had my mask off and could smell the sweet odor of burnt flesh that hung over the mineyard ever since the fire. You just don't get used to a thing like that. It seems to be in the air even when it isn't. The sky was grayer than before. It felt like it took an hour just to count off those bells.

A few women were wandering through the rows of bloated corpses. You couldn't stop them from doing that. They had to come and look. They'd hold handkerchiefs soaked in camphor over their faces so they could stand the smell. I could tell them it was useless. But that was useless too. It was a sorry sight, not something a woman should have to see. One hundred sixty-two by last count, corpses with black and swollen faces, fat cheeks like melons, noses buried, lips split and fingers big as butcher sausage. I'd carried over twenty of them up myself, but just thinking about what some poor woman had to carry the rest of her life left me cold.

I headed for the cage right away. You see, I was on the crew that checked the twenty-four hundred yesterday. There was nothing in that crosscut. I mean nothing, not one body anywhere.

Me and Tom O'Brien climbed in the cage together and went down to have a look. We found some boy. He kept telling us there were others. I believed him, but Tom said, "We got to get you out of here." Which we did because the boy got sight of a water keg by the station and a powerful urge was on him to have a drink. I had to hold him back. Ain't nothing more poisoned than water that's been through a fire.

There was a wind blowing. I didn't notice it myself, before that is, but when we got the boy up top, he started shivering and the bumps on his naked skin rose up. We got him to the dry fast as we could. Tom told the big boss that there were others down there. We must have walked right up to their bulkhead and turned around. Shit, I thought, and my stomach went tight, though I knew the best thing was not to think about it.

I had seen some awful things in the last three days, like the two station tenders who rode the cage down to find out what the smoke meant. That was the beginning of trouble. By the time the hoistman finally got scared, it was too late. He hoisted the cage and brought the fire right up the shaft. I was in the mineyard at the time. All we could do was stand there and watch. The fire just leaped up and surrounded the cage. Roasted those two fellows. When we took their bodies out, their shoes were even burned off them. It had cooked their arms and legs so they loosened and dropped off when we tried to lift them out.

So when I volunteered to go down in the mine and bring up the rest I knew I couldn't let myself get worked up by thinking about anything. If you do, you get emotional and first thing you know you're not any help at all.

We went for the others and brought them up two by two. Twenty-six of them! For the first time, the numbers seemed to count. I wanted one of them women to run over and throw her arms around her husband because he was alive. I wanted the clouds to lift and the sun to show itself. I wanted somebody, anybody, to come over and tell me the rest of my life was going to be all right and that I was going places.

Then this miner named Leonard started calling for Manus Dugan. It had got dark. There was no moon. Me and Tom went back down and started climbing the manways. We found three men. Two were lying on the ground. One was hung up on a ladder, caught from falling by the rungs. He had short curly hair. He looked clean and trim somehow. Tom helped me lift him down. They were dead. Smoke had got them. I checked the pockets of the one we found on the ladder and found his name on a piece of paper. Manus Dugan. A couple of notes were folded behind it. He had a wife and a child somewhere. I kept telling myself I had work to do and that I didn't feel a thing, not a thing—nothing.

A Woman among Them, Painting

Melissa Kwasny

*In the cave with a long-ago flare
a woman stands, her arm up. Red twig, black twig, brown twig.
A wall of leaping darkness over her.
The men are out hunting in the early light
But here in this flicker, one or two men, painting
and a woman among them.*
　　—Muriel Rukeyser

IN JUNE, IN THE FORESTS OF MOUNTAIN PINE, a smoke lifts, not from the whole forest at once, but from one tree, this one, the one I am looking at. The yellow pollen drifts on its way to another the way spirit, they say, lifts from a body when someone dies. If I stand below it and shake the limbs, my feet will be yellow-dusted. The moon, of course, has yellow dust to give me. It is ours and always has been. No one else wants it, how it changes, the swelling and then the fading, like the sound of wind soughing through trees up the mountain. Women know only too well of this. We come together for a reason. We part for a reason. "Spare me," she has said as I touched her bare shoulders.

She lies across the bed on top of the sheets, blankets pushed to the side, and I have never seen anything more beautiful. Mine, I start to say, but this isn't true. It is hers and when I reach to touch her, it is with hesitancy. I wait for a groan, a move toward me. If there is not, as there often is not, my hand comes back to me. She is not mine, her body tells me, but she lets me see. Her narrow hips, a boy's hips she calls them, but I don't agree. Her warm stomach and below, the sea-threads of black hair. Too much, she says, and backs away.

I have imagined different roles with different women. I think of D., who was aggressive, left bruises on my thighs, who thought it too submissive to let me touch her. I have been the young boy on top, with faces, eyes closed, beneath me, have felt myself swell beneath my jeans. I have sometimes imagined myself taken by more than one woman or by men. I never imagine her as a man. I do not *imagine* her at all. It would degrade us.

God the Father, Mother Earth. I scorn the sayings, change them both into genderless things. No, that is not quite true. I change them—earth, sky, water, mountain, even Coltrane, Dolphy whom I love, Rothko, Pollock, the painters she has taught me to see—I change them into sisters, friendly, holy, swarming between the idea of a god and me. Not god, the tender green threads of bathtub light. Not god, my woman and her cats who sleep, closed like fists. Not god, who, I have been warned, would try to separate us. I would like to imagine without gender, a presence like a touch, light traveling.

> *I have only my hard breath,*
> *my reason and my madness.*
> *I cling to the vine of my prayer*

writes the poet Gabriella Mistral, she who named herself after the wind, she who lived her life with another woman.

My prayers are sent into the air like the webs of spiders or nests of birds, collected from her hair, her denim, her eyelashes, the thin smoke trail from her cigarettes, the tiny lines filled with oil paint in her palm, threads pulled from between my teeth like the skin of apples. I am Solomon draped in chains of sunlight. I, too, feedeth among the lilies.

She is neither woman nor man if to be a woman is to be unsure and a man insensitive. She is not effeminate. She has muscles from stretching and building her own stretcher bars, from covering her huge canvases with a palette knife. She owns tools and knows how to use them. Woman? No, she is too sure of her genius. Ever since I first met her, she has told me she will be a great painter. She has narrow hips and the eyes of a child—maddening how they can scorn me and, minutes later, open with a trust I could never betray. Some gypsy in her heart, perhaps, something nomadic. Those red lips, her black eyes. It is amazing to me that she is often mistaken for a man.

Where she is rooted, I am blown free. My limbs are gangly, motional. Every feeling sends them into a thousand spasms. My hair—brown, red, the pale of cobwebs in it—should be tied down, but I never use a scarf so it flies, flies to each of the directions. I frighten myself often with its shadows. Am I female? Yes, as female dodges the world as an act of self-preservation. I am female as light is female, not content to lie in one shape under the pine. I am diamond, circle, star. Am I male? Yes, as I shy from dependency. Yes, in my anger, my pure selfishness. Female in my distractions and male in my love of women, especially this woman, who would focus me (inarticulate murmuring of danger), who I circle around.

She sees. She is a painter. I hear voices in dreams, from birds, myself as a child, and the legions of those who hate me or are like me. I write what these voices say. Sometimes, I am concentrating so hard I can't hear her. There are times, in her studio, when she can't see me. We come together for a reason. We part for a reason. "There are times in my life when I don't want to be sexual," my friend Liz says, "when I need to be absorbed into other things, into animals, insects, the earth, my art." Liz, who quit her job so she could paint full-time and, within a week, had a new lover. Liz, who now complains to me how her new lover gives her no time to paint.

"Quit early," I say to Nica, "and we'll make love before dinner."

"We'll see."

"We'll see?"

"It depends. I might be into something."

I walk away from her. Slam the door to my study.

"Please," she says through the closed door. "Don't start this. Don't be mad at me."

"I *am* mad at you."

"Please?" she begs. "How am I going to work?"

I sit at my desk, heart-broken, tired, feeling like my mother, resigned to the meager instead of the celebration I wanted. I feel like my father, angry at not getting the response I expected, the response I had decided beforehand was mine. I will punish her with my silence. I will punish myself with it.

"Why don't you write about me instead of making love with me?" she asks through my closed door.

Dear Nica,

I have always known there would be someone to replace me, someone as brilliant as you are to me, as honey-colored, someone who could match you. I imagine it this way: a woman with green eyes, in faded, torn jeans and straw hat. You, staring across the bar as only you can stare. Like a hero in a movie, not flinching. Your bravado and, at the same time, your bravery. Your brave eyes like the soft tunnels the bugs make in trees, perfectly round as is their nature. One smiles. Which one? One moves her chair across the room. Soon, the jokes have double meanings. You will guess each others' birthdays or have the same birthdays or be reading the same book. While I, the frumpy gray-haired one, wrapped in a blanket, read and wait for my young wife who has gone dancing.

I have heard stories, usually old tribal stories, of virgins being swept away by spirits, never to be seen again. One day—it is always a fine day, bright with singing birds and the sound of water—a young woman is picking berries or gathering firewood or hanging clothes to dry on the line and next, a wind from the north comes, fluttering her clothing and . . . she is pregnant. Or she can't get him out of her mind. Pining away, they call it, that sound the evergreens make even as the breeze moves down the slope away from them. Until the day he returns, cold, unearthly, and takes her away forever to a land where she forgets all she has known before, her family and friends who she can see now only from a distance, as if she were looking through a long, narrow tunnel. All over the world, women awed, rumpled, ravished, their berry baskets lost to the ground.

I am not a virgin and Nica did not come looking for me. But Nica arrived in these mountains, my mountains, the place I was born, like that, dramatically, unearthly, in disguise, and petulant as any wind. It was a wonder to me that no one else noticed. Or that no one noticed my fear. Because you see, the young woman in the story is frightened, too, although she is also enchanted. After all, she has powers of her own: to read minds, to become invisible. She had come to depend on them for their ability to sway opinion or favor, a skirt of sorts, though she never wore skirts. They had seemed large powers at the time, the way she could get women, or men, to follow her. But when she compares the power of her charms to the wind, she is wary. The distance she could fall to the ground as they speed through the sky—the wind's domain, not hers—would kill her.

How did I meet her? I met her in one of our small cities. We were both carrying a communicable disease, a tiny parasite that burrowed under our skin and exhausted us. It was impossible to get rid of despite the doctor's chemicals, despite packing up everything we owned and letting it bleach in the sun. This wasn't as difficult as you would think. Our belongings weren't much. We lived in tents on the abandoned outskirts of the city, separately, since we did not yet know each other. There was little else to do. The doctors were still busy trying to find a name for it, much less a cure. We had seen their patients—nauseous, bone-thin, standing in the long lines of the clinics.

We met in an empty room without furniture. We filled the bath with herbs to kill the parasites and took turns soaking in it. There were others there, other diseased men and women. In between baths, we would lie naked on the bare floors in the half-light of the waxing moon. No one turned on the lights. She had perfect breasts, dark shoulders. How startling it was to see her naked. "I am always too intense for them," Nica told me, her damp hair curling at her neck from the steam. "I tell them I'm going to die. I frighten them away." I watched the beads drip slowly from her hair, down her face, down her shoulders which are narrow, unlike mine.

We met in a stone village in the most civilized country in Europe. I was middle-aged, a widow, by the time I knew I loved her, child-faced though with the most brilliant cornflower eyes that I had trained to look past anything I didn't want to see. Weak-brained, but blessed like Saint Francis, I knew all the plant names, whether ovate, palmate, or umbel. They called to me with their own uterine luck. I could place a leaf on my tongue, a petal, and know what it healed because inside me, as in a tea cup, floated all disease. I could feel them shift, dissipate: self-reproach, apprehension, bitterness. I knew the names of the plants and the ailments, and she knew how to prepare them, who needed them. It was only natural that we would become partners.

I knew things. She knew things, but she kept what she knew secret, had the enviable belief that it belonged to her. This was the source of many of our fights. She thought I was too sloppy and intrepid, my nose so close to the ground that I would miss any change in weather. True, I went into the woods often, even the king's forests, for my roots. I wondered off into those pure sylvan forests, so dark, so large it was like pawing between the toes of a giant. So dark I would sometimes use a flare. What did I care if anyone followed—and why would they?

The religious have always been my enemy, how they come with black robes, imperious, pale-skinned, with hatred poisoning their blood. Their arrival is always bad news for women and children. It was wrong that they took her. I admitted my guilt freely. I talked to plants, of course, and listened. How else would I know how to help? I couldn't read the Bible, but I had been taught as a child that god lived in the herbs and large trees. The priest said that was wrong. *Do not talk to snakes, God said, talk to me.* I died in the flames. I give up easily. Why should I suffer for what I know? I heard she suffered. I heard it in my dreams. She, of course, would admit nothing. She was different from me. She believed in her own goodness. While I believe in grief.

I met her over a hundred years ago on the plains of Montana. She was Ojibway, as you can see from her features now, the high cheekbones, the dark skin. You think you grieve now with the loss of beauty, the endless avenues of discount stores replacing the cottonwood, the forests transformed before our eyes into subdivisions, and the songbirds . . . the songbirds disappearing. No, there is nothing you can do. There was nothing we could do then. The endless soldiers, the waves of the future we did not believe in—they are the same.

We rode out toward the carcasses from opposite directions. We didn't know each other. We were from different tribes, different homelands. We rode our ponies out to where the railroad lines divided the world into before and after. You have probably seen the photographs: men leaning out of the trains with their guns, the buffalo, thousands of them, on their sides, stinking, their tongues cut out so they could no longer speak. Black, dried mouths.

You mention your Jesus, but you weren't there with him. Here were a thousand Jesuses. Our bread, our blood, our wine. She dismounted, walked up to them. I watched as she offered a few drops from her water bag. It made the desiccation shine like oil. I did the same. All day, we made fresh dark blood together. Though we were from different tribes, different lands. She would stoop, I would, to the great destroyed mouth of the source of our lives, offering water to what was already dead. Our men watched from opposite sides, unable to fight or leave, while we transgressed the field as if watering flowers. When we were through, she went back to her people and so did I. The look we exchanged has kept us together for lifetimes.

Nica arrived in these mountains, my mountains, the place where I was born, while we were still in our twenties. The mountains were not unfamiliar to Nica. She had, even then, friends all over the world. We met at a party, a women's party it was called. Now, even if only women attend, we simply call them parties. I noticed her immediately. She was dressed like us, in worn jeans and flannel shirt, work boots. She was very quiet, but aware, not dreamy as some quiet people are, as I am. There was something troubling her, too. I could see it in her concentration which was cast inward, a balance like a tree will do in wind.

"Not like a city girl," I said, "but a girl who should be riding horses, a woman who should be sleeping under stars."

"You are misled by the boots," Liz said, "It's the style now in the city."

Nica was across the room, curled in a chair, studying a large book of plates by the Canadian artist, Emily Carr—dark green, blackened, surreal landscapes swirling like flames or water. Mountains and an Indian presence, too, if not an Indian motif. Tragic. Haunting.

"A little like Van Gogh," I said, balancing next to her on the arm of the chair.

Nica frowned. "She studied in Paris, which was a rare thing for a woman of her time and limited income, so, sure, she knew of him. And of Franz Marc, Kandinsky, Picasso, even Duchamp. But these," she said, running her fingers over the page, "are like bad weather, stronger, darker, more serious than Van Gogh."

"How could anyone be more serious than Van Gogh?"

"She lived by herself in a trailer in the wilderness of British Columbia with her monkeys and the giant ravens who flew down to be fed from her hands. She raised and bred dogs for a living. No one ever sent her money. Her sisters hated her work. She had, as far as anyone can tell, no lovers."

I leaned closer to the photograph of Carr standing in a clearing of tall, primordial trees, the legendary monkey on her shoulder. "She never had money for materials," Nica was saying. "Everything she made was funky, like mine."

"So, you're a painter."

"And I heard you are a poet," Nica said, brightening.

"Well, yes," I hesitated, "most days. Some poems take longer than others, of course. There's been days I've spent. . . . " She was grinning at me. "You got me," I said, laughing.

"And I wasn't even trying."

"Do you," I asked, "paint every day?"

Her amusement faded. "No," she said seriously, "I can't afford to, but someday, yes, I will."

Her confidence shone back at me foreign, unlikely for a woman. I was strangely discomfited by it. "What do you paint?"

"Canvas," she said and I could see she wasn't joking. "Oil on canvas."

"Landscapes? Portraits? Abstractions?"

"Yes. And color. I'm very interested in color."

"Any specific one?" I teased.

"There is no such thing as one color. Look," she said, pointing out the window. "Look close to the evening star."

"Blue," I said, "Indigo. Cerulean. Azure. Aquamarine."

"Keep looking."

I concentrated again on the spot she had shown me, enough to see how the color was broken into tiny specks of light and to see them moving, pulsing, dimming, swirling. The longer I looked, the more they traveled.

"My eyes are playing tricks on me."

"Good thing you're not a painter," she said. "You don't trust your eyes."

Dear Nica who falls in love with beautiful women,

I am not beautiful. I am not of your class, which is regal, smooth as china plates, a private beach, your hair. My hair is frizzy and your lovers are expensive. I am cheap. You are pure. You are a genius. I have a muddied, rain-choked intelligence. You are an artist. I am vagabond, illicit, undisciplined. You are beyond sexual. I am sloppy in my lust.

"She is the fairest," I told Liz, "the fairest one of all. She will never want me."

"If you were a man, you'd be proud of her beauty, not jealous of it. You could wear it on your arm. It would reflect on you. It would show your good fortune, your excellent taste. Would a man ever say, 'I am too ugly for her?' Never!"

"But, I'm not a man. Women are supposed to be beautiful."

"To be beautiful," Liz said, "is a matter of health, not pretense."

"But what do you do when you want to be adored?"

"Is that really," Liz said, "possible between women?"

Someone is in love with me. I paint my lids plum, dust my hair golden. I slick my lips. I wear red. I go barefoot, grow the sleek hair on my legs, under my arms. Someone is in love with me. I pick the summer peas in the rain, eat a peach the color of August on my deep blue plate. I read poetry, only pages at a time. I can't stand more. The words send me dizzy and profound into the weight of the green hills. *Dear Nica, I am slim this summer, tan like a boy, dressed in t-shirts and Nikes. I climb easily, alone, pray that green will enter me so the sun can plunge through me. I pass into cold pools. I touch the eyes of the trout we call rainbow and am surprised how even in death they are soft. I catch two fish. In one, I find a slim red sack of eggs, shining like rubies. In the other, a bloated sack of yellow sperm. Now, I can see underwater. When I sleep, you should see it! They dart under my eyelids, thousands and quick like inspiration. I am blue-veined as lake water.* "With beauty before me may I walk," the Navaho say. "With beauty behind me may I walk. With beauty above me may I walk. With beauty below me may I walk." *I am the color of a candle flame, a nectarine. I am a poet in painter's clothes. I can see through your eyes.*

To be a muse, to have a muse. Health and Pretense. I chant the names of chokecherry, ale, soft cheeses, whisper the words blue and stone and bird. "However, a woman is not a poet: she is either a muse or she is nothing," writes Robert Graves. The muse as driven, in work clothes she has had to petition the law to wear—Rosa Bonheur, her hair unbrushed, painting pictures of animals. The muse with animals, Frida Kahlo with monkeys and parrots. The muse with big, strong, training dogs like Emily Carr. Camille Claudel living alone in a stone studio with high windows and her twenty cats. The muse as genius, who doesn't cook, keep a clean house. The muse as man? No, it is impossible. The woman, inspiring, responds: to touch, to music, to Dolphy's bird-flute—how he used to sit on the sea-cliffs, listening to them—to the ripe skin of anything. She takes out the red tablecloth, which has faded to rose, and we eat outdoors. She takes out the red tablecloth, lights candles.

Men are easily inspired. With women, the flirting must have a strength to it, a confidence. What we lack, we are attracted to in others, softness or drive, always capability. A hat, say. My grandfather's Stetson. I put it on. To wear with what? Then, how many others, men or women, wear felt hats? Then, I could never wear it in public, at my job, for her. Wait, *a tall woman in a brown man's hat walked in. She always wore pants and men's black oxfords. She never wore jewelry or lipstick. She never giggled. She was very good at what she did though some were uncomfortable with her around their children.*

"Nica," Liz said, "is always in and out of love with women. You? Who knows if you're a lesbian. Lesbians don't act like they've found the only love of their life."

"I have always," I said, "wanted to marry a genius."

"And not be one?"

"No one told me that I would have to choose."

I am in love with someone. I neglect her, showing her the seriousness with which I take my art, writing love poems, slipping them under her door when I know she's not home. I bring her wood for her fire, spend days stacking it in the rain. I want to take care of her, protect her. I will discipline her children, beat the arrogant, youngest one in pool. I will lift it, pay for it. I am proud of my strength. I bring her a fish, cleaned of its heart. I ask her to cook it for me, but she is against killing. I push her onto the bed, undress her quickly, my fingers inside her. It is only later, when she is turned against me, that I find it was too quickly, that I may have hurt her. Or was it her, waiting with honey and lemon after the wood was stacked in her favor, was it her head thrown back in pleasure against the pillow? I am in love with someone. I become a young boy, awkward in all but the grandest gestures. No, I will not remember the napkins and the pinot gris for our picnic. I will pick up turkey sandwiches and beer and make her laugh. I am in love with someone. I hike the mountains alone. The animals come close. They can feel my vanishing skin. And the valley? The valley below me is rounded the way her hand would draw it. Blue. Green. All line and uninterrupted color. Not like the way I see it, finding the one broken limb that resembles a bird, spending hours on the tail feathers, the crooked, the filigree, the jade or emerald eye. I am in love with someone. Suddenly, terrifyingly, I am seeing through her eyes.

Imagine this. You are walking through an old-growth forest near dawn. All around you, you can hear them waking, the giant pines who murmur. The air begins to smell like white clover after rain. Before you in a clearing, where the sun is spilling through in the shape of shadows, is, unlikely enough, a bed. The blankets are old lace, open-woven, the pillows embroidered with all animals and birds who have ever come near to bless you: the hummingbird trembling on its pale nest, the night-deer like ghosts in a dream. You are sleepy and you have been walking all night. As you move toward the bed, you see there are already two people in it. What do they look like and what do they have to say to each other? Do they speak the same language? Do they fight or make love? Does one wake while the other is sleeping? How do they sleep? And who is awake now? If one is a child, which one? If one is big, soft-bodied as a snail, if one has long hair like in a Renaissance Madonna, which? Which one wears the earring? Which one is darker, lighter? Which one is turned on her side, toward the other? "Why do you hate me?" one asks slowly. One scowls and says, "Why don't you wake up to the world?" One wants sex fast and doesn't want to woo to get it. One smokes Canadian cigarettes. Which one? Which one eats pale, sweet baked things? Which one surrenders like a dog on her back, approached by one who is stronger? Which one *is* stronger? Which one is needy, scares the other one away? One has picked the roses that bloom in a vase on the bed-stand. One has built the bed out of the white-barked aspen. One is a Romantic. One is a Modernist. One is a colonist. One is aboriginal. Which one supports them? Which one works with her hands?

Nica comes into the clearing. She sees the bed, walks past it. "On my way to paint," she says.

Things might have been different, I tell myself, had she not been in love with someone else when I first met her, when she arrived without warning, breaking limbs in my quiet, wooded mountains and then, as quickly disappeared. She promised to write. I told her she was always welcome. She lay on my couch at dawn, her arms for a pillow, smoking and bemoaning the betrayal of a ranch girl, how they had guessed each other's birthdays, were both reading Klee's journals. I stood at the window, watching the first lights go out in the town below us. "Like stars going out," I said.

Nica had come up behind me. "No, the light is far less complete."

She stood so still, I felt compelled to say something. "Why do you paint?"

"What else would I do?"

"Bake bread, grow a garden, design cities, drop nuclear bombs, a million things."

She nodded. "I paint because the world I see outside me is not the one I feel inside." She turned to me. "Isn't that why you write?"

"I write to make things happen, to draw things closer."

"So, you are a maker of charms," she said. The sky was white with pre-dawn, and we were shadows. "Are you going to charm me?"

from
"BILL'S BONGO PARTY,"
an endless loop

Bill Borneman

(Take One)

What is Bill's Bongo Party? Where is it? When?

It is beginning now.

It is? Who's invited? Why?

Yes. Everybody. Listen.

These are songs without words or music.

Shorthand for reverberations in the soul.

Sure, we bring our bongos. Djembi drums. Shakers. Rain sticks. Wood blocks and frogs. Tambourines. *Too many instruments to name.* We bring anything! Flutes, guitars, poems, turntables, beer bottles. Polka dots and moonbeams. You'll see.

Let's get started.

Listen to this dreamy harmonica phrase I found at a yard sale. (Jerry Murad's "Fabulous" Harmonicats. The melody from "Cherry Pink and Apple Blossom White.") I've put this little phrase into a five-second loop so that you hear a brief sequence continually folding around itself and bending as it flows, now above and now below the note we know is supposed to be there—*but never is.* As we listen, we think, "I know where this will end." But the note we expect, that we already hear in our heads, never comes because I've re-started the loop before it arrives.

We are left with an imaginary note floating in space, a Mobius sound loop forever approaching the implied note from a little above, a little below, then twisting around the center of the note but never passing through to hit the tone that will resolve this yearning. You never hear the note you know is there, buried somewhere in the orbiting harmonica.

While we're listening to this hopelessly inexpressible harmonica loop, tribal drumming grows louder and louder followed by a deep male radio voice cutting through the world exotica percussion:

If the natives are peaceable it will be possible to determine whether the road is passable. We will petition to have the competition held towards the beginning of next session. They have a permit to set the machinery in operation. I will protect the business in your absence.

These handsome sentences are from THE PITMAN METHOD OF PHONOGRAPHY (1901). Practice sentences for student stenographers learning to take dictation:

The administration declares in favor of protection. The audience made a demonstration of approval of the administration. I will adopt the work if you can adapt it to my special needs. I admonish you not to diminish your watchfulness. My carefulness will suffer no diminution in consequence of your admonition. I will follow your advice and put this device to immediate use. Our representatives promise to devote all their energies to defeat this obnoxious measure.
My daughter told the editor that the auditor would notify the debtor.

My italics. Taste the italicization, as though a layer of frosting has been spread on the sentence.

My daughter told the editor that the auditor would notify the debtor. *What a delectable cadence.* Reminiscent of the Lord's prayer, isn't it? "Thy kingdom come, thy will be done, on earth as it is in heaven...."

Welcome to Bill's Bongo Party, where fresh relations are discovered as the rhythms of the participants interact. One ethnomusicologist has described Bill's Bongo Party as, " . . . a way of getting down to more significant concerns: its context is a context of action, of social life; its reality is that of community. The continuous music consists of many rhythms, and the 'beat' emerges from the way these rhythms engage and communicate with each other. While various rhythms may be more important, no single rhythm can provide a complete focus, and in this sense there is no central point of unity. . . . "

Meanwhile, all the drumming and singing and dancing has been increasing in intensity until noise, text, music, and cacophony comprise a wall of sound that is suddenly—*instantaneously*—cut off. It is not difficult to describe this phenomenon of sudden silence. As DJ Cliché puts it, the silence is "*def*-ening."

It would be wise to acknowledge at this time that the sentences above are from Lesson XXIV of THE PITMAN METHOD OF PHONOGRAPHY. The Pitman Method was one of several modes of taking dictation that flourished around the turn of the XXth century. However, it suffered from a lack of flow to its graphology—even using on occasion the dreaded right angle. Hence, it rather quickly and quietly died out, replaced by a more efficient and elegant form of transcription.

Whatever happened to Annie K. McDonald of Anaconda, Montana? She was the owner of this book so dear to Bill and his Bongo buddies.

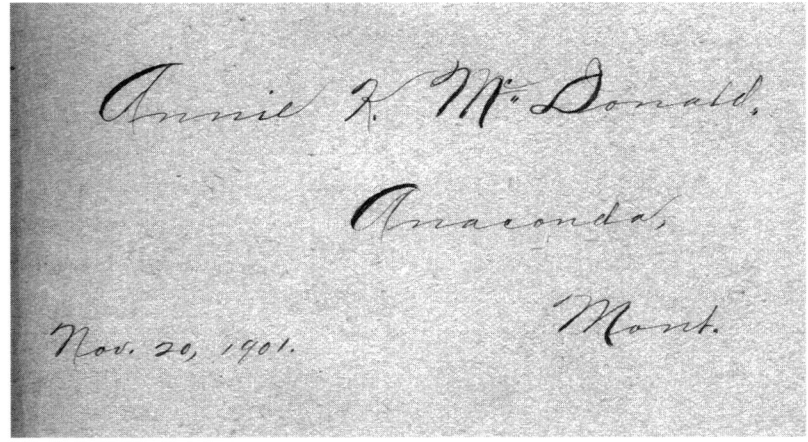

[Tonight's bongo party is dedicated to Annie K. McDonald whom I assume is safe in heaven dead.]

We are here to unearth our names. Embody our phonography. Therefore, we sometimes inquire of the participants as to whether they might enjoy shouting out affirmative ejaculations into the air while raising their arms above their heads. Then, we urge them to clap their hands together thus creating a percussive acoustic disturbance.

Suppose, however, a participant is unable to bring to mind spontaneous syllables of raucous joy to accompany his or her clapping?

The Pitman Method can aid us once again! Select words from lesson 79 to shout while your arms are raised in the air swaying to the rhythms.

> VARIABLE CONSONANTS 33
>
> WRITING EXERCISE.
>
> (R and Ray, Lay and L.)
>
> **79.**—Row, oar, rack, ark, rag, argue, rub, hub, pair, parry, chair, fur, furrow, shower, showery, jury, arch, rich, urge, ridge, earth, wrath, revive, arm, army, remove, re-hash, room, Rome, live, alive, ledge, lobe, elbow, limp, like, alike, limb, long, lion, pull, pully, deal, delay, chill chilly, gill, galley, issue, shape, shank, shipwreck, shabby, shocking, fish, fishy, bush, bushy, militia, girth, forth, mileage, demolish, failure, dirty, apology, home, hem, ham, hump, hack, hug, hog, humming, hearing, why, hop, hip, hill, hole, wholly, help, helm, Helena, howl, hail, hear, here, hair, hire, harsh, hark, hinge, hero, hurry, her, harangue, hectic, hemp, whip, whack.

Bill's Bongo Party will return after a brief pause.

Perhaps you notice that "Helena" appears in this exercise list. Now why is that?

Why not Anaconda? Chicago? Spokane? New York? Philadelphia, PA?

Helena happens to be where "Bill's Bongo Party" is taking place tonight–by *sheer coincidence*. And yet, it is no secret that serendipitous synchronicities frequently occur at BBPs. After all, the point is to improvise, to improve, to multiply connections between all the elements comprising our world. In Ralph "Where's Waldo" Emerson's words: "It was at a BBP that I coined the fossil phrase: 'Where the air is music . . .'" And is it not the very air itself that reverberates with the waves of sound after the hand has struck the drum? The beat goes on where the hand has been. Drumming is a lot like prose. Written, spoken, or thought—there is no end to it. As Von Humboldt wrote: "Poetry can only belong to individual moments of life and to individual moods of the intellect. Prose accompanies man continuously and is evident in all expressions of his intellectual activity. It clings closely to every idea and to every sensation."

Listen to these sentences from the same lesson as above but without quotes, simply incorporated into the text as though they occurred here naturally. By unanimous decision no mention was made of the anonymous communication.

The stream has its origin in the region of perpetual snow.

It is an undoubted fact that we are indebted to him for material assistance. A potato will satisfy his appetite. The passionate individual was advised to be patient. My patron pledges himself to prosecute the oppressor of the poor. Your success will be proportionate to your preparation.

The avenue is broad and bright. Yes!

This is where Bill's Bongo party takes place. On the lonely avenue; broad and bright though it may well be. Bill is one of the citizens of this town. I propose that we support him in his efforts to establish a party devoted to the principles of rational celebration.

Let's try to get a handle on this PHONOGRAPHY, this transcription of bongo fury into well-formed sentences of business English.

Come with me and listen to the echo.

"Come with me and listen to the echo."

(Take Two)

This party is about drumming and being.

(We may need to see some identification.)

It is not our intention to observe rituals; rather, we seek the ritualization of everyday life.

Tonight we are joined by Ibrahim Abdulai, master drummer from Ghana: "Drumming has no end. And to talk of drumming, you cannot talk of it and finish. As we are drumming, every drumming has got its name, and again, every drumming has got its dance. Every playing is different, and in drumming everyone has got his hand. So no one can know everything about drumming; everyone knows only to his extent. If you want to know everything, what are you going to do and know it? The knowledge you have today and you are taking to bluff, there is someone somewhere who knows more than that."

Tonight, Bill's Bongo Party begins like this:

You hear a bowling ball rolling down the hardwood lane . . . . . . and smashing into the pins.

The crash of the pins is sampled, slowed down, slowed WAY down and, Lo!—a bass line begins to emerge from the rumble.

Add the sizzle of hi-hat cymbals; brushes on a snare drum. . . .

MC Pastiche grabs a microphone and exhorts DJ Du Jour to deliver a lecture upon the subject of philosophy. To be precise, upon the phenomenology of internal time consciousness during bongo party participation.

Du Jour obliges:

Time is music made manifest. Music enters your body and you break into blossom. Feel the deep blue juice that through the green grooves drives the power chords of the apocalypso.

>Are you ready?
>Where is the one?
>Who's on first?
>Who takes the first solo?
>*Are* there solos?
>Does it matter? Whose tempo is in command?
>Are we a marching band of ornery Xtian soldiers as to war?

Or partisans of the peace-loving poets of percussion?

Set your keel to breaker at the Bongo Party. Check out DJ Du Jour's black cap with the infinity symbol in white. Trademark of philosophy? Logo of the *Logos*?
>Listen to the echo.
>*The echo.*
>DJ Check Mark is here, as is DJ Shopping Cart.
>Listen to the relations between the various rhythms happening at once.
>DJ Cliché, meet MC Tongue Tied.

Cliché says, "It's a pleasure to meet you." And Tongue Tied, true to form, can think of nothing to say.

Nonetheless, the two get along like P-Diddies in a pond, like water ducks lined up in a row of corn-fed chorus girls.

Frequently, life-long friendships are formed through attendance at one of Bill's Bongo Parties. Just last night I over-heard this exchange between Paul Valery and Bill.

"The passage from prose to verse, from speech to song, from walking to dancing—a moment that is at once action and dream," said Valery.

"Exactly. Bill's Bongo Party is the unity of action and dream," replied Bill.

"Last Call!" shouted the bartender, Jim Crumley.

Yea. Last call for us all, mumbled Yosemite Sam Beckett at the dark end of the bar at the East Gate Liquor Lounge in Missoula, Montana one night in 1976.

SHELTERBELT

from "Why Do the Heathen Rage," a novel in progress

Kim Zupan

THE SWAYING PINETOPS BURST PINK before anything else, the dark lying long on the ground like a seamist and then the birds heralded with ruthful screeds the blazonry that fell down through the black boles and onto the sage and finally into the gullies and canyons of the Breaks spread out below me. A bull bellowed and coughed somewhere nearby in the timber. On a far promontory a herd of deer fed nervously through a patch of rimed wheatgrass, froze like lawn statuary as two dull rifleshots resounded from the Judith bottom. A fawn stuck its head into his mother's flank.

A mile down the tortuous descending road to the riverbottom, a Hereford bull came at a trot toward me, his great polled head upright and his sack penduluming under a sleek belly. From above, his voice had come clear and seemed very near though I had driven at least a mile. He pulled up short and stood roaring claim over an enormous pasturage unfenced as far as I could see, a glorious red ogre possessive of a harem long since driven to wintering ground. He stood looking up at me from among thick twisted sage nearly to his shoulder. He seemed to have been waiting for me. Steam rose from his back in the first warming light of the morning. He lay his head back and blew long moist disquisitions on blooms of dragon's breath.

Beyond in the frosted grass his tracks told of a furious and bounded transhumance, a meandering meaningless crosshatch of one small steep-sided gully, while the great Breaks lay east and west for hundreds of miles with only the river as barrier. He would winter in there, nothing to hold him but his own life. He was master of it nonetheless. I stood on the roadberm, inconsequential suitor for his remote raw gulch and dimly recalled breeding dams, his trumpeted challenges stilling the birdcalls and subsiding with forlornness altogether human as his wind wheezed liquidly from the huge cavity of his chest.

At Bohemian Corners that night I had bought a six-pack of beer, a loaf of bread, and a bottle of hydrogen peroxide. I leaned against the Dodge's quarterpanel, flushed down three stale slices with a warm Lucky. The sage blued in the low light. The bull walked up and back below me with a pink eye cocked upslope. He brayed and tossed his head. Shortly he took up a position opposite me and began to run his nose through the grass like a weaning calf. I was no threat to him. I had become as insubstantial as the ghosts who haunted me, more a shadow for all the cowardice Yvonne had seen on me that night at poolside like the phantasmal fire that fell down on becalmed ships. Even this dull animal would defend the memory of his kind, while I ran from them, over the whole huge country, running my nose along the fences of my cowardice telling myself it was freedom I wanted. Even Gustovich had turned to face those dogs of life that pursued him toward madness.

In this place where the trees were dwarfed and tortured by wind, not a branch moved. Magpies and crows from their roosts regarded me in silence. As I drove toward the river the bull's clear pibroch rang in the enormous calm and articulated the nobility of great loneliness that I could never hope to know.

On the bottomland the car's shadow ran alongside over bleached barkless deadfall lying among the knurred trunks of cottonwoods like the bones of mastodons eroded to the surface. The headlands that had seemed with their cool pines lovely respite from the monotony of stripfarms and sere CRP now from below were glowering wigged visages, sprouting from their dour foreheads volcanic plumes of stratocumulus gravid with snow. The road ran to the riveredge and stopped, as though enticing travelers in the face of such barrenness to choose the consolation of cold perpetual sleep.

I watched the brown water slide past. The current ground at a fissured cutbank, the roots of distant cottonwoods adroop in the air from it and suspending above the surface in their withered fingers and elbows the globular rocks of an ancient riverbed. A flotsam of leaves and farm trash floated by like a kelp bed. The clapper of the ferrybell tinged softly against the sound bow and on the stifled breeze from upstream I heard the lowing of a cow.

On the far bank I saw a man come out of a trailer and stand looking at me with a pair of binoculars. He dropped his hands to his sides, turned, and spit. I went to the bell and jerked the clapper cord. The man disappeared into the engine hut and shortly emerged and the ferry began to chug into the current, the cables tautening and screeching across the barberpole deadmen. Halfway across I could hear the laboring engine and at the same time the cable tower atop the bank beside the Dodge began a maledictory groaning, one rotted leg tipped from its footing.

The boatman spread-legged on the deck began to call out to me. I strained to hear as I stood above the water's edge, cupped my ears toward him to block out the hiss of the river churning at its banks and the pulley whines and scraping of the cables across the deadman. The tower set lightly down on its ruined leg like a lighting heron. I stood between the car and the water leaning to hear some instruction or warning and then I could hear him, singing. I couldn't make out the words but the tune on a wafture of breeze dappling the water roused a memory that seemed suddenly important to remember. The boatman sang. He stood with his legs spread wide on the deck sailor-wise, his voluminous trousers flapping about his legs. A hundred feet out he began working the nose upstream to meet the road, cranking around a sidewheel with a ratcheting of rusted cogs that drown out the words, just as I was about to hear. He motioned me back. The hull rasped gravel and with a jolt the ferry stopped, all cables sagged and the endgate fell slowly down.

"Pull 'er straight on and I'll tell you when to whoa." I pulled the car ahead up the ramp and the old barge squatted in the water. The boatman held up his hands crossed at the wrist.

"Put 'er in gear and set the brake, would you please." He was a good-looking man in his fifties, high-waisted like a bronc rider. He wore a feedstore hat jauntily tipped on his head. "Okay, then. You're supposed to stay in yer rig but I don't care."

The boat slid off the streambed and nosed slightly downriver and the cables began their squalling. The ferryman ducked inside the tiny engine shack to light a pipe and in that dark closet his face glowed above the bowl. A wheelless tractor was bolted to the deck, its engine throbbing, the operating cable windlassed around an axle drum.

I got out and stood at the rail. The 4 x 10 deck was split at the boltholes and strewn with dried gumbo and gravel from a season of rainy day crossings. An aluminum lifeboat lay against the windward rail secured with a chain and padlock. The water bulged against the upstream hull and slid by, a flat ruckled reflection of the sky, its opacity belying a bottom of cragged menhirs and fathomless mudholes filled with bones and like the bowsprits of sunken ships a chaos of blasted treeboles and tentacled roots lodged and slowly rotting.

From the Dodge's trunk I lifted out my warbag. I took it to the aft ramp and for a moment watched the water boil in the wake. I slid it beneath the railing and pushed it over the edge with my foot. It bobbed and trailed along briefly after in the churned wake and then heeled over and went down. After a moment a dead carp boiled to the surface in its place and submerged again with a languid sideroll. A fair enough trade.

A gust of Prince Albert preceded him and then the boatman appeared beside me. He held the pipe in his teeth with the bowl turned into the downstream breeze to feed the fire.

"What was in it?" he said. "A body?"

That's about right, I thought. "Just some things, clothes and things." We leaned together at the rail staring into the dirty moil. He sucked at the pipe and it produced a faint woodnote like the chirrup of a tiny bird.

"What was that song you were singing?" I said.

He lifted his gaze to the receding bank where now a cow had materialized from among the brush and cottonwood and waited in the road on the shore as though to cross. "Wasn't singing no song," he said.

"On the way across I mean, while I was waiting. I think I remember it from when I was a kid."

"Wasn't singing at all, son. I don't even sing in the shower. I'd scare off everything in the country." He pulled his pipe and pointed its stem toward the cow rubbing a haunch against the deadman. "Go on, gal," he called, and then to me, "Bank caved in there with her calf. She's been hanging around a month now, poor gal. Got her wattle stuck under the cable one day and I had to stop and go on back and get her loose." The power cable bucked against the hole in the engine hut and he tested it like a guitar string with a gloved hand.

"Are you a history buff?" he said.

"Not to speak of."

He pointed upstream. "The governor of the state of Montana fell off a steamboat drunk ten miles upstream of here and they never found him. But I got a notion I have. I been all up and down here. Hard, though, because sometimes the river's here, sometimes it's there. I've had to keep a chart just even to go to the same exact place every year. And it's a place that ain't there 'til August when the river's down. Sort of the river's junk pile. The first years I come up with deer skulls and things such as that, and garbage. Tires and stuff. Car junk. But now last year I dug out a whole buffalo with an arrowhead stuck in a rib. Got the skull up at home on the mantelpiece. So you see I got his honor Francis Meagher bracketed-like. He's somewheres in between the cars and the buffalo. Now it's just move up and back, up and back, in a pattern. It's slow work. And then it's start again after high water."

"Sounds like a lot of work."

"Keeps me out of trouble."

As we receded from her dim vision, the cow bawled miserably from the riverbank then fell silent as her own voice, dwindled and remote, fell back on her from the implacable bluffs. She turned and began trotting toward them.

"See there," the boatman said. "Poor dumb gal. She hears her calf in her own echo. I expect I'll find him down there next year with the rest of the junk. Probably your bag, too."

"You're welcome to it," I said.

He smiled faintly around the pipestem and raised a hand from the rail as if he might touch my shoulder. "Sorry you won't be needing it," he said. "Those horses, though. They'll bust you up."

I watched as he began once again to crank the nose around with the side wheel. The cables thrummed with tension and in the shack the tractor engine began to lug and heave under the strain like a plow horse.

The ferryman called out, "Come on, Sweetheart. One more time." He went across the deck and clutched it into a lower gear just as the bottom rasped ashore.

After I had pulled the car off onto the road, I walked back as he shut down the engine and offered him the five remaining beers.

"They're kinda warm but they might drink alright with a little help."

"Ordinarily I'd say no thank you, but I might take one off you today.

I was just fixing to take her out of the water for the season when you come up."

"I appreciate it."

"Shoot," he said. "It's a long ways back the way you came."

He worked at his pipebowl with a folding tool. A white-muzzled Lab shambled from under the trailer porch, snuffled his master's pantleg and lay down there with a possessive forefoot across his boot. He raised up his face adoringly when the boatman said his name, rheumy lactescent eyeballs searching blindly for a hand to lick. "You old sorry thing," the man said. He tousled the dog's ear. Across the road in a bosk of forgotten apple trees choked with brush a rooster pheasant croaked hoarsely and the dog sat to attention, vaguely leonine and youthful. "Thinks he's pup yet," the man said. "Go on, now. Go lay down, John."

"Well, I guess I better let you get to work," I said. "Good luck with the governor."

"Come back next year and I'll show you him. Might have your warbag for you, too." He smiled ruefully. "But then maybe I'll leave it be."

I climbed stiffly behind the wheel of the Dodge. "I won't be needing it," I said. "Thanks again."

"Yup."

He squatted on his bootheels, stroked the blind dog's head gently, and went to work on his pipe. I started the car, levered it in gear, and began to pull away. A child's bike leaned against a slim tree. A curtain fluttered from an open window of the trailer and from the blighted orchard a flock of starling rose up in a great black Catherine wheel and swept from sight. I stopped and rolled down the window.

"Where do you go now the ferry's done?" I said. "What do you do?"

"Right here," he said. "This is home. I piddle around. I stay busy." He stood up. "This winter, I believe I might try to quit this damned pipe." He knocked it against the heel of his boot and stuck it like a pencil in his breast pocket. "That's what I'll do."

As I ascended the striated and sage-covered carved north rims of the Breaks the song that had come to me like the voice of a ghost below on the river began again to sound in my head, and among the endless stubblestrips on top it played on until at last, as I sped past a schoolhouse in ruins, its tottered flagpole flying only a strand of cord in the wind and from its spire a paneless meniscus looked bleakly down, the childish words formed up, falling from my mother's lips through the years:

> *Down by the seashore, Mary Ann*
> *Down by the seashore, sifting sand.*
> *All the little girls love Mary Ann*
> *Down by the seashore, sifting sand.*

Now that the words had come, I could forget them. I could forget her, too.

In an hour of driving gravel I met only the sway-topped ungainly crane, moving as slowly as a migrating dinosaur toward its appointment with the ferry. The man in the tiny cab seemed less a driver than part of the thing itself. He raised a single index finger from the wheel in salute.

The clouds hung down along the hilltops as I dropped into the Marias bottom, the river reduced at this late month to muddy ribbons wending among the islands of willow and squamous sandbars rippled their length like dunes. Gulls wheeled above the cottonwood tops. What houses there were, set back beyond highwater line, gaped skeletally sprouting from their doors and windows tangled chokecherry and the spinous suckers of grove trees that spanned the swagged rooflines with their branches.

At three in the afternoon on the Meeks Bench Road I parked at a gate to a large field, the fences bordering it five sagging wires, the posts canted at odd angles and some merely hanging from their staples above the ground. The rotted buttends stuck like broken teeth from a berm of blowsand. From the far corner of the field a cloud of smoke rose up and an instant later the croup of a diesel engine came rebounding from the hill's bald battlements like the calfless cow's blatted knell at the ferry landing. The umbers of early evening crept imperceptibly down the lee couleesides toward me as the sun fell away.

With a rag soaked with hydrogen peroxide I bathed as best I could the claw marks on my back. My undershirt stuck to them and came away bloody and pus-stained and I threw it into the borrow pit. Looking at it there, unfurled and fluttering from a weedstem, a filthy flag emblazoned with my own blood, the struggle in the hotel suddenly seemed less a horrific dream long past. Without even the impetus of a salvivic conviction I had twelve hours ago probably killed four men and set fire to a building, or a town. I had fulfilled the Gustovich legacy and cut and run. Even my grandfather had watched the effects of his work, had stayed behind, and built from its ashes a kind of life.

From out of a depression in the field's far corner a tractor came lumbering, drawing behind it a cloud of dust and shortly, as I watched, a white wake of gulls, circling and dropping and scrabbling afoot for whatever small life was unearthed there from the dry ground. Worms. Centipedes. Pink infant mice. They leapfrogged each other and before long it appeared as though the machine was disinterring from their netherworld a legion of gulls and they sprung up holding their wings aloft and jouncing like inexpert fledglings testing the air.

As I put on a clean shirt from the back seat, at the far corner of the field the tractor stopped. The driver had seen me and sat riding the clutch, while about the cab dust spun like a swarm of wasps and the diesel smoke columned from the stack. In the adjacent field two horses cantered along the fenceline toward the idling machine, one running with his head inclined oddly sidewise to the wire. He reached the corner first, flinched, and shot out a rear hoof as the other horse came alongside.

The tractor moved on, rumbling down the sectionline toward me for all of ten minutes, stopped idling at the next corner, came on parallel to the road, came abreast, and stopped. For a moment the driver sat in his glass box looking me over, then threw open the door. I stepped across the fence. The gulls, undaunted by me, fought among the broken clods. Presently one would fly off with some treasure, gag it down jerkily, fly back to the others. Some brazenly lit and scavenged among the polished chisel drills. The engine muttered smoothly and the stack cap percolated up and down in a tinny rhythm. The old man looked down. He removed his cap, wiped the sweatband with a rag, and tugged it back in place. He waited.

I stepped up onto the first rung of the cab ladder.

"Got a pretty fair gull crop this year," I said. He leaned closer and cupped a hand behind his ear. I said it again.

He turned in his seat to look out the rear window. "Oh, about average, I suppose." He smiled. "Might have done some better if we got a little more rain."

"Did that snow slow you up any?"

"We didn't get it. Didn't even get a sprinkle." He looked back the way he had come. "It's an odd year. Never plowed this late before."

"I came through it from the south."

"Whole different world, seems like, just the other side of the river." He went on for a moment in a voice hardly audible about the barriers the country afforded, ("Just my own theory, there's those who'd say it was malarkey") not only mountains but rivers and flats making weather, how he'd watched clouds strung out above the river like another river in the sky with its own cloud trees and great popcorn plates of cloud hovering above the sage prairie and he could tell where the hills were in Canada even without seeing them because there would be their twins floating over them like a reflection. But that it was just a theory and I might think it was malarkey but he's made a kind of study of it.

When he finished he seemed embarrassed to have gone on and turned to the dash, tapping the tiny round windows of his engine gauges. I stood on the rung below him. The knees of his jeans had been patched and repatched, stitched by hand. I hadn't planned anything while I watched him going around the field. I hadn't been thinking of anything. Then there it was.

I said, "I wonder if you were looking for any help."

From habit he doffed his cap again, smiling wanly, his low forehead deadwhite above the capline and he swept back a frieze of white hair that had fallen wild and somehow boyish over it.

"Well," he said.

I pointed back across the field where he'd stopped earlier. "Those your horses?"

"Just what you see."

"Got a blind one, I guess. Or halfblind."

"Bit by a snake. Don't know why I keep the sonofabuck. Head swole all up but then come out of it with one eye." Together we stared out through the rear window at the pair of horses standing like a team at the fence regarding the stilled tractor expectantly and the gulls began to gyre up and plane toward the river with hardly a wingflap. Some sat the right-of-way fenceposts like vulgar flagstaff ornaments, hawking imprecations soundlessly beneath the diesel-drone.

"I'm not much of a mechanic but I know cows some and I could fence or whatever."

"Well. Now." He looked at his boots, looked over my head at the Dodge at the borrow pit. "Don't keep cows no more. Not since the Mrs."

I stood on the rung. "I understand," I said. I swung down into the stubble. The old man sat studying the jumping gauge needles.

"Can you cook?" he said.

"I don't think I've killed anybody."

"You'd have to cook 'cause there isn't no Mrs. or gal."

"Alright."

"I can keep you on until the weather shuts you down, doing some things. That could be any day, you understand."

"That would be fair, sure. Thank you."

"Did you come up from the ferry?"

"This morning."

"Then you passed the house. About three miles east back the way you come. I'm going to finish this field. You can wait up there." He said his name, Verl Gosst, and held his hand down to me. "Help yourself to the icebox. I'll just eat cold tonight."

When I got to the car, one of the gulls tugged doggedly at my fouled shirt tangled among the ditch weeds. It pulled free and the bird flapped with it awkwardly up onto the roadbed where it was set upon at once by the four or five demure post-sitters in a flurry of feathers, obscene nebs and feet and womanish screams and croaks that drowned out even the tractor engine chuffing down the field.

It may have been when his wife was alive that he came home to kitchen noise or the sound of the radio from an open window broadcasting cattle futures or percentages of rain or her singing (he told me later she loved to sing when she thought she was alone and he would stand quietly outside the house to listen), but as I stood in the yard that first evening I heard only Hungarian partridge calling each other softly from the olive windbreak around the house. They had fluttered up from the yard as I drove in and sailed into that cool shelter and there was only that sound and nothing more.

Where his rutted inroad crossed a cattle guard a half mile from the county road the fence was in disrepair. A polled cow skull hung from a post, its sockets stuffed tight with nesting and a wren or sparrow peered serenely out. From some past day when he'd kept cattle, a hide lay across the cattle guard rails and it was reduced to a curled glabrous parchment tethered there by a reticulum of weedbines. The house, like the outbuildings clustered around it, was white clapboard, a weathered twenties bastion of hope. The porch had been enclosed at one time and I could see two chairs beyond the glass. On three sides the yard was protected by the shelterbelt and on either side of the house stood two bare elms like temple columns of a lost race.

The Huns chirred in the olives. I stood in the yard for a while and watched the hills across the river blaze in the last light of the day. In half an hour he would be summerfallowing with the lights on.

Though the woman was dead, she was everywhere yet in the house, in the head-darkened doilies on the backs of chairs, the tasseled throw rugs, statuettes of porcelain deer. Verl Gosst had preserved of her what he could. On the mantelpiece among the deer and miniature clocks synchronized and faintly ticking was her picture, a small plain woman with her arms thrown around the neck of a horse, smiling a smile from its warmth familiar because it was so like his and just from that I knew he must feel a loss that would make anything I might have felt at that moment or any other some pale selfish remorse. It must have been a courtship photo as she had signed her name angling across one corner appended by her great lie: Always, Evelyn.

It may have been that Verl Gosst wanted us to get acquainted, his wife and I. I waited for two hours, first at the small dining room table where through the long window I could see a bend in the river over the near rimline and for a while, before it came dark, the pillar of dust and smoke he rose, out of sight to the west. Ducks silhouetted themselves against the sky and then disappeared into the darker bluffs, one after another like a returning squadron, enveloped by shadow. Sitting in a stranger's home, among the artifacts of a dead wife, I felt oddly at ease. Once or twice I caught the scent of lilac, as if from the folds of her dress that redolence drifted on the slipstream of her passing. I remembered when Yvonne and I had first stayed at the hotel I'd opened the door to a rush of perfume from the hallway and thought some woman—another ghost maybe, the woman the old sheepherder had sought—had just been standing there. Or that Vera, the battered chambermaid, had been eyeballing us through the keyhole. But downstairs in the coffeeshop a luncheon group of old women gabbled and moved down a buffet on their burdened thighs and their combined musks filled the room, overflowing into the stairwell and hallways and rooms like a ground fog. But there, in that house, with only the ticking of her tiny clocks from the mantle in the darkness, the scent was a frail ghost waiting at home.

    I idly fondled one of the miniatures, a speckled fawn no more than two inches tall. The clocks tolled softly the half-hour. When I returned the deer to its spot, one of the legs caught on the mantle's edge and snapped off. I set it in place quickly among its kin, balanced on the tiny leg as though nothing had happened. I stood back. My hand shook, hung down from my shirtsleeve as if it was not part of me: a defiler of shrines. Her face stared out. The gears ground in the clocks. I had begun to sweat. I sat down achingly on a wagonwheel divan in front of the painted geegaws, animated suddenly with a clangor of metallic heartbeats. I would have to tell him.

The first day Verl Gosst set me to picking rock with apologies and I drove down the hill on a Fordson tractor with a flatbed trailer behind and for eight hours I piled rocks on the trailer and unloaded them in a long windrow like a heather fence in the field where the two horses were pastured. The two of them watched me all day with interest and at noon I petted the long nose of the blind horse while he stood as gently as a hound.

    After work and dinner of soup and bread, what the bare pantry provided, the old man sent me to Fort Benton for groceries. He signed a blank check and gassed up the Dodge at his tanks. At the IGA in town I loaded two shopping carts and when I filled out the check and handed it to the clerk he looked me up and down, turning the check over and over in his hands.

    "Working for Verl, are you?"

    "Yup."

    "How you get along with the Mrs.?" he asked.

    "Look, here's my license. You can call him up if you want."

    "No, no, that's okay. Just that he hasn't kept a hired man for a while."

    When I got back it was fully dark and a wind had come up and the branches of the elms, enjoined in their upper reaches, creaked and rasped against each other overhead as if engaged in some slow rancorous wrestling match. The old man had cleaned out the bunkhouse, made up the bed with clean sheets, and pushed aside boxes of magazines and old letters and lady's hatboxes so that there was only the bed with a narrow aisle on each side. The room had long ago been given over to storage. The walls were hung with rolls of coiled rusted wire and handsickles and broken-toothed mower blades, and that night, as the milk heater glowed orange in the pitch black, the blades tinkled softly as the wind bore through the walls. I went to sleep by them.

I picked rock for two days and then set to fixing the fences in the same field in the company of the horses while the old man continued his plowing through the odd warm days, each morning standing outside the front door, smiling wryly at the frostless landscape and peering long into the north sky as though expecting the appearance of a mushroom cloud or like Blueback God Himself rolling forth horribly as explanation.

One evening after supper we sat in the chairs on the porch with the lights off, looking into the clear southern sky, its paillettes adorning the highest branches of the elms like sidereal Christmas ornaments. The furnace pulsed through its ducts beyond us in the house and the old man's chair or his bones creaked a slow rhythm. He got up and I heard the springless back door bang shut and shortly the squeal of its hinges opening. He came back with two glasses of bourbon and water and we sat drinking, wordlessly nurturing our separate vacancies. The old man would suck in his breath and point at each shooting star like a child.

The night before among the clutter of boxes in the bunkhouse I had found a framed aerial photo of the ranch, from above an ordered geometry of house, outbuildings, shelterbelt. From that view I could see a pathway through the Russian olive trees from the northeast corner of the main house that led to a fenced square that may have been a hay corral. It sat on the edge of the hill and beyond it the bottomfields we had been working and one glistening loop of the river. I had hung the picture from a nail above my bed. I mentioned it to him.

"Feller came around some years back and I couldn't say no to him. He done a nice job of it."

"It's a nice picture."

"But you know, I took it down after a while. I have no desire whatever to be reminded every day of how small my life is." The creaking stopped and I could hear him absently swirling the liquor in his glass. "Ah, look there." A meteorite flagged a cold tail for an eyeblink across the immense firmament. "And then it's gone," he said.

The bunkhouse when I entered it from the windy interstice was as warm as the main house and the milking heater whirred, its coils casting into the close darkness an irradiant bell as soothing as a hearthfire. The old man had turned it on when he'd gone out to make our drinks. I undressed in front of the heater and lay down in the cool sheets. The wind stirred the sickle blades on the wall. But it wasn't a weather-bringing wind, only the breath of that country, even on the stillest of days a sigh ruffling the grasstops and the leaves on the infrequent trees, mourning its own perdurable emptiness. After a while I got up and took down the picture from its nail on the wall and leaned it behind a stack of hatboxes.

The next evening, coming from the field I'd worked, I saw the old man still disking through a huge bottomland. I went across to him. I stood on the bottom ladderrung as I had that first day. He said he'd work late and seemed otherwise disinclined to talk. The diesel pothered its black plume up into the still air. He turned in his seat to glare north, south, east, west and long again and uncomprehending into the featureless north sky, his face tired and vaguely apparitional under a fine powdering of dust.

I set dinner to warm in the oven and walked into the tunnel through the Russian olive I'd seen in the aerial photo. Ahead of me through the umbrage of brambles and bent wild wheat the birds who make their home there rushed invisibly and some flushed out of sight beyond the tangled bosk with reproachful clucks. The path was well worn and came into the open at a small run-off coulee whose bottom and sides were furred with some soiled matting as if from a burst mattress. Opposite it, on the highest point of the bluffs overlooking his bottomfields and the river with its gaunt cottonwood sentinels, was a fenced burial plot. The grass inside was cut back and the wires around it on steel posts strung tight. As I stood in front of her stone a pheasant burst from the windbreak and sailed on set wings toward the river. The tractor made a black stripe below in the stubble and churned up a vortex of dust and salacious gulls. Her name and days of her birth and death were listed there and beneath it Verl Gosst's simple approbation: Wife. Beside that another stone with his name, date of birth, Husband.

The gray woof lay about stuck in the grass and some in tufts hung from the barbs of the fence. Otherwise the Gosst cemetery was as neat and tended as a rose garden. A hand sickle hung by its blade on a steel post and revolved slowly on a sigh of breeze. I sat in the grass there watching below me as the stubble was chiselplowed to sod in anticipation of the coming snow, from that promontory the field turning with each tedious round from umber to black until there was only black and the night closed down on him. I saw his truck lights wend toward home.

Because I was the cook I began to take as my duty the mixing of the drinks, which we drank together that night at the table overlooking the bottomland of the Marias as the late autumn sun dwindled by degrees ever southerly behind the gumbo blufftops.

He began to talk even before I sat down with the drinks. He sat his chair in the semi-dark, the crick-squeak like a heartbeat, crick-squeak, facing the emblazoned sage benchland beyond the river, the sun a fingerwidth from extinguishment behind the rim of the seeming world.

"I saw you up there," he said. "She was a beautiful woman, by God."

"I see from her picture."

"Oh, she was beautiful thataway, too. But she was just pretty through and through. I had some pet names for her, silly things, but she called me by my name. Though sometimes she called me Love."

A rooster pheasant croaked so close in the Russian olive that I turned in my chair to catch a glimpse of him and the old man laid his hand on my arm.

"Don't go in just yet now. I mean, finish your drink."

"No, no," I said. "I was just." The rooster squawked again. "Just that old cock."

"A cock has got to crow."

"I guess what else does he know."

"That's all. Not much different from a man in that way. Cock's got to crow and a man, what? A man's got to work and grieve and then die. If you're unlucky. If you're lucky, you just die and the grieving goes on without you." He paused to drink. "But I wouldn't have wanted her to have to do that. It was better this way, I believe. I wish I was better at it, is all."

The pheasant called again and we could hear his wingtips fan the underbrush, he was that close, and then the sun lit his outlandish breast feathers, just a flicker of color at the end of a gray day and then he was gone to his harem of dull hens quavering in the arbor.

He said, "One thing that gave me hope my whole life was what my father told me. He told me nothing lasts and that everything will come around at last. He talked German to us at home. *Alles waechst und webt, und alles kehrt wieder.*" He stopped abruptly. "How do you like that? Haven't heard nor spoke that in thirty-five years or better." He tapped his white temple. "Just rattling around in there." For a long moment he sat in sad distant wonderment, slowly shaking his head. I set my glass lightly down on the table edge but it seemed to rouse him. "Anyway but what I mean to say is this: you have a bad year and the next could as well be good. Or the next after that. One year you buy hay to tide you over a drought, the next you're getting three cuts. Hail this year, forty-five bushel that. The good'll come around. I lived with that notion in my head and it saved me my whole life practically. And I thank God I was an old man before I come to see it was wrong. Some bad things do last. I never got over that old woman dying. I figured to come around but I never did. You see me. You see my place. If I would have known that what he said was such a lie, I would have laid down long ago. He figured on that. Sure he did. Wouldn't be fair to tell you otherwise."

He sat for a long moment looking down into his open hands, as if to divine in their cloven phalanxes like a palmist a differing future or past.

"But you're a young man with a lot of strength in you. A lot of good in you. Like Bill Alfredsson there. I to tell the truth never thought much about him before Mrs. Gosst died. Lost his little girl in the river two years ago, but he keeps on. He's a fine man. You see a man's character in how he holds up to such a thing as that."

"I don't know him," I said.

"Must have met him, though. Runs the ferry. Hard-working man. Always digging in the mud for some old dead man or some darned thing. You see the man's character." And so I pictured the ferryman again just then, rigidly astride his deck and lullabying his cold daughter somewhere below in her watery desolation. He sang to mollify her loneliness, not his own. He had strength enough to spare a manly tenderness on the likes of me while at the rail staring mildly down at the water that had taken his child.

"But me," Verl Gosst said, "me, I've wanted to die everyday since she went." I was embarrassed for a moment, to be so close to such emotion with so little defense against it. I took a long drink. I realized that one thing I was to Verl Gosst was a reason to say things aloud for the first time that he had been holding in for an excruciating year. Or maybe he had been saying them, to the windbreak coveys or the snakebit useless horse patrolling his pasture fence or to the picture with its vast untruth there on the mantelpiece. What could I possibly say that could bring comfort to an old man grieving with such perfection? Like the drowned girl, the woman from the mantelpiece regarded the living from behind her more transparent pane.

"If it wasn't that I couldn't bear to think of all of it just going to wind and ruin. I would be letting her down, letting go all that we worked at for so long. It's her garden. She called it that, all this." He swept his arm before him, encompassing with it all the forsaken fields and slack fence and rock piles and weeded pastures devoid of cattle. "All this, her garden." He set his drink on the floor beside his foot and that close I could see his thick hand grip the chairarm. "But it's not anymore. I've let it go. I'll admit that."

"It's not so bad."

"I just don't have the heart," he said. "Not anymore." In the blue fall dusk we sat, as though she were there again lending her strength, the air which had been a warm breath from the furnace ducts became a chill wafture of her springtime perfume. Still the old man, who had seemed for these weeks such a part of the austere hard land, languished instead under her calming hand. First through sighs and then in his perfect stillness I felt him move from his tangible life beside me in the darkness and nearer the coterminous shadowland of his patient Evelyn. He lay his head back against the doily she had made and I felt as though I were in the presence of some intimacy between them. He slept. I took our glasses to the sink, washed them up, and went out to my narrow home amid the litter of their happy life.

A Map for Hummingbirds

Ellen Meloy

MONTANA'S WILD GEESE MIGRATE IN FAMILY UNITS. They navigate by memory and topography—the shape of a mountain, a curve of river—and by an internal compass that responds to the earth's magnetic field. The point bird in the distinctive V-shaped formation is usually a gander, although the geese change position frequently. Updrafts of air behind each wing in the V reduce drag for all but the leader, who must drop back to rest. Think of the V as a single creature: aerodynamically fluid and energy efficient, adjusting its flight pattern with loud honks.

Borne by sturdy bodies and powerful wings, the geese stay aloft for hours. The peoples of old did not underestimate the endurance of migratory birds with large body mass. They also observed, correctly, that hummingbirds migrate, but presumed that such tenderly small creatures—birds that must eat constantly to fuel a rapid heartbeat—could not fly long distances on their own without dropping dead. Thus, according to folk belief, big Canada geese would carry tiny, fragile, hitchhiking hummingbirds on their backs when they migrated.

A cold front can trigger migration in the fall, although the precise moment of departure is never predictable. Not all goose families are of like mind about staying or leaving or when. One minute they might be nibbling succulent plant bits in a serene valley, the next minute they rise into the clean blue air above the Montana-Idaho border. Below lies a rumpled cordillera of rocks and ice and a pickup truck winding along the Interstate highway. Inside the truck are two humans, also migrants, also at odds about staying or leaving or when. Cranked on for the first time in months, the truck heater smells like melting chihuahuas. The man drives. The woman, who never wears socks south of Pocatello, takes off her battered desert sandals, pulls on a pair of woollies and shoes, then stares down at her feet as if they were freshly embalmed mummies. Paths cross. The distance between sky and road, wing and tire, diminishes sound but not a vague sense of air flowing in opposite directions. The southbound geese comb our northbound hair.

Birds respond to changes in their environment by migrating. In temperate North America the best strategy is to move south for the winter to warmer terrain, where better menus flourish, and to return north in the spring, where the mild season and longer daylight hours favor mating, nesting, feeding, and growing up. Nature, of course, never quite sticks to the grid. Some birds head south when they should head north. My ornithology book defines reverse migration as bird movement that proceeds in the direction opposite the one expected for the season. If a storm or heavy winds sweep them off course, for instance, the birds fly back to the beginning or to a point where instinct orients them to their preferred lane of passage.

Reverse migration is the metaphor of my life in Montana. My husband's seasonal work as a backcountry ranger and a home we built in southern Utah keep us in the desert during the hottest months, from early spring until late fall. Our slightly delirious Utah life, spent largely outdoors, unfolds in the sensuous red-gold light of a heat-scorched, tense, skinless earth fissured with deep canyons and upthrust in sandstone monoliths. Each winter I haul my lizard pelt and desert soul back to our Montana home, blue-starved. For months I have not seen so much light at this end of the spectrum: thick conifer forests the color of malachite, steel-gray peaks creased with cobalt shadows, lofty cornices underlined with blue-violet cusps of snow. Montana is a sojourn in northern light.

The truck moves through an indigo dark. The geese push onward to open water and a rest. At this point in our migration all other vehicles have fallen off Idaho, whose edge meets an abyss into outer space—or so it seems. Our vehicle slips solo up the massive plateau that hovers above the rest of the continent like Coleridge's Xanadu ("That sunny dome! those caves of ice!"), a distant, glittering place undercut by something dark and alluring. The night beyond our high beams obliterates all horizons, all distinctions between land and sky. The lights of scattered ranches become stars. Nothing but the ground beneath me tells me that gravity exists. Away from towns spread like islands in

Montana's vast space, few travelers are immune to the floating sensation caused by this blanket of darkness.

Geographers often describe Montana's size with the how-many-states-can-fit-into-it measure. Nearly three Connecticuts. A couple of Vermonts. One slightly distended West Virginia. Stretch the analogy further: overlay Massachusetts onto southwestern Montana, where I live. The Crazy Mountains impale Boston, tossing half a million people downslope into a rude heap. Cape Cod's curled finger tickles a paltry number of sage-freckled acres west of Twodot, and the Connecticut River disappears into the Missouri like a lost noodle. The Berkshire Hills form a dust cover to the Scapegoat Wilderness. Cowboys from Deer Lodge sell Housatonic gentry a few sizable cattle outfits. The city of Butte pierces the overlay, startling everyone in New Bedford with a giant open-pit mine. Yellowstone National Park, however, now sits conveniently in their backyard.

Montana easily fits Gertrude Stein's remark, "more space where nobody is than where anybody is." The journalist Joseph Kinsey Howard called Montana "the space between people," implying that a vehicle and a few tanks of gas are needed merely to bring you close enough to see if the other person's eyes are blue or brown. So much space fosters deep introspection, philosophic distraction, fierce independence, and narrative inventiveness—desirable traits for writers, cowboys, and that up-and-coming New West prodigy, the golf pro. Under the Big Sky, human and landscape exist in the right proportion to one another; comfort is found in one's own insignificance. As a young, insignificant woman I believed that Montana's humbling scale would provide the proper vessel for my terminal restlessness, my notion that home could be found in movement itself. I felt that rootlessness might find root in a place of this size.

Some birds, notably young gulls, herons, and egrets, do not always migrate in predictable seasonal directions. Juvenile wandering can be linear—the young birds head north as the rest of the colony heads south—or explosive: they move in all directions and at considerable distance from their hatching areas. When immature birds cannot compete successfully for food with older birds, they must wander until they find an adequate food supply for themselves.

Years ago I came to Montana as a juvenile wanderer, a native westerner exchanging one rural home for another. Behind me I dragged previous lives—student, lifeguard, hermit—and ahead lay a buffet of new ones. I made a living in technical illustration, churning out laboriously stippled pen-and-inks of bones and feathers, detailed diagrams of geological strata, and the cell divisions of anxious amoebas. The medium enriched my knowledge of science and gave me thumb calluses, thick reading glasses, and the revelation that my art, so meticulous in nature, was also extremely uptight. For relief I painted barns.

In the Rockies' brief growing season I jump-started my garden seedlings inside a junked farm truck, its cab and windshield facing south, its windows adjusted for ventilation. This greenhouse yielded seedlings for tons of unlikely tomatillos and one cantaloupe the size and flavor of a used tennis ball. Montana's weather crossed Seattle with the Yukon. One storm covered the land in humid, brooding skies, the next in brittle, frigid air that burned the skin like poisoned needles. Contrary to predictions, winter didn't kill me. I boldly crawled under the house to thaw my pipes with a blow dryer. When a more severe cold snap froze every molecule of liquid in my house except a tumbler of whiskey, I drank the whiskey. I survived winter's cold but not its length. Each year I fled to the desert to cheat it.

In Montana I married a man who called his sleeping bag "Doris" and lived three blocks from where he was born. At the time of his birth, in the fifties, the neighborhood boasted a hospital, a convent, modest family homes, and one active and at least five former brothels. On one of our first dates he took me to a bird refuge in a remote valley, where he shot a duck and served me its tiny butchered breasts for dinner. Before I could decide how I felt about dead duck, he told me its name: bufflehead. We were eating bufflehead breasts.

In Montana I learned to flyfish, row a river raft, belly dance, and herd sheep. I frost-nipped my feet on cross-country ski trips in moonlight and rearranged my knee cartilage on treks across mountains with a heavy pack. The land seemed so vast, each season so deep, adventure became irresistible, even if moments of exquisite beauty had to be earned by extreme pain. These years matched youth to place, reckless energy to a land that does not yield easy living to anyone.

Perhaps the southbound geese that flew above our northbound heads picture their winter grounds as an enormous open-air restaurant; their primary occupation is to eat. On my feeding grounds on the upper Missouri River, I exchange the lusty, brainless, overheated, intimately physical life of the desert for winter's distinct mood of reflection. I trade summer's harlotry of color for what Melville called a "fixed trance of whiteness." I trade the wild for shelter.

My street abuts a million acres of timbered high country along the Continental Divide, possibly the last street until the next town nearly ninety miles away. Here, edge of town means a distinct, palpable border. On the tamed side of the wilderness, below our house, lies the old red-light quarter and, wedged into a narrow gulch, a dense cluster of commercial buildings with ornate facades of sandstone and granite. Montana's innards—gold, silver, copper, lead—paid the bill and fed the town's aspirations to worldliness. A delirious mix of architectural elements borrowed from the Italian Romanesque, French Renaissance, midwestern American Gothic, and mining-camp Baroque doesn't quite hide a frontier soul. Similar opulence is found on the downtown's other flank, merely a gulch away from the whorehouses, in a neighborhood of stately mansions built at the turn of the century by mining magnates who followed a cardinal rule: The dirtier you mine, the farther you live from it. They lived here, close to their banks.

What could be more western than an endemic confusion of virtues? As towns like mine outgrew their frontier motleyness, civic pride called for churches, schools, and other refinements. Visitors from the East wanted mud and bugling elk and virile men who mumbled about posses and punched each other's lights out. As the nation paved its highways in the 1930s, Montana, short on funds and long on need, stretched its blacktop budget by building its highways as narrow as possible. Not that it mattered; traffic was negligible and everyone drove all over both lanes anyway. These days, however, *los hombres de global economy* dress like Wyatt Earp on weekends but demand a four-lane to the ski lift. Everyone wants Montana to be not a state but a state of mind.

The downtown district recently sprouted a thick crop of espresso bars. From my house I can walk this gauntlet and arrive overcaffeinated at my favorite bookstore. The cafés, and weekly calls from realtors hoping to wrest our house from us, portend Montana's demise as a faraway, hostile, possibly coffeeless place. The great interior West is filling. Hoarding the limelight are white supremacists, golf pros, a ranch-hungry Hollywood elite, and nearly everyone else from California who saw the flyfishing movie. The state's soul, however, perches precariously between its own myth as a paradise of raw nature and a backwater of rural primitives in love with sheep and assault rifles.

In winter Montanans become a hearth people, content to shut the door against the howling wilderness. The season exacerbates an insularity in the Montana character, an ease with keeping to oneself without diminishing one's community. A few cope by shooting their refrigerators. Others embrace the pleasure, if not the necessity, of friends and neighbors, one of whom might someday pluck them from a snowdrift. Ranches a tenth the size of Belgium keep a lot of people far apart. Early homesteaders often built their houses on adjacent corners of their sections and lived close to one another. Before long they moved to the other side of their holding, ostensibly because their chickens got mixed up together. Something about this extraordinary land accommodates a desire for privacy without loneliness, seclusion without solitude.

The winter solstice marks the midpoint of our stay in the far north. This calendar suspends me in the purity of a singular season; winter's most evocative qualities freeze-frame in a landscape that wears them to perfection. Days unfold in preternaturally bright sunlight or under a pewter sky weighted against snowy hills with its impending storm. Nights are sudden and complete, with a faint glacial scent. The moon is lilac as it rises, silver at its zenith. As a winter resident I never see the seasons change in Montana. I never see the green, only its scheduled death. For me Montana is always cold, the original and ultimate state of the universe.

January brings the coldest days, bone-chilling polar air that leaves no slack. Every surface freezes so hard it would rip yours lips off if you kissed it. Car exhausts spew dry-ice fumes. The air crackles with helium, ozone, neon, argon—air that can be 108 degrees colder than me—yet somehow I remain liquid. Not counting my bathtub, the aquariums in the local pet store have the only open water for miles. Winter's worst grip sends me there for the solace of gurgling water and a fecund, tidal humidity. The same Arctic front sends the derelicts to the library. Some sit cozily next to the heat vent in their baggy parkas and unlaced pac boots. Another sleeps at a table, snoring face down on *La Technique: Cooking with Jacques Pépin*.

Despite the pervasive lethargy of hibernation, things get done. Ravenously hungry after the cold spell, cedar waxwings—tawny birds with black bands across their eyes—strip my crabapple tree of its frozen fruits then fly off like masked bandits. My husband cleans the basement. Someone resuscitates all those Bostonians heaped at the foot of the Crazies. According to the news, Romanians are selling their excess bears. I order two. The legislature, which meets here every two years for ninety days, undoes the laws that the previous session repassed in response to laws depassed by the session before that, making everyone so dizzy, we wish they would meet every ninety years for two days. I send out postcards with photos of typical Rocky Mountain ungulates and letters that note a ski trip to the valley of the bufflehead breasts, the length of icicles, the blizzards and the chinooks, the shock of exploding color from arriving seed catalogues, an epidemic of imploding marriages among friends—all the riches and wrecks that mark life as *Homo sapiens* on a wobbly, spinning planet that tilts its northern hemisphere away from the sun.

Then the season turns and the light slowly climbs the orb.

Before migrating a bird must eat a great deal, storing energy in the form of subcutaneous fat. The bird must also become predisposed to migrate by a metabolic state called migratory restlessness. In spring this condition is controlled by the pituitary gland, which in turn is stimulated by periodicity, or changes in day length. Fat, restless, and physiologically prepared, the bird now needs only the external stimulus of a drop in barometric pressure, the moist, southerly air of a warm front, before it loads those little hummingbirds on its back and takes wing: northbound.

For me the migratory impulse manifests itself in too many trips to the pet store aquariums. The geography wars, the tension between allegiances to two places, escalate. One day I will press my face against a window that frames Montana's crystalline winter purity and I, too, will long for hummingbirds. Fat, restless, physiologically prepared, aching for the desert, I will turn winter's bend with the geese and take wing: southbound.

Journey of Small Deaths

Tom Elliott

Her husband once told me that she had beautiful nipples. Actually, he wrote a poem about her, about their hippie tribe, a lake, about her nipples. It was a poem that left me longing to be with her, to jump naked into the water and to splash and dance and be a part of their merry tribe.

There's something to be said for knowledge without the reality. Nipples that take your breath away. It could mean anything.

I

It was bad enough the dumb calf was born with a big head, but now she had to die so that Phelps could use her skin to graft a bum calf onto the dumb calf's mother. "Damn," he thought, wishing for a sharper knife as he straddled the big, dumb calf and hooked his arm under her throat, sawing through the soft, shiny black hair into the flesh, the skin, the thin layer of fat until the blood started to seep then spurt in thick blue-red steaming spurts onto the snow at his feet. The calf opened her eyes wide, pivoting her gaze onto Phelps, full of fear, smelling her own blood, letting out a bawl that gurgled in her throat, watching Phelps, kicking her leg, pawing at his leg pulling back as the blood flowed out onto the snow. So much blood, Phelps whispering, "I'm sorry calf, I'm sorry calf, I'm sorry calf," thinking for a minute it was a mistake, maybe he could stop the blood, but the calf stopped kicking and slumped against his leg and her eyes glazed over, looking at Phelps, until the purple tongue lolled out of her mouth and her body shook and gave a last jump and she died.

"I'm sorry, calf," Phelps said, stroking the soft black fur as he girdled the legs with the knife and slit the calf up the belly and carved around the nape of her neck and slowly peeled the skin off the thin body with short strokes of the knife until the naked flesh of the calf lay steaming in the snow and Phelps held the warm, heavy skin in his hand, thinking "Damn, damn, damn."

He walked around the cabin to the pens and flopped the skin over the pole fence. Then he climbed over the fence, cornered the gaunt-looking calf in the pen and wrestled him to the ground. Whipping out his pigging string, he caught three of the calf's legs and dallied the thin rope around them. Then he grabbed the hide, wrapped it around the calf and tied it in place with pieces of twine. "You better live, you son-of-a-bitch." he said, and pushed the calf in front of him into the pen with the dumb calf's mother. "You better live."

2

Phelps is driving down the road, clear, blue Montana sky, endless highway that rises over hills, follows the river bottom and sinks into the horizon. The road today is lined with death, road kill, mostly deer bloating in the sun, legs splayed, bellies burst open, tongues hanging in the dust. Magpies are everywhere bringing death full circle, cleaning the bones. Coyotes, rodents, insects cleaning the charnel grounds. Ahead, magpies are lifting off the road slowly as the vehicle bears down on them, slowly with their bellies full of death, rising into the sky, disappearing into the luminescent blue. Phelps is wondering, "I don't know what it is they find up there, but they always return to the earth, bellies empty, to feed again on death."

Well, death was on his mind. It was all around him. Not just the reality of death, the smell of death, but the idea of death, driving down the road, surrounded by death. Struggling with the weight of the knowledge of death.

Magpies in front of him on the road. Watching the birds rise out of his path, the vehicle closing on them, wings starting to move, closing on them, Phelps thinking how the cushion of air from the truck will lift them into flight, birds rising slowly, Phelps letting off the gas, too close. One magpie veers to the left, blooms into full flight. The other, full of plunder, swoops too low, smashes into the grill, rolls over the hood. In the rear view mirror, a flutter of feathers and a black and white body that skids along the pavement, settles with one wing up, blowing in the breeze. Road kill.

3

Phelps was standing in the moonlight, 3:00 am, pissing beneath the huge birch tree next to Foster's house when he noticed the cross. At first he couldn't figure the light, something pulsing in the night, a pale light, pulsing in the night. He followed the light up, through the branches of the tree to the steeple of the white-framed church on the corner. It was a neon cross blinking steadily in the night.

He laughed. It might have been a religious experience had he not been holding himself, pissing into the night. "Weird," he said to himself, zipping his pants, thinking of Marie, feeling slightly guilty, but buoyed by the rush of clandestine sex.

She had walked into the bar dressed in a tight black skirt and knit top that was scooped to reveal her shoulders and her full breasts. "No one will ask me to dance," she said as she walked up to the table. She was the friend of a friend. A woman he had only just met, but he knew why no one would ask her to dance. She was plenty attractive enough, a beautiful woman with short brown hair wound in tight curls and a body that promised pneumatic bliss. But he knew no one would ask her to dance. Every cell in her body exuding a lifetime of quiet, angry desperation. Dance with her and you'd be one more sacrifice to this woman's bottomless avenging pit. A lifetime of anger in those eyes. That look on her face!

So she sat for a while. Phelps' friend, Foster, polite, but unusually distant. He knew. And he didn't want Phelps to get sucked in, maybe wanted to protect his friend, maybe to protect his friend's lover. "Faith," Foster projected.

They talked around the table. Small talk about her paintings. Exquisite Montana landscapes rudely split by incongruous objects in the sky. Something that would totally dominate the beauty, so incongruous, so ugly—split like a knife, this woman, who knows what she might imagine? Small talk.

Finally, drunk on dark beer, knowing faith was out the window, Phelps asked her to dance. They danced slowly around the floor, close enough to feel the heat of her breasts, close enough to touch his lips in her hair. She had a small tattoo on her right shoulder blade. A swan. His hand resting in the small of her back feeling her move against him, wanting to stroke her swan, to slip this knit top slowly off her shoulders, stroking the swan, gasping at her breasts when they swung free of the stretched fabric.

Phelps knew it would happen and he knew she was poison and he could hardly wait to follow her home to that long blue sofa beneath the painting of the craggy mountains and icy snow-melt stream with the gigantic razor blade slicing through the sky. Marie on her back, one leg astraddle the arm of the sofa, toes touching the painting. Tasting her, smelling her scent, listening to her gasp, thrashing in each other's arms, the tangle of their legs, salt licking skin, clutching bodies, hearts pounding and hardly a word spoken until he whispered, "I've got to go home."

Pissing under the tree, the cross, the long road home to find Gina sleepily cuddled beneath the quilts. Slipping in beside her, feeling her reach for him, roll into him, wanting him, wanting him, now.

Afterwards, holding her, their bodies damp, flushed, touching everywhere, watching her softly, her eyes closed, breath warm against his beard. She had lost everyone to death, one at a time, all of her family—everyone gone. And now he brings her more death.

Phelps strokes her softly as she rolls into him in her sleep, wondering, "How does a body hold so much grief?"

4

He was thinking about the new kid in his daughter's class at their small rural school. Stephanie. Fifteen years old. A very pretty girl. Long dark hair, eyes that flashed with the excitement and beauty of youth.

Thinking about all of the pubescent posturing that surrounded her. How difficult it must have been for her. The other kids in their little cliques, their subtle exclusions.

He was thinking of a particular moment at an inconsequential basketball game. It was near half-time. Their team was enjoying a comfortable lead, and the coach sent her in to play out the half. She was new to the team, not a particularly good player, not even very motivated, preferring to skip practice to flirt with the boys. But the coach puts her in near half time.

With only seconds to go, the guard brings the ball down court, full court press, fake left, passes right to Stephanie. She feints a shot, ducks under the defense, dribbles, shoots. The ball arches slowly towards the basket, everything slow motion, bounces on the rim, once, twice, then drops cleanly through. Her hands come together, she turns toward the crowd, clasps her hands, jumps up and down with glee. The look on her face, such beauty! Such joy!

Two weeks later Stephanie is driving the family Bronco down the gravel road, too fast, teenager fast. Hits the washboard at a bad angle, too fast, turning to catch the road as the rear end fishtails out, adrenaline rush, fear, wide-eyed loss of control as the vehicle rolls over the edge and Stephanie's head bounces against the wheel, then the windshield, then her lifeless body is hurled out the door and the vehicle rolls to a stop upright, roof smashed, but, damn, you could still drive it. Body lying next to it, limp, head cocked at an angle, arm draped over sage. Lifeless. Damn.

Phelps breathes slowly, grateful for the breath. He thinks of his own daughter, thinks, "God, protect my child," feels the grief coming over him. Crying now, he can see Stephanie's face, see the ball arching slowly towards the basket, everything slow motion, bouncing on the rim, once, twice. . . .

5

Phelps had a fever that winter, the kind that strikes you down, holds you in bed shivering, sweating, delirious, thinking about dying, about letting go of the body and drifting into the light. It was the winter of the fever and Gina nursed him faithfully, cheerfully. She brought him soup, books, changed the sheets, talked him into taking antibiotics. In his fever, he wanted her to go away. To let him crawl into a quiet place to either live or die.

One night in the early spring, he woke from a deep sweat, bedding drenched, feeling oddly separate from himself. He arose from the bed, cool from the sweat, full of a fearful calm, and walked into the bathroom. Looking in the mirror at his two selves, he asked, "What do you want?"

Phelps ran his hands over his face slowly. "What do you want?" he said to the other self. That day the fever broke.

6

Phelps was eating Chinese tonight while he traveled on business. He followed the young hostess to his seat, watching her long blond hair, pleasing hips, indulging in an old man's fantasy as they wove their way through the restaurant. Phelps nods to the two older couples sitting at the table nearest his—heavyset older folks, the women's gray hair cut short, curled tight. Men slumping in their chairs, hands resting on their paunches.

The waitress comes around, he orders fried rice, lo mein, egg roll, sitting uncomfortably in the room, feeling alone. He listens to the conversation at the table next to his.

"Harold," she is saying, "Harold wouldn't see the doctor, even Dr. Biggs. One day Dr. Biggs sat me down in his office, you know he was that way, that kind of doctor. Florence, he said, you've got to get Harold to come in for a physical. So I said, if you say so, Dr. Biggs, I'll get him in here. That was before we knew Harold's heart was bad. So I finally made him come in, that was when I was still working for Mr. Jamison. Well, Dr. Biggs said, you'd better get up to Albuquerque right away. They need to run some tests. I think Dr. Biggs saved his life, he would have died years ago if it wasn't for Dr. Biggs. And now they're both gone."

"Hiccups," said the heavyset man wearing a striped knit shirt sitting to her left. The group collectively turned toward him. "What?" they said.

"I was saying I had the hiccups after my heart surgery. Hurt like hell. I just lay there waiting for another one to come on, thinking I was going to die. Finally I grabbed the nurse, it was a male nurse. Jimmy, I said, I got the hiccups, it's about to kill me. You gotta do something.

"Hold on, he says, I know what's going on. You see I was laying there with these two tubes going under my ribs, big suckers. He says, it's the blood coagulating under your ribs near your throat. You just lay there, he said as he undid my gown and pulled it back from my chest. You just lay there and tell me when you're about to hiccup. When you do, I'll just whack you as hard as I can right here, under your throat. It'll scatter that blood, give you relief. This is one problem I know how to fix.

"I lay there quiet like, kinda braced and ready, just laying there, waiting for the next hiccup, waiting. After a while I says, I guess they've gone away. Jimmy smiles, says, They always do. Just like that. Scared them right out of me!"

Food passing around the table, plates heaped with sweet and sour pork, chicken wings, rice. "Who was that doctor that died in the plane crash?" the other woman asks.

"Dr. Taylor," this first woman answers. "My, he was handsome, but all business, not like Dr. Biggs. And rough, too. Terrible to die like that, so young, family and all. Wonder what happened to them?"

"Moved back to Nacogdoches, I heard," chimed in the other man.

The waitress slips between the tables, spreads out Phelps' meal, lo mein, rice, egg roll. Phelps spoons it onto his plate, chop sticks stabbing at the noodles, flecks of red chili, slivers of carrots.

"Those tubes," the man says louder. "Jesus, they were was big as a garden hose, stuck under my ribs to drain the fluid. Jimmy came around one day, kinda sits on the bed down low where I can't see him. I'm laying there on my back like this. Sits there where I can hardly see him and says, I'm going to take one of your tubes out today."

Phelps stirring the noodles, feeling his heart pumping blood, feeling the spot where he broke a rib, never quite right after that, so close to the lungs, stirring his noodles, staring at the food.

"Quiet like, kinda sneaky, Jimmy says, here goes! and jerks sudden like this. I feel nothing! I'm thinking, man, this guy is the best, when all of a sudden, he grabs the tube and really jerks that sucker out. Whooeee, sucked my brains right out of my head. Jesus that hurt."

The first lady says, "They used a balloon on Harold." The second says, "I didn't think they had them back then." "Oh," she says, "it was very experimental. Harold was one of the first."

Phelps feeling the blood in his veins, the crack of his jaw as he chewed his food. Belly uncomfortable, the rib, breathing carefully, wondering about his heart, feeling hot, clammy, stabbing at the noodles.

"When I came out of the recovery room, the nurses wheeled me onto the elevator at an angle, like this. But when they angled the bed, wham!, the wheel dropped into the crack by the door. Then the door closes, wham, and closes again, wham! Quick, says the head nurse, get an orderly to help us. I says, I'm pretty heavy, get a man. And hold the goddamn door. Jesus, I hurt. That head nurse, she was from Dallas, God was she embarrassed!"

Phelps started walking out of the restaurant, a little queasy, paying the bill, the cute young hostess saying cheerfully, "Have a good night, sir." The "sir" lingering longer than necessary, too respectful, distant. Back at the table he heard the man chortle. "When they finally got me to my room, the nurse says, Are you sure you're all right? I says, Hell, yes, I'm all right. You all done your best to kill me, but I still think I'm going to live."

Phelps walking slowly out of the restaurant, careful of his heart, his broken rib, walking gingerly and feeling—feeling very bald.

7

They both thought she was going to die. Phelps couldn't remember when they realized it, but they both thought she was going to die. Gina had lost her family to cancer, one at a time, and now she, too, was going to die. Something always rushes in to fill a vacuum and she had given too much, given so much that she created a great open space in her soul and that was where the cancer began.

They had been through the surgery and some of the treatment, refusing finally to be subjected to any more of the grotesque and humiliating witchcraft of modern medicine. Choosing macrobiotics and the possibility of welcoming the disease or death, learning its lessons, inviting the disease to diminish. But the cancer did not diminish, and even though Gina ate brown rice and fruits and vegetables, the cancer was there to teach a lesson larger than her body could hold. Still, they were glad of their choice and, though she grew weaker in body, her face and spirit assumed a calm and luminescence that was surprising to them both.

"It's me in here," she said softly, adjusting the colorful knit tam that she wore over her head, "it's me in here." And she was right. Even in the hollow agony of her disease, she was there, full of love, concern. Phelps feeling her body fading, the shame and sorrow of his own weakness sinking through him like the oncoming winter frost.

A few days later he was walking the ridge behind their cabin, wildly aware of his living step, the sounds, the smells on this mid-October day. Walking the ridge, tracing a deer trail that winds its way through the silver gray boulders, around thick moss-covered ponderosa pine trunks, Phelps ducking under low branches. The soft soil beneath his feet, cushion of needles, wheat grass, smell of pine, whistle of wind in the branches. To his left, a great grassy plain that slopes off into a dry lake basin. To the right, a steep, rocky, pine-covered ridge that tumbled into the river valley. Faint sound of the stream tumbling over beaver dams evoking the memory of deep, still ponds followed by the foaming, swirling rush of water downstream. Everything very clear, crisp, feeling his breath, the tread of each step, the cool air against his face.

Phelps walked quietly to a shallow cave that was partially hidden behind three yellow-bark pines. In the cave, a place he had visited many times before, he kindled a small fire and sat cross-legged to meditate, facing north across the vast plain. He was breathing deeper into the meditation, almost sleeping, breathing peacefully, when an old man appeared in his thoughts. "What do you want?" Phelps asked.

"How would you hunt an antelope?" the old man queried.

"I would follow his tracks," Phelps replied.

"And if there were no tracks?"

"I would follow his trail."

"And if there were no trail?"

"I would follow his scent."

"And what if there were no scent?"

Phelps closed his eyes and pondered the question, rolling it over in his mind. Finally letting go of the mind, thinking, "Then I would be the antelope."

When he opened his eyes to test this response, the old man was gone and he saw Gina standing there briefly, vibrantly, her hair streaming in the breeze. Like before the sickness. Dreaming. Settled back into the meditation, losing all sense of boundaries, molecules of thoughts vibrating into what? The old man? Gina?

In his dream, Phelps felt very calm, very quiet. In his dream, he followed Gina down the ridge toward home.

When he entered the house that was their house he knew she was dead. Everything still, quiet. Her death marked by the absence of vibration. Only a faint hum from the refrigerator in the kitchen. He could even hear the incandescent lights as he switched them on. "Gina?" he asked.

Walking into the bedroom, he found the bed empty, covers tossed aside.

Suddenly he remembered the time when he was a young boy, when he had tried to nurse an injured bird back to health. When the bird died, he cut two doors in a small Kellogg's cereal box, wrapped the bird in a tissue and placed it in the box. Then he wrapped the box in tin foil and carefully buried it behind their house. He thought that the bird would go to heaven if he prayed hard enough. In his dream he saw himself as a child fervently saying the Lord's Prayer night after night so full of hope, faith, so full of Presbyterian possibility.

After a few months had passed, he dug the box up to see if God had answered his prayers. When he opened the first door, there was no body and he was elated, the prayers answered. When he swung open the other half, there, in the corner were a few feathers and a tiny shriveled bird.

Only a dream, feeling dazed, walking through this part in his dream, looking for Gina beside the bed, under the bed, afraid of what he might find. What if she were dead? His mind working through the agreement they had made, Phelps gathering her in his arms, carrying her into the bath where he would gently sponge her body clean. Looking into her face, "Oh, Oh," he moaned, dripping water over her shoulders, rocking back and forth, washing her arms, her fingers, feeling the odd sensation of her cool flesh, even the water warmer, more alive.

Somehow, Foster was beside him, carrying a shovel and his hoop drum. He put his arm around Phelps' shoulder and stood there quietly for a long time. Just like they had arranged, Dr. Mandry had agreed to sign off on the paperwork, the tedious approval of a gravesite on the ranch—all very legal.

Together, the two men turned to wrap the body in the colorful quilt that Phelps' great grandmother had sewn. Phelps gathered her in his arms, but, in the dream, it wasn't Gina anymore, it was Phelps' mother. Pathetically shriveled in her body, the face bloated from drink, leaning unsteadily toward him, cigarette in hand, long drooping ashes about to fall as she slowly stabbed at an ash tray, leaning towards him, until he could feel her besotted breath, staring fearfully into her bleary, rheumy eyes. "Mother?" he said, and was suddenly fourteen, "Mom?" watching her on the floor, slobbering, crying, drunk, then dead, thinking, "If only I'd loved her more. If only I'd tried harder." Watching her melt into a mist that moved through the doors and walls, hearing her voice, "The seeds of death. . . . "

Hearing a voice behind him, turning to see Gina standing in the doorway saying, "I, I don't know what it is. I feel better."

"What?" he said, trying to hear the rest. Then Gina dead again and Foster walking up the trail in the afternoon sun, Phelps in front, Foster walking slowly behind, beating a soft dirge-like meter on his drum.

Together like this they carried her to the grave that they had been digging up on the ridge. The grave wasn't quite complete, so the two men laid the quilted body beneath an ancient pine and took turns digging in the hard, rocky earth.

When at last it seemed deep enough, Phelps gathered pine needles and made a cushion in the bottom of the cold, dark hole. Then he laid on the cushion while Foster and Gina sat quietly by the edge, feeling death move through him. Death. "The seeds of death. . . . The seeds of death are sown at birth." Of course. And now he was deep in the grave and the first handfuls of earth falling very heavy. "Wait," he cried, but the earth rained over him and he felt his body dissolving into nothing, into everything.

Foster began drumming, a slow rolling rhythm, three strokes, over and over, earth rhythm over and over. Gina danced in the clearing, trailing a scarf, danced, whirled. Phelps was with them, surrounding them, inside them. He broke into a song he'd never heard, a bone song, a chant for calling the darkness, a song that grew louder into a deep, wailing song that rolled over the tree tops, bringing the dark to his calling, folding the dark into his song.

Phelps woke, feeling calm after the bizarre dream, stretched his legs. He could hear the water flowing in the stream. Over the horizon, just beyond the dry lake, the moon was rising.

Breathing, breathing, hearing the deep rhythm of Foster's drumming, feeling the beating of his heart, he stood slowly, and peacefully turned away from the moon towards the shadows. Phelps smiled, stepped into the darkness, trusting the earth would rise to meet him.

8

When I think about my friend's wife, this is how it is. I see her standing naked on the rocks next to the shore of a mountain lake in the warm summer sun, breasts full, glistening in the light, nipples that take your breath away. She walks to the edge of the sparkling granite boulder, shakes her hair, raises her arms, and in one smooth motion arches gently through the air and into the cold water of the lake. Hardly a splash, her smooth youthful body gliding with gravity in a rainbow arch, slow motion, hair streaming, nipples pointing to the lake, then slicing deep into the cool dark water. Hardly a splash. I stand near shore, waiting for her to rise out of the frigid lake, waiting for her to rise shaking the water from her hair, her face, her breasts. Waiting for her to rise. I stand waiting in the warm sunlight, waiting for her to rise out of that cold dark place.

This Is How We Got to Be Three Pods and a Pea

Lynda Sexson

I'VE GOT THREE AUNTS AND NO MOM. Not a breath of a dad and no uncles. One grandaddy who says I've got too many aunts. Grandaddy says he was cursed with all these females. That's counting me too.

The aunts all agree to the date. It was sixteen years ago. Before me. He was saying his grace every night at supper, and the aunts all agree down to the letter that he prayed, Lord, too many girls, get a man for at least one of them or pack me to Heaven, where there's sure to be lots of men and not hardly a woman. Except when my aunts cried, he allowed that their momma is one female who must surely be in Heaven. His wife. My Grandma Fernie. I only get to see her in pictures Aunt Tish shows me, looking younger than my aunts look now. We were young like you then, they tell me. So young it could hurt their feelings, as they had to listen to him grumble about all these girls, even as one was missing from the table, their mom, her empty chair almost still warm. Aunt Fern says I sit in her chair. Aunt Celie says that I'm just lucky not ever to have had a mom, because when she's dead and gone it's sadder than a naked bird.

He complained, they tell me, about the aunts' roast beef and pies. Even the peas weren't as good as Grandma Fernie had made. They still cried all the time for her, they say, hating to hear Grandaddy complain to God about Grandma Fernie in Heaven and not in the kitchen, where his girls were so bad they burned water. So that was the year they tricked him. He's been so mad ever since that he gave up, Aunt Tish says, praying for his virile heaven and has, he always says, to suffer in a house with not one plumb wall and clotted up with all these old girls. Can't blame him completely. Except that he says the one young one's turning out the same. But I'm not.

My aunt Tish sees me painting the cat's fingernails and sits down with me on the rug and says it was really my Aunt Celie's doing. She means when Aunt Celie ran off, got as far as Deer Lodge, Montana, and the fanbelt popped. A prison town. There she was, a saggy old silk scarf holding back her in-a-hurry hair, in her jeans she'd put on and sit down in a tub of water, just so when they were dry, you'd know exactly who was inside them. She poked every record and nail polish she ever owned into the Falcon, plus all the mascaras and shadows belonging to Aunt Tish and Aunt Fern, plus all their sweaters and story books. Then Celie and the Falcon ran to a sweat across the hot summer.

Aunt Fern remembers it too, and tells me, it served her right, Celie stole my angora sweater and Grandaddy's station wagon right out from under our noses. It served her right to break down right in a prison town. It was a sign. That car's fanbelt dropped her right where she belonged. In jail almost.

Aunt Celie saw it as a sign, too, but on her side of things. It was so hot Celie had to make herself a shirt out of Grandma Fernie's hankies, the only pretty things left me, says Aunt Fern, aside from Grandma Fernie's own frilly name.

That's one female down, Grandaddy must have thought. He must have prayed her away, and he was thinking he could get rid of the lot of them by prayers if not by marriage, Aunt Tish says.

Aunt Celie showed me how to make a hanky shirt once. Forty-five seconds in a real emergency, she says. I don't know what kind of emergency.

Even though the mechanic told Celie to stay where it was cool, she walked around the hot town of Deer Lodge so she wouldn't have to sit and smell the oil, look at how sad that Ford was, and hear again and again how it was the damnedest thing, every size belt hanging there but the one you need, it never fails. I can almost see them myself, says Aunt Tish, those imperfect bands of infinity, hanging on nails in the dank garage. Celie called the car the Falcon, never the station wagon, as Aunt Celie never likes to humiliate anyone, especially not a car that tried.

Celie didn't realize it was a prison at first. Tish explains that it looked like an improbable castle, built by men with small hopes and a big pile of rocks. It must have been made by the first prisoners themselves, working hard to wall themselves in. Aunt Celie looked at the wall.

Walked right up to it and put her hand against a stone, leaving a damp handprint that evaporated so quick she almost forgot her name. She felt the shock of the hundreds of men penned in there.

Aunt Celie went to the drug store, scraped her knuckles on her Levis pulling money out of her pocket, sucked on a Coke and thought about those men. She knew they could sense her presence too. Every single one of them. The woman in the drug store told her a thousand men were locked up and somebody should throw away the key, not worth a dime, the lot of them. It came to Aunt Celie in a flash they were worth more than gold, and she was destined to make one of them, the jewel of them all, happy after all his suffering. Aunt Celie tested the nail polish and spun the paperback rack. She picked out the Name Your Baby book so she could look up the names of the men in the pen. The drugstore woman gave her a real sympathetic look when Celie paid for the Name Your Baby, and tossing her head toward the stone walls, asked, You here for a visit? How do you visit? Aunt Celie asked her.

The fanbelt was still on its way from Butte. Celie stayed all night in a motel painted turquoise. It must have exactly matched my ring, Aunt Tish recalls, the ring that was your Grandma Fernie's and the ring I told Celie she was to leave in my dresser drawer and she better not wear it one step outside of this house. Aunt Celie had stuck it on her pointer finger just before she took off in the Falcon.

That night Celie untied the hankies and washed them out so she'd have a fresh blouse in the morning when she followed up on her plan. She would go to the prison, she schemed, and tell them she was looking for her brother, but only knew his first name. They'd been separated as babies after their parents had been killed in a flood, maybe a fire. Celie was making a past to fit like skin. She paced around half the night in the little motel room, naked, holding a pencil, consulting her lists, her hankies drying on the shower rod. She had to decide on a first name in order to get to the second, in order to get to the man. Aunt Tish shakes her head at the logic of it. The fated one from among all those one thousand inmates. Celie reasoned that men named Sedgwick didn't get to prison and men named Thorkild deserved it. Henry would be too bald; John was in for crimes against nature, Leonard against the state. Tom stole a pig, Percy was in for larceny. Charles for bigamy, Victor for moving boundary lines, Mike for inciting a riot. Sheridan, maybe. It was a chance, a Sheridan caught for a horse thief. Yes, a horse thief would be all right. A car thief too dull. A crime of passion, as long as it was not too gruesome or too common, was what she wanted. Passion itself is a crime and he's still committing it in there, longing for me, Celie thought. She walked around her motel room, burning her image into the minds of those one thousand sleepless felons.

The next morning, sure at last of the name of her made-up brother, really her secret lover, Celie went right to the deputy warden, got right in with her clean shirt—Grandma Fernie's hankies in knots. I got a brother in here, she whispered, his name is Drake. The assistant to the absent warden was sorry, he said, no Drakes. Well, the people who took him in called him Sheridan, maybe he's enrolled under that name. Sure am sorry. I got to find him, she knew it was her last chance, her third gamble, her final wish. Grandma Fernie always called him, she hesitated as she and the warden's assistant looked down at Grandma Fernie's—or legally Aunt Fern's—hankies wicking moisture between her sweet breasts, and inspired, murmured the word Lacy. Grandma Fernie always called him Lacy. The name hadn't even been on her list. She nearly cried. Lacy, the deputy warden nodded, don't say. About twenty-six, you say? Yes. She hadn't, but yes, she would. What color's his hair? Celie could feel all one thousand perpetrators catch their breath and flex their restless backs. She mustn't make a mistake. She looked into her fog, trying to see the color of the hair of the brother she believed in more than God, and burst out crying, because firm and handsome as he was in her forged memory, he was wearing a hat and she couldn't see his hair. He's wearing a little hat, she sobbed. The deputy warden took it for evidence of her shattered childhood instead of a clue to her fraud, and confirmed, Lacy's your brother, all right. There's a proof, that little hat. He handed her a Kleenex, since he noted she could hardly spare a hanky. He wrote down the prisoner Lacy's last name and long number, giving her instructions to come back the next day at two.

It was all right with Aunt Celie, because first Butte forgot to send the fan belt, and then the Greyhound misplaced it and routed it on to Seattle. At least it's a fan belt that likes to run around, Celie said to the garage man, who felt so bad about the mix-up. Aunt Celie went back to the drug store and got some potato chips, red hots, and a Coke. The woman at the drug store said, you got to eat good now, even though it's hot, and gave her a cheese sandwich and another Coke.

Next day at two p.m., Celie lined up like a visitor and felt like a movie. Someone put a scratchy cardigan over her shoulders, saying, no sense asking for trouble.

Lacy came curious to his side of the fence. He liked her free story. He liked her run-away hair. They looked at each other and both of them knew for sure they were brother and sister. His hair was common brown, she could have guessed. Lacy looked strong and innocent, just as she expected. They touched fingertips and cried and their laughter twined around each other 'til that gray place was like paradise.

That was when Aunt Celie realized she'd outsmarted herself. Aunt Fern says Celie was all hot to mate up with her inmate, but she wasn't about to commit a crime against nature. She had failed, Aunt Tish explains, in her mission to pick a pearl from among those thousand lonely men; instead, she found her long-lost and newly-minted brother. Trying to fool the guards, she fooled herself.

So, with the Falcon belted and gassed again, she promised Lacy she'd write, and came back home. Aunt Celie never got married, never even wrote the prisoner Lacy a Christmas card, so nobody could figure out how she came back pregnant. Had you nine months to the hour of her visitor's pass at Deer Lodge, Aunt Tish tells me. We always said she was your aunt to preserve her feelings and to keep you from looking among the criminal element for some dad, our counterfeit brother. That wouldn't be good for our girl. But Celie, Tish says admiringly, could always take just what she was after, even through guards and guns and dogs and stone walls. And I guess it was you she was after. I guess it was. It was me she was after.

But Aunt Celie, when she catches me staring out the blind window, wraps me up with her in Aunt Tish's afghan and tells me it was Aunt Fern who ran off that summer sixteen years ago. This is what Aunt Celie tells me. Fern always knew where she was going and headed straight into the old calendar picture of Sedona, Arizona. It was the calendar page facing up when Grandma Fernie died so Aunt Fern didn't know how to turn the page, to go past it.

Karla, her divorced friend, was left with nothing but custody of the nine-year-old dog, Sharp, the three-year-old boy, Geoffrey, and the eleven-year-old van, Van. Karla didn't know which way to turn, so Aunt Fern gave her an idea, showed her the picture and they headed off toward it. Aunt Fern tended Sharp, Geoff, and Van while Karla sulked. Every time they let Sharp out to pee, he ran off following new scents, and they'd lose another hour. Geoff regularly threw up every time the Van turned a corner and had to be bathed and soothed back from motion sickness. Aunt Fern used baking soda and psychology and a road atlas. Van lost its ability to go in reverse, which was hard on Geoff because it caused more turning, but was a sign to Aunt Fern to keep going and keep taking care. She missed Grandma Fernie so much she still needed to nurse anything sick.

Aunt Fern's still like that, nursing everything: even the African violets so fussy they kill themselves if they even touch a drop of the very water they need to drink, even the cranky lawnmower that pitches parts of itself across the yard, even me when she mashed strawberries for me when I had tonsillitis.

But next thing they knew they were smack up against Cathedral Rock and Aunt Fern said, this is where I get off. I can't listen to anything louder than a stone, and put her hands over her ears when Karla said she didn't know who had used her more, that worthless guy Eddie or Fern, who hadn't paid a dollar on Van's gas. Karla herself had no business in some red rocks. She left Aunt Fern by the side of the road, waving to Geoff and Sharp. Aunt Fern turned around and suddenly, just like Aunt Celie had, she felt like she was in a movie. At least maybe a commercial. She listened to the red rocks, the curled scorpions, the tenacious plants, until all of them were too noisy. She climbed the rocks until her own blood was dry, red dust. With just a little more effort she would petrify. Aunt Celie calls her the rolling stone every time she takes off to visit some scene she admires in a magazine.

Still, Aunt Fern in trying to be a rock was actually turning them over, looking for something human. Maybe a man who would not jangle her reverie. Maybe her mom.

She discovered the old Indian graveyard and set up her camp in the cemetery, taking turns sleeping on each grave, her ear to the ground. Any grave too talkative, she'd get up and move in the middle of the night until she found one sufficiently quiet. In the morning, Tish says,

Fern examined the tracery of her sleep like hieroglyphs of the spectral conversations left in the red dust. All our socks, Aunt Celie remembers, came back pink and would never bleach white again. We thought she was trying to hear from your Grandma Fernie, who was one-quarter blood herself, through those graves. But your Grandma Fernie was always quiet, even when she was alive she never said much.

Fern slept there until she thought the old Indians would talk her ear off and she thought she might as well be at home. They almost sucked the air out of her just so they could keep talking. Before she left, I guess it was the bones under the ground, gave her a present. Or maybe Grandma Fernie saw to it that those dead Indians gave Fern a little drawing of a person inside her, just like on the stones. I don't know, they were not her tribe. And really old. Anyway, Aunt Fern came home pregnant. We never wanted to tell you, Aunt Tish confides, because we didn't want our little girl trying to find a daddy in a boneyard, not even among magic petroglyphs. That was really what Fern went out to get from that calendar page, it was you, my girl.

It was me she wanted.

Grandaddy shuffles around the aunts and they dose him by the spoonful with sweet words and chicken gravy. All the rest of us eat little cups of yogurt and it really makes Grandaddy angry. He's afraid we'll slip yogurt into his mashed potatoes. He caught Aunt Tish at it once, he says.

This is what Aunt Fern says, pulling the book out of my hand and snapping it shut without a marker, crawling into midnight bed with me to tell me it was Aunt Tish, left alone in the house that summer sixteen years ago, left alone with the screen door banging, flies knocking into the windows, and her heart beating. Tish had to streak her hair and bake her flesh with bottle sunshine, Aunt Fern says, because of staying indoors. Aunt Tish wouldn't go out for the mail, the movies, or the Fourth of July. Wouldn't go out for ice cream, she was tied to the telephone like chains. She watched the fireworks from the tiny attic window and felt like two movies, like she was in black and white and the sky was in color.

She ate the nasturtiums she could reach from the porch railing. She coaxed me to try that, too, hanging by my knees, without using my hands. She can still do it. Tish wore her cut-off shorts, measuring to get the legs exactly even, pulling threads from one side and then the other. She couldn't go out until she got them even, she said, and ran out of material before she ran out of summertime, snipping her scissors, pulling threads, 'til there was little left to quarrel over, with a difference, Aunt Fern says, only Tish herself could discern.

She'd wait for the phone to ring. She'd listen to any offer, aluminum siding, any prize she won, ten free bowling lessons. Put my name down, Tish said, but wouldn't go out of the house to stick her fingers in the face of a bowling ball. She was even polite to the kids who called to say the refrigerator was running and Prince Albert was in a can. The real reason she wouldn't leave was because of the wrong number. Who became the insistent caller. Who became the only breath in the house. Her wrong number persisted, calling at odd hours in a cast of characters, a dozen voices. The voice started out as an obscene call designed to shock, but it made Tish laugh. Then the voice called back as the president. Then a swami, then Gregory Peck, Betty Davis, Bugs Bunny, a leprechaun, the next-door neighbor, even as a fortune cookie. I would like to have heard that one.

Anyway, it was the day after Independence Day and a storm rose over the mountains, belittling the fireworks of the night before. Tish answered the phone on the first ring. The caller was doing another fancy voice, making Tish laugh, telling jokes about Heaven in the voice of God. Aunt Tish was very interested in the Heaven jokes, always hoping to get news of her mother. Then the phone crackled, the maple tree around the corner got a big lightning gouge in it, and the line was broken. I can still see a trace of that lightning strike. We've all put our hands into that old wound, where the tree went smooth with fire that night. We never told you, Aunt Fern says, because we didn't want you to reach for the phone every time it rings, expecting a dad to call you up, it's no way to live. I actually heard once that the Virgin Mary got pregnant from the Dove talking in her ear, but we're Protestants. That caller with all those voices never called again. Tish never needed to hear another word. The caller had told her everything.

It was me.

Grandaddy doesn't go to work any more, so the aunts send him after newspapers and thread. Otherwise, now that he doesn't get to go off with his lunch box, he sits on the porch still trying to puzzle out which one of his bad girls is the worst. They bring his lunch out to him in the old lunch box.

I don't mind being as pure as Jesus. Maybe more pure: not only no dad, not even a mom. But I think I'll get out of this house, get a guy, and get a baby the regular way. But now Grandaddy's started following me around, thinking he can keep it from happening to me. Whatever it was that happened.

The three aunts, Celie, Fern, and Tish puffed up all at once, like a sudden magician's bouquet. It nearly killed Grandaddy to have three—he didn't say the word *pregnant*—daughters. He claimed he would have killed any one of them who got herself knocked up, but with all three wearing smocks, a man couldn't kill three women, and three little ones, he said, if he let his mind follow up. Where are my cousins, you ask? Well, my aunts fooled Grandaddy. Only one was pregnant. Only one shell hid the pea. The other two were pretending just so Grandaddy couldn't kill the ripe one, couldn't kill her or banish her or pick on her. He didn't know which way to aim his shotgun, not a suitor in sight, his three girls puking, then sucking ice. Then his three girls gnawing on raw potatoes, then chewing licorice, then eating bread and jam, bacon and eggs, eating him out of house and home. Then his three girls learning to knit and his three girls packing up toothbrushes and layettes.

They took off in the Falcon, late one night. We still have a picture of that car, with the aunts all young, all legs and hair and laughing, draped all over it. Don't call at the hospital, they ordered him, we're going to another town so there'll be no gossip. They liked being the only news that spring, but they wouldn't submit to being mere gossip. Paint the spare room, they ordered him. We'll come home to a nursery. Grandaddy was ashamed at the hardware store to ask for pink or blue, so he cleverly asked for yellow. And yellow my room still is.

It was bright as a daffodil when the three thin-again daughters came home with one basket, one baby, three big smiles, six swollen and leaking paps, Fern brags. Grandaddy asked, who lost, who's grieving, whose is this? And all three said, I'm her aunty and you're her grandaddy. Then Grandaddy realized he'd been tricked by three evil daughters. Only one of those gals had strayed and the other two just pretended, to protect the bad one. He watched all bird-eyed, but couldn't figure whether Celie, Fern, or Tish was the real momma. I'll get a knife, then, and divide it up in three parts, he threatened. We didn't fall for that old ploy, Aunt Tish says, there was no wisdom in it. Grandaddy complained, you all paraded around town in those hatching jackets without the sense to be ashamed, but not one of you hags will own up to being a mother. There's not a creature on earth behaves this way. You gals are witches and this child's an orphan. Three aunts can't equal one mother, and that's the last he said. Grandaddy's new name rattled off their sharp little tongues, and the baby, that was me, changed them all into aunts.

And here I am.

And Grandaddy thinks if he figures out which aunt's a mom, then he'll be happy. What he's forgotten is that whichever one he chooses, he'll still be stuck with a riddle. If he decides which aunt got me, he still won't know where I came from. The aunties think their daddy is a cross to bear, so not one of them would have inflicted a dad on me.

I sit with Grandaddy on the porch swing and he raps me on the knees with his newspaper when I swing too hard. So I tell him what I think. It's this. The aunts missed their mom so much, my Grandma Fernie, they just thought such mom thoughts they had a miracle and got a baby. You ought to be caned, Grandaddy says, whopping me with the rolled-up newspaper.

About the Contributors

Ralph Beer spent much of his life on his family's cattle ranch near Clancy, Montana, but now makes his home in Colorado. His books include the award-winning novel, *The Blind Corral,* and the collection of personal essays, *In These Hills.* For many years, he wrote a column on the ranching life for *Big Sky Journal* and is a former contributing editor to *Harper's Magazine.*

Bill Borneman lives in Helena, Montana, with his wife, Patti, and son, Karl. He works as a house painter, dabbles in the "book business," and plays Lo Prinzi guitars. His degree in philosophy from The University of Montana aids him in each of these endeavors. Borneman is currently a member of the poetry performance quartet, The States of Matter, a group devoted to the sonic realization of poetic occurrences. He is perhaps best known as the genial host of the literature reading series "Naked Words" at Miller's Crossing, a Helena watering hole.

Phil Condon teaches Environmental Writing for the Environmental Studies Program at The University of Montana. He is author of the collection of stories, *River Street,* and the novel, *Clay Center,* forthcoming from Eastern Washington University Press. Condon received the 1991 A. B. Guthrie, Jr., Award at *CutBank,* a 1993 National Endowment for the Arts Fellowship, and the Novel Award in the 2001 William Faulkner Creative Writing Competition, sponsored by the New Orleans Faulkner Society. He makes his home in Missoula.

Sandra Dal Poggetto, born in Sonoma, California, earned her Master of Arts degree in Painting and Drawing from San Francisco State University. A resident of Helena, she divides her time between making art, writing, and producing the weekly National Public Radio program "Home Ground: Changes and Choices in the American West," hosted by her husband, Brian Kahn. Dal Poggetto's essays on art and hunting have been published in *The Structurist, Gray's Sporting Journal,* and *Northern Lights.* Her essay, "Duccio in the Eye of the Hunt" will soon appear in an anthology of women's writing on hunting, published by Stackpole Books.

Debra Magpie Earling is a member of the Confederated Salish and Kootenai Tribes of the Flathead Indian Reservation. She is the author of the novel, *Perma Red.* Earling has also published stories in *The Last Best Place: A Montana Anthology; Talking Leaves: An Anthology of Contemporary Native American Short Stories;* and *Circle of Women: An Anthology of Contemporary Western Women Writers,* as well as in journals such as *Ploughshares, Northeast Indian Quarterly,* and *Northern Lights.* She is an Associate Professor of Creative Writing at The University of Montana.

Tom Elliott recently retired from his position as managing partner of the N-Bar Ranch near Grass Range. Elliott is a published poet, short-story writer, and author of various public radio commentaries. He co-founded the Flatwillow Arts and

Philosophical Society, an artist's group in central Montana. He is a frequent keynote speaker, panelist, and educator in the fields of agriculture, sustainable food systems, chaos theory and organization design, and marketing. In addition to his business and literary activities, Elliott is current co-chair of the Montana Community Foundation, past chair of Alternative Energy Resource Organization (AERO), and a past board member of the Montana Committee for the Humanities, Northern Plains Resource Council, and Feathered Pipe Foundation.

Ron Fischer grew up Jewish in Anaconda, Montana, where his father worked as a smelterman and his mother as a cook at the State Hospital in Warm Springs. He received a teaching degree from Western Montana College, Dillon, and then his MFA from The University of Montana. His play, "A Dance on Crumbling Earth," won a Montana Centennial competition and was produced by Butte's Broadway 215 in 1989. His collection of stories, *Journeys in Open Country,* won the Montana Arts Council's First Book Award for 1992. After teaching for some years at Western in Dillon, Fischer entered a doctoral program at Idaho State University, Pocatello, and wrote his dissertation on Native American literature. He currently teaches at Minot State University, North Dakota.

Pete Fromm is a three-time winner of the Pacific Northwest Booksellers Literary Award for his novel *How All This Started* (2000), his story collection *Dry Rain* (1997), and the memoir *Indian Creek Chronicles* (1993). Fromm has published four other short story collections, as well as more than a hundred stories in magazines. His new novel, *As Cool as I Am,* is forthcoming from Picador. He lives in Great Falls, Montana.

Fred Haefele received his MFA from The University of Montana in 1981. His essays have appeared in *Outside, Wired, The New York Times Magazine, American Heritage,* and *Newsday.* Haefele received literary fellowships from The Fine Arts Work Center, the National Endowment for the Arts, and Stanford University. He is the author of the motorcycle memoir, *Rebuilding the Indian* (1998). Haefele currently lives in Missoula, where he works as an arborist.

Tom Harpole, a known associate of recognized experts, teaches writing in Eskimo schools along Alaska's Bering Seacoast for a few months every year and is writing a book about the Yup'iks. He hails from a long line of accomplished liars from Deer Lodge and lives near Avon, Montana, with his wife, Lisa, a potter. Harpole's articles and stories have appeared in *Sports Illustrated, Smithsonian, Left Bank, Outdoor Life,* and *Northern Lights.*

Poet, novelist, and singer **Krys Holmes** is a fulltime freelance writer and editor. Her essays, memoirs, and poems have appeared widely. She has recently completed her first novel, "The Magdalena Chronicles." Holmes lives near Montana City with her husband, writer Charlie Atkins, and daughter Tara Leigh.

David Horgan received an MFA from The University of Montana in 1987. His collection of stories, *The Golden West Trio Plus One,* was a winner of The University of Montana's Merriam-Frontier Award. His work has been anthologized in *Best of the West, Volume 2*, and he has published fiction and essays in a number of magazines. Guitarist for the Big Sky Mudflaps, he lives in Missoula with his wife, artist and musician Beth Lo, and their son, Tai.

Allen Morris Jones worked for five years as editor of *Big Sky Journal*. His novel, *Last Year's River*, was released by Houghton Mifflin in 2001, and by Mariner Paperbacks in 2002. He is also the author of *A Quiet Place of Violence: Hunting and Ethics in the Missouri River Breaks*, published by Bangtail Press. His magazine work has appeared in *Men's Journal, Town and Country, Gray's Sporting Journal*, and *Sports Afield*.

Melissa Kwasny is the author of a collection of poems, *The Archival Birds* (2000), and two novels, *Modern Daughters and the Outlaw West* and *Trees Call for What They Need*. Kwasny is also editor of *Toward the Open Field*, an anthology of writing on poetics by modern poets, to be published by Wesleyan University Press in 2004. She makes her home near Jefferson City, Montana.

Novelist, humorist, and poet **Robert Lee** has recently retired from the U.S. Postal Service and makes his home in Missoula. James Welch wrote of Lee's first novel, "*Guiding Elliott* [The Lyons Press, 1997] is a gem of a book—small, faceted, and polished to a bright light. By turns quietly moving and belly-busting funny...."

David Long was a student of Richard Hugo and William Kittredge at The University of Montana in the early 1970s. He is the author of three short-story collections, including *Blue Spruce* (Scribner), and the novels *The Falling Boy* and *The Daughters of Simon Lamoreaux*, also from Scribner. His novel *Purgatorio* will be published in 2004. A long-time resident of northwestern Montana, he now lives in Tacoma, Washington.

Ruth McLaughlin grew up in northeastern Montana where her grandparents homesteaded. Her stories and nonfiction have appeared in small magazines and in the *Best American Short Stories* and *Circle of Women* anthologies. She received a 1998 Montana Arts Council Individual Artist Fellowship for her memoir-in-progress. She lives in Great Falls and teaches community memoir writing workshops around the state.

Neil McMahon is the author of the novels, *To the Bone* (HarperCollins, 2003), *Blood Double*, and *Twice Dying*. He is a former Stegner Fellow at Stanford University, and his short fiction has appeared in *The Atlantic Monthly, Boxing's Best Short Stories*, and other publications. He lives in Missoula.

Deirdre McNamer grew up in Conrad and Cut Bank in north-central Montana and lives now in Missoula where she teaches creative writing at The University of Montana. She is the author of three novels, *Rima in the Weeds* (1991), *One Sweet Quarrel* (1994), and *My Russian* (1999). Her essays and stories have appeared in *The New Yorker, Ploughshares, DoubleTake, Outside*, and other publications.

Ellen Meloy's *The Anthropology of Turquoise* uses memoir and natural history to guide the reader through landscapes of pure sensation, from southwestern deserts to turquoise seas. It was a finalist for the Pulitzer Prize in nonfiction, a *Los Angeles Times* Book of the Year, and winner of the 2003 Utah Book Award in nonfiction. She is also the author of *The Last Cheater's Waltz* and the recipient of a Whiting Writer's Award. *Raven's Exile*, her account of living on Utah's Green River, won the admiration of readers and river lovers everywhere. Meloy no longer migrates to Montana seasonally but lives in southern Utah year round.

Born and raised in Helena, **Maile Meloy** was educated at Harvard and the University of California–Davis. She is author of the collection of stories, *Half in Love* (Scribner, 2002), and the novel, *Liars and Saints* (Scribner, 2003). Her award-winning stories have appeared in *Paris Review*, *The New Yorker*, *Ploughshares*, *Ontario Review*, and *Best New American Voices*.

A native of Kalispell, Montana, and a founding board member of the Montana Center for the Book, poet and cultural journalist **Rick Newby** served as co-editor of *Writing Montana: Literature under the Big Sky* (1996) and *An Ornery Bunch: Tales and Anecdotes Collected by the WPA Montana Writers' Project* (1999). He is also editor of the rollicking Western novel, *A Most Desperate Situation: Frontier Adventures of a Young Scout, 1859–1864* (2000), by Montana pioneer Walter Cooper. Newby's most recent book, *The Suburb of Long Suffering: Poems and Prose* (Bedrock Editions, 2002), is distributed by Riverbend Publishing.

Aaron Parrett is a writer and musician and Assistant Professor of English at the University of Great Falls, Montana. Parrett has recorded several CDs of original songs on the Pizzle Label, including *Left of the Mason Dixon Line* and *The Legend of Jim Collins*. His book, *The Translunar Narrative in the Western Tradition*, will be published in 2004 by Ashgate Publishing (United Kingdom).

Caroline Patterson has published fiction and nonfiction in *Epoch*, *Alaska Quarterly Review*, *Big Sky Journal*, *Newsday*, *Northern Lights*, *Seventeen*, *Southwest Review*, and *Sunset*. She received a 1990–1992 Stegner Fellowship in fiction at Stanford University, the 1990 Jackson Prize in Fiction from the San Francisco Foundation, a 1992 Henfield Prize in fiction, and fellowships from the Montana Arts Council, the Ludwig Vogelstein Foundation, and the Money for Women/Barbara Deming Fund. A fourth generation Missoulian, she currently lives in her hometown with her husband Fred and her children Phoebe and Tobin.

Born in St. Ignatius, Montana ("half bohunk, half Scots/Irish"), **Matt Pavelich** grew up in Lonepine. Educated at The University of Montana and University of Iowa (where he received his MFA), Pavelich is the author of *Beasts of the Forest, Beasts of the Field*, which won the Montana Arts Council's First Book Award. He has been a Michener Fellow and received an Individual Artist's Fellowship from the Montana Arts Council in 1998. His novel "Our Savage" is forthcoming from Shoemaker & Hoard in 2004. Pavelich is employed as Tribal Prosecutor for the Flathead Nation and lives in Polson.

Though he works as a teaching librarian at Western Washington University in Bellingham, **Paul S. Piper's** heart remains in Montana. He received his MFA from The University of Montana in 1992, and he owns (with his father) a small cabin on five acres near Condon, Montana, in the Swan Valley. He visits it religiously every year. Piper is co-editor of the anthology of personal essays on fathering, children, and the natural world, *Father Nature* (University of Iowa Press, 2003).

Lynda Sexson teaches at Montana State University, Bozeman. Her books include *Ordinarily Sacred, Margaret of the Imperfections* (which won the Pacific Northwest Booksellers Association Award), and *Hamlet's Planets: Parables*. A prize-winning teacher and author, she was honored with the Montana Award in the Humanities.

Cultural historian, poet, and fiction writer **Noelle Sullivan** lives at the western edge of Yellowstone National Park. Her work has appeared in *Kinnikinnik, The High Plains Literary Review, Poetry Northwest, Fourteen Hills, Puerto del Sol,* and the *Bloomsbury Review*. In 1998, she received a Montana Arts Council Individual Artist Fellowship for her fiction, and holds an M.A. from the University of New Mexico.

Melanie Rae Thon's most recent book is the novel *Sweet Hearts* (Washington Square Press, 2002). She is also author of *Meteors in August* and *Iona Moon,* and the story collections *First, Body* and *Girls in the Grass*. Originally from northwestern Montana, she has taught at Emerson College, Syracuse University, University of Massachusetts, and Ohio State University. She now divides her time between the Pacific Northwest and Salt Lake City, where she teaches at the University of Utah.

Florence Williams is a graduate of The University of Montana's MFA program in creative writing. Her articles and essays appear regularly in such publications as *Outside Magazine,* the *New Republic,* and the *New York Times*. She has won four national article awards from the American Society of Journalists and Authors and was listed as a notable mention in *Best American Essays 1996*. She lives with her family in Helena, Montana.

Poet, playwright, and fiction writer **Elizabeth Wood** lives in Roundup, Montana. Educated at San Francisco State University, she has participated in the Writer's Voice "Poet on the Prairie" program and was co-founder of the Roundup Arts & Culture Committee. She is also a founding member of the Flatwillow Arts and Philosophical Society and co-editor of the ranching memoir, *Cowboys Don't Walk,* by Anne Goddard Charter.

Kim Zupan grew up on the east side of the Rockies in Stockett and Great Falls. Before and after earning degrees in English and Creative Writing at The University of Montana, he worked for several ranches in the Judith Basin, and he spent a decade as a professional bareback rider with the Professional Rodeo Cowboy's Association. He received his MFA in Fiction in 1984. His work has been anthologized in *Where We Live* (Spring Creek Publishing, 1997) and *Hunting's Best Short Stories* (Chicago Review Press, 2000). Zupan lives in Missoula and divides his time as a writer, finish carpenter, husband, and dad.

Grateful acknowledgment is made for permission to reprint the following copyrighted works:

"Virgin Everything" by Deirdre McNamer © 1998 by Deirdre McNamer, originally published in *DoubleTake,* reprinted with the permission of The Wylie Agency.

"Snow Country" by Paul S. Piper. Copyright 1991 by Paul S. Piper. Originally published in *Northern Lights*. Reprinted by permission of the author.

"Haircut" by Ruth McLaughlin. Copyright 2000 by Ruth McLaughlin. Originally published in *The Cream City Review*. Reprinted by permission of the author.

"At the Edge of Things" from "Lady," a novel in progress, by Ralph Beer. Copyright 1999 by Ralph Beer. Originally published in *Big Sky Journal*. Reprinted by permission of the author.

"Fruit in Good Season" by Caroline Patterson. Copyright 1997 by Caroline Patterson. Originally published in *Epoch*. Reprinted by permission of the author.

"A Lot of Living to Do" by David Horgan. Copyright 2002 by David Horgan. Reprinted by permission of the author.

From *PERMA RED* by Debra Magpie Earling, copyright © 2002 by Debra Magpie Earling. Used by permission of Blue Hen, an imprint of Penguin Group (USA) Inc.

"If It Is So Far," from "Our Savage," a novel by Matt Pavelich. Copyright 2002 by Matt Pavelich. Reprinted by permission of the author.

"Cranes" by Pete Fromm. Copyright 1999 by Pete Fromm. Originally published in *Willow Springs*. Reprinted by permission of the author.

"The Difference between East and West" by Florence Williams. Copyright 2002 by Florence Williams. Reprinted by permission of the author.

"My Cat Chuck" by Tom Harpole. Copyright 2001 by Tom Harpole. Originally published in *Northern Lights*. Reprinted by permission of the author.

"On Drowning," "In Uncertain Light," and "First Winter", from SWEET HEARTS by Melanie Rae Thon. Copyright © 2000 by Melanie Rae Thon. Reprinted by permission of Houghton Mifflin Company. All rights reserved.

"A Black Convertible" by Elizabeth H. Wood. Copyright 1991 by Elizabeth Hughes Wood. Reprinted by permission of the author.

"Side of the Road" by Aaron Parrett. Copyright 2003 by Aaron Parrett. Reprinted by permission of the author.

"Four Lean Hounds, ca. 1976" by Maile Meloy. Reprinted with the permission of Scribner, an imprint of Simon & Schuster Adult Publishing Group, from HALF IN LOVE by Maile Meloy. Copyright © 2002 by Maile Meloy.

"The Last Photograph of Lyle Pettibone" by David Long. Copyright 1985 by David Long. First published in *Antaeus*; reprinted in *New American Short Stories*, Gloria Norris, ed. (New American Library, 1986); and reprinted in *The Flood of '64*, (The Ecco Press, 1987) by David Long. Reprinted by permission of the author.

"Dogs and Dogs" by Phil Condon. Copyright 1997 by Phil Condon. First published in *The Seattle Review*. Reprinted by permission of the author.

"Warrior" by Krys Holmes. Copyright 2003 by Krys Holmes. Reprinted by permission of the author.

From "Journeymen," a novel in progress, by Neil McMahon. Copyright 1999 by Neil McMahon. Reprinted by permission of the author.

"A Fine Spring Day, with Regrets" by Allen Morris Jones. Copyright 1999 by Allen Morris Jones. First published in *Big Sky Journal*. Reprinted by permission of the author.

"More than a Hiding Place" by Fred Haefele. Copyright 1996 by Fred Haefele. First published in *Newsday*. Reprinted by permission of the author.

"Relict" by Sandra Dal Poggetto. Copyright 1999 by Sandra Dal Poggetto. First published in *Northern Lights*. Reprinted by permission of the author.

"New Deal" by Noelle Sullivan. Copyright 2000 by Noelle Sullivan. First published in *Alkali Flats*. Reprinted by permission of the author.

"Big Ears" by Robert Lee. Copyright 2000 by Robert Lee. First published in *cold-drill*. Reprinted by permission of the author.

"Manus Dugan" by Ron Fischer. Copyright 1991 by Ron Fischer. Originally published in *Clear Water on the Swan & Journeys into Open Country* (Montana Arts Council/SkyHouse Publishers, 1992) by John Holbrook and Ron Fischer. Reprinted by permission of the author.

"A Woman among Them, Painting" by Melissa Kwasny. Copyright 2002 by Melissa Kwasny. Reprinted by permission of the author.

From "Bill's Bongo Party" by Bill Borneman. Copyright 2002 by Bill Borneman. Reprinted by permission of the author.

"Shelterbelt," from "Why Do the Heathen Rage," a novel in progress, by Kim Zupan. Copyright 2002 by Kim Zupan. Reprinted by permission of the author.

"A Map for Hummingbirds" by Ellen Meloy. © Copyright 1997 by Ellen Meloy. Previously appeared in *The Place Within: Portraits of the American Landscape by Twenty Contemporary Writers*, ed. Jodi Daynard (New York: Norton, 1996). Printed with the permission of the author.

"Journey of Small Deaths" by Tom Elliott. Copyright 2002 by Tom Elliott. Reprinted by permission of the author.

"This Is How We Got to Be Three Pods and a Pea" by Lynda Sexson. Copyright 1996 by Lynda Sexson. First published in *Hamlet's Planets: Parables* (Ohio State University Press, 1996) by Lynda Sexson. Reprinted by permission of the author.